Mystic Sweet Communion

JANE KIRKPATRICK

Multnomah Publishers *Sisters, Oregon*

MYSTIC SWEET COMMUNION
published by Multnomah Publishers, Inc.

© 1998 by Jane Kirkpatrick
International Standard Book Number: 1-57673-293-2

Cover photograph courtesy of the Fort Lauderdale Historical Society
Cover design by D^2 DesignWorks

Multnomah is a trademark of Multnomah Publishers, Inc., and is registered
in the U.S. Patent and Trademark Office.
The colophon is a trademark of Multnomah Publishers, Inc.

Printed in the United States of America

For information:
MULTNOMAH PUBLISHERS, INC.•POST OFFICE BOX 1720•SISTERS, OREGON 97759

Library of Congress Cataloging-in-Publication Data
Kirkpatrick, Jane, 1946–
    Mystic sweet communion / by Jane Kirkpatrick.
        p. cm.
    ISBN 1-57673-293-2 (alk. paper)
    1. Stranahan, Ivy Cromartie, 1879?–1970—Fiction. 2. Fort Lauderdale (Fla.)—
History—Fiction. 3. Florida—History—1865– —Fiction. 4. Seminole Indians—Fiction.
I. Title.
PS3561.1712M97   1998
98–30162
813'.54—dc21   CIP

03 04 05 — 10 9 8 7 6 5 4

This book is dedicated to teachers
of all ages and places,
and to Jerry, for abiding with me.

Other books by Jane Kirkpatrick:

DREAMCATCHER COLLECTION
A Sweetness to the Soul
(winner of the Wrangler Award for Outstanding Western Novel of 1995)
Love to Water My Soul
A Gathering of Finches
Mystic Sweet Communion

KINSHIP AND COURAGE SERIES
All Together in One Place
No Eye Can See
What Once We Loved

TENDER TIES HISTORICAL SERIES
A Name of Her Own

NONFICTION
Homestead
A Simple Gift of Comfort
(formerly *A Burden Shared*)

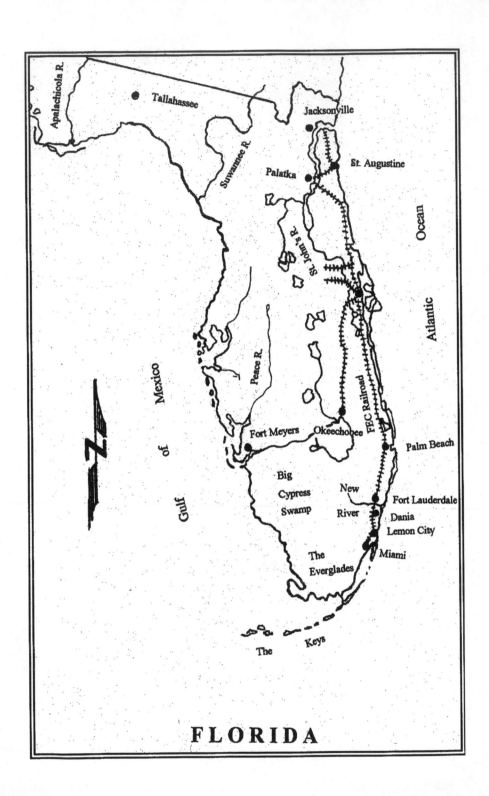

FLORIDA

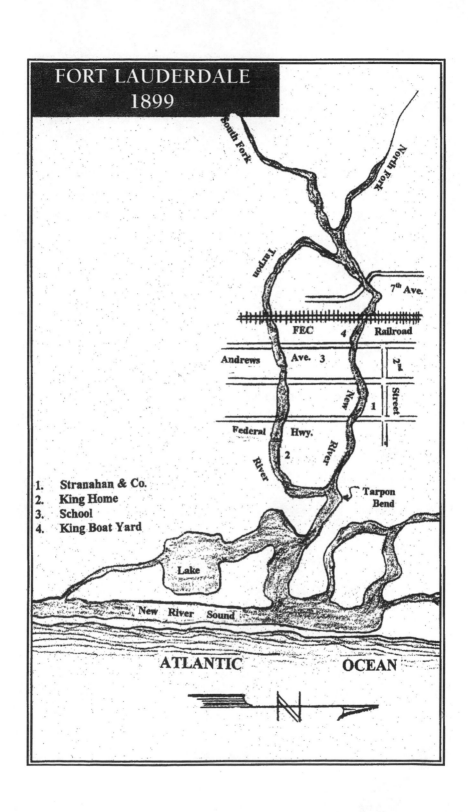

He that dwelleth in the secret place of the most high
shall abide under the shadow of the Almighty....
He shall cover thee with his feathers, and under his wings shalt
thou trust.

PSALM 91:1, 4

Commune: To exchange thoughts and feelings; to distribute and share.
American Heritage Dictionary

ACKNOWLEDGMENTS

Mystic Sweet Communion is my version of a remarkable story of faith, protection, and perseverance. It is fiction based on fact, and I could not have told the story without the treasure of material Ivy Stranahan left behind. She selected sound keepers of her experiences, and I am grateful for their allowing me access to facts, books, files, photographs, tapes, and speculations that document what Frank and Ivy did and permitted a glimpse into who these remarkable people were.

Special appreciation goes to Alice Cromartie Cassels of Tallahassee, niece of Ivy Stranahan, for her gracious time of remembering, loan of newspaper clippings and books, review of an unedited version of *Mystic,* and confidence in my ability to tell Frank and Ivy's story. I thank Greg Cromartie, Ivy's great-nephew, for first mentioning this story and for remembering who I was two years later when I began to pursue it.

Appreciation goes to Barbara W. Keith, executive director of the Stranahan House on the New River, for her work to preserve the Stranahan home, responsiveness to phone calls, and a personal tour; and to her and Sandra Casteel for their reading of and providing suggestions for an unedited manuscript. The publications of the Stranahan House—in particular, *Stranahan House, Frank and Ivy Stranahan: New River Pioneers,* and a video production about Ivy—proved invaluable.

The docent manual prepared by the education committee of the Friends of the Stranahan House provided details about the region, the house, Frank and Ivy, and even archaeological results. I am grateful for access to this well-researched compilation and the warmth and care conveyed through it.

Access to another history used for docent orientation at the Stranahan House, compiled by Pam Euston while she was director of education for the Fort Lauderdale Historical Society, was very helpful. Ms. Euston's book *Cruising down the River: A Self-Guided Tour of the Historic New River in*

Fort Lauderdale, Florida offered a rich accounting of life along the New River as well.

The work of the Fort Lauderdale Historical Society in compiling the more than two dozen boxes of letters and articles and hundreds of photographs related to the Stranahans is exceptional. Special thanks go to Susan Gillis, curator, and Dan Hobby, director, as well as others who answered questions, and who with enthusiasm offered ideas about the why and who of the man and woman so instrumental in the founding of Fort Lauderdale. I appreciate permission to reference these materials and for the use of the photograph of the Stranahans' home on *Mystic's* cover.

A 1979 article in the Broward County Historical Commission in Ivy Stranahan's own words offered documentation of the Baptist involvement with the Seminoles. The work of Dr. Harry Kersey Jr., especially his book *Pelts, Plumes and Hides,* provided an important view of the trading culture in south Florida at the turn of the century. His conversations with me, his sharing of research from his own forthcoming historical work about the Stranahans, and his willingness to let me refer to Tony Tommie's letter to Frank Stranahan were greatly appreciated.

I thank Dr. Betty Mae Jumper for her time and remembrances of Ivy Stranahan and for confirming the bond of friendship between and influence of Ivy and Annie Tommie as a formidable team.

The Seminole Nation's Ah-Tha-Thi-Ki Museum at Big Cypress, whose name itself means "to learn," afforded me hours to do that, walking the boardwalks into the cypress, talking with men and women carving and sewing, viewing the exhibits, and allowing my mind to imagine life one hundred years earlier, if only for a time. That I discovered its existence through the Seminole tribe's Web site seems a perfect blend of the old and the new.

Patsy West, of the *Seminole Tribune,* is both a fine writer and a gracious interviewee. Her Reflections series offered a sensitive glimpse into the lives of the Seminole people and their land as they remembered it with insight and wisdom.

James Lafayette Glenn's letter published as *My Work among the Florida Seminoles* and edited by Harry Kersey Jr. provided images of day-to-day life in the early years at Dania and a view of non-Indian involvement in the affairs of another nation.

My thanks go to the National Archives staff, especially Richard Fusick of the Archives 1 Reference Branch. The material I found there provided primary documentation of a singular woman's efforts on behalf of a people, the often frustrating efforts to rid squatters from reservation lands, and Ivy's unrelenting commitment to social righteousness on behalf of native peoples.

Karen Davis's *Public Faces, Private Lives: Women in South Florida, 1870s–1910,* August Burghard's *Watchie-Esta Hutrie,* Stuart McIver's *True Tales of the Everglades,* Calvin Stone's *Forty Years in the Everglades,* and Theodore Pratt's novel, *The Barefoot Mailman,* provided additional material about the people and ideas that were south Florida at the turn of the century. Jan Dargatz's book, *Women and Power: How Women Can Use the Power God Has Given Them to Further His Kingdom,* offered insights that seemed fitting for Ivy's character and life. My appreciation also goes to Anne Galbraith (now of Massachusetts and Annie Beck's namesake) for her remembrances of Ivy's devoted friend.

The New History of Florida, edited by Michael Gannon, provided a panoramic view of the third most populous state in the nation: her past and passions, and the effects of climate, people, and change over its 485 years of recorded history. Samuel Proctor's and William W. Rogers's pieces in this edition were especially beneficial. A transcript of an interview by Dr. Proctor and Ivy proved valuable as well.

I thank the people of Florida who talked about what they love and lament about their state and its history. Especially I thank my husband's daughter and her family, Kathleen and Joe Larsen, Floridians who made their home available while we researched and who answered phone calls throughout the seasons such as "what do you hear right now, what's the weather like, what's blooming...." Thanks too go to Kay and Don Krall, Blair Fredstrom, Sandy Maynard, Millie Voll, Matt, Melissa, and Mariah Kirkpatrick, the Hurtley clan, and my agents, Joyce Hart and Terry Porter, for their encouragement and for keeping things going while I wrote. Teachers in my early life served as models for Ivy's excellence and endurance: Virginia Schroeder Everson and Ellwyn Hendrickson in Wisconsin; and Bob Shotwell and Bob Welch in Oregon. My admiration goes to all.

I thank Bill Sidnor, a Florida teacher and artist whose painting of Ivy and Frank's home served as inspiration throughout the writing of this novel.

To the colleagues, friends, teachers, families, and children I am privileged to work with on the Confederated Tribes of Warm Springs Reservation in Oregon, thank you for tolerating my schedule changes and talk of Florida on wintry Oregon days.

To Rod Morris, my editor and fine teacher, and to all the people at Multnomah for publishing and marketing stories that permit the past to teach and touch us, I give my thanks.

Finally, to my husband, Jerry, who is a partner, teacher, and friend: thank you for understanding, persevering, and abiding with me.

CAST OF CHARACTERS

*Henry Morrison Flagler–owner of the Florida East Coast Railroad

*The Cromarties of Lemon City, Florida

    * Augustus and Sarah–parents of Ivy

        *Ivy Julia Cromartie–Florida teacher

        *Bloxham–brother of Ivy, employee of Stranahan and Company

        *Pink Elizabeth–Ivy's only sister

        *DeWitt–brother of Ivy

        *Augustus (Gus)–brother of Ivy

        *Albert–brother of Ivy

*Ada Merritt–Ivy's tutor

*Isidore Cohen–owner of trading post on Miami River

 Jan Nordstrom–grove owner, beau of Pink

NEW RIVER (later known as Fort Lauderdale)

    *Ed King–boat builder, school builder, provided Ivy's first home

    *Susan King–wife of Ed

    *Louise King–daughter of Ed and Sarah

    *Eleanor, Wallace, Byrd–children of Ed and Susan

    *Frank Stranahan–owner of New River trading post

    *Will Stranahan–brother of Frank, bookkeeper

    *Tom Kennedy–pharmacist, doctor, and farmer

    *Cap Valentine–founding resident and justice of the peace

    *William H. Marshall–Fort Lauderdale's first mayor

    *Lula Marshall–wife of William and soloist

    *Annie Beck–Ivy's friend

    *Alfred Beck–a pharmacist, husband of Annie

    *Reverend Holding–Methodist minister

    *Brother Frost–a communicant at the Methodist church

    *Randall Moss–a developer and husband of Pink

    *Lucien Spencer–Bureau of Indian Affairs agent at Fort Myers

    *W. C. Kyle–banker and friend of the Stranahans

*Reed Byran–friend, hotel owner and builder of the dredges

*W. O. Berryhill–businessman and partner of Bloxham's

*Oliver brothers–purchasers of Frank's Stranahan and Company

*Susan Byran–a Broward County teacher, sister of Reed

*May Mann Jennings–wife of Florida Governor, leader of Florida's
    Women's Clubs

*George Zapf–owner of West Palm Beach saloon

*IVY'S FIRST STUDENTS

Minnie Bellamy, Wallace King, Lula Marshall, Tenley Bellamy, Edgar
    Bellamy, Sally Marshall, William Powers, Mack Marshall, Vasco
    Powers, Louise King, Cora Powers, Irma Bass, Byrd King, Frank
    Marshall

AMONG THE SEMINOLES

*Billy Osceola–friend of Frank Stranahan and provider of alligator
    contracts

*Johnny Jumper–a medicine man

*Mary Gopher–Johnny Jumper's wife

Esther–a Seminole child, later a mother

Julia–Esther's daughter

Stretch Johnson–a trapper and Esther's husband

*Annie Tommie–medicine woman and daughter of Johnny Jumper

*Tony Tommie–the first Seminole to attend Fort Lauderdale schools

*Willie Jumper–brother of Annie, of first to go to Dania

*Jack and Pocahontas Huff–grandchildren of Annie, of first to stay at
    Dania

*Betty Mae Tiger–first Seminole to graduate from high school, later first
    Native American woman tribal chairman

*Ada Tiger–Betty Mae's mother

*Billie Osceola–a student and later pastor

Squirrel–a Seminole widower

Dav-id–Seminole man in Miami

SQUATTERS AT DANIA
 *King Solomon Branham
 *Mr. Williams

*THIRD-GENERATION CROMARTIE CHILDREN
 *Dale, Margaret, and DeWitt Jr. (children of DeWitt and Frances)
 *Billy, Alice, and John (children of Augustus and Vera)

MIAMI
*Mary Munroe–a plume trade protester and protector of the Everglades
*Hiram Byrd–president of Florida Audubon Society

*denotes historical person

GLOSSARY OF TERMS

bar	a netting dropped over the bed in the evening to protect against mosquitos
bell boy	a rattlesnake
chickee	Seminole home composed of six posts holding a palm-leaf-thatched roof and a floor made of half logs raised two to three feet from the ground. People sit on the platforms rather than go into their houses. Stranahan trading post kept chickees for visiting guests.
chizy winks	little biting bugs nearly impossible to see
cootnie	a flour or starch made from a root. Pronounced Com-tie or comp-tie in the Muskogeon dialect; coon-tie or koonti from the Mikasuki dialect.
Florida Crackers	non-Indian natives of the Everglades
FEC	Florida East Coast Railroad
hardwood hammock	several trees growing in a mound
Mikasuki	dialect spoken of those Seminoles in the Big Cypress and Biscayne Bay area of south Florida, near Miami
Muskogeon	dialect more often spoken by Cow Creek Seminoles
ojus	word used by Seminoles to mean "good"
saw grass	sharp, toothlike grass growing in ponds in the Everglades
scratch well	a shallow water hole dug by hands in the Everglades. Muddy water is taken out in three or four cups with clear, though warm, water remaining
sofkee	a corn-and-water mixture that is served as a drink by Seminole people and south Floridians
wyomee	Seminole slang word for liquor
watchie-esta hutrie	Seminole word meaning "little white mother," affectionate term for Ivy

PROLOGUE

*W*hat is it about water that makes me dream of it so often? The lapping of the New River against pilings outside the camp, perhaps, sounds that now send me to sleep? Maybe it's the memory of 1896, sloshing through land still saturated by hurricanes, wet toes a constant even in the wagon that should have been dry but never seemed to be with six children scrubbed feet first by south Florida's steamy-water milieu.

In my dreams I hear the manatees again. They blow and twist at twilight as they leave the safety of the sea bays in search of hyacinths, on a path so ancient and ingrained I simply gaze, amazed. Sometimes snakes twist there, white-mouthed moccasins lazing across cypress-darkened waters. They pursue me and the Seminole child I swim with in my arms. "Ojus," the child says, though I cannot see the good in it just then. They back us from the river, the snakes do, where we seek refuge in Frank's arms, arms large enough to hold us all, just as he once held us in his heart.

Dreams are formed of fragments and shavings of hope; life and faith make the rest. I have a story to tell, of life and hope and dreams, of challenge and teaching and lessons to learn. It was what I longed to do those years and did, I believe. Never waste time doing what someone else can do, that was my motto. Still is.

Some have said I didn't really know, didn't really cover what I cared about. How could I, just a small white woman, unfamiliar with their practices and lives, just one person trying to right wrongs? What could I do—change being ordained, after all? But Frank knew and I did, too, in time. Time. That's what it took, time washed with vision, faith, patience, and commitment. In the process, I was taught, too. Such are the nature of true communions, mystic and sweet though they be.

I must begin farther back, before Frank and I met and agreed to our terms. That he concurred marked *our* beginning, but my momentum had come before and must be told of first.

Part One

CHAPTER ONE

Lemon City, Florida, 1898

Squirrels chattering brought me, Ivy Julia Cromartie, seventeen years old, from my dream-filled sleep. Tropical sun spilled over the split leaves of coconut palms outside the window. It was early sunshine, light washing away dark. The day had barely begun but it promised to be a still and sultry one.

My heart pounded as I shook myself of wet and fought it before realizing there was no water, only mosquito netting brushed against my face, the bar letting the protection drop low. Good. It wasn't a fearsome thing pulled up out of the ooze of my unconscious, just a residue of sleep.

"Time to rise, Pink," I said.

The soft, warm form that was my only living sister moaned beside me.

"It's the big day," I said.

"Your big day," she said after a pause, her throaty voice hushed by the pillow's down. She rolled over and pulled the linen sheet from us as she did. Warmth from her slender body brushed beside me, releasing a scent of citrus from her tousled hair. "I'm jittery as a frog jig." She yawned and laid there, languid and lethargic.

I laughed. "I'll put my jitters to rest if they arrive as yours," I said.

"You don't look worried at all," Pink said. Her blue eyes blinked against shafts of light beginning to pour in through the cracks of shutters. "Are you really, sister?"

"Honest to truth?"

She nodded, moistened her lips with her tongue.

"I've poured as much into my head as Ada Merritt could find inside all her books and years of experience, and today I find out if I can pour it back. It's enough to set the soul on edge."

Pink stretched her arms, white as beach sand, over her head. Her sandy hair spilled onto the pillow slip's embroidery. She was fourteen months younger than I but taller and more willowy, though with the same narrow hips, the same eggshell complexion. More sickly she was, too, always first to get the summer fevers that arrived with rains and mosquitoes. She'd been healthy so far this season and we'd reached the approach of winter without her being ill.

Pink had the look of a ripening mango, a state we all hoped would defy the yellow fever said to be moving our way. Maybe the south Florida drought kept her tuned that year.

My sister stared at me, eyes like a Key deer, attentive and gentle. I thought she'd make a fine mother when that time came, after her schooling, after she'd exercised her mind.

"You'll do well, sister," Pink said. "You're always outperformin' yourself. My jitters come from knowin' you'll be gone soon after that."

"Know-ing," I corrected. "Don't drop your *g*s, it's unbecoming to a lady. Makes you sound unschooled."

She rolled her eyes, the shape of plump almonds that always looked sleepy even when she wasn't. "You'll be just fine," she said. "Correctin's in your blood." She rolled back over.

"Is that really how it comes out? I just want you to know what's right, that's all. Pink?"

No amount of gentle jabbing against her chemised back brought even a giggle. I knew I may as well begin my morning regime without her.

Leg stretches first, while still in bed, as the drift of bougainvillea floated through the air. "No need to rise before exercise," Ada'd told me once. "Discipline may as well begin early."

Ada was the sister of the school superintendent of Dade County. She lived in Miami, a distance away. Ada wore discipline as though it were a whalebone corset meant to keep one rigid and straight. Once, she confided, a bone had broken and brought blood to her rib cage before she could gracefully excuse herself for repairs.

That morning, rigid and straight was what I needed to keep control over butterflies batting at balls in my stomach. I stretched my fingers to my toes. It was a mindless, soothing task, these exercises. Simple routine had a calming effect on one's soul. I stood up to touch my toes. A mockingbird insisted itself into my thoughts, chirping outside the window.

I stretched my legs, then reached for sky. Both hands overhead, then forward to the ruffles of my pantaloons circling my feet. Like a palmetto in a hurricane reaching green to sand, I touched the cloth, then the rag rug, my hands always flat against floor. Twelve more stretches, exactly.

My deep breathing must have finally roused Pink.

"Couldn't you skip that once?" Pink asked.

She was named for a flower and her cheeks reminded me of it as she sat up, finally, her hair spilling over her sleeveless arms.

"My exercises, my walk? Not today, especially. Routine creates a sense of competency," I told her. "Doing the same things every day is a way to build character, a Greek word meaning 'to chisel,' Ada says."

"Builds boring, too," Pink said.

I sat on the rug now. Bleached bloomers over opaque legs formed the letter Y. Bend chest to knee, fingers gently tugging at toes. Now leg over neck, chest to the floor.

Pink groaned, flopped herself back on the bed. "You're like a noodle."

"I can hope such stretching will result in a lengthened spine."

"Hasn't in seventeen years," Pink said.

"Think how short I'd be if I hadn't. Besides, Ada says there's nothing wrong with being routinized."

I'd looked for the word in Noah Webster's book, deciding when I couldn't find it that Ada had made it up. She could do that, make up things in the flick of a fawn's tail. A great storyteller, she was and trained me to be, a valued lesson for sharing a home with five younger living children.

Still, if "routinized" meant establishing a discipline, one with predictability and precision, then I fit it as sure as the summer season brought rain.

I stood, slipped out of my sleep clothes, splashed tepid water from the bowl onto my face. I allowed myself only a small splash what with the cisterns so down. Even troops leaving Key West for the Cuban war had run out of water and had to bring barges in to supply them. South Florida waited for rain while the army built distilleries turning salt into liquid the soldiers would drink.

"Such a marvel," Papa'd said, "how the government can change even the sea if it's a mind to."

I donned my own corset, clasped front hooks to snug at my bony hips, and stepped into three light petticoats I tied at the waist. Looking up, I caught Pink's image in the mirror and watched her dab at her eyes with some linen.

"You're not crying, are you? Please don't. I may not even get a contract offered."

"You will. Then you'll be off."

I wiped a slice of lemon over my forehead and cheeks, swept my hair up in a knot at the top of my head. A white cotton shirtwaist drifted over my corset. I cinched a belt and reached for my straw hat before coming to sit on the side of the bed. Pink's face lay hidden now beneath the sheet.

"It won't be for long if it happens," I said, "nor far away, I'm sure of that." I wondered when I said it if I was being honest. "And if it is, I'll bring you along. All of you, keep you safe and sound."

"You can't know," Pink said. "I heard you say to Mama."

"Miami's growing. So is Lemon City. Maybe I'll get a position right here. Could be. Anyway, it hasn't happened yet, so don't you go away in your mind. I need your help, today especially, with the Baby Bugs. Pink?"

Her body remained still as a deer at twilight.

"I'm taking my walk, and then when I get back, be ready to eat with me, all right? It really would help calm my nerves."

"Whatever you say," Pink said. She lowered the sheet to just below her eyes. "But you look as far from nervous as New York is from Richmond."

"Things aren't always as they seem," I said, hoping to hide the relief in my voice. I headed out.

A creature of habit, I am, a quality I think befits all productive people, and I most assuredly wanted to be that. Prayers came easily to me on my walks. My hat shaded sun and my bare feet kicked at the tiny white-rock paths that led past vines and lilies out toward the bay. I expressed my gratitude and confession, asked for calming and direction; then my mind was free to soar while my feet marked the mile or more I walked each morning. Usually I'd swim but not today, one small exception to routine.

Sun sparkled bright off water. The smell of distant smoke, from one of the lightning-sparked fires that always came with drought times, drifted on a breeze. A cluster of clouds hovered off the coast, a long way off but close enough to remind me it was the season. I made a mental note to warn Papa, have him set the boys to boarding windows, then decided to turn back. There'd be much to do for safekeeping those I loved while I took the teaching test in Miami.

As I walked I wondered if the boys had caught up enough spiders for their pet lizards. I'd have to check. In the distance, two small forms appeared and squatted on the white-rock road, and I thought at first it might be my younger brothers. But these boys were dressed in long shorts with bare, pink-skinned backs. First-time visitors, I supposed, and not aware of how hot the sun could be even in the morning.

They poked at an object with a stick and when it came to me what they were doing, my face felt hot with fury. I could not abide an uncorrected wrong.

"Stop that! Turn him over. I'll find your parents, I will."

Startled, they turned and stared, their eyes wide. I stiffened my back like a bed slat. Papa said I could "get my back up over the smallest things," but by the size of their eyes, I suspected they would not describe my state as small. They looked from me to each other, then dropped their sticks and ran crashing through ferns and palmettos. "Don't stop 'til you hit Ohio!" I shouted, shaking my finger at them as they disappeared from sight.

The turtle lay on its back, vulnerable and exposed, its legs with thin green stripes pulled in for protection then reaching out to right itself. I lifted the creature with both hands. His legs pawed against the air and brushed my fingers as I turned him over. The turtle sat for a bit, head inside its shell, not unlike Pink's had been that morning. Oriented and secure, he poked his head back out, saw my toes, pulled back in, waited. We each moved our separate ways, our heartbeats back to normal.

Back at the house, I heard stirring.

Bloxham, the brother closest to my age, had left early to help Papa. DeWitt, Augustus—Gussie, we called him—and Albert, the baby bugs as I called them outside of their hearing, were up already and Pink had served them, setting mugs of canned milk beside their plates of eggs, biscuits, and pear-shaped guavas. I considered challenging Pink's use of milk, a luxury in south Florida, but didn't. She looked so serene in her faded plaid dress the color of beach sand and peach pits. She'd tied a wide cloth belt at her narrow waist.

"How's Mama?" I lifted my straw hat and hooked it on the rack. The blue ribbon hung limp in the heat.

"Tired," Pink said.

"But she's rousing," I heard Mama say behind us. Mama's soft, breathy voice spoke from the doorway where she leaned, her dark hair laced with gray pulled back from her face with a wide black ribbon. "And will be taking you to Miami."

I loved the Miami trips with my mother though they'd been few, given her health. We usually didn't take the younger children along, except for the baby, so the trips became my time alone with Mama. We had things to do, of course. Gathering supplies, picking up harnesses and items repaired, and once, a special trip for my picture. But I had become the children's second mother, wiping faces, washing bloomers, entertaining them with stories and games; and the weekly trip with my mother permitted me to forget that and be just a child of hers. Today would be special, a major alteration in my life. She would share the stitching.

"Come sit down, Mama," I said, patting the back of the chair. "Pink's got things settled this morning."

She was a bent palm-tree woman, our mother, hinting at an earlier sturdiness and more strain than sleeplessness caped on her bony shoulders.

"I could even drive the cart alone, you know."

"Can I have more milk?" Gussie asked.

"May I."

"I guess you can," he said to me, looking bewildered.

"She means you can if you're able but you may if you want," DeWitt told him, swirling his milk in the cup so it came almost to the lip but didn't spill. He ignored my right eyebrow raised to him. Albert waddled into the kitchen chewing on a piece of hard bread, his eyes exploring worlds from his height of everyone's knees. Mama must have already been up and fed him before even Pink and I moved around, as he was dressed and crumbs of éclairs dribbled onto his shirt.

"And miss the drive with you?" Mama said. "Not my plan." She lifted a wisp of tawny hair from my temple, pushed it back into place. "Let me look."

She held out my arms with her cool fingertips, motioned for me to turn around. She brushed at a tuck of my collar. The scent of rose hips drifted to my nose.

Mama stood withered as a fig leaf facing me, eyes with lines formed too soon on her face. Always pregnant so quickly after each baby, I wondered if she wasn't tired of conceiving and then either birthing or losing or burying a child every other year in a different plot of Florida ground. She never complained, not once, never mentioned scattered graves out loud, nor my part in one.

"You know how proud we are of you."

"I know, Mama, but first I must get through it. Then we can celebrate. May I squeeze you grapefruit? You don't look strong this morning."

"You change the subject when it comes on you," she said. When I didn't answer she smiled. "Yes, I'll have grapefruit if you take it with me. You, too, Pink and you boys. We've time. We'll propose a cheer to our Ivy, who walks out the door today a student and will return a teacher."

"At least she hopes to have the trappings of one," I said. "We'll have to see about the title."

Mama kissed me on the forehead, her lips cool and soft. "I know it's what you've always wanted, to teach and teach some more. Lord knows you didn't get that from me. And you, not able to school for as long as you wanted, us always on the move..." Her eyes pooled as her voice trailed away.

"It'll be fine," I said. "Isn't that what you've always said? Just have faith and all will be fine."

She blinked and looked away.

"You can take the test again and again until you pass it, can't you, sister?"

"Such a vote of confidence."

"I only meant to cart away a worry," Pink said. Her bare toes made circles on the floor. "You've carried off plenty of mine." She slipped in beside me then; her arm squeezed at my waist.

"If I fail, I can take it again," I said. "It's a good thing to remember." Pink grinned so I didn't add that it would be another year before the test would be repeated, another year before contracts would be let, another year of waiting before attempting to reach my goal again.

Gussie said, "I'll marry you and you'll never have to go away." He stood up, put his little arms around my skirts, and hugged me. He was warm and smelled of sleep.

"Or bury your head in the sand if you fail," DeWitt said, holding his fork in the air as though announcing election results. "That's what I'd do."

"I'll bury *you*," I said, reaching over Gussie to tousle his brother's brown hair. "Did you feed the lizard?"

"Who's burying whom?" my father said, bending as he came through the door. Bloxham, straight and tall in suspenders and rolled-up pants, stood behind him, fresh earth dribbled onto his bare feet. A heel rubbed against toes. Bloxham's grin proved infectious and as supportive as Pink's, though he was quieter than she, kept his ideas more to himself.

"Papa home," Albert squealed and dove out from behind Mama's skirts to the knees of his father.

"I wondered if you'd make it back in time to say good-bye," Mama said.

"Now, Sarah. You didn't think I'd forget my girl on her big day, did you? You didn't look as though you were up to that Miami trip this morning."

"Why, I'm just fine," Mama said.

Then to me he said, "Not every day a father gets to see his daughter step over the threshold into independence."

"Even if I pass I'll have to have a contract offered, and that might not happen for months," I said, not liking the weight they placed on this day. "You may not be rid of me as soon as you'd like."

"My girl'll be snapped up in minutes," my father said, and I warmed in his confidence if not in his grasp of the facts.

"I wished you wouldn't go at all," Gussie said. He added an extra *d* to *would* and so it sounded like "wood dent." He had tears in his eyes, and I noticed then he hadn't touched his breakfast.

"We'll all have to leave," I told him. "But we won't go far away."

"Not me," he said. "I'm staying here for always. And not you, neither, I wished."

I squatted down beside him and patted my heart. "You'll always be here," I said. "Whether I become a teacher and move away or grow old playing marbles with you." He leaned into my shoulder and I felt his little bony back shudder. "It's a scary time for me, too," I whispered.

"It is?" he asked, leaning away from me.

"Yes, sir, change is scary. How could we turn it into fun?"

His mind worked while he chewed on his lip. "'Member when we saw that train?" he asked.

"All the smoke and noise and fearful machines? I remember."

"We had fun after I put my scared in a sack," Gussie said. He wiped his eyes with the back of his hand.

"Then that's what we have to look for," I said. "A sack to put the scared into so we can take the fun part out. I'll remember that. Thank you, Master Gussie."

Gussie beamed then began to eat.

DeWitt cleared his throat and said he'd squeeze the grapefruit if Bloxham would help him climb the tree. Activity shifted, and hands and feet were now engaged in bringing in fresh fruit for my send-off, which one would have thought was to Richmond or Tallahassee rather than to Miami and the superintendent's office.

Papa sat at the table. My mother served him a soft roll while they exchanged information about the small grove he nurtured. The younger boys chattered and swung their feet while Pink licked the grapefruit juice from the palm of her hand. I watched Mama, her head leaned to each child who spoke even while she nodded to my father's words. Her wardrobe was a shirtwaist dress and weariness. The meal finished, I stood, picked up my hat with the netting, and took Gussie's hand to walk outside, shading sun from his eyes with my palm. The clouds off the beach had grown longer now.

"That time of year," Papa said, standing behind me. He moved around us to put my carpetbag of overnight things into the cart, then walked to the front of the mule to brush a mixture containing turpentine around the animal's nostrils and eyes. "Should hold the chizy winks for a while," he said, setting the pot into the footwell. "Better start battening down the hatches, boys."

"Doesn't feel like it," Bloxham said, gazing out toward the sea. He was named for a former governor, a "wool hat" democrat like my father. All the boys had been named for patriotic men.

Papa squinted toward the beach. "Seen too many not to recognize the early signs. Too sultry and silent not to be worrisome. A few days off, though. We've got time. Step up, Ivy. Best we be off."

"Isn't Mama taking me?"

"I'm replacing her on your monthly trip," Papa said, "if you can stand to have your old man about."

I lowered my eyes. "Of course, Papa."

My mother didn't protest his decision, but I thought I read disappointment in her. She held Albert on her hip and used the doorjamb to support them. Albert reached out to me. "Miss me I gone?" he wiggled his arms to me. "Miss me I gone?"

"I'll miss you when you're gone," I said, and touched his nose until he smiled. "Are you feeling all right, Mama?"

"Fine, girl, just fine."

I tried to put sense into my unease about her words and the way she chose to say them but could not cut out the pattern. "Want to walk partway with us, Gussie?" I said instead. "Couldn't he and Pink, Papa?"

"I can?" Gussie's eyes lit up with my father's nod.

"You certainly may," I said, squatting down to his height.

The child squeezed my hand in his, then released me only to cling to my neck. "I'll be back," I said. "Honest to truth, I will."

I pulled his arms, as thin as sticks, from around my neck and motioned to Pink with my eyes. She stood behind him and eased him into her softness.

Papa pushed his hand at me again to help me up into the cart, then stepped up himself. My fingers smelled of turpentine when he released them. I pulled my hat netting down over my face to ward off the bugs, then opened the umbrella kept in the footwell.

"I'll be back soon," I said. "Maybe just two sleeps."

Mama waved, too, a tired motion. Papa was probably right, she was just worn.

"One sleep," Gussie said, holding up his finger.

"It's not so far away," I said.

He and Pink fast-walked beside us now. Papa slapped the reins on the back of the mule and we picked up the pace just a bit while the rest of my kin waved and shouted.

"She leavin' us!" Gussie wailed.

"Not forever," Pink said, waving vigorously. "And she won't never let us go."

I thought to correct her, to not present hopes that couldn't be met. But we'd left them behind. I turned my eyes to the road ahead, aware that something of value had ended.

Children were my life's greatest treasure. There had never been any question in my mind about that. When I thought of my brothers and sisters, a fullness stretched the measure of my heart. But I also knew that babies arrived through an ocean of pain, a condition I planned to avoid at all cost.

Gussie's words about leaving stayed with me. I didn't want to think of how they'd feel when I truly did leave as I knew I'd have to. There'd be disappointment and pain. But safekeeping, too, I hoped, in the end. That was my plan: to leave yet take care of them all. I always had some kind of plan.

Papa kept glancing toward the sea, and his unusual quietness, not even singing a note, made me repeat my suggestion. "I really could go alone," I said.

The crunch of wooden wheels against the white rock filled the silence. "Wouldn't want you doing that," he said. "Got enough to think on with the test. This way you can use the time to memorize. I'll keep quiet so you can."

"Thank you, Papa."

"Need to make the best use of your time," he said. "Once that minute is gone, it's gone forever."

The mottled shadows of sun through palms and ferns that lined the road made me more sleepy than alert and brought back the memory of my early-morning dream.

It wasn't of the New River then, the water of my dream, but of the Suwanee, in an area where I'd been born; at least I supposed that was the dream river's source. It might have been the Peace River or even the St. Johns. I'd walked beside a string of streams in my native state, my father being of the wandering kind, taking his family with him.

The Seminoles appeared often in the watery dreams. They pressed into my sleep shortly after my first Seminole encounter, in Miami. I had been fifteen and newly arrived in south Florida. It was our first day at a mercantile along the Miami River.

A straight-backed Indian man used broken English there with the trading post's owner, whom I later learned was named Isidore Cohen. That day, they traded dried alligator hides and egret plumes for calico and knives. Papa, Mama, and my five younger brothers and sister had stepped out of our wagon, tired, and for me, more than a little wary of our future.

Papa'd seen his friends lose everything in the big north Florida freeze of 1894–1895 and word had it that Papa could farm again, if he would follow that wealthy Flagler constructing a railroad farther south. That's what I'd overheard him tell Mama.

With the extension of the Florida East Coast Railroad, the FEC, we called it, my father and other farmers in south Florida would have a way to send produce north for the first time. The land promised to be free of frost always, and so we'd headed for the potential of Biscayne Bay, Lemon City, and a little town called Miami.

Lemon City was bigger than Miami and had a better dock off Biscayne Bay. But with northern folks seeking sunshine and the railroad to bring them, Miami, like a voluptuous younger sister, soon outgrew us.

We'd driven our cart to Miami first as that was where the FEC would eventually end. Mosquitos and whisks of tiny bugs they called chizy winks welcomed us, along with new beginnings.

"Take that," the big Seminole man said, pointing with his chin to an umbrella of all things. He handed over pelts stretched on a board, and Mr. Cohen lifted the umbrella from a bin of them, a trade apparently having been made.

"Finest in Florida, Charlie," Mr. Cohen told him. "Pure Chinese silk. Keep the downpour off you day or night and the sunshine, too."

Mr. Cohen opened it for him and I noticed the eyes of several children get large as they huddled behind the colorful skirts of a woman I assumed was their mother. She stood solemnly near the door. The scent of onion and peppermint from the shelf of candies filled the small post.

Charlie Tigertail grunted. He located the button to close the umbrella, pushed his wide thumb into it. He examined then closed the silk, turning it this way and that and then proceeded to a counter where he picked up a gold watch bob with the tip of his new umbrella.

"How many hides, this?" he said, and Mr. Cohen's eyes sparkled in anticipation.

"Oh, that's a special one," he said. He winked at my father and grinned, a kind of complicity that surprised me, even at fifteen. My father had no connection with Mr. Cohen except that he was not dressed like an Indian.

"Solid gold, it is. Fifty hides for sure."

Charlie used the closed umbrella to bring the chain to him and let it cascade into his palm. He ran the links through his fingers as though washing it in water. "Twenty," he said.

Mr. Cohen looked as if he'd swallowed a fly with no salt. "You know better than that, Charlie," he said. He had a pouting look to his face now, jowls hanging low. "I set a fair price."

The big Seminole laid the chain back down on the counter. It was heavy and clanked against the wood. "*Ojus,* or we not trade here," he said.

"*Ojus,* yes, good. I'm glad you know that," Cohen said. He rocked back and forth on his heels, his fingers pressed against the Dade pine counter, his aproned belly rubbed against wood. "So you agree it's a good price? Look pretty on your blouse there."

"Don't have fifty worth one. All mine good for two. Chain not worth that."

Cohen hesitated, followed by additional moments of discussion, but neither changed the value of their products. Charlie raised his umbrella and pointed to the bag of flour set beside the counter. "How much?"

In my later years, I learned that trading could go on all day like that with egret plumes bringing twenty-five cents apiece and buckskin dyed with red mangrove bark bringing a dollar a pound and the price of alligator hides varying with the vagaries of seasons and the garment industry interests in New York.

Glass beads for Charlie's wife and possibly her sisters and books of cloth began to stack beside otter pelts by the end of the day, item by item.

One had to be patient behind Seminole trades.

I turned and caught a glimpse of strong dark eyes, the Seminole woman's. She stood back, showing no sign of impatience.

"Who are they?" Bloxham asked. His voice cracked, and his Adam's apple bobbed in embarrassment. He pointed his then thirteen-year-old finger toward the window of the post. Mama and I looked in unison and saw several Seminoles standing outside beside dugout canoes lined up at the post's dock.

"Sh-h," Mama said as she turned. Her voice was sweet and weary. "Not polite to point, Bloxham, dear."

They wore head turbans and knee-length shirts, the men did. Through the post's windows, I watched as they leaned into their canoes, lifting out bundles wrapped in canvas, their brown legs exposing curious scars that laced across muscled calves like saw grass trails through the glades.

Their children simply stood in line beside their mothers, better behaved than Mama's at the moment as each of my younger brothers and sisters began to show signs of fatigue.

Besides me and Pink and Bloxham, eight-year-old DeWitt and seven-year-old Gussie waited for Papa while Mama patted the napkined bottom of baby Albert, but two months old. She shifted her weight from foot to foot to soothe him. My little brothers picked up iron dogs and horses sitting along the counter, the toys soon chasing each other. I touched their shoulders and shook my head no.

DeWitt said, "Can't we go?"

"May we," I said. He stuck his tongue out at me. I looked to Mama, seeking support. Mama rested her chin on Albert asleep on her chest, her own eyes closed too as she hummed a low tune, their bodies swaying in the heat.

"When Papa's finished we'll go," I said, turning back. I held my voice in a whisper then. "Let's just see how many things we remember. Look at everything, and when we're outside, we'll make a count, see who can recall the most items for sale."

They began counting and I returned to my own gaze. The Indian children let me stare and acted as though they were alone as they walked to the shade of the palmetto-thatched huts Mr. Cohen had constructed next to his post, apparently for their comfort as no one else sat beneath them. They acted as though we did not exist. Another clerk finally came to help Papa. I herded DeWitt and Gussie away from the boxes of alligator eggs, jars of sweet candies, bins of pickles in a salt brine that made my nose itch when I approached it.

We purchased supplies including precious canned milk, survival liquid for Albert, Mama's milk being almost dried up by the trip.

"Heard there's land for sale," Papa said, pocketing the change into his coin purse. "Good farming?"

"Saunders still has a few parcels," the clerk said. "Up north a bit, near Lemon City'd be my advice. State lands for lease that way, too. Ad's there, if you've a mind to till soil."

He pointed to a placard hung beside the door where various needs were promised to be met by locals or strangers.

"I certainly do," Papa said. "Augustus Cromartie's the name, sir." He reached to shake the man's hand then turned to adjust his spectacles to better read the posted advertisement.

Land prices were already inflated because so many of us sought refuge from the ravages of the frozen north and visionary men, who, being human and born with the seed of greed left unchecked by Christian love, had found a way to make a dollar out of human misery. Chance had gotten them to south Florida's rich land before us though I'd like to believe my father would not have been a speculator even if he'd had the opportunity.

Still, he must have carried a heavy ache for all we'd lost. "No sorrier sight than rows of blackened citrus trunks," he'd said. The trees looked like charcoal drawings against a royal sky reaching as far as a child could see; and that's what we'd left behind. Papa had lost all he planted and what he made through teaching, and his music to supplement his farming had barely fed the little ones until we were certain the trees were dead and unrecoverable and we once again picked up and moved.

We'd treaded through water always ankle deep, often deeper, as we crossed the territory first in Sumpter County, then east to Juno and then south, the whole of Florida still wet from the big storms and folks still suffering from the memories of blackened trees. Here in south Florida we hoped to stay a while—at least I did—and replace trees, adding tomatoes and the opportunity to finally finish school.

Charlie Tigertail finished his trades about the same time Papa announced we could leave the post. Bloxham's eyes lit up. We waited for Charlie to go out, followed by his family. I gathered up my brothers and sisters, putting eggs back in the bins and returning toys to their shelves. We opened the door with the bell jangling over it and stepped out onto the boardwalk that lined the seawall. Afternoon sun scorched our faces.

Several Seminoles had already gotten into their flat canoes and begun poling out toward the swamp. Their poles, silent as tears, barely broke the calm water. Charlie's wife held the umbrella over her head, a picture I will always remember, as Papa called us to follow his cart.

The Cromartie family made its way slowly the five miles north from Miami to Lemon City, a place named for a few old lemon trees. Wild orchids and other plants now scented the atmosphere. Frost was an absent aunt here, never invited and never expected.

"Think this is the place, Mother," Papa said. He scanned the horizon of little houses and fields of citrus trees branched out like broccoli in the distance.

"It has a good feel to it," Mama agreed.

That was enough for Papa. We found a small house and stayed.

The Seminoles stayed too, in my mind. I thought of their quiet presence at the post, the blend of Everglades and umbrella as they left. The encounter pierced me and burrowed there, found a place of belonging before I ever knew one of them—or ever thought I did. They belonged to the landscape, from what I could see, brought swatches of color into the green, not unlike the parrots and egrets. Something distant and distinctive settled over them as they eased their canoes beneath deep-reaching trees, and I often wondered about their lives and the changes we newcomers brought with our umbrellas and hat-shaded eyes.

We rarely saw Indians after we settled so I expected them to ease from my memory. I had growing up to do and work: staying at home with the youngsters, washing clothes like a day lady, clearing weeds from tomato patches. I earned what I could for the family, helping another farmer or two pack tomatoes for shipping north. Bloxham and Pink and I weeded and worked our shoulders, and you knew by the end of the day you'd accomplished a task, that was sure. Learning by doing sears things into both brains and backs.

But the fieldwork offered thinking space, too, a quietness, with room for memory and dreams to swirl and settle. That's when the Seminoles slipped in, my curiosity and wonder about how others lived moving from daydream into nights.

Once when Mama and I hitched up Nellie and the wagon for our weekly drive south for supplies, I'd seen a lame Indian, a child carried in a cloth bag on his father's back. His thin legs, with contrary knees, stuck out of the striped sack. His eyes didn't glance away from mine as he perched over his father's shoulder. He stared at me not at all afraid. It made me wonder what had happened to him to be so brave—and bitter looking, too, now that I thought of it—while he hung like an extra limb on his father's or uncle's or brother's stout back.

"Wonder what happened?" I said to Mama.

"He's surely too young to be a war casualty," she said, watching.

The last battles had ended nearly forty years before with the United States Army in defeat and the Seminoles scattered without any hope of a protective treaty.

"Why wasn't he protected?" I asked.

"Who's to say what happened," Mama said, her response sharper than I'd expected. "Someone has abided with him through the years, cared for him, or he wouldn't still be alive," she said. "Perhaps he was born that way, and his father is doing his best to provide for him, carrying him in his own turban, I suspect."

She nodded her head toward the colorful cloth worn by one or two other men on their heads to protect them from the sun. The boy's carrier was bareheaded.

"He's maybe even preparing him for a life that moves on a troubling trail, regardless of one's race."

I'd turned to look at her, surprised at her voice that quivered a bit while her eyes stayed straight on the road, her hands wrapped into reins.

I'd caught a glimpse of them, that same boy and his keeper, a second time when I turned sixteen. Mama and I had driven in to have a photograph made of me at Hand's Studio in Miami. The boy's torso had lengthened but his legs were just as bent and short and he seemed to be no weight at all to his large-chested father. I'd decided the man was his father as they bore a resemblance, the same wide nose with one nostril that flared when they spoke. The sack that carried him was a bright twist of calico stripes this time, tied at the man's waist and his shoulders. His son's eyes had a depth to them, like a dead-calm sea with just a hint of the pull of rip-tides beneath.

I'd stood and watched so long, Mama came back out of the studio. "Not polite to stare," she said.

The picture of them stayed with me, though, a portrait of shelter, a willingness of the parent to wander through life with such unexpected linkage.

Inside the studio the photographer positioned me, and his quick-stepped wife brushed imaginary lint from my bare shoulders and plucked at an orchid in my hair.

"Such a pretty thing, you are," the photographer's wife cooed. "Heart-shaped faces come out so lovely on the plates." Her damp fingers lifted my chin, then fussed with my upswing of hair. "Let's see the velvet collar, dear. Your neck has such graceful lines. I do surely envy you your hair, too, all thick and bodied. Moisten your lips, dear. Just deep blue eyes. My, my."

I swallowed and looked away from the lens, not liking my picture taken, nor the extravagance of it.

I couldn't brush the Seminoles from my mind, though, and that night I dreamed again of them and of another river.

Oddly, when I awoke, I'd remember the fear of the dreams but also the assurance that I would make it through, that greater things awaited if I just persisted. I might not know the outcome of a thing or why I was there or how I'd come to be holding that child, but I sensed that if I did not let fear and fact as I knew it deter me, I would prevail. I would look after those I loved. I would protect them from the hurts and dangers of life and succeed with my plan, whatever that proved to be.

It was a belief that inspired me and one I relied upon as I sat beside a silent Papa and headed toward Miami on the first day of my testing.

CHAPTER TWO

Spect Ada's waitin' on you," Papa said. He pulled the mule up short in front of a two-story pine building. It was early afternoon, a time of new beginnings.

Endings come wrapped in new beginnings, I've decided since. Woven and overlapping, they send shards of light and luster onto action. They attract us and can blind us, the way the sun glints against glass beads that grace a Seminole woman's neck.

"I hope that road hasn't bounced out everything I knew," I said, standing to stretch then sitting again to lace on my shoes.

"Just have to adjust," my father said. He tipped his hat at Ada when her large frame filled the doorway, then handed me my bag as she approached. He said, "God be with you both," turned the cart about, and left.

I knew important things awaited him at home but his distance and departure left a void, deprived as I was by the chance to say a proper good-bye.

"Come along, child," Ada said, her arm around my shoulder. "Your Papa's busy and has given us time to study before tomorrow."

"I thought I'd be taking it this afternoon."

"Did you? Perhaps I suggested that. But after such a tiring trip, I thought the full day tomorrow would be better, give you time to rest and remember just a little more."

"I like getting things taken care of," I said, trying not to sound challenging.

"Patience, my dear. The first lesson to be learned. Come along. We'll study a bit, eat a light supper, and get a good night's rest. Then the test."

We did study, until twilight nudged. Ada served me cold broccoli soup then lifted the mosquito bar of the bed and plumped the pillows. Dressed in my nightdress, I crawled inside and fell asleep in the fresh linens and never knew until morning that Ada had slept on the other side of her four-poster bed.

We exercised together in the morning. I did not tell her how my stomach burned and fluttered as it fought off a growing fear of failure.

The test consumed two days. Leaves of the prolific palmettos growing outside the window clattered to break the sound of my labored breathing, deep breaths designed to calm.

"Don't give this too much weight, not too much weight, not too much," I repeated. I remembered Pink's words. "You can always take it again."

My ruse of repetition meant to relax myself did not work. I still felt clammy and noticed my shallow breathing. I wished I'd brought dried bread to absorb the bile I was forced to swallow while I wrote. The fear surprised me, appearing as it did when I'd begun the day feeling confident.

Of course I'd put too much weight into it, this teaching and testing. It had been my wish all my life to open doors of learning and understanding, to broaden thinking from the sheltered places I saw so many stay in just because they did not have tools to think or see beyond their own small world.

Teaching was in my blood, my father told me. I saw it as a gift that I'd been given, one meant to be shared. That I could earn money to help my family by doing it, that was a sign of abundance.

On Sundays our family attended the Free Methodist Church and in the evenings we read the Bible, studying it as a text, Papa often pointing out the phrases of God's promises and faithfulness to those who followed in His ways. I'd been certain that teaching was His way for me, a belief that kept my envy at bay when I watched the younger children—from October to May—walk to school in Lemon City, leaving me behind since only the lower grades were offered.

My father had done his best to teach us when we'd moved from town to town and even state to state. I'd been born near White Springs; Bloxham had been born in Georgia, and each of the rest in a different part of Florida, but we'd always learned along the way.

I'd started school in the north, along the Peace River not long after the phosphate boom brought hundreds to the area to mine fertilizer for export,

Florida's land always luring others to its riches. On weekends we walked to the Peace River with Papa encouraging us to call out our sums and multiplications as we skipped. At the river we filled bags with white sand we carried back to spread on the floor of the house, to keep it tidy and clean. Bloxham and Pink and I learned to write out our names in that Peace River sand.

We moved then to Arcadia, north of Fort Myers. There, Pink and I hung shoes strung over our necks as we walked five miles to school. We watched for snakes and panthers and tried not to be startled when wild turkeys flapped their wings in the branches beside the road. As we neared the school, we'd stop, brush sand from our feet, and put our shoes on, saving the soles for as long as we could, money being scarce and footwear even more so. Then we'd face the new children, often just learning their names before moving on.

Always, Papa spoke of our responsibility to do our best to ourselves, our family, and our country, and even talked of it around the cooking fires when we traveled in our high-wheel cart across Florida. We'd build fires on fallen logs, finding them the only surface not saturated by ankle-deep water.

Papa might have aspired to greater things than being a farmer and a music teacher and a wandering man, but he never demeaned what he was. "Got each other, a pair of shoes each, and the love of fine music. Don't know what more a body needs," he said, a phrase he repeated when his offspring dared to complain.

He called himself a democrat, my father, lifelong, one who wove duty into every date in history he made me memorize. He believed in frugality, honesty, and efficiency in government and life—and in white supremacy, as did all his democratic candidates, but not because he thought anything wrong with other races. No, he paid the poll tax at voting time without complaint, he said, because it was the way to ensure that only learned people's decisions directed government; only people with the discipline to educate themselves and use their minds would be allowed a say in larger things. He answered, "Discipline," when I asked him once why no Africans nor Indians nor Cubans came to the schools we'd sometimes stay long enough to attend.

He sat silent, sipping sofkee, a mixture of cornmeal and water, when my mother noted once that many women she knew were both educated and disciplined but nonetheless excluded from the vote.

Ada thought me well disciplined. She said I had a fine memory and a clear way of organizing my thinking and compassion. "All a teacher needs, dear—that and being a little bit of stage actor, nursemaid, musician, seamstress, diplomat, preacher, and, of course, rodent killer."

She'd laugh then, breaking up the tension of our tutoring sessions, telling stories of her first schools and people she'd lived with while she taught.

"Remember, women aren't encouraged to teach once they marry, Ivy," she admonished. And while it may have been her wish to marry, Ada never did, and so continued all her life in classrooms. Eventually, Ada stopped staying with school families and moved in with her brother and his wife. But she'd smile, wistful and remembering of her first students and the home they provided her.

"Savor the light in a child's eyes as they get brighter, dear; that's how a teacher takes wages. When a child discovers a new idea, some new truth about themselves and the world they never knew until you helped them find it, then you'll forget all the hardships and inconveniences in that one moment of communion."

Her eyes would lift into the past.

"Study now, Miss Ivy," she'd say, and tap the table beside my open book, her palm holding a crumpled handkerchief with embroidered edges. "You will become a good teacher, but you must be a disciplined student first."

The old writing desk Ada sat me down at to take the test was made of Dade County pine, planed and hand-rubbed smooth as a satin ribbon. I spread my fingers across the test pages, lifted the lead, and began to write. The lead slipped in my wet palms. I swallowed, trying to remember my routine.

I concentrated on my numbers and geography and history as I knew them, pulling dates and names and numbers from places I hadn't known existed in pockets of my mind. Newspaper accounts of Cubans and the Spanish, the war and its toll on our own; stories of ancient Rome and ruins, wars and leaders; all tumbled in my head mixed with my Father's booming voice as he taught us of government and civic responsibility, music and math.

If I could pass the teacher's exam, I could teach in whatever town a school board would have me and live in the homes of my pupils, at least until I'd saved enough to live alone. It was my dream, one I saw as lifelong. Like Ada, I did not expect to marry.

You can recognize a person from a long distance off by the way they walk, their gait and posture, the way they hold themselves against the wind or sun. So I knew Gussie and Pink and little Albert walked to meet us long before I saw their faces. Dark dots on the white-rock road, they must have been watching for me every day, none of us knowing when Ada'd be bringing me back. I watched Gussie break rank and run toward us.

"Could you stop? I'll walk with them on back."

She pulled up the mule. I stepped out and opened my arms.

"Did you pass, then?" Gussie asked when he reached me.

"Much too soon to tell that," I said, wrapping my arms around him. He smelled of sun-dried cotton.

"Was it hard, sister?" Pink asked.

Albert gestured to ride on my back.

"No more so than getting you out of bed before dawn. There's a five o'clock at the beginnin' of the day too, you know."

"I prefer the one just before supper. Haven't you always said that efficient people never repeat themselves?"

I bumped her with my hip while Albert squeezed his legs around my waist. I wished I had a striped sack to hold him instead of having to reach my arms around behind me to balance him bouncing against my back. Gussie skipped backward in front of us to hear what we said, his blue eyes all curious and lighting his lean, narrow face.

Once home, everyone hugged me and graciously encouraged, thanked Ada for bringing me and invited her to supper, an invitation she accepted before leaving to spend the night in the nearby hotel. "Thank you, Ada," I said, walking her out to her buggy. "Whatever comes of it, I thank you." I handed her a string-tied box of embroidered handkerchiefs I'd sewn for her.

"Why, thank you, child," she said, opening the package. "I certainly need these. Winters always makes my nose itch, seems to come in with the tide. How thoughtful."

"Nothing compared to what you've done for me." I lowered my eyes.

"Just part of who I am," Ada said. The breeze pushed against the puffy sleeves at her shoulders. "I could always see more in you than my other students. You've great potential, Ivy, if your heart is pure, you stay disciplined yet allow yourself to make mistakes, and you take a few chances now and then. Why, even the lobster grows the most when she's out of her shell, exposed. And laugh a little. You can be a tad serious."

"Yes, ma'am."

I thought her eyes got misty before she straightened, brushed something from the tucks of her shirtwaist, adjusted her wide, plumeless hat, and said, "I'm off, child. I'll bring news of the results just as soon as I've heard."

All my family acted pleased that a tension of our lives had passed. For them it had and I hoped my own wondering did not spill into their days.

It would take several weeks before I'd know the results. The county seat was up in Juno now, and the exam made its way for correction by train to the school board there.

As the week progressed with no word, I did my best not to be short with my brothers and sisters. A weight of uncertainty pressured my chest, though, in that place of the heart that wants to respond, just respond, whatever the result, not have to wait to act. It was not knowing that bothered me, not being able to "do this all well" that drained. It was not a position I liked.

Some people are better waiters than others. Bloxham never rushed. He gathered information and thought about a thing, presented possibilities and problems and chewed them around until solutions had passed and he still hadn't decided, telling me, "See? Patience pays off. Making the choice is what gets my stomach twisted. Gathering facts, that's adventure."

It was the opposite for me. I gathered facts and figures just enough to choose, knowing I could always adjust, always change my mind later if good cause arose, if someone offered a reasonable doubt. I considered that difference in us, how my brother would have waited out the exam results, and commented on it to him.

Bloxham laughed. "Why, I would've never taken it," he said. "At least not the first year I thought of it."

"Why not?"

"Timing," he said, tapping his temple. "It's all in the timing."

It was what we were discussing when the first rush of wind hit the house and we felt that late October storm move onshore.

Papa'd been correct in his assumption about a hurricane approaching the morning I left for the exam. The heaviness brought a growling darkness off the coast, a hovering on the horizon. It built up to attack, I imagined, the way soldiers take in courage before battle. We citizens of south Florida went about our daily tasks of tending bean fields and docking ships, unloading rail shipments and hanging out sheets, always looking over our shoulders at a force we could not prevail upon, hoping dark would move north over the ocean, away from our shores, anyone's shores, just move out to sea and disperse.

We'd nail down shutters as wind picked up. Bring in objects that could be lifted and driven through isinglass or thin roofs. Hand tools got tossed into sheds, and pets, if people had them, huddled under steps watching hurried feet bring things in from outside.

The storm hit in yellow twilight, an uplifting of palm and palmetto branches began like a sigh, and then the night turned into a rage of rain driven through shutters. Trees abandoned their leaves, clinging to their roots. Coconuts pounded roofs and crashed through bougainvillea vines. Winds raced against the clock in a swirl, so dark in the day we lit lanterns at noon. The roar continued two days before calm.

It was always a troublesome calm, this dead in the midst of disarray. "Marks the middle but could be worse to come," Papa said.

We relished it just the same, the stillness, the shriek of the wind gone so babies could sleep and mothers could sweep paths to the icehouse and skim leaves from the rain barrel while fathers checked shingles and restored kerosene fuel and new candles. And then the wind began again, in the opposite direction, tearing at oaks and stripping wild grapes of their fruit.

And rain, so much rain, with nowhere to go but inside your shoes if you ventured outside or in fields, collecting in pools in places always known to be dusty and dry. The ache of the weight of the storm dove deeper with time, deeper, inside of skin.

In the midst of it, we sang songs and I read stories and made up more. Albert fussed and coughed and pulled at his ears that drained with the rage of the wind. Mama made hot poultices for them and to place on Pink's chest when her cough came back. Pan breads bubbled on the stove, sweetened with coontie root, a gift from a neighbor's mill. The boys carried chairs and tables up the narrow stairs, stacking things there for later, in case. At night we said prayers of thanksgiving that the worst of it must have gone farther north or south since our house still stood.

When the storm subsided, we waited for the tidal surge that could come, each hurricane bearing its own personality, its own way of approaching the land and then blowing itself out.

It came, water in a wail of reverberation.

We lived on Sixty-sixth and Second Avenues, higher up, and the line of trees and depth and width of the bay broke it before reaching us. We had only rain damage to respond to.

We found Papa's music sheets soaked, my boxes of papers and notes smudged by the roof leaks, limp with the scent of dampness. Legs of chairs showed a white high-water mark where water had seeped a few inches over all the floor. Albert's leather ball bobbed about table legs before the sun came out and began drying the earth and we could sweep old rain into the street.

In the morning, we woke to skies so blue our eyes hurt to gaze at it. Seaweed and kelp cluttered beaches. Often treasures from ships caught unaware landed there on sand. Along with other young men, Bloxham walked to the docks to help with salvage operations while Papa and I, Pink and DeWitt and Gussie began cleanup of the yard and the fields. Water standing in white-rock trails just hours before sank away, and with them, the snakes and the turtles.

My uncertainty still hovered, but action and recovering from the storm salved the sting from my not knowing how I fared on the exam.

Ada delivered the results herself, stepping out from the shade of her buggy just a few days later. Her eyes were thin lines of delight buried inside a chubby face, and the joy on it gave me the news before words and made me forget I had waited.

"You, I am so proud of!" she said. She held me at arm's length, both shoulders kneaded in her large hands, one holding her always-present hankie. "To only go to school those few years and to still perform with such knowledge, such skill, it is a thrill for me! I shall never forget you!"

"Good students are born of good teachers."

"A gesture of kindness I accept with humbleness," she said in her booming voice. She hugged me, my cheek pressed against the watch pin attached to her blouse. She smelled of lavender.

"We shall have a ceremony, yes?" She spoke to my father now as much as to anyone. "With a certificate and cake and a speech or two. Yes, we will have a small ceremony at the Lemon City school. I will speak with my brother about it. And then, we will find you your students."

Ada and Zachariah T. Merritt held court in Dade County Schools, he being superintendent, she, his sister. Thanks to them, my third-grade teaching certificate arrived, we had a ceremony followed by squeezed limeade sweetened with precious sugar, and I became a certified teacher in search of her life.

Most contracts had already been let by October, school sessions running from then into May. So I told myself it was no failing when I passed into the new year of 1899 still at home, still cooking and cleaning and weeding—and teaching, but only my brothers and sisters.

I worked once or twice at the vegetable-packing plant at Dania, getting the fruit ready to ship north. Pink and Bloxham sorted with me. I made friends there with young women my age. Along with Pink, they spoke of flirtations and how they would someday marry.

"What about you, Ivy," Jessica Bassett said once, "will you marry a man from Miami?" She spoke the city's name the Florida way, with the *i* sounding like *ah*. "Maybe that photographer's son?"

"Not me." I laughed. "I'm going to teach for years once I start."

"I'll wager you marry before any of us," Jessica said. "You being so forward and all."

"Forward?"

"Walkin' forward, I mean," she said. Her hands were wide as wagon tongues, and she packed three tomatoes to my one. "Headin' for something you're so sure of. That's just the thing to make a man take notice." She lifted a dark, wayward curl from her cheek, pushed it back behind her ear with her wrist. "They think you're not interested in marriage and won't even know they've taken to you until they're totally smitten."

"But I'm not," I said.

The others laughed.

"It's true," I said, irritated by their smallness, their inability to see another way for a woman to enter her future.

"She's goin' to teach," Pink said, her long lashes framing her wide-open eyes.

"Aren't we all?" Jessica said and laughed again.

"It's a woman's calling," another said, "even if our students share our age."

They couldn't know how sure I was that teaching children was the way I'd take care of my family. I held a conviction confirmed when I'd enter our home and see Mama, sweet and kind but oh, so tired. She loved us dearly and pushed herself to do all she could to care for us. But she'd never really come back after Albert's birth. His had been one of her worst deliveries. Apparently it didn't get better with time. Albert had been her twelfth carrying.

Bloxham and I were invited for a ride on the yacht *Skipjack* in late March, the wind washing our faces. Ferns and wild iris bordered the shore, hinting at romance. I suspect Master Williams's invitation had not meant to include my handsome younger brother, who'd soon turn sixteen, but he made no objection when I broadened the courting to include Bloxham's presence.

I had my share of suitors. They did not appeal to me the way they did to most other young women. They interested me more for the diversion provided from my waiting, my knowing I would someday be leaving. I enjoyed their company, the picnics in small groups and the camaraderie, but more, I liked the opportunity to study human nature. I watched with detached interest the beguiling, the pomp they presented when attempting to win affections. I found the conversations they had with others equally fascinating, especially when one would join us at our family table and talk politics with Papa.

The Cuban situation proved a lively topic along with that upstater named Broward and his wild idea to drain the cypress swamps, move what was left of the Seminoles out to Oklahoma, and sell the land to cold-climate citizens seeking Florida's warmth.

I discontinued time with one young man when he prattled on about the New Year's Day bird kill begun just that year and how successful he'd been.

"Best way to count them," he said, "is see how many we can shoot in a day and multiply that by whatever number the birders choose, to see how they've reproduced during the year. You young ladies have a big demand for feathers," he said smiling at me. "Made plume hunters out of half of south Florida."

"Not on my account," I said. "Horrible practice, slaughtering birds just for their foliage. I'll never wear one on my head."

"The way you look in a hat, I'm surprised," he said, pulling on his mustache, leaning back in his chair to study me like a specimen. He winked at my father. I didn't like mustaches.

"Plume hunters and rum runners seem to have settled south Florida," I said, "but no reason to continue such practices among civilized people."

"Finest women in the country rely on birds' plumes," my father noted. He scraped at his fingernails with his knife.

"Not forever," I said, more to Mr. Jason than to contradict my father. "There are laws being proposed to protect them."

"Make half the citizens here smugglers if that happens, won't she, Mr. Cromartie? And all of the swamp Indians, that's sure. Why, their survival depends on fashion needs from New York to Paris."

"President McKinley's signed the reserve near Dania into law," Papa said. "Maybe they'll go there now. Have a place where they're not pushed about."

"A reservation? Prime land, I suppose," Mr. Jason scoffed. "Hope he doesn't lose his lunch over that. Look what happened the last three times the government tried to force the heathens out of the swamps."

Papa nodded his head. "Twenty million dollars and thousands of good soldiers."

The face of my father's guest began to turn red as he warmed to his subject. "None on any reservation, either, still as free as birds, no treaties controlling 'em. Call themselves 'unconquered.'" He sniffed at the word. "'Less they sign a treaty, they shouldn't get nothing but land that's used up and finished. Like they are, or should be. Western tribes that signed in 1855, they got both land and protection. Seminoles had their chance and sank it poling back into their swamps."

"Was a bit disappointed the army arrested Osceola under the white flag, though," Papa ventured.

"Soldiers do what they got to," Mr. Jason said.

"Surely capable men can find more creative activities to occupy their time than the killing of snowy egrets just to fluff up a woman's fashionable felt," I said, "or defend wicked ways of war."

"You tell that to the veterans setting about at Cohen's post," the mustached man said, one eyebrow raised. "I don't have the courage."

"Doesn't seem that plume hunters and government soldiers are in the same league," Papa said.

"Both certainly change the landscape," I said and left the room.

It was a landscape I loved. The lifting of weighty birds as they pierced the aqua morning sky, flashes of feather white or red viewed through the fans of palmettos and ferns, provided intrigue on my walks. I relished the quietness of herons, a statue on one leg beneath the arch of red mangrove roots, patiently waiting to fish. And the sight of a cormorant perched on a snag holding out its wings like one crucified, unable to fly until wind dried, never failed to sway me. It was an act so vulnerable, so exposing, and yet required if the bird was to survive. Its peril stayed imprinted on my soul.

Every walk I took in these tropics held lessons for me. The birds and the way of water and land were Florida's free treasures, the mainstay of my education.

That the birds could be destroyed for their plumage sickened me, though I confess I had not thought through what might happen if the government passed laws to stop it.

Spring turned into summer. Afternoon rains began as predictable as mosquitoes. Pink weakened, and I worried about yellow fever. It had flared up again, the "black vomit," as people called it, a thing turning skin yellow. In fact, a few hours north on the New River, people couldn't cross by ferry unless they held a doctor's certificate saying they were well and hadn't been near anyone with fever.

I read that a Dr. Kennedy living near the old army fort named Lauderdale on the New River had been cited by the Miami Board of Health for treating yellow fever victims.

Well, he wasn't actually a doctor; he was a pharmacist, which was what caused the fracas. He'd been treating people and quite successfully, too, I'm told. But he held no diploma or degree, so they fined him then told him he could submit his bills for reimbursement. Odd, but somewhat just, I thought, since no other doctors were available and people suffered less with what he did, degree or not. Rumor had it he would take the money he received and go to school, come back as a doctor with a diploma.

My own lack of a degree ached in a corner of my mind when I read the news account. If only we had stayed in one place long enough, I might have finished school. I had only a certificate, but I knew that like "Doctor" Kennedy, I could perform the service I'd been trained for and at least I had a paper to prove it.

Pink's health troubled me more than usual that year. She became so pale and ached, clutching her stomach, and though feverish and hot to touch, she often failed to perspire.

"Like it when you fix the vinegar packs," she said, looking up as I laid the pungent rags on her forehead. "Rub my legs?" I nodded and sang softly 'til her eyes closed in rest.

I sewed little gifts for her and sometimes we'd wind up the gramophone I'd won in a contest requiring no skill, just luck, with my name pulled from a hat. Music seemed to ease Pink, or perhaps the company did. Neighbors came to sit on the porch in the early evening, waving funeral fans as fat as elephant ears to ward off mosquitoes and bugs until dark, while strains of Italian tenors drifted across palms toward Biscayne Bay.

We watched the horizon for signs of hurricanes but it appeared we'd be spared that fall. September came. No harsh storms followed. I still lived at home, still with no contract.

"Think I'll write that Dr. Kennedy," I told Mama. "Find out what he uses to treat fevers. It might not hurt for Pink to have such remedies at hand, even if she lacks all the yellow's symptoms."

"How thoughtful," Mama said, dabbing at heat moisture beading at her lip.

But I didn't have to write: I could meet the man in person though it meant leaving Pink—and everyone else—behind.

Ed King arranged it, though neither of us knew at the time just what he would begin. He arrived by train down from the New River area where he chaired the school board and represented five families with children. He met immediately with Z. T. Merritt about acquiring a teacher.

Until recently, the New River community had consisted of three or four men and twenty or so Seminole families camped along the stream, well out of sight in the cypress. He wasn't counting Seminole children, he told me later, when he spoke with Z. T. Merritt of the nine children needing teaching.

It was a well-known fact that Seminoles abhorred the teaching of reading or writing English.

"Only conquered people learn their captor's language," Papa said. "'Spect that's why it's one of the few offenses gets significant punishment, even banishment from the Seminoles, never losing a war. Take their punishment serious. Don't forget old Charlie."

I remembered hearing about Charlie No Ears, a Seminole who had warned the Cooley family a few years back of an impending massacre, and though most of the white settlement had died at Cooley's Hammock, some lived—because they'd been warned. When Charlie's people learned of their survival, he paid the price of his ears for having defied his own kin.

I shuddered at that story of shelter, risk, and repercussion every time Papa told it. No, Seminoles would not be counted by Mr. King's school board.

Mr. King cultivated oranges, mangoes, and avocados, and built buildings, too. He promised Z. T. that if a teacher would be assigned, they'd chop through trees and vines and build a school so classes could begin in October 1899, just as everywhere else.

Z. T. told him he had a teacher in mind.

My train left Lemon City at 6:00 A.M. All my family came to see me off; even Pink stood there at the station, hugging and holding me despite her wan appearance.

"We ain't never been apart, sister!"

"I'll be back in the spring. Worst weather's over now, so you'll be fine. Drink lots of rainwater and take moderate doses of subnitrate of bismuth if you start to feel ill. I'll find out more when I talk to Dr. Kennedy. Papa will get a supply of morphine if things get worse. Here, pull that shawl tighter. It's chilly this morning."

"I'm not worried about being ill," she said, "except from sadness." Her eyes were puffy from crying, her voice huskier than usual.

"I can visit. And we'll write. Just tell me you need to see me. Send it by post."

"You'll come if I write?"

"Of course, Pink. I'll check every day."

Papa said again how proud he was of his little teacher, and Mama wept openly and so profoundly against me that Papa had to pull her off and hold her, reassure her more than me.

"Don't flirt too much with those New River men," Bloxham said. A thatch of his straight, dark hair drifted close to his ocean blue eyes. "I won't be there to rescue you now."

He tipped his head forward when he talked, as though the ground held more interest than the sky or another person's eyes.

"You come visit in the spring," I said. "Start deciding now. Give yourself plenty of time."

He laughed and reached for me, crushing me into his chest. He smelled of good earth and sun-dried shirts, and I squeezed back and swallowed fast, surprised by the press of tears against my eyes.

"It'll be all right," I said, stepping back, pulling the V of my jacket down over my hips.

"Who are you convincing?" he said.

"Whom," I said, and dabbed at my eyes.

He laughed from his belly.

"Head on, sister. You're ready."

DeWitt and Gussie stood off to the side, watching the brakeman and eyeing passengers in dark suits and plumed hats. The smoke and smells took the boys' interest from me. Pink held Albert now and I kissed his little face, pressed them both against me then hugged the younger boys and Bloxham again, quick and sure, just to feel each once more, smell the cleanness of their hair, the slender bones of backs I'd often bathed.

The whistle blew and the call came for me to board, and I reached for the handle to help me step up. I turned toward them all and waved a gloved hand, then took my seat beside a narrow window.

For as long as I could see them, I watched the faces blink up at me, then begin to fade away, just shapes, then tiny dots that marked my whole life, disappearing through distance and smoke.

The journey was my first alone. Brave was how I felt, to be leaving all I loved and held dear, to enter a frontier town, to begin life in the career I'd known I'd always have. This was adventure, making a thing happen even though I rode alone. Alone, but sure of who I was; so sure of everything at eighteen years of age. I didn't let myself feel sadness at the growing distance between my future and what I left behind. Instead, I let the memory of their faces gazing up at me nourish and sustain me.

Ed King met me at the railroad station two hours later. Several others at the stop, which looked to be nothing more than a boxcar, greeted friends or just lounged about, the train arrival and departure apparently one of the few entertainments along the New River.

"I've your valises, Miss Cromartie," Ed King said. "And I'll come back later for your trunks." His brogans vibrated the boardwalk as we walked toward the railroad dock. "Easy now."

He reached for my hand and steadied me as I stepped into his moored boat.

"I've only one trunk," I said.

"Unusual," he said. To my raised eyebrow in question he added, "I've got two daughters and a wife."

He tossed the soft bags behind me, pulled the docking rope, and sat down next to the engine. Set in the middle of the small boat, the engine popped six or seven times, idled quietly, then popped once or twice more. It had its own rhythm that one could set music to.

He touched the rudder and we headed east, up the main avenue that consisted of a crystal clear river lined with sea ferns and white lilies. An impressive two-story building with a row of dormers titled Byran's Hotel stood near the tracks and promised a burgeoning community.

"We live back that way," Mr. King said, lifting his voice so I could hear between the explosions of unmuffled engine. He nodded southeast with his head. "But I wanted you to see our downtown."

I spied fish in the water, dark shadows darting about. Birds called, loud enough to hear above the pop-pop of the engine.

"You being a native, don't suppose I need to advise you about the water moccasins and rattlesnakes," Ed said. "Nor alligators or brown recluse, either."

"I'm aware of their practices," I said, speaking rapidly into the unexpected silences of the pop engine.

He nodded and eased the boat closer to the north shore where I could see occasional huts and tents nestled in palmettos, a few wooden structures set back from the water. Another with a covered porch and boat dock before it Ed called Stranahan's Trading Post. A small stream invited canoes to dock along the west side. A ferry, maybe twenty by thirty feet long, sat docked there, marking the end of the cable that hung like a weary clothesline across the river.

"Pick up and post mail there. Ferry bell's on the south side, where you'll be." He pointed to the opposite side of the mango-shaded river. "Ring the little one so Frank'll know you're on foot. He'll bring the rowboat over to fetch you 'stead of the ferry. Not cost you a cent, though it used to. Twenty-five cents. People didn't use it 'less they really needed to then. Now the county pays him to run it."

"I thought it was quarantined, that you had to have a certificate?"

"State pays him a quarantine salary not to run it, county pays him to get them across. Gets paid for sure, one way or the other. He's a savvy man, that Frank." Mr. King chuckled. "I can pick things up for you if you need," he said. "Go right past it most every day."

"Thank you," I said. "It'll take some getting used to, what works best here. Just part of my schooling, I suppose." I pushed my straw hat onto my head, held my hand there to resist a flush of ocean breeze, straightened my back. I inhaled the scents of the river and sea and felt surprisingly at home.

Mr. King nodded and revved the engine, and we popped up the New River to my new life and what I hoped would be the accomplishment of my deepest, lifelong dream.

CHAPTER THREE

The New River, Ed King said, was both "sturdy and stubby, as rivers go." It rose from dark swamps of cypress, formed two forks, then flowed east to the Atlantic past this little village, twisting into a basin that paralleled the shore as a lake before surging into sea. A wide river, the distance of three ferries strung end to end, it was also deep. Some said it was called "new" because it had simply appeared one day, following one of the region's havoc-making storms. Fluffed clouds reflected in its water that day. Yellow dots of bonnet lilies floated at the edges and camouflaged secret dangers of so deep and swift a stream.

Mr. King's craft chugged easily along. People like to talk about their acquisitions, I've found, and just by asking of it I learned that he'd built the boat and operated the King Boat Yard, a site we passed.

"Build coffins, furniture, houses, schools, too," he said. "Though the one we're working on'll be my first of that line."

"Did you say 'working on'?" I shouted above pops. "So it's not finished yet?"

"Made a good start," he said. "Should have it ready to open by mid-October. Take you there as soon as you're settled in at home."

The Kings, with whom I'd reside, lived in as fine a home as appeared to exist in the community. The single-story pine house, with its rain sack hung over a coopered barrel beside the porch, could be seen on the river just around a loop of water Ed said was called King's Creek, "though it's on maps as Tarpon River." Their square house sat on high ground. Just beyond, I could see land sloped into the thickness of mangrove and leggy cypress that marked the swamp.

At the dock, I met his wife, Susan, and three of the children I'd be teaching: Byrd, Louise, and Wallace King. Eleanor, the oldest, was already married to a Smith. Wallace reminded me of a younger Gussie as he shyly clasped his hands behind his back and bowed his head when his father introduced us. Byrd, a tall drink of water quite unlike his father's form, had a spirited smile. Louise, stately and slender, looked not much younger than I. I realized she'd be in the eighth grade at least. I held only a third-grade certificate, and two of these three were well beyond that.

"Set the rules clearly and sternly, the very first day," Ada had said. "You can always go easy later, but once discipline is gone, you'd more easily wrestle alligators than get it back."

Even before I met the other students, word would get out about me, how firm or fun, how strict or how stern. So though I wanted to put my arms around Wallace, wrap him as I might Gussie or DeWitt, and perhaps share stories with Louise as a sister, I did neither.

Instead, I shook Wallace's hand. "It's a pleasure to meet you," I said, my words crisp and clear. "And you." I turned to Byrd and Louise and nodded my head once, keeping my hands clasped in front of me, resisting the urge to smooth my wet palms against linen.

"You must be tired," Mrs. King said. "Would you like to freshen up or perhaps lie down a bit? No? Take a glass of fresh juice with us, then?"

"Juice, yes," I said. "And after, if it's not too much trouble—" I turned to Mr. King, a short, square man, and said, "I'd like to see the school."

"Merritt sent money for lumber. Supposed to send boards as well," Ed King told me as we sat at their round oak table divided with an embroidered runner. "But Marshalls and Bellamys are bringing the load, and we'll have us a raising. Windowpanes arrived last week. Frank took them off the FEC at the station. They're at the post. Put them in as soon as we've walls."

"How old are the other children?" I asked Mrs. King. I remember keeping my back straight, tight against the ladder-back chair.

Louise answered. "I'm the oldest. Sixteen." Her voice held a hint of whine to it. "There are two who'll probably be in their first primers and the rest are spread out. The youngest Marshall girl isn't quite six. Where did you teach last year?"

"I didn't."

The words popped out before I had a chance to censor them. Louise's right eyebrow came up. "Except for my brothers and sisters," I added. "Four of them spread across the classes gave me a challenge. I'm really quite prepared."

"Of course you are, dear," Mrs. King said. She passed a platter of pecan cookies that I passed up even though I loved pecans. "I do hope you won't mind the chatter and rush of these children around you after a day's teaching," Mrs. King said.

"Oh, no. It'll feel just like home."

"Come along, then, and I'll show you what's there," Ed King said. He pushed his hands against the table and rose. "Marshall's got four and Bellamy's two, so with our three, we had enough for a school. Town's sure to grow. Wasn't sure we'd be able to find anyone willing to come this far out, though." He laughed.

"This is a perfectly lovely place," I said.

"Might not have thought so a few years back. Mostly thatch shacks, Indians, and traders. Until the railroad, there was just the Refuge House keeper, the postmaster, and Stranahan. Why, during one of our early elections, Captain Valentine, a founder, got pecked almost to death on his bald head. By bluejays. That's how frontier we are."

"Teach him to wear his hat," Louise said, gathering up her younger brother.

"And perhaps imbibe a bit less so he'd notice. Hatless in this sun," Mrs. King added. "Imagine that." She clucked her tongue but smiled, and I guessed she was fond of this Valentine. "We were more worried that the epidemic would keep people away. We've had several cases."

"I hope to meet Dr. Kennedy."

"Not yet, he isn't," Ed King said. "But should be. Works all day farming tomatoes and all night treatin' people. Rows that boat of his up and down the river, tows it well after dark, until everyone's been seen. Couldn't ask for a more dedicated man even if he has been known to amputate a leg with a handy saw! Patient survived," he said to my widening eyes. "Poured tobacco juice over the blade to clean it." He shook his head but in awe. "Tom's his name. Not much taller than you. Used to be a pharmacist up north, they say."

"My sister, Pink, has afflictions. I thought he might have some remedies I could share with her."

"We'll pop on up to his farm later, if you want. Ready to unearth where you'll be spending your days?"

We stepped out behind their house. Ed King led, followed by his children and then me. He pushed aside dense growth of woods and palmettos, spindly branches that grew without thinking, their roots spreading and lifting up palmlike leaves like a fan from the ground. Someone had chopped a narrow path through them, not much wider than the hoe used to hack back the brush. It smelled damp and musty, familiar. I looked above me, watching for snakes, and down, too. A covey of quail darted single file across the path, then flushed and fluttered into the tangle of brush. Different surprises awaited me here, but definitely surprises.

The next surprise appeared at the site we approached a half mile down the path, a clearing in the midst of oak trees dripping with moss and a stand of pines. The air smelled fragrant with the scent of cut lumber. In the center of the clearing rose a floor set on short stilts a foot aboveground. Makeshift steps pushed against the pine floor. Off to the side, lying on flattened palmetto, was the outline of a wall. Two window holes stared at us on either side of a hole that hoped to be a door. Palmetto roots poked through openings. There were no standing walls, no windows, no roof, no school.

"Families are bringing the rest of the lumber over tomorrow. We'll finish walls in a day or so and add tin. You'll hear the first raindrops, that's sure. Set windows, finish the stairs, and we'll be set. Give us a day or two. Water from that pump over there." Mr. King pointed to the blue cast-iron pump with long handle. "Good water. Kind of a strong smell of iron in it, but tastes all right and better 'n scratch. We'll get a rain barrel, too. Wasn't really sure we'd have someone, you know, to teach this quick. It'll be a proud place. We'll use it for church services. You'll see how it'll turn out."

"It looks just fine. As fine a school as I've ever seen. Or will be," I said.

In Louise's bed that evening, listening to the night sounds, the crickets and bullfrogs and the growl of alligators in the distance, I thought of Pink, sleeping alone in her bed for the first time just as I slept alone in this one. I curled my knees up to my chest without touching a back. It felt empty and odd.

Families and others in the town did come the next day to finish the school. I met the infamous "Cap" Valentine, former postmaster, who swept his hat in a low bow before me. He had tiny bumps on his head; I imagined they were from bluejays' beaks. The scent of ale fluffed from his breath as he spoke of books he'd read.

"I wish I'd kept my favorites in my possession, dear lady. They'd be yours to use," he said. "But, alas, I've loaned them on. I'll ask Frank to gather up more. He's the other bibliophile in town. You haven't met him yet?"

"Lots of new people to meet," I said, fanning my face with my handkerchief.

"Frank secures me classics," Cap Valentine said. "Got me my favorites, *Moby Dick* and Mark Twain's *Life on the Mississippi,* though I think Twain's a bit harsh on the south. I found *The Strange Case of Dr. Jeykll and Mr. Hyde* no stranger than evenings I've spent at Zapf's establishment after a night of imbibing. I think I loaned that book out when I stopped being postmaster," he said, replacing his hat, "or maybe I still have it. I'll have to look. I hope you like being here, Miss Cromartie. Everyone's pleased as crisp pickles to have their own school. Becoming an important place, just like Palm Beach and Miami."

"It's my pleasure," I said.

"Got to get you books for your school," he said. "Nothing more important than learning to read."

"My sentiments exactly, Mr. Valentine."

"Call me Cap," he said. "Everyone does."

We began the year without books, but I had a school bell, which I rang on October 17, 1899. The parents all brought their children the first day. We'd decided on a grade based on their age and their recitation to my questions. The remainder of my teaching tools consisted of desks, benches, a globe, a dictionary, blackboards, a chart, and our imaginations.

My days began early, even earlier for some of my pupils as they traveled long distances to come.

Children mostly arrived by pop boat. We lacked a formal convenience house but had land full of palmettos behind which one could disappear in an instant. The children excused themselves to go there. I disciplined my body never to need the palms and ferns during the schooldays.

On the first morning without parents present, the bell called nine pupils in from the pump they hovered around. I set out to memorize each name immediately, knowing there was something special about one's name, hearing it spoken with attention and care. I was determined to be as respectful of them as I expected them to be of me.

Mack Marshall received the challenge of clearing the room of critters in the morning, he being the biggest boy if not the oldest. He seemed to relish the responsibility, and it lessened a prankish look I noticed in his eye the first day he arrived, grinning and stuffing something into his pocket as he ambled last up the steps.

"Let's see what you have there, Mack. It is Mack, isn't it?"

"Yes, ma'am," he said.

"Let's have a look, Mack," I said and put out my palm. We stood near the entry and all heads turned our way.

Mack was probably ten years old and had no neck at all, just stocky shoulders and a square face with a broad forehead. He reluctantly reached his grubby palm into his pocket and pulled out a black snake. A couple of the girls squealed, but I could see it was just a Florida brown water snake, so I took it from him and showed the others, walking among them. A few of the girls moved to the back or put fingers to their mouths as though to keep from screaming. The boys moved their eyes from side to side, watching the way I held the snake's head. When its tongue darted out, little Edgar Bellamy, the youngest of the boys, stumbled over himself walking backward. Louise steadied him but kept her eyes on the snake.

"It's so smooth," Wallace said, running his small finger down the back of the reptile when I asked if anyone would like to.

"It's not even wet," blond-haired Lula Marshall noted. "You said they were slimy and wet!" She gave an accusing look to her brother. "And that slimy would rub off if it touched me."

"It could," Mack said.

"Could not!"

"Could too."

"It couldn't, Miss Cromackie. Could it? I mean Cromarkie. Oh, I don't know what I mean," she said. A blush moved up from her neck to her face.

"Let's just call me Miss Ivy," I said. "And no, the slime won't rub off."

We spent a few more moments discussing snakes and reptiles and how they lived and what they ate and which ones were dangerous and which ones weren't.

"Just remember that little pygmy rattlers, not much bigger than this one, are just as dangerous as larger ones, so don't pick up just any old snake. You were very wise, Mack, to know which reptile was safe." He sent a smile to his little sister.

"I think we ought to let him go now, though. All this attention isn't doing its little heart any good. Mack, would you please?"

"You want me to take it back?" he said.

"Yes, though I do so appreciate your sharing it with us as our first science lesson. Trees and palmettos, the fauna and flora—do you know what I mean by those words?—they're good lessons for us. It's important we not disturb in ways we can't put back. It's our responsibility," I said, "to be careful of the plants and water and to live side by side with God's creatures and respect them."

"The Indians too, I suppose?"

Louise spoke the challenge.

"All of creation," I said, gazing into the eyes of the youngest children, sensing that Louise's ways were already set.

The stocky boy took the snake from me and for a moment I thought he might poke its head toward Louise or Sally, his older sister, but he didn't. With shoulders straight, he marched right outside and released it and came back in, slipping into an open space on a bench, eyes forward, hands folded, ready for school.

After that first day, Mack came early, and with a stick or palm branch would beat along the schoolhouse walls scaring out squirrels and raccoons, spiders and snakes. When finished he'd shout, "All clear," and we'd go into our one-room school, Mack's day already begun with success and contribution.

On cool mornings, it was Frank Marshall's job to start a fire in the iron stove. I asked little Lula Marshall to bring water from the pump and keep the pitcher filled that I set on my desk made from salt-pork crates. Her scrawny arms strengthened some with the task. Children should never want for water, and Lula kept them from wandering outside to get it.

Each child was given a task, a responsibility, something that told them others depended upon them for their safety or their health or even pleasure. We would talk about the task and how it touched the lives of others and even speak beyond our little school, of how what they learned that day could affect their lives tomorrow.

They eagerly learned. Lula, not yet six, had been recruited to fill the needed nine slots that would bring a teacher to this isolated area. Her blond hair bobbed busily in the front row and she answered with pride the question I asked the first day: "How many fingers do each of you have? Lula?"

"Ten," she said, beaming. Her hand had been first to shoot up.

I shook my head. "No, you have eight fingers, Lula, and two thumbs, which are not considered fingers. But you were right to want to answer quickly and to know your numbers," I added, thinking of the merit of Ada's ways as I watched color work up Lula's neck.

They discovered my standards of respect and care for others, accuracy and risk, and reaching, even if the possibility of failure loomed. And after the first day with Mack Marshall's snake, I had no trouble with these frontier students, not a one.

I made my way to the trading post, planning to send a letter to Pink and to see if any awaited me there. I'd survived the first week. No, *triumphed,* I decided. I'd memorized all the children's names, assessed where each fell in ability, and begun designing lessons just slightly beyond their skills to give them something to reach for without discouraging their efforts. My evenings were busy preparing lessons and thinking of games to play to make learning fun. Children always learned more if they were laughing. Adults, too, I suspect, if we'd admit it.

Evenings at the Kings' had been pleasant, too, and I'd allowed myself moments to laugh and play with the King children, deciding that with a little effort I could separate my life as a teacher from my life as a boarder paying fifteen dollars a month to the Kings for my fare.

Louise remained aloof, stirring her limeade in silence, just watching, while I played checkers with Lula. Louise studied me, I thought. She proved a bright student, quick with her answers, and a fair writer, too.

That first Saturday morning of my first week away from my family, I walked to the schoolhouse, crossing the old Tarpon Canal on the two-board bridge, grasping rails on each side. I strode out long with no children with me and realized I'd have to find a way to walk more or farther. I felt better when I exerted myself each day. Swimming had always been a love of mine. I'd have to find a place to do that here.

The school building looked forlorn with no children about. Inside, the smell of lumber and chalk dust mixed as I walked between rows of benches toward the front. So simply furnished, so little to begin with, and yet already I had seen the light of insight fill the face of each child. A word spoken, a look, a smile, a gentle touch on a shoulder had been enough to brighten each child's day, if only for a moment. Their minds opened up like a door, with only the gentlest knocking. And then they were off, looking at bugs or bringing in plants, pointing to words in the dictionary that would lead us to look up others, and exploring the ideas the words put together could mean. It was like watching a pot of stew bubble into something savory and rich.

Something about the scents and the physical presence of this place welled up inside me, and I sat on a bench, aware that tears could stream down my face if I allowed them. I felt guilty to experience such joy, unworthy and yet full.

I stood to leave, then saw the shadow, just out of the corner of my eye. It sent an eerie feeling like spiders running down my back. Just a large bird, I supposed. It moved out of sight as I opened the door and disappeared by the time I stepped out. All stood still and quiet.

I walked away, then glanced back. The building looked unrelated, set into a hacked-out area of palmetto and pine.

"I suppose it has to be," I said out loud.

Ada had once quoted Robert Browning, saying that "progress was the law of life." But the quotation failed to cover the sense I had that the school looked more like a wound on this land of vibrance and green than the result of any natural law of life.

So I said a prayer, one of thanksgiving for this school's presence and one of request, that what we would do here would only nourish and not hinder, that it would be what God intended.

I strode out toward the New River then, and waited for a wild turkey to land and outrun me down the path. One like it had probably whisked past my view at the school, bringing on the shadow.

At the ferry cable, I rang a small brass bell on the south side of the river and waited for Frank Stranahan to bring his rowboat to take me across.

It was a glorious October day. On my way past the Kings', Susan had said some of the young people would be going out to the House of Refuge later for a picnic and I was invited along. It was a two-mile boat trip down the New River, ending up at the site of the third fort that Lauderdale and his Tennessee Volunteers had built during the Second Seminole War.

"You'll see the famous Sentinel Palm if you come." The tree marked the inlet for sea captains on the Atlantic.

I thought as I stood waiting for the ferry boat that I should find Dr. Kennedy instead.

A slender man left the trading post and stepped off his dock into the rowboat, then pushed off toward my side.

He had his back to me as he rowed, each bite of cypress oar slicing into the water deep and firm, the movement of a man accustomed to the rhythm of rowing. Large ears, slightly smaller than the leaves of a young elephant ear plant, set themselves off from the side of his head.

The boat thumped against the dock on the south side and the man jumped out, agile and quick. He tied the boat and reached to remove his hat, only to find that it didn't exist. His forehead furrowed for a moment and he spoke out loud as though I wasn't there.

"Getting daft in my old age, going off and leaving my hat."

He looked up at me then, as though coming from a deep fog, just discovering that I stood there.

He didn't smile, and his eyes wore a kind of wariness, as though a hurt lived there in those pools of blue fed by tiny lines of experience. He reached his hand out to help me into the boat. Warm, firm fingers held mine, and I realized it was the first time I'd been touched since Mr. King had helped me into his boat the week before.

My rower released my hand and moved out of the way so the brim of my straw hat did not bump him. He smelled of leather and lye.

Settled in, he began rowing, and we were halfway across before he spoke again, his voice a good baritone, deep and well timbered. "You must be the new schoolteacher."

"The new teacher. Yes, I am," I said.

"Know everyone else here, as you might imagine."

"I imagine you do."

"Been hearing about you." I sat quietly. "People are pleased to have their own teacher in these parts."

"The pleasure is mine. I've heard of you, too, if you're Mr. Stranahan. That you're a book collector."

"Cap Valentine," he said, and I nodded.

A drift of brown pelicans eased overhead and gulls screeched. I heard the high pitch of a parrot in the distance. Water lapped against the boat.

"Got a letter for a Miss Ivy Cromartie. From Lemon City. That's you?"

"My family lives there. And yours?"

"My people come from Ohio," he said. "Youngstown."

I thought about asking him why he'd come here or how and when, but he didn't give the usual signs that he wanted to converse. He asked for information and having received his answers showed no interest in pursuing more.

I smiled, let my fingers drift into the water. I wondered if the sea turtles came in this far. The water felt cool. Frank didn't smile back.

He was a stern-looking man, now that I faced him. His eyes were piercing and veiled. He was older than I'd thought when he first stepped out of the boat. I imagined he was in his mid to late thirties, not all that much younger than my father.

"Thought you'd be a bit older," he said then, surprising me that his mind rowed beside mine. "Taking on a new school and all, away from home."

"Did you? My father always said it wasn't the age of the tree that mattered but its root system. It's what's beneath that determines how well a tree will weather a storm."

The oar cutting the water splashed. I noticed beads of sweat form on his forehead.

"Your father's a philosopher?"

"A farmer," I said.

"Same thing," he said and this time the tiniest movement of his mustache told me he harbored a smile.

We arrived at the dock, and I looked more closely at the trading post.

A wide covered porch surrounded the shingled, single-story building set up off the ground by a foot or two. A window in the dormer of the roof was pushed out to let air circulate. Beyond, a thatched-wall building with a tin roof could be seen. It resembled a chickee, a hut similar to the one Mr. Cohen's Seminoles used to store their stocks when they came in to trade. A couple of tall pines stood to the east; mangoes and palmettos and palms clustered behind.

A nimble man with a circle of hair like a halo met us. He said his name was "Jack Wallace, ma'am," as he tied the boat and helped me from it.

"The missus works for Stranahan and Company, too, and she's as excited as a hound on a hog's trail that you're coming this way. Here, let me move this crate out of your way there."

He pushed at a salt pork box and helped me up three steps. A deep thunk of our feet marked the boardwalk to the post.

I turned to look over my shoulder, intending to thank Frank Stranahan, but all I caught was the cross of his suspenders as he strode with long steps around the back of his store.

He was already inside and standing behind a small counter when I stepped through the front.

"Letter for Miss Ivy Cromartie," he said and handed it to me. He nodded his postmaster head—marked by a visor over his eyes—then left the main room.

Pink's letter felt damp but was filled with good news.

i am better, sister. feelin my oats, papa speaks. bloxy and me chopped an acre of tomato vines then gone to the beach. met a boy there, sister. made him pink in the face. ha ha. mama makin some marmalade now. me and gussie walkin mornings. keepin you with us. breezes cool. bed cool without you.

I read the letter through, right there, and felt a twinge of longing so intense, so hollowed out, I thought I would be ill. I wished I was home with them, the baby bugs, Albert, Augustus, Bloxham, and especially Pink. Wishing, I stood there, wishing that things did not have to change at all, that all could stay the same.

"Always nice to get mail from home, ain't it? I'm Mrs. Wallace."

She didn't wait for a response, just chattered nonstop while I pretended to wipe dust from my eye. The interruption gave little time to grieve my family's distance.

"You'll find bonnets are accepted just fine here. No need for straw hats all the time." She had a singsong kind of voice. "We've lots of fine cotton bonnets right over here." She took my elbow and directed me. She stood half a foot taller and I guessed weighed twice as much as my one hundred pounds: I didn't resist.

"Lovely ruffled blouse. You make it?" I nodded.

"Your waist is much too tiny, though. I don't see how you can breathe in this heat. It's quite all right, you know, to set the whalebones aside here." She leaned into me, revealing cabbage-laced breath.

"I'm quite comfortable," I said.

Even though the idea of wearing cotton without the rigid stays sounded appealing, it was not the proper thing for a young woman to do. There were standards that I had told myself must be met and kept.

I picked up a wooden spool of O.N.T. thread and a needle, fingered the books of calico the store stocked, but didn't buy any. I put my purchases in my hand purse and asked Mrs. Wallace where the bell was to take me back across.

"Oh, Mr. Wallace can take you right this minute, if you like. Can't you, Jack?"

Her husband hustled over, tipped his hat at me, and took my elbow as we walked outside.

I was decidedly confused by my disappointment that Frank Stranahan was nowhere in sight.

Ed King did motor me out to find Dr. Kennedy later that morning. The pharmacist or doctor watched us arrive from a distance, then leaned his hoe against the side of a thatched-roof shed, brushed his hands on his dark flannel pants, and ambled toward us, wiping his forehead with the back of his forearm.

"Haven't been by for a coon's age, Ed," the doctor said. "Then you show up with beauty by your side. Does Susan know?"

"She told me to get out from underfoot. Had to pack a picnic. Guess she'll live with my fine choice here. Miss Cromartie, Tom Kennedy."

Ed helped me from the boat and the men shook hands.

"New schoolmarm," Ed said.

"I've heard you treat yellow fever with success," I said.

"Don't know that anyone really does that," Dr. Kennedy said. "Someone suffering recent, are they?"

"My sister, in Lemon City. She's almost seventeen and has a tendency, especially in winter. Trouble breathing sometimes. We've followed various treatments but without much success. I worry that she's susceptible to plagues and things."

"She live close to water?"

I shook my head. "You can see the bay from our home, but not feel evening breezes."

"That'd be my first advice," Dr. Kennedy said. His eyes were a deep brown and his face wore a few days' growth of whiskers that said he became too busy with other things to worry over shaving. "Since you've already looked at medicines and such, get her close to breezes. They push at the bugs, I think. Don't have no proof of this now, but I believe the mosquitoes and such bring on the fevers."

"Bring her here, to the New River," Ed said. "Another pretty girl would be a welcome sight."

"Won't promise such would stave off the fevers, but it couldn't hurt," Dr. Kennedy said. His mule behind him stomped in the dark muck, switching flies with its black tail.

"A good doctor's prescription," I said. "I'll see what I can do." The thought of bringing Pink closer pleased me, and it would be for a good cause, not just because I missed her. She might be the first of my family to come. Maybe then I could convince Papa. The breezes might be good for Mama's health, and the baby bugs and Bloxy would follow.

A greater sandhill crane stepped gingerly in the distance as we said our good-byes and left.

The House of Refuge, station number four of five built, staffed and stocked by the government every twenty-five miles from Miami to Bethel Creek, was a small frame structure. It existed to assist sailors surviving sea wrecks off coral reefs. It had become the perfect place for picnicking.

The Kings had packed more than enough. We had no need to pop by the post but headed east and out to the point. We motored up the river to a site sheltered from the Atlantic. The beach here extended long and white like the graceful feather of an egret.

Mr. and Mrs. Fromberger operated the Refuge, and the mister of the pair stood laughing with six or seven others, some with pant legs rolled up to knees, dragging the beach with their toes. Two women walked arm in arm, barefoot, with umbrellas to ward off the sun. Children darted about picking up shells and racing to mothers sitting and fanning themselves on blankets in the palm shade. I recognized several; they were my students, their younger brothers and sisters, and their families.

Most women wore either light calicos or alabaster day dresses with fabric belts and full skirts marked by three rows of satin ribbon circling the bottom. Several spring green umbrellas shaded sun. A few adventurous girls donned bathing suits, the navy skirts falling just below their knees. That's what I had on, the top bearing a sailor collar with short, puffy sleeves.

"Let's build a sand castle," I said to Louise.

"I didn't bring a suit," she said. "I find them so common."

"Honest? I adore them."

I signaled the younger King children and soon several others joined us. Our shouts of laughter must have lured Louise, as she ventured closer, her umbrella shading us as we bent over our creation.

"What do you think, Louise?"

She shrugged her shoulders. "Maybe a moat, over there?"

"Show me where."

She dug with her heels, then squatted when her brother and sister squealed in delight as the seawater filled up the channel. Soon she was sitting, white sand clinging to her stockings, the umbrella pitched beside the shore while she dug and shaped with her hands.

Finished, she stood, brushed sand from her skirt, then admired her creation.

"Look how the water moves around the edges," I said. "You've made a good improvement."

She nodded. "Dredged out, real channels, I mean, could float big steamers right up the New River."

"But why would you? It would wreak havoc with the fish and birds. The plants as well. Honest to truth, Louise, it would."

She shrugged her shoulders and her lower lip pushed out as her eyes dropped. "Broward says it can be done without damage. Papa thinks so, too."

"Well, you've a fine eye for design at least. The moat gave our castle much better proportion."

After a pause she said, "Thank you." Then she hugged me.

At least I thought it was a hug, just one light press of hands to my shoulders, a breath against my cheek before she quickly walked away.

I stood watching her, both startled and warmed. Her touch and the hot sand at my feet and the sound of laughter brought back the fond feeling of home. I let warmth settle on me instead of the talk of a dredge.

Susan King headed my way, pausing to lean into her daughter striding back from the sea. They stood and talked while I turned to the water. Aqua in layers like chiffon lined by silk smoothed out toward the deep, darker blue. I licked the salt from my lips. Children swam near the white sand, and a few men in their striped suits braced themselves against temperate waves. Gulls dipped and pitched. No women walked barefoot.

"Let's take our socks off," I said to Susan when I felt her stand beside me. "My feet are screaming for the sea."

"Grand plan!"

She dropped to the sand, began untying her laces. I stuffed my stockings inside her shoes. She hiked up her skirt, and hand in hand, we waded into the warm, salty sea.

Whistles rose from behind us. "Just Ed," she said fondly. "Noticing women. Ignore him."

I liked that I shared the category of "women" in her eyes.

"Now, this feels like I'm home," I shouted to her over a noisy breaker that splashed against our calves.

Hands clasped, we stood, letting the edges of our skirts turn dark with wet while our toes sank into sand.

"Mother!" Louise called from a distance, more offense than petulance in her voice.

"Louise harbors a bit of stuffiness," her mother said. She smiled, threw her head back so that the ruffles of her cap caught in the wind. "But she has a good heart."

"It's time to eat, Mother," Louise shouted again.

I heard laughter in the distance and turned to see people gathering near the food, Ed signaling for us to come in.

"Guess we'll have to go," Susan sighed.

Together, we turned to push against the waves that were already lapping at the sand castle.

That's when I noticed a man lounging off to the side under a palmetto thatch. He leaned on his elbows, dark hair lifted by the breeze. He stared off toward the ocean, no one close by except a sandpiper walking between him and the sea. But I knew who it was and I was surprised I'd failed to notice him before.

Susan King and I sat on the sand, air-drying our feet.

"No need to rush, Ivy," she said. "They've plenty of help. Hurry too quickly and we'll be set back to work."

"Thought I'd just invite the gentleman lounging there." I nodded with my head and she stretched her neck to look behind me.

"A man who does love his creature comforts," she said, turning back. "I suspect he'll follow his nose to food whether invited or not. But go ahead. He also loves to flirt with lovely ladies."

I slipped on my stockings, laced up my shoes, and walked toward him, kicking up soft sand, pondering Susan's observation. I felt a gentle energy move through me as I approached, a feeling I described as the anticipation of meeting an old friend. I was quite sure I knew him, given the size of his ears, but he didn't strike me as someone all that interested in the ways of flirting with women.

CHAPTER FOUR

I didn't really think about my boldness. He wasn't watching me approach, didn't realize I was there until I addressed him as "Mr. Stranahan."

"Yes?" He turned, surprise washing his face.

I proved the more surprised.

Prominent ears apparently marked the family clan.

"I'm so sorry," I said. "I thought you a Stranahan, someone I met earlier today."

"I'm a Stranahan. You must've met my brother, Frank." He stood and brushed sand from his pants. "He has the well-manicured mustache. His pride and joy. I'm Will, his wayward brother. Work with him at the Post but can't get him to take time off much. Perhaps when he learns that a pretty young woman mistook me for him, he'll be more interested in the beach in the future."

He smiled more easily than his brother. I lowered my eyes at the compliment.

"No need to mention it," I said. "It was quite bold of me to have addressed you. My favorite teacher, Miss Ada Merritt, would say that it's the very reason one should refrain from conversation without proper introduction."

"Know a Peter Merritt. From Lemon City. Builds bridges. Served on a committee to bring the road through, between there and Juno. Know him?"

"I imagine they're related somehow. We're such a small place, aren't we?"

"Used to write for the paper and covered politics of road-building. We were the overnight spot for the Bay Biscayne Stageline, even before the road. Reason Frank came, that and to deliver the mail at first. Ever take the stage?"

"We walked it more, though my father had a cart."

"Like the barefoot mailman."

"We never carried mail," I corrected.

He looked at me, his head cocked to one side. "No, of course you didn't."

"Your brother's had a varied experience."

"Hard worker, Frank is," Will said, his long, bare toes digging into sand. His pants were rolled up around his calves. "But that's what makes success. That and a good dose of patience and being at the right place at the right time, as I am today."

Susan King called my name, rescuing me from the consequences of my forwardness, and Will walked with me to the blue-checked tablecloth dotted with baskets of chicken and fruit. The group ate slices of smoked venison and cornmeal muffins with wild grape jelly, pickled green beans, fresh tomatoes, and boiled swamp cabbage. We drank lime juice sweetened with cootnie root and generous with water now that cisterns had been refilled from October rains. Slices of watermelon and guavas were our dessert. The tide came in, and in between bites of melon, I watched the castle disappear. Will's interest in me had waned with the presence of food and men's conversations. He and Ed and the others spoke of Flagler's investments in Palm Beach and the hope he'd build a hotel near our village. Other men gathered around and I heard words such as *"Maine"* and "Cuban fighting" and "Broward's gun-running" lift above the chatter of children and the drift of cigar smoke. Men stood downwind of the baskets we repacked. There being few mosquitoes this close to the ocean, we had small need of their usual smoky assistance.

Louise introduced me to Susan Byran, a woman of my height and age.

"How do you like teaching in our little village?" she asked. She had a gravelly voice, like someone hoarse from shouting at play.

"It's wonderful."

"I grew up here, almost," she said. "My father built the hotel by the railroad." Sunlight filtering through the pink silk of her parasol gave her face a rosy hue.

"You must be Reed's sister."

She nodded. "I've always wanted to teach," she said. "I'm going to take the test next year, as you did. Was it hard?"

"Consuming," I said, "but not exactly difficult. I didn't want to learn the material just for the test, but to hold on to it."

"Oh, of course," Susan said, the umbrella handle spinning in her hands. "That's what I'd do, too." She exposed her straight, white teeth with her smile. "And I'm hoping that this state will come to its senses before long and permit married women to teach. We teachers don't intend to stay single all our lives." Her dark hair flounced loosely around her oval face as she talked. "I fail to comprehend why I should have to choose one over the other just because I wear skirts."

She'd lifted her voice and looked beyond me, I thought to see who might have heard. I couldn't have agreed with her more but something kept me from saying it.

"A woman's place is at home," Louise said from behind her, hands clasped tightly in front. Her lips could have held a dozen pins for easy plucking. "Providing for and protecting her children."

"Unless she has none," Susan said. "That does happen, Louise, despite our challenge to be fruitful and multiply."

"God wouldn't tell us to do something and then not provide the means," Louise said. "It's a question of faith."

"You can be so stuffy sometimes, Louise," Susan Byran said.

Louise stiffened. The bun at the back of her neck never bounced when she turned in the sand and stomped off.

Susan shook her head.

"She certainly feels strongly on that subject," I said.

"Who'd have thought someone so young could be so rig—Why, hello." Susan's face lit up like a lightning flash at the young man who offered his arm.

"I'd love to stroll," she said. "You'll excuse us, Miss Ivy?" Susan waved her fingers at me over her shoulder, making me wonder just how long that budding schoolmarm would remain single.

I found an uncertain relief with them gone, the sand still warm under my feet. It seemed a good time to head back, and I wondered how long it might be before Ed King's boat would take us down the New River sound and home.

"I don't want to intrude into your time," I told Susan King. "The children are having such fun. Maybe there's another boat?"

"I'm sure there is," she said, turning to see who else had come for the day.

"What we need is a good excursion boat," Will said. "Mind if I take you back? It's a little craft I have, but sturdy. They'll vouch for me. I'm educated. I'm safe." He grinned. He had eyes clear as tide pools and just as inviting.

"The educated part, yes," Ed King said. "Not so sure I'd bet money on how safe."

"Now that he's announced it, I think you'll be just fine, Ivy," Susan King said.

"I would mind, actually," I said to Will's surprised eyes. "I think I'll just wait and go back with the Kings."

"She doesn't seem to need protecting." Ed laughed in that high-pitched way he had, and Will smiled.

"I don't mean to be rude," I said, feeling a blush move up my neck. "I just thought perhaps I should wait rather than set any tongues to wagging."

"Too late for that," Ed King said. "Though it's wise decisions we'll be chortling about, right, Will?"

Will laughed. "Some other time, then," he said. He plopped his bare heels together in the sand and bowed before leaving. I turned with relief to the sea.

Each day at school, I taught reading, writing, and arithmetic to the children, and it became "my school." My ideas and designs washed across minds in ways I planned. It surprised me a little that most of the children knew the alphabet even before we began studying letters on the chart, though only the older ones knew how to put them together into words. As with my family, their parents apparently knew how to read. Until I came, they'd taught their children themselves. My brothers and sisters and I knew about that. Except for occasional stays in one place, a father who tutored us had been our only hope at expanding our horizons through words.

As was my own habit, I began the children's schoolday with exercises.

Palmettos held in each hand worked as flags to lift and swoop and drop so it looked as though we performed a dance instead of merely stretching muscles. Younger children liked doing what the bigger children did, and moving their limbs was a good place for it. I took to breaking up the day with exercises, sometimes only for a few minutes. Children always returned with alert minds, ready for thinking.

With no individual slates, we'd go outside to practice writing in dirt and sand when it didn't rain. When it did, I'd set the primary children to the blackboard, practicing their letters while I worked with the older group discussing geography, science, and world matters.

Cap Valentine loaned old newspapers for reading practice. The articles enhanced our discussion of history (depending on how old the papers were) or current affairs. We spoke often of the fighting south, in Cuba.

"Do ya know anyone fought as a Yankee in the War between the States?" Byrd asked one day.

"Uncles," I said, being honest. "Four of six of my mother's people."

"Fought for the Yankees?" Mack's eyes were large as mangoes.

"For the North, and then were not allowed back inside their family home," I said, "so I have never met them."

"They was wrong," Byrd said with the sureness of a child, "so sending them away's fair punishment."

"*Were*, Byrd, though not all things are so clearly right or wrong," I said. "Exile from one's family is a terrible price to pay for expressing one's convictions."

"What's 'convictions'?" Lula asked.

"My Pa says the Creeks do that," Wallace said. "Make people go away when they mess up. They cut 'em first, on the legs and such, if they don't listen, then next time they send 'em off."

"Something that matters to you very much," I told Lula.

"Like my turtle?"

Wallace laughed. Lula looked at him, her face a puzzle.

"More like something you believe in," I said. "Have faith in, like that your Mama will fix supper for you or that God will answer your prayers."

Lula's eyes sparkled. She opened her mouth to speak but Minnie Bellamy interrupted. "And some Christians do, too," she said. "Send people from their home when they mess up."

She wore her cashew-colored hair pulled tightly back from her chubby face and held in a bun at the neck. She was ten but talked with the authority of some preachers I'd heard. Her head leaned forward so she could look at Byrd sitting two children down from her, studying with the older group. "Papa says where he grew up, he knew a girl told not to come to church ever again because she was doing something she wasn't 'sposed to with this boy, I can't remember his name, and—"

"I'm sure your Papa has a very good memory," I said, "but I think you can go back to your letters, now, Minnie. I believe the Indian people in this part of south Florida are called Seminoles and some, Miccosukees," I said. "We can use their correct names. But right this minute we're discussing the Spanish War, over Cuba. It's important to keep one's mind on the topic and not be led astray, Minnie."

"Yes, Miss Ivy," she said and sank back into her seat.

I found that the younger children would often hurry through their lessons so they could listen to older students recite their multiplication tables or poems they'd memorized. I knew I needed to increase the level of their own challenges. Minnie had given me the latest sign.

The following day, I brought in my china doll—one my mother had given me to soothe the pain of a time I did not like to remember. We took one dress apart, and using it as a pattern, placed it on the cream-colored silk of an old umbrella Mrs. King provided when I expressed out loud my need for material.

"We'll learn measurements and fractions," I told the boys, who acted as though I'd asked them to eat worms when I told them to lay out the dress onto the unshattered pieces of silk.

"It's a girl's thing," Wallace complained.

"Saddlemakers and tentmakers certainly know how to cut and stitch," I reminded him.

"I'd like to make a dress from my own pattern," Louise suggested. "One I have in my head."

"One in your head? How creative."

"Not yours if you stole it from those magazines you're always staring at," Byrd told his sister.

"Now, Byrd, new ideas are always helped along by old ones. It's the joining of them in our imagination, sewing them with new threads, subjecting them to different patterns in our minds that makes them unique. It's why you're here in school, to be exposed to ideas and facts and—yes, Lula? You may put your hand down."

"Conbictions?"

"Even convictions."

I gazed over them, wondering how each would change the world because of what they learned now, while they were young, while their minds were willing to see differently and take risks. "Each of you will swing off from those ideas and beliefs in your own way," I said. "It begins with knowledge. I simply don't believe we can imagine what we know nothing about."

I noticed other little dolls, small and soft, dressed in bright colors, for sale at Stranahan's Trading Post the next time I went there. Though mail came in three times each week, I thought it unlikely I'd receive letters that often so I made only a weekly visit.

I saw Will there occasionally. He acted pleasant. Mrs. Wallace's chatter had been cut back by her cooking up catfish for lodgers who stayed in overnight tents Frank provided at the back of his property. Sportsmen filled them mostly, men who took hounds into the Everglades hunting wild boars and turkeys or who hired boats to take them out for tarpon or silver kings. They were northerners, mostly, with both time and money burning holes in their tailored pockets.

Stranahan and Company was an active place though I wouldn't say bustling. A man Will called Nelson, an African man, unloaded heavy crates and barrels and moved them to the storage room at the back. He kept the bins of ammunition stocked and never spoke to patrons that I saw.

Several customers were waiting that sunny December day when Frank Stranahan came out from behind the counter to talk with me. I pressed one of the soft dolls between my fingers, thinking I would send one home for Pink.

"Made by Seminole women. Trade goods."

"I haven't seen any Indians around."

"In swamp camps," Frank said, pointing with his chin. "Won't be long. They'll pole in. Every six weeks or so 'til summer. Tourists buy them," he said, nodding toward the doll now. "Sportsmen take them home to their children."

"Soothing their conscience for being gone so long?"

"I suppose. They're popular in Pittsburgh and even Ohio."

He turned the "o" at the end of Ohio into a soft "ah." "Made of palmetto. Fibers." His wide hand gentled under mine while his flat-padded finger moved across the doll's face. "One black stitch for eyes."

He held awe in his voice—no, respect, I'd say it was. The doll's arms stood straight out like a cormorant's wings, exposed. A twist of hair marked the head; colored cloth composed of horizontal stripes formed the skirt.

Frank still held my hand in his. He looked at me then, eyes clear yet probing.

"I've some letters to post," I said, holding his gaze but pulling my hand from his.

He lifted the doll from my palm and laid it delicately in the basket that held one or two others. He stepped back and nodded formally, then bowed stiffly at the waist. "Your letters, please?" I made sure our hands did not touch when I pulled the envelopes from my cloth bag.

When I looked up, I noticed Will watching with an eyebrow raised in question.

One letter went to Pink and another to Ada Merritt. Frank stamped them and placed them in a leather pouch. I paid him and turned to leave, trying to remind myself what else it was I'd come to do.

Frank said, "You have letters. Two."

I looked at the handwriting as he handed me the rectangles.

"Beaus from home?"

"My brother. And my mother."

Was that a rash I noticed on Frank's neck? I didn't ponder it. I felt a little guilty that I'd almost failed to pick the letters up. I'd somehow become muddled. Pink had not written. Ed King had posted my letter to her, asking her to think about joining me here, for her health, and I'd expected a reply.

"Interested in Seminoles?" Frank asked. He stood beside me again. He nodded back toward the dolls.

"I'm curious about the children mostly, their educational opportunities, as you might imagine, my being a teacher and all."

"They take no stock in formal education. Forbidden to read or write English."

"Seems sad to me."

"Learn their lessons differently. Pretty wary of what we white folks offer. Good cause. Almost wiped them out in the last war. Just now coming back. No help from us."

"But their children would love the structure of school, I should think. They're like all children. They play with dolls, after all."

"I suppose," Frank said, hesitation in his response.

"They come here, so they have some trust with non-Indians."

He actually chuckled then, the first time I'd heard it, the sound bubbling up from his belly. "First morning here I woke up at dawn, surrounded by them. Guess they decided I was all right, snoring next to them on a palmetto thatch just off ground. Snores probably kept the skunks away. Hadn't heard them come in but there were a dozen canoes pulled in by morning and men and women sleeping sound."

"You must have been very tired."

"They're extremely quiet people."

"But you've done well with them? You've taught them English?"

"No, no. They spoke English before I came. Enough to get them by. But yes, we've done well together. They bring in goods regular. I meet my orders up north. I stock items they want. See for yourself when they come in, maybe a month or so."

"I'd like that."

"I'll send word."

He poled me back across the river with settled silence. Just as we bumped the other shore he said, "We have a good exchange. Beyond trade, it's at their invitation. They don't extend it often or to many. You should know, being who you are, that the two they're most wary of are strangers and teachers."

Frank did make it out to the beach for the community's picnics once or twice that season, but I learned he had to ready someone else to man the ferry when he left and that wasn't always easy to do. I wasn't sure what arrangement he had with his brother, but I did discover—through Ed King—that the "Company" part of "Stranahan and" wasn't Will but had been someone named Welles. "Will," Ed told me, "is a well-educated wanderer at heart."

A dark shadow across the schoolhouse door materialized as Frank one Saturday afternoon as I rushed to finish so I could join the Kings at the beach.

"Heard you worked here even without children around," he said.

"It's quiet. Gives me time to think."

"Not wanting to intrude. Thought you might like to see the source of the New River. Brought my boat."

Hesitation visited me for a moment. "Perhaps I can use something from the journey for my science lessons," I said.

The boat gave an excuse for not talking much, what with the popping and all. Watching him, I decided Frank must be about thirty-five years old. Little lines fled from the depth of pain in his eyes. The sadness intrigued me, but I didn't pry. The timing for sharing burdens, after all, belongs to the bearer.

Sometimes Frank shut the engine off and he'd row. "Like the stillness," he said.

We inhaled the fragrant criniums, the white lilies that draped over the water like waterfalls. He pointed out farms and various trees and talked about the royal and coconut palms he'd planted soon after he arrived. A bright burst of color he called the Carolina parakeet flitted through the Spanish moss-laden trees. We moved on past the homes of a student or two, and Minnie Bellamy stood sour-faced on the palmetto-dotted bank, waving only once as we passed.

Farther into the cypress, the banks closed in. Huge birds roosted in trees laced with Virginia creeper and blooming wild orchids. A roseate spoonbill, the flashy pink of its chest and wings cutting through the shadows and moss, stood in the shade of the lilies, its bill deep in the water. We floated so close I could almost touch it before it started, splashed, and lifted as we eased by. Moisture formed below my nose. Frank handed me a Ball jar, and I lowered the metal clip, lifted off the green glass cap, and drank. The air dropped a humid anchor on us. But even the mosquitoes we fanned from our faces couldn't dampen the beauty of it, the succulent splendor that defined the New River.

As the stream narrowed into a fork, we approached a spot Frank said was probably as close to the source as we'd find, what with the water and saw grass almost indistinguishable from each other farther in.

"Spent much time in the swamps?" he asked.

"Only when we came across."

"Pole through the saw grass," he said, speaking of the slender green leaves edged with sharp, teethlike ridges that rose from the water higher than our heads. "Grass folds down." He pointed to where we'd just eased our way through. A subtle slice in the landscape formed behind us. "Leaves a path to follow back out."

"If you know what you're looking at," I said.

We floated on water thick with greenery until just this side of what looked like a stream. Frank pointed, and I twisted about.

A waterfall flowed and spilled into a pool. It wasn't much of a drop, maybe the height of one step at the school. Feathery ferns and white lilies arched over stillness. Black-striped fish fanned their tails in water so clear it was like looking through sky.

"Oh, Frank," I said. "This is beautiful. What a perfect, peaceful place."

"One of my favorites," he said. Something in the catch of his voice made me look at him. He had straight though slightly topaz-shaded teeth he showed when he smiled, which he did now, his eyes sparkling like gently swirled pools. He took in a deep breath, and the grin that developed as he gazed at me was so full I didn't really mind his dark mustache.

He talked a bit more then, about his first coming to the Lauderdale area, how he'd helped drive the stage, then created the camp that served passengers staying over before heading south to Lemon City or up north.

"Worst year was '95," he said. "Three hurricanes in one season. Rebuilt after that. Glad my shacks set two miles inland. Can't imagine what it would have been like at the station."

"That's the year we came across from Arcadia to Lake Worth," I said. "I remember how wet everything was."

"Goes with the land," Frank said. "Places like this take the sting from those days."

"It's important to find salves for wounds. Heal them well. Otherwise they just eat away at a soul."

"I suppose," he said. His eyes dropped from mine.

Twilight approached as we popped back toward the Kings'.

"I've something more," Frank said, "if you don't mind being out yet."

"I'm fine."

Frank eased the boat to settle beside the shore across from his trading post, close to the ferry bell. He shut off the engine. Night-blooming jasmine powdered the air. Bull alligators began to serenade us. Birds chattered like children blowing tiny whistles while water lapped at the wooden boat.

But it was the sound that rose from the river that capured me.

"What is it?"

"Listen," Frank said.

A burst of air, like a swimmer gasping after winning a race, then a blowing breath followed by a flush of water. Shadows moved at the surface. Dark, long shadows that rolled then disappeared. Another burst of air followed by a spout of rising water I could barely see in the twilight.

"Sea cows," Frank whispered.

"The manatees."

"Come in most evenings this time."

In moments I could anticipate their rhythm, when they'd lift and roll and raise their backs above water, dip and sink to dive, return to the surface to blow. There must have been a dozen grand mammals as long as horses and twice as thick.

"Seeking hyacinths," Frank said. "Scavenge the bottom. Bring in their young."

I felt a shiver course through me at the sight of them, their hugeness and haunting dance. "Oh, Frank, they're magnificent."

"Suppose 'magnificent' does describe them."

I decided then that I would stay in this village called Fort Lauderdale, built along the New River. A little stream that seeped from the thick wetness of the Everglades became this: a river wide and deep that lured the manatees and served those who sought safe harbor sheathed with harmony. It became a symbol to me of something pristine and promising that flowed from the vast darkness of the past, flowed out to change tomorrow, flowed on into forever.

A pageant, with students memorizing their parts from my Bible, became the project. By Christmas, five more students had joined us as new families moved in to farm and stay. Cora, William, and Vasco Powers attended now, and Irma Bass, a little girl who lived with the Joyce family, and Tenley Bellamy, who had the scrawniest arms I'd ever seen. Thin and pale, he looked constantly in fear of his brother, Edgar, who didn't smile the whole first week I taught him. I eventually gave Edgar the task of wiping down each wooden bench with a palmetto branch before we began each day, making sure no brown recluse spiders had made their homes there.

The additions meant we had plenty of angels wearing their flour-sack dresses and lilies woven into halos. Palm branches formed wings. Those playing shepherds wore palmetto robes and pulled dark fibrous stuff from the plants' centers to make soft beards. They carried poles used to push canoes for their staffs. My china doll with new umbrella-cloth clothes became the baby Jesus, and Mary wore a tablecloth loaned by Susan King. A scene composed of palm leaves and poinsettias Frank had brought down from the north filled the front of the school, giving the place a festive and hopeful sense the whole week before the events.

That afternoon, everyone came. Clove and orange and lemon scented the air. Following the Christmas story read by Cap Valentine, each child recited a poem of several stanzas they'd learned or written themselves, scratching at the backs of their knees with their feet, fidgeting with their fingers behind them. Even Tenley wrote a poem, each line beginning with a letter of his name, something he decided on his own.

T-Tenley attempts
E-even alone.

N-notices everything,
L-looks for the spoonbill,
E-every day searching
Y-yesterday's light.

Polite applause greeted his bow from the waist, but I could tell by the furrowed frowns that the poem confused many. I smiled at him and he grinned as he sat down. I liked words that weren't always encased in form and structure all the time. Insights could come from them, stinging like bugs or just brushing past like a butterfly's wing. Tenley's effort created images, thoughts that poked about inside his mind and others', if they allowed it.

I wondered what he longed for, a child so young with wisdom spilling into his words.

Several recited the "Children's Hour," which many parents knew and the audience applauded warmly. The children stood in front of community and family fanning away at the bugs with their palm branches or funeral fans. As had most of the women, I'd stuffed newspaper beneath my stockings to deter mosquito and horsefly bites and crinkled whenever I walked to the front to introduce the next presentation.

When the formal portions were complete, we sang carols. I loved it; it so reminded me of home! Frank and Will Stranahan, the Wallaces and Cap Valentine and the Byrans all came. Even Tom—Dr. Kennedy—stopped by, briefly. He asked after Pink and nodded his balding head when I told him Mama said she was fine.

"I thought she'd come up," I said. "She loves a good gathering."

"This certainly is," Susan King told me as she swished by with a platter of pecan cookies I only looked longingly at.

The train whistle interrupted us once and Frank slipped out. The children reached in their stockings then and ate their candy and played with small toys I'd purchased for each one from the Sears catalog that Frank had ordered for me. We all drank limeade and ate cookies the girls had baked on the Kings' woodstove and brought for the occasion. The adults caught up on news. A successful school, I decided, was a place where families found joy for themselves and their children. My day was darkened only by the less than pleasant greeting of Mr. Frost, one of those who served on the local board of instruction.

"Don't know what you were thinking with that youngest boy's recitation," he said. "Doesn't seem like much good comes from that kind of free thinking."

"Great ideas come from poetry, Mr. Frost. Look at Longfellow or the poetic prose of Robert Louis Stevenson. Surely you enjoyed *Treasure Island* as a boy?"

"Didn't have time for that," he said. He was a butternut squash sort of man, round at his middle with narrower shoulders and bulges of pinkish flesh at his neck and jowls. "Learned my numbers and letters at home. Only poetry worth reading is in the Bible. Doesn't seem like we should be paying for teaching more."

"Oh, now Hiram, don't give the schoolmarm here a hard time," Ed King said. "She's done a good job for us. Why, my Wallace is already reciting his tables into the fours."

"She didn't do no recitation like that today," Hiram Frost grunted. "Not much religion, neither. School can't survive without religion."

"Whole town's gotten used to no church, Hiram. Can't expect it to happen at school instead."

"We'll have a church afore long if I have a say in it," he said. He straightened to his full six feet with those words.

"Well, this is a festive event. Come on now, let's see if we can't find a way to lift your old spirits."

Ed clapped him on the back and turned him away. They joined a group of men talking muckland and crops with only Mr. Frost standing out with his sour face.

Several people came to tell me how pleased they were, how happy to see their children learning so much and so quickly. "Even that Tenley had something different to offer," Cap Valentine said. "Whole new way of thinking out there in these young minds, isn't there?"

"My sentiments exactly," I said.

I hovered here and there, making sure plates were refilled, that the children served their parents, that flies were kept at bay. I wasn't sure why, but something about how the children behaved reflected on me. Mr. Frost's comments bothered me more than they should have. After all, not everyone could approve of me, unless I stood for nothing.

I did not go home for the holidays. The train's schedule prevented my going down and back in one day, so I sent letters and packages wrapped in calico beneath the newspaper for my brothers and sister and parents.

Pink did write back at last. *not worryin, sister. bisy with bugs and mama helpin.*

At the Kings' on Christmas morning, presents with my name on them sat wrapped in yarn beneath the tree. I was touched by their gesture. A hair comb from the King children, a new white lace blouse made by Susan.

I'd embroidered a handkerchief for each girl and bought spinning tops for Wallace and Byrd at the post. I'd asked Frank to order a special enamel baking pan for Susan, a woman I now considered my friend, different than Ada had been for me. For Ed, I'd ordered a new wooden encased tape measure. Neither had arrived in time.

"This way we'll extend Christmas into the Twelfth Night," I said.

"Always turning something discomforting into a strength, aren't you?" Susan said. "It's a good trait, believe me. Especially in a village like ours."

"Let's eat," Ed said. "I'm half starved."

Chairs scraped against wood; children chattered; Louise and I ferried platters from the kitchen, setting them on the sideboard so we almost didn't hear the knock at the door.

"Thought I heard a pop boat," Ed said when Frank stepped over the stoop.

"Just bringing packages. For Miss Ivy," Frank said.

"You deliver now, do you?" Ed winked at his wife. "Things must be slow at the post. Here, take a load off your feet." Ed's eyes sparkled, and I saw him glance my way and then to his wife again. Byrd giggled. Wallace got up to stand by my side.

"They're presents for your parents," I said in my teacher voice.

"To open after we've eaten," Susan said.

Byrd stopped laughing.

When Frank sat down, I noticed his boot. It had a slice with jagged edges across the arch. The sides and back were scraped.

"What happened to your boot?" I asked.

"Stepped in a trap," he said. His eyes looked at his foot, glanced back at me and over to Ed.

"Not a steel trap?" Ed said. "No. You're lucky you still have a foot."

Frank's mouth and mustache twitched and his ears turned the color of ripe tomatoes.

"How'd you do that? Not coming here?"

"Not today," Frank said. He cleared his throat. "A few days back. Ah…" He started to wheeze a bit as he talked. "Planned to see Miss Ivy at school. Got a new catalog in. I was late. She was gone."

"Maybe another eligible young bachelor saw you heading this way," Ed said.

"Set out a detour for me," Frank finished. He laughed and it went into a cough.

"Well, I'll be," Ed said. "Best you make your move then, Frank. Not too many eligible young ladies in Lauderdale. The competition could get brutal." He looked at Frank's foot. "Maybe even fatal."

"These children look hungry," I said.

"Let's say grace, shall we?" Susan said.

Frank didn't stay for the opening of gifts. He didn't, or couldn't, he said, because of the post.

"But if you've time later this evening," he said to me, "I'd like to come by and perhaps we could go for a ride. The moon's full. And I still have that Sears."

Now the King children almost snorted trying to keep from giggling.

"I'll check for traps," Ed said and howled his high-pitched laugh.

I thought a ride might be pleasant, inhaling the scent of night-blooming jasmine beneath a full moon. But it would create too much misguided talk, so I declined, correctness a higher calling than companionship.

Several of us did go on out to the beach late the next afternoon, though. We swam. I wore my leggings and blouse and fluted hat and we threw a ball about in the massaging waves. Susan Byran was there and Eleanor, the Kings' oldest daughter, with her husband, who worked for the railroad. It was a contented place and aptly named, this House of Refuge beach. Only Mr. Frost's presence and his talk of "proper things" pierced the amiable day.

We celebrated the New Year and the new decade with a dance held at the Kings' instead of the school. People sought a porch to sit on and a lawn to lounge on, things my schoolhouse didn't offer. The whole community, now fifty-two strong, received invitations. Even Mr. Frost attended though he maintained a constant scowl, and I wondered why he tortured himself so, participating in an event he so obviously disliked.

Heavy tables and chairs were pushed back against the walls while young babies were laid like fishes packed head to toe on the floor in a corner near the woodstove. We'd begun the evening with a small fire to take the chill off the unseasonably cool air, but by the time the accordion player finished the first reel, the room was warm and no one noticed the weather.

I danced and danced. It was something I loved to do, and there were plenty of young men I hadn't met before, coming in from the mucklands willing to swing me and Louise and Susan and even Cora Powers and Irma Bass—still schoolgirls, but able to twirl.

"They act like they've got white lightning in 'em now," I heard Mr. Frost complain to another farmer standing near the punch. "Wonder where it goes in the morning when you need 'em to work."

Even the married couples joined us in the square dancing and the old ones waving their fans kept the bugs from lighting on the food.

Frank came for a short time. He clapped his hands and tapped his foot to the music but made no effort to invite anyone to dance. When a White-hall woman approached him during women's choice, he declined, and no amount of teasing or cajoling made him change his mind.

I was aware that he watched me dance and aware that a few others did too but I didn't care. A new decade began, a new century, and we were young and entitled to enjoy it.

At midnight, several of the men meandered outside and blasted their shotguns into the air; and then we all sang "Auld Lang Syne" to the scents of swampland and the low calls of frogs.

By February, I had taken a night ride with Frank Stranahan. It was on my birthday, the 24th, but I did not tell him this nor any others. Such an announcement would have been frivolous and self-serving. Instead, we talked of him that evening, more than he'd shared with me before.

Frank told me of his poisoning in the steel mills of Ohio, how he'd inhaled arsenic used to process metal and how the big furnaces had burned his lungs. He'd come south for his health, originally. "Folks come to keep cold from their bones, usually," he said. "Stay through the winter then leave before hurricane season."

"But not you."

"No bone problems. Just breathing and sometimes my legs. Arsenic affects blood and nerves. Except for bone, I'm not sure what else there is."

"You certainly chose an occupation that needs good lungs," I said. "All that rowing you do. And standing. And the need to stay healthy, be available all the time."

"Been fortunate." His face had a hollow look to it reflected in the kerosene lantern that sat between us in the boat. A smudge pot burned beside it. The moon cast a camber of light onto silver ripples.

"Appreciate your stepping out with me," he said.

"I'm not really 'stepping out' as I see it. Just having a conversation with a friend. Perfectly harmless."

"I suppose," he said after a time of silence filled only by the growl of alligators deep in cypress and saw grass.

"Found something here I never had in Ohio, or even the years I worked in Melbourne for my cousin."

"And what would that be?"

"My life with the Seminoles," he said.

"I see. You don't actually live with them."

"Something about the way they are, though. Formed a good friendship with the Osceolas and Jumpers and Tommies. Quick in their thinking, fair and honest. Demand the same from those they trade with. Reliable to a fault. Couldn't have made it without them."

"Mr. Frost says they have liquor problems."

Frank cocked his head at me.

"I'm not judging. Just what I've heard."

"Not limited to Seminoles. I don't stock it in my post for that reason."

He sounded hard, almost severe in his commitment against drink, and I liked that about him. I liked that very much.

"You're able to give them something back," I said.

He didn't speak at first. "In small ways, I suppose. Been asked a time or two to bring my mule and wagon. Help with a burial out at their camps. First time it happened it took me a bit to understand what they wanted. Makes it easier for them, to move a body by land."

"They must respect you very much to ask for your help."

"I suppose. I pay them in cash more than other traders, I've heard."

"They wouldn't have to buy from you, then?"

"Usually do."

The bullfrogs had become so loud Frank was half shouting. He noticed and moved closer so I could hear.

"Meet my contracts up north, buy parcels of land down here. Eventually hope to give back to this village. What I'd like. Seminoles make it possible."

"It's interesting that you should have come so far from home, from Ohio, to find such challenge and satisfaction in your work," I said. "All because of the Seminoles."

He sat quiet, the oars at rest across his knees. I could almost feel him thinking things out before he said them.

"They've been shabbily treated," he said. "Hunted down, sent to Oklahoma and places where they don't have swamps. Just dryness and dirt. Those who hid out in their homelands, they're coming back. Raising families and all. Close to two hundred I'd suppose."

"And now there's that talk of draining the Everglades," I said.

"Take even their swamps."

"That's really just a wild scheme, though, don't you imagine? How could they really drain half a state? I'll bet the Seminoles can stay right where they are if they like.

"You put a nice brush on a picture, Miss Ivy."

"Looking positively on life's presentation is the best way." I swept lint from my skirt, reached for the water jar, and drank.

He rowed for some time without speaking and then said, "My father says there's a difference between blind optimism and hope."

"What did he feel were the distinguishing features?"

"One lets you hide from the facts; the other, the hopeful part, urges action toward accomplishing a thing worth doing even if you don't know how it'll end."

"Is your father a farmer?" I asked.

"A philosopher."

"Ah, if I remember what you told me, they're the same thing."

The crease on his face changed in the moonlight and I felt more than saw his smile. The thought of it warmed me in a way I hadn't planned.

CHAPTER FIVE

They'd been in the village several times during the winter months. I'd seen them cooking in the chickees, thatch shelters Frank kept for them near the post, or standing at the counter inside when I came to fetch my mail. But I'd never been there when the Seminoles came in. That was a sight to behold.

Frank had no need to send word to me. It was the first of March and I stood glancing through my mail when Nelson, in that quick-step way he had, moved among us, telling everyone inside, "They on they way, they sure are. They on they way. Best hurry along now."

Frank urged Hiram Frost and his other customers there that day to finish their purchasing and get enough to last for a few days so they needn't come back right away.

"Don't worry over that," Hiram Frost told him. "Wouldn't even trade here if you weren't the only store in town, Frank. Patronizing with those heathens."

"Fraternizing," Will said and winked at Frank, who acted like he hadn't heard.

"That's what I said," Hiram said.

"I wouldn't be here if they weren't," Frank told him.

Hiram wiped his hands on his pale green vest then lifted his string-tied package from the counter. "I'll send my boy if I need anything," he said. "And pray I don't." His brogans rattled the shelf of kerosene lanterns as he thumped heavily out.

I stepped onto the covered deck behind him and beheld a sight I could never have imagined in any of my dreams.

Dugout canoes, maybe fifty or more, long and lean like dark cigars, rode low against New River waters. Four and five abreast they came, as far back as I could see. The canoes were poled by men with short-cropped hair wearing colorful shirts that stopped just above their knees. Belts tightened them and their white undershirts. Turbans, twists of cloth, surrounded their heads, with a single dark plume fanned up from the back. Behind them sat their families like lily pads, surrounded by pigs and chickens and rounded stacks covered with sandy-colored canvas. In the stern, skinny-tailed dogs panted, front feet up high, the breeze blowing their ears back from their faces.

As they drew closer, I saw women dressed in capelike blouses of red and white and yellow stripes separated by narrower rows of purple and blue ribbon. Most wore draping strands of necklaces of tiny, colorful beads, some burdened by so many they appeared as starched collars to their chins. Thick, dark hair sat stacked on top of their heads in twists as fat as French bread. As the lead canoes moved up into the shaded stream west of the post, I noticed men wearing turban rings while others sported necklaces of silver. They were all dark-skinned, almost shiny in the winter sun, and they shared the same expression on their faces: distant and deep.

Frank stepped out onto the covered porch next to me, and I saw the man poling the lead canoe change his expression. He lifted his hand in greeting along with a smile showing broken teeth.

"Welcome, Billy," Frank said, raising his hand. He stepped off the porch to approach him. "Good to see you. Good to see you."

Something wonderfully exciting passed through me as I watched them dock. A feeling warm yet rousing. Frank straightened his shoulders as his hand stretched out to greet the Seminole man.

"You have hides for me," Frank said. "Ojus. And eggs."

"Wrapped. In leaves," Billy said and nodded to a large basket set before the bare feet of a woman I assumed was his wife. Billy leaned back into the canoe and lifted out his rifle, handing it to Frank.

Dogs began barking as more canoes approached the dock. A few tied up to the front of the post, others eased into the stream west of the building. People called out words I didn't recognize; dogs took up positions by canoes, barking at whomever passed by. Canvas packs were handed over by the women who rose up from their seats like brightly colored umbrellas fluffed out, revealing full, multicolored skirts. Brown fingers pinched to lift them as they rose from the canoes as gracefully as herons stepping out of the swamp. A rainbow of color swirled as they turned to lift loads to the dock.

I'd given my mind free rein, built fragile mental castles in the sand out of stories I'd heard of them, the romance of their arrival. I didn't see them as individuals then, but as all mysterious, faultless, and unknown. The colors and the canoes shimmering in the water, the sounds and the smells of pelts and corn and swampland mesmerized me, made my heart beat faster.

Then the children stirred. They moved about the canoes in flashes of color, carrying and stacking: boys in knee-length blouses clearing places under the thatched roofs and open-sided chickees, girls in long dresses watching younger sisters and brothers while handing tied cloths fat with produce to their parents. They sent their gazes outward, looking neither right nor left. They were bright-eyed children, strong looking and as princely as their parents.

As they finished their tasks of unloading and settling into the chickees, their mothers spoke to them, giving final instructions, I imagined. As a group they marched toward the trading post door where I stood.

The children advanced and I smiled. But they walked on past and disappeared into the shadow of the porch as though I didn't exist.

Through the window, I watched them chattering, pawing at the bins of items, squealing, showing friends, laughing among themselves.

As the adults entered, Mrs. Wallace came to assist as did Will. Other men scurried about with loads. They moved crates on the porch to make room for the canvas packages and hides stretched on long boards brought up by more Indians. Though most locals had left, a few stood like I did, spellbound by Seminole presence.

I stepped back inside the post then and leaned against the doorjamb, watching the children so interested in the world before them, so full of energy and concentration. My straw hat shaded my eyes.

I was whisked away for a time, watching those children playing there at Stranahan's post, carried off by their exuberance and the promise in their eyes. I thought of Pink and Bloxham and when we were young, moving from place to place, at first excited by a trading post we'd stop at, curious about what was different in Juno from what we'd seen at the Peace River up north.

We'd been excited by change in the beginning, the color and smell of it; and then tired by it, all the adjustments required.

The children's chatter in words I did not understand interrupted my daydreams. I looked to catch an English word someone said from another part of the store. The children gave no sign to indicate they'd heard a thing nor knew I stood there gazing at them: a teacher, learning. I coughed once or twice to see if they would lift an eye or turn a head my way. Not a child did. Not a one.

The Seminoles stayed for nearly two weeks, moving in and out around the village. After they sold the alligator eggs to Frank and their otter pelts (turned inside out and pinned to wooden slabs they stacked against the pine walls), a few rode the train up to Zapf's establishment in Palm Beach.

"To buy liquor," Frank said, shaking his head.

From the time the canoes arrived, the men had already stacked their guns in an area Frank set aside for this. They had no need for weapons while in the village, and the assurance of them stacked in Frank's post while they made their trips north kept the rest of the community secure as well. Frank said that at least one of the clan was designated not to drink or imbibe when they visited Zapf's and that one ensured the others got back to the chickees safely if not sober.

Daily, the scent of wood smoke rose from their cooking fires, blanketing the village. Every time I went to the post those weeks the Seminoles were in, I watched women at the White sewing machine Frank let them use, the needle singing in rhythm as they turned the ribbons and tiny squares of cloth into clothes. Often, Frank bent over a woman, giving her quiet assistance as she sewed strips of reds and blues and purples together then cut and sewed them diagonally across.

"They don't cover a woman's ribs when they reach," Louise had said when I'd commented on the sewing going on, the diagonals that made up the capes and shirts.

"Very efficient, though," I said. "Lets the breezes cool and yet the capes cover their arms and still keep the insects away."

"A long-sleeved brown frock tucked in at the waist would be more proper and modest, don't you think, Mama?"

"Reminds me of quilting a bit," her mother said and winked at me as Louise turned away.

But always, it was watching the children that intrigued me most.

April came, the season of new life.

"I can't believe the school year has scampered past, with only a month or so left," I told the children one day as they readied to leave. "Only one month left."

"Scampered ain't the word for it," Irma said then pinched her lips with her fingers.

I would have corrected her but the pop of Frank's boat interrupted.

Frank popped up to the Kings' or the school every time I had a letter now, not waiting for them to accumulate for my Saturday visits. Ed quipped about the "irresponsible proprietor of the ferry leaving his post so often." Mrs. K—as Frank called her—admonished him with her eyes but she looked at me with curiosity, too. I knew they all did.

It wasn't that I was encouraging Frank. I wasn't. I did enjoy getting the letters in such a timely fashion. And I enjoyed the times we made the trek up the New River to fish for snapper and trout and bream, or when in a crowd with the Byrans and Smiths and others, we laughed and sang and picnicked at the beach. Sometimes we ventured toward the lake or farther north to the Hillsboro River inlet, putting up a sail on a leisurely day, usually with a group, though we had gone out alone in his pop boat often enough for others to take notice.

Frank was well read and an easy man for me to talk with. I'd assumed he spoke that way with most people, friendly but in a formal and abbreviated sort of way. His father was a Presbyterian minister in Ohio, and Frank embraced the theology of human compassion and rational discourse that marked that denomination. He spoke well of his family. And he had a great memory for detail, a quality I liked in a person, since to me it demonstrated both discipline and a fine mind.

I certainly liked the look of the man as well. Lean and wholesome. What evidence existed of his poisonings those years before was well camouflaged behind a straight posture, muscled though slender arms, and not an ounce of fat as far as I could see. He did cough and wheeze at times. That was probably a residue of his steel mill experience. Still, it was nice to walk out with him on the beach, someone pleasant to share a Saturday with.

I liked his convictions, too: "I don't sell vanilla at the post," he told me. "Got alcohol in it."

His presence with the Seminoles was admirable. He didn't urge them this way or that. Both gentle and kind with the women, he showed them beads, special glass ones with many sides that he told me he ordered in just for them.

"Most women like the little black or white ones," Frank noted, "for your long dresses. Seminole women wear them as necklaces. Difference in fashion."

Frank took long hours looking over alligator and deer hides, giving their providers the honor due their preparation and care.

He worked hard, paid his bills, or so I was told, treated people with dignity and fairness. He was a thoughtful person and a generous man, especially to the children. He saved sweets for them and small toys hidden behind the counter that he gave them rather than take their parents' efforts in trade.

The trading post proprietor is a gentleman, I wrote to Pink.

Though honest to truth, I don't have time for Frank Stranahan or any man, not really. Too many other things to consider, finishing up the school year and getting ready to come back home. Hope Mama's feeling well. Sure wish you'd come to see me, Pink. The breezes here are cool and I don't know for sure if I'll be coming back to this New River. I don't want you to worry yourself nor mention this to Mama and Papa, but no one has spoken of the next year's contract though I'm leaving in just a few weeks.

Perhaps I've offended. You know I can be corrugated as a road in how I say things, not as smooth as I'd like. Maybe now that they have a local girl interested in teaching—Susan Byran's her name— they may have no need for a Lemon City teacher. I'd be distressed by that. I've come to love this little village and I want you to come visit here next year. If there is a next year here for me. I know the money I've sent has been useful, at least Mama has written her thanks. It will be an interesting few weeks, my dear little sister. I so long for the comforts of home.

I was sure Louise would enjoy having her room back at the end of May when the term ended and the rains began. The Kings had been gracious hosts. And I'd been blessed with being able to remain with them the entire term rather than spending a few weeks here and there, shuttling between families, adjusting to a new set of children and routines as most teachers did in other parts of the state. I'd dreaded spending a term with the Frosts and was pleased at Christmas when the Kings had asked me to remain.

But my salary of forty-eight dollars per month would cease in a few weeks and I'd take my savings, buy a train ticket, and head home. I had hoped the board of instruction would offer me the contract before I left and certainly intended to take it if they did.

A few short days before I planned to depart, Frank popped by and asked me to join him.

"School's about finished. Can't be too busy now," he said.

I accepted, glad for the diversion.

"I'm quite a bit older than you," Frank said. He faced me in the little boat, the oars resting on his thighs. An aqua sky spanned over us, not a cloud in view.

"I'd guess fifteen years."

"I'm thirty-five. Does that fit your figure?"

"It does."

We were at the place where the fish swam in the pool surrounded by delicate green.

"I've enjoyed time with you this past school year, Miss Ivy. I hope you'll be returning."

"Most contracts aren't let until nearly the end of the summer, when they know how many children there'll be. Lauderdale's growing."

"Yes."

"I would like to come back. To this place especially." I fanned against the chizy winks that fluttered like cobwebs against my face. "So beautiful."

He cleared his throat. "I can't promise much." His palms rolled the oar back and forth across his legs. "I may be speaking well out of turn here, but you'd have many suitors if you permitted and I might not be the first to declare myself. And I'd want to be. In case there was a chance…"

I let my hands drift in the water, aware that my chest had tightened as he spoke.

Frank's Adam's apple bobbed up once or twice and I realized he was gasping a bit, but he took a deep breath and began again.

"Ivy," he said, "I'd like for you to consider me in marriage."

My fingers lay still in the water. I had expected something about permission to write, to court, to continue spending time together, not marriage.

"Frank, I—"

"When it appeared that the steel mill had taken my health, or a good portion of it, it didn't seem fair to encumber a vital woman with the trappings of uncertainty. Coming south, alone, making my place, gave me back some confidence. But I've taken no liking to anyone. Until you."

My fingers no longer wished to linger in the water. I needed to move.

"Is there a place we could walk?" I asked.

"Hammock over that way," he said. He nodded toward a canopy of mahogany, the tallest trees clustering the center, smaller dropping out toward the sides. "Have to watch for bell boys, though. They like this higher ground and don't always buzz their intentions."

He used the oar to pole the boat through the saw grass until the bottom scraped against solid ground.

There really wasn't much room for walking with the ferns and thick growth, but we could stand and stretch a bit while watching where we placed our feet and what hung from overhead.

"I almost prefer the cottonmouths," I said. I could hear myself becoming formal and stiff, moving into exile. "They don't seem to mind intruders who keep their distance while the diamondback comes on whether threatened or not."

"At least they warn you."

"They usually warn you, yes."

"Just entering their territory intimidates them," he said.

We heard the heavy splash of an alligator surging into water beyond us. Frank cleared his throat again. "Ivy—"

"I'm not sure how to answer."

"Like you being here, on the New River. People have taken to you, parents and children."

"Mr. Frost would disagree. And I think the Joyces. They haven't been too pleased by Irma's progress."

"Perfection's a poor standard to set for yourself."

"I doubt anyone disapproved of Ada Merritt, my teacher," I said. "Compared to her, I fall quite short."

"My father always advised against comparisons like that," Frank said. "Better to find qualities in people we admire that we can admit live inside ourselves, too, instead of looking only at what we don't think we live up to."

"Your father has interesting advice."

"And I'm sure he'd advise me to pursue my question with you."

"Would he?"

It was cool on the hammock, the foliage so thick it looked dark just a few feet from where we stood. A gray squirrel darted out across purple paurotis palm berries, saw us and twisted, disappearing up the back of a tree.

"You seem at home here," Frank continued.

"I've settled in well enough."

"I've come to care for you very much, Ivy. I think of you and wonder how your day is and whether you'll come in for mail. When I haven't seen you for a week or so, I find myself thinking of excuses to bring something to you. Not like me at all, that isn't. I wonder about how you spend your spare time, what your favorite color is or your favorite memory of growing up. I imagine myself sitting across a room from you, both of us reading and feeling, oh, contented would be the word for it. I don't know if that's love but I believe it could become that, if it isn't already." He paused. "And I wonder if you've had any similar thoughts."

It was almost painful watching him expose his care to me. I could tell he had seldom done it, if ever. The words were practiced but came with the fear of rejection, of wanting to be sure he hadn't miscalculated, made a mistake. Had that happened before?

"Perhaps we should go back," I said.

He bent to pick up a twig and broke it, throwing little pieces of it into the saw grass, watching it slowly swirl out of sight. The water beneath the grass moved as gentle as a sigh.

"There's another," he said.

"Oh no, Frank, no one. Unless you count Vasco Powers and Mack Marshall and Tenley Bellamy. And my brothers and father. Those are the men in my life."

"Like to be in their company," he said.

He took my hand to help me back in and held it for a moment and looked at me. "I'm not very good at this," he said. "I would think a young woman would want to hear these kinds of words spoken with passion but that isn't my way. You should know that, though my feelings are no less intense. What I'm offering is an opportunity for you to be loved until the day I die, to be cared for and protected, best I know how. No one will ever love you as much as I do, I promise you that, Ivy. Stay and live here along the New River, stay, and be my wife."

He leaned to lift my hat from my head, and then he kissed me. It was a soft brush of mouth, then firmer, gentle yet strong, my first kiss. The prickle of his mustache poked at my lips and when I pulled back he gentled my head against his chest, still holding my hat but now behind me, using it to fan. I could hear his heart pounding, still taste the peppermint of his breath. It was a warm and welcome place to settle for a moment. Comfortable was a word that came to mind. Comfortable with a twist of gentle stirring.

He moved the hat into his other hand, then stroked the back of my head, lifting the tendrils of hair that escaped from the upsweep. I felt his fingers tucking them back into the ribbon.

"I've wanted to teach my whole life," I said, still letting his arms encircle me.

"Figured that. Something about the way you are with the children. Like a calling, almost."

"A calling, yes. That's a good word for it. I've known I would teach since I can remember. I think all children know their life's pathway when they're young but then the adults in their lives rechannel them, push the saw grass around so they can't find their way through."

"Rare gift to be able to do what God's pressed onto your heart as a child."

"I wouldn't be able to if I became serious and married."

"Considered that. Times are changing, all over Florida. We're growing. It's more a matter of custom than requirement that married women don't teach. At least until after they start their family. I'd stand with you if you wanted to pursue the matter. It might even carry some weight in the fight if you were Mrs. Frank Stranahan."

"I've never been one to back off from a good argument, not one based on conviction," I said.

"Just not sure that marriage to me would be worth the fight."

He said it with such sadness and such sureness that I pushed back away from him to see if his face matched his voice.

"Self-condemnation does not become you, Frank Stranahan," I said.

"Don't expect it's my usual fashion."

"Well, I hope not. You have accomplished too much to feel unworthy."

"Enough to win your hand?"

"It's not about that, Frank, or you. It's about, well, marriage and teaching."

He stepped back, moved toward the boat. He offered his hand again to help me step in. Once inside, he pushed off with the oar and we headed back out through the sedge to the place where the waterfall flowed.

"No need to have an answer right away," Frank said. He hesitated now, wheezing. "I thought you'd want time to consider. If we found a mutual agreement and you were inclined, we could marry this summer. You wouldn't even have to leave, except to visit home, of course. I'm sure you could stay on with the Kings until then."

"I have to go back to Lemon City," I said.

"Could we write back and forth? I'll be sure the letters'll be posted."

"I'm sure they would," I said and smiled.

He oared back in silence and when we reached the broader river, I was pleased to have the pop-pop-pop of the engine to fill up the space.

The school term ended and the school board sat silent; and on the day I planned to leave I received a letter from Mama saying Pink was ill and could I please come home without delay.

The Florida East Coast Railroad left midmorning and I was to be on it, my trunk and bags brought up by Ed King while I rode with Frank in his pop boat to the station.

"I'll write," I said. "And we can carry this on paper. Perhaps clarify things and have the advantage of giving each of us time to think it through."

His forehead furrowed as he nodded. He turned back to ease the engine up. He flicked at his ear.

When the trunks had been loaded, we stood, a foot between us, at the station. The sounds of steam building up, dogs barking, three or four others with family and friends saying good-bye, all became background noise.

"I'm sorry about Pink," he said.

"I hope it's just her usual, that time of the year when the rains come. I'm sure it will all work out fine." I looked around to see exactly where I'd board.

"Like looking at the bright side of things, don't you?"

"Keeps fear at bay that way."

"Good lesson for me," he said. "I'll hope that distance in this instance makes the heart grow fonder." I turned back at his words. His mustache wiggled slightly.

"You could lose the cookie duster," I said.

He touched his face. "If it'll finalize the arrangement, you can rest assured I will."

"I'm not going that far," I said. "But I do promise to give this matter my greatest thought and my deepest prayers, Frank Stranahan. More than that, I cannot promise."

"It's enough for now," Frank said. "I'll wait for your post. Actually look forward to gathering up the mail from the FEC now."

"You always have," I said, resettling the hook of my umbrella over my arm. I brushed at the whiteness of my traveling suit, wondered about the soot floating in the air from the engine firing up. I set my shoulders back and took a deep breath. One last gaze around the New River; it might be my last.

I'd given it my best. I'd met the challenges of a dozen children in various stages of their learning journeys. I'd profited from my mistakes and hoped not to repeat them. I'd even formed a kind of truce with Louise, a young girl whose changing emotions marked her walk across the bridge from childhood into adulthood. If they wanted me back, I would come. If they didn't, I would move on to another school, another set of challenges, another tongue or two to wag like Mr. Frost's. It was he I suspected was behind my leaving with no offer. We saw the world differently. I doubted I would ever meet his expectations.

"Where're your thoughts?" Frank asked.

"I gave a moment to Hiram Frost," I said. "Waste of time, I know. And I was thinking of the children, whether they'd received as much as they'd given."

"Wouldn't wonder over that. Heard—"

At the pop-pop of engines and the squeal of voices, we both turned. Tenley Bellamy and Mack Marshall jumped first out of the boats, Mack hurrying forward with a handful of gardenias. His grubby fingers clutched at the short stems of the ivory blooms.

"Do I have to worry about a snake hidden inside these, Mack?"

He blushed. "No, ma'am. These is flowers. For your going-away time."

Tenley caught up with him and breathlessly said, "So you'll know to come back, Miss Ivy. You have to come back."

I looked over their heads at Frank and he shrugged his shoulders in innocence. "Speak for themselves," he said.

To my surprise, several other families hurried to the platform. Louise hugged me one more time followed by Byrd and Wallace. Even Minnie forced a smile onto her face as water pooled in her blue eyes. I spoke each of their names and thanked them for coming.

"You be encouraged now," I said. "And don't forget your lessons over the summer."

Tenley pulled at my sleeve. "What do you do to encourage yourself?" He said it loud enough for all to hear but I knelt beside him to answer.

"That's a fine, fine question, Tenley," I said. "And important. I try to remember what I think I'm supposed to do and trust that God has given me all I need to accomplish what He asks." I dabbed at a smudge on his face with my thumb. "And I—"

"Last call. All aboard."

They swarmed me in a group then, this first class of mine. The smell of them, the strength of them, the feel of their arms and their faces, the absolute honesty their presence conveyed pushed at me and I couldn't hold back.

"Discipline, be gone." I sniffed as I felt Frank's hand on my elbow, pulling me free.

He helped me step up on the train, my arms full of flowers.

"You write, now," he said, adjusting his hat, walking quickly to keep up with the groaning train. "Don't forget me."

"I won't, Frank. And none of you either," I shouted to the waving hands behind him.

I missed them all the minute I left.

At the last picnic gathering announcing the end of the school year, Frank had asked the well-known photographer R. E. Restler Jr. to take a photograph of us in front of the school with all the little ones standing on the steps around me. I pulled the image out now to gaze at it as I rode away, the little schoolhouse that had been my first.

The windowsill of the train made a dark line of shadow flickering across the photo but the faces stayed imprinted on my soul. I slipped it back inside my wrist purse and sighed.

I felt the same emptiness I'd had when I left my family those months before. It was a kind of sickness wrapped inside a shortened breath, not a grieving really, but a loss just the same. I would miss Frank's easy chatter, that place in his presence where I felt accepted just as I was. Why couldn't we just keep it a friendship, a companionship, I wondered? Why did strong feelings have to turn into puzzles? I dabbed at my eyes, grateful for the excuse of the smoke.

The train pulled into the station in Miami and Papa was there to pick me up, waiting in the high-wheeled wagon. Albert joined him. Apparently he'd been exploring rocks and salamanders while he waited. Bloxham eased from foot to foot. Both boys had grown and filled out.

"In only six months you two look like you've aged two years," I said.

"That's what Mama says," Bloxham said with a laugh. "Though she says the years have been added to her life by Albert's racing about."

"He has lost that baby chub," I said. "You'll be tall and lean like Bloxham when you grow up, won't you, Albert?"

"Yes, ma'am," he said.

"Oh, someone's been teaching you well!"

"Not as well as you did, Ivy," Papa said. He patted my shoulder. "It'll be good to have you home, girl."

"How's Pink?"

"Better," Papa said. "It seems to come and go with her. I wonder if it's her spirit as much as the vapors that come every summer."

His own shoulders looked bent as he leaned into the reins he slapped on the old mule's back. "You'll do wonders for that," he said. "She's missed you so."

"You'd never know it by how often she wrote. Why, I think I only had six letters from her the whole time I've been gone."

"She's been busy looking after, you know, things. For your mother."

I was immediately ashamed. Of course Pink had little time to write. She'd been doing her work and mine, too.

"I graduated higher school," Bloxham said.

"Did you? How wonderful. I wish I could have been there."

"Just a little ceremony," he said. "But the school is growing. More people coming and staying longer."

"So what will you do now?"

"Don't know. Work in the packing plant this summer. Help Papa, too. We'll see about the fall."

"The New River is a lovely place," I said. "Good air. Nice breezes. It would be good for Pink, Papa. Maybe even Mama."

"Our lives're here, girl," he said. "Grove's doing good."

The clop-clop of the mule against the white-rock road was as soothing as sleep and I let it fill the silence now. I nodded off once or twice, my head bobbing against my father's shoulder as we made our way home.

Pink awoke in an instant when I sat on her side of the bed. She opened her arms and hugged me.

"Tell me all about him, sister," she said.

"Who?"

"Who-oo," she said in a singsong that didn't sound all that ill. "This Frank. It sounds so romantic, goin' for moonlit boat rides and dancin' 'til midnight with an older, experienced sort of man."

"So you did at least read my letters," I said.

"Over and over. They're so wonderfully dreamy. I can just picture him. Tall, handsome. Those northern men are all so mysterious."

"I didn't say any such thing."

"I read between lines," she said. "The best things're said in empty spaces."

I laughed. "Such a vivid imagination. Frank's a very unpretentious man, modest and chaste. He's nice looking. With a mustache and ears that stick out a bit."

"Yes, but with dark eyes, harborin' deep secrets," she whispered as though we were conspirators in a crime.

"Oh, Pink." I poked her side. "He seems quite transparent to me, presenting just what he is."

"Oh, pooh," she said, sitting back on the pillow and crossing her arms over her chest. "Where's the fun in that?"

"In quiet conversation and introspection," I said, patting her knee that poked out beneath the flannel sheet. "That's where there's fun. He's just a good friend. That's all I'll ever let it be."

"I'm wantin' adventure and passion," she said, "not just friendships."

"We've got to get and keep you healthy, then."

"I'll do better now you're here."

Pink improved and everyone accepted me back into the rhythm of their days as though I'd never gone away.

It was different for me. The change surprised me. I'd had a taste of setting my own pace with time alone to think and write and be. It was a luxury invaded now.

My dear Frank.

How are Mr. and Mrs. K these days? And the Frombergers at the House? A Saturday came and I was neither at school working nor at the beach. But I thought of all of you and thank you, especially, for writing me so quickly. How strange it seems to me now to be at home and yet be a stranger. It's as though I've moved into a different place. Even the linens appear new and belonging to my mother rather than the faded pillow slips I embroidered myself. Pink kicks the covers and I long for a bed of my own. Selfish, I know. Mama looks to be improved. Her color is rosier and she is gaining needed weight. I'm sewing more, exercising, taking my walks, swimming, and enjoying the conversations with the children. But I feel homesick, in the oddest way, since here I am, at home.

Diversions surrounded us. Bloxham knew everyone, and so invitations to beach parties and boating were frequent and fun. Pink was permitted to attend as long as I went and I found the amusements pleasant if not invigorating. I took the cart one day to visit Ada and we laughed over my experiences at my first school.

"You," she said, "didn't I tell you it would be wonderful?"

"Wonderful. Yes, that's just what you said."

"Do you know anything about the contract for next year?" she asked, one eyebrow raised. "Will you go back?"

I shook my head. "I hoped you might know, through Z. T."

"He'd tell me if there'd been any discussion," she said. "No news is good news, I always say, so just assume the best. You'll be going back to teach, I'm just sure of it."

I wasn't so sure. Frank wrote three times a week. His letters were newsy and gentle. He spoke of building a crude boathouse, to keep the rain and wind off the pop boat. He said Mr. Marshall had begun picking children up in his boat and taking them to the Sunday school Hiram Frost and several others had started. They held church now in our little building. He told me that Nelson had some compadres, what with six Africans now living in Lauderdale. He teased me about spending too much time at the beach and how he hadn't gone himself since I'd left. He'd been swimming in the New River for his daily refreshment, making his way out to the island where the pond apples grew.

They were community letters with little beads of personal words strung through them. True to his word, he was giving me time. He never mentioned my teaching contract nor his marriage proposal.

Then he wrote of a visit he planned to make.

I'll be coming by train to Miami and if it should please you, I could come by to see you and meet your folks as well. I must check on pelts. I'd hoped to come sooner but Will decided to head north and make buys while there. Someone needs to man the post so I'm selected for the next three weeks at least. I don't mind being here

*alone and managing the bookkeeping but I do wish my brother
would decide, giving me a little more time to prepare. He also fails
to write frequently when he's gone so I rarely know where he is nor
when to expect his return. Makes planning trips of my own difficult. Never mattered so much as now when I am longing to see
you.*

I wasn't sure how I felt about his coming. A part of me looked forward
to seeing him, hearing news of the river. Another part of me knew that if he
came and the subject of marriage persisted that I would have to speak of
wounds of my own, wounds I'd kept buried quite tidy and deep.

My father liked him immediately though I could tell he was a bit taken
aback by Frank's age. They seemed to understand each other, both being
men who loved to read and had a sensitivity to commerce and the land.

Mama liked him, too. "He's not truly a Yankee," she told me while we
sliced tomatoes for supper. "His being from so far south in Ohio. And then
living in Florida for what, almost ten years?"

I waited for Bloxham's estimation, knowing it would take more than
one contact. But he surprised me. The two walked out in the groves
together, though I've no idea what they spoke of. When they returned,
Bloxham winked at me.

The younger children took to Frank fine, as did Pink, though she
agreed he did not have the "high romantic look" she had expected.

"But he does have a broodin' quality to him, sort of a veil over his
eyes."

"I think that's the pain he's been through, with his health," I said.

"Maybe. But I'm a good judge of people," she said. "Better than you,
who are much too logical. It's the heart that matters, sister."

"So how would you gauge his heart?"

"Oh, he adores you. Listens to every word you say, watches all of your
moves, takes them in like he's takin' in sugar. I think his sadness is deeper
than he lets on, though. He's a kind man, too, I'd say. Gentle as a butterfly.
But I agree about his ears."

We giggled like schoolgirls, our heads together as we sat on our upstairs bed. Then Pink stopped and looked puzzled.

"Say, I thought you said he had a mustache."

"Doesn't he?"

She shook her head and laughed. "You're messin' up on details, sister."

I hadn't even noticed that Frank had shaved his beloved mustache off.

CHAPTER SIX

By mid-July, I had decided. Something about Frank, when I thought of him, when he brushed my hand, when he watched me from across a room, offered passion tempered by tenderness. Love, I imagined, and more; a sheltered island from which I might launch and then return for nurture and protection. It could work. It could get me back to Lauderdale with or without the school. Frank could make it possible to bring Pink, then Mama, then perhaps all the rest until my whole family lived there, safe and out of yellow fever's way and closer to my own protection.

Frank needed to know of one important thing before we went further. I had failed to find a way to say the words when he had visited in June, despite my seeking guidance. I'd written to him, to open the shutters before letting the gale force in.

> We need to speak frankly, of a subject I've been reluctant to convey to you. Perhaps on your return trip we could meet at the hotel for noonday meal and talk there. After that, we'll both know how to proceed with this communion between friends.

"Your letter sounded solemn," Frank said when I met him at the train. "You usually put the sun on things."

I'd come alone. We would drop his bag at the hotel, lunch there, spend the day walking and at the beach, and then join my parents for our supper.

Where to begin? Frank filled my silence as he took over the driving of the cart. With the whisk broom he brushed at the base of my dress, knocking off the white sand.

"Mrs. Fromberger looked startled to see us," Frank said.

"Tongues will be wagging now, I'm sure."

"Sorry for that."

"Oh, don't you worry a twit about that. We're doing nothing wrong, just meeting to talk."

"We did come to talk."

"At the hotel," I said. "Look at those butterflies. Almost transparent, aren't they?"

"I can wait, Ivy. No need to distract."

"Now," Frank said. "The solemn subject."

"I should have spoken of it earlier, before I let this go so far."

"Don't say your feeling's not returned, Ivy. I know it is. I can see it in your face. We've become more than fond of each other through the distance."

"I missed you more than I can say."

"That's a worthy start."

He had a deep valley beneath his nose that widened to his thin lips, features his mustache had hidden before. A tiny cleft in his chin showed more, too, without other distractions to the eye. Thick dark hair curled like a broccoli flower at the top of his head. He wore no part and no sideburns, instead shaving close to his scalp at the temples. "Easier to slap at mosquitoes threatening my little ears," he'd told me once, straight-faced. "They can't escape into side hair."

The waiter took our order and I brushed my fingers over my forehead, lifting up wispy stray hair to tuck under my hat.

"Look lovely in blue, Ivy," Frank said. "It's your favorite color, isn't it?"

"I like white, too." I picked at the ruffles on the blouse I'd sewn new, to wear that day. The high collar scratched my neck.

"Such piercing azure eyes," Frank said.

"Your letters are so interesting, Frank. The everyday detail. I like detail."

He reached a hand across the table to cover mine. I started to pull it away, but didn't. His touch held comfort in it, safety and warmth.

"If we should marry," I said, emphasizing the *if,* "there is something we should agree upon now. And you may not wish to. I'll understand, of course, but it must be said."

"Couldn't surprise me," he said. "Except to say the feelings weren't returned."

The food arrived. I watched his face as he leaned back to permit the serving of Spode plates against ivory cloth. Nothing changed in his eyes or his mouth. He kept staring at me. The waiter bent at the waist, retreated to leave us alone. Rain dribbled and ran against the windows.

"Go on," he said.

I played with my soup spoon. "If we marry, we must never...I must never...conceive. I could never, ever have children."

"You don't want a family?" he said. He leaned back from the table but reached to quiet my moving hand.

"This is the best way. I've thought and thought and decided early on that if I ever cared for a gentleman, he would have to know this was my way, the only way."

It felt hot and humid, and the ceiling fans remained motionless. Thunder rolled off in the distance.

"I have seen my mother's life ebb and flow with the size of her," I began. "The months she's carried babies, the delivery pain and then afterwards, too. Each child took more out of her than the last and still she continues, wants them, adores them. Wanted to please my father, I suppose, while grieving so many lost."

"There were more than you six?"

"Twelve pregnancies, as far as I know."

"Great loss in her life."

"Loss, yes. And still she continues. 'We'll see them again,' she tells me. 'A lost one is as much of a birthing as one that takes on a breath of their own.' She names them, each one, grieves them by name. Her body goes through labor worse, I think, than when she actually delivers. She says it's all part of a larger plan. 'It's my way of serving,' she says."

"God does have plans we don't always understand."

"It isn't a question of faith," I said. I felt irritated that I couldn't make myself understood. "It's a matter of decision and discipline, of self-control. Of commitment to an end and staying with that. Of protecting ones you love when you can. I wouldn't want to put you through that, Frank. Nor anyone else I cared for."

"You can't protect people from loss," Frank said. "Only prepare them for it."

"I wouldn't survive a pregnancy. I doubt I'd endure the delivery and I think there are other ways a woman can...serve, as it were."

"Ivy, there's no reason to believe you'd have the same complications."

"It's a decision I've made."

"Trying to fix it," he said.

"My mother doesn't question it anymore," I told him, looking away. I poked my spoon at the lemon slice shriveled inside my crystal water glass. "She says it sets her off. Feels as though she's failed me, not shown me the gift children are and how much the pain is worth it. 'So short-lived, the pain is, compared to all you receive,' she says."

"She'd like for you to have that joy," he said.

"I intend to find pleasure in diverting such energy toward other worthy causes, things that can make a difference for the lives of all children, all families. I do love children, Frank. I truly do. But I've decided to place such maternal urges as God's given me toward other matters."

"Such as?"

"Teaching. But others too, things I don't yet know but will when the time's right."

"You're so young to be so sure."

I felt drained, exhausted as though I'd exercised for hours. I pushed pieces of watermelon around the china.

He coughed awkwardly. He had the look of protest.

I shook my head. "No. Chances."

He took a drink of water then and the lemon slice sank slowly toward the upturned bottom. It camouflaged his face. He set the glass down on the thick linen. He picked up the napkin and pressed the cloth between his fingers, folding it over and over. We sat a long time in silence. His watch chain gleamed against his light coat, but he never looked at his timepiece.

"If you'd like more time to consider," I said, "I will understand. Or if you wish to withdraw your offer."

"Wanting to understand, is all," he said. "Not what a man prepares to hear, that a woman cares for him but wants no offspring from the union. Doesn't even want the…ah, union, if I understand you."

"I want us to be together, Frank. I believe we can give to each other and care in ways no two other people could. You are my best friend. I've discovered that during our separation. And I love you beyond measure."

"I'm glad of it."

"That part of a marriage, the physical, intimate part, is just a small portion," I continued.

"Suppose," he said. He leaned back, his head cocked as he looked at me. Ferns on stands beside us cast splintered shadows across his face.

"I made a terrible mistake once, Frank."

He looked puzzled.

I sighed, knowing I would have to tell him but wishing there was a way to avoid the disdain and disappointment I expected in his eyes.

He put his hand on mine. "You tell me if you want, Ivy. But it won't change how I feel."

I could put it away most of the time. But when I brought it to the surface, it felt like a sharp scissors had cut the memory out of yesterday, though it had happened when I was barely ten.

I was alone with my mother. Pink and the boys—all but Albert, who wasn't born yet—played in the next room, played and waited. We lived in Sumter County then. Our fourth home, fourth move, home and life and education interrupted by travel and change. Mama twisted in the bed trying not to cry out, trying not to scare me as she readied to birth her sixth child, complete her eleventh pregnancy. She'd lost one since Gussie, and he had just turned two. This one she'd carried almost full term.

The baby sought the world a month early. No one expected it. There was just me to assist.

My mother's hands were strained, grasping the sheets on the bedpost, and she writhed in pain, panting. In between she swallowed screams and then would tell me not to worry, that it was all right, that all would be fine.

It had gone on for hours. I'd checked on the younger children, fed them, pulled the bar over them to nap. But what I remember most was sitting in the chair next to my mother's bed, close to her footboard, where I could stare at her feet and the mound of her stomach.

I felt immobilized by her pain, my limbs heavy, my legs like old carrots. I thought I should go get my father but she didn't want me to leave her. She'd say, "It'll be fine, Ivy. Just fine."

I made no sense of the incongruity, of her telling me that all was fine while her body heaved and contorted, her face strained with pain. My mind left me for a time, walked on the sandy beach, heard cries that were sea-gulls. The strain on her face and the heat of the room belonged somewhere else so that when the baby came, all slithery and wet, I didn't notice at first.

"Pick...the baby...up, Ivy," my mother panted. "Pick it up. Put it on my stomach now. Pick it up, dear. It's all right now."

A small, jerking thing laid against her, slipped near her legs, still bound to her through the cord. I couldn't move. Didn't move. All the blood, the squirmy wetness. My stomach twisted. I tasted something awful in my mouth.

"I'll drop him."

"No, no. It'll be fine. Ivy," Mama ordered, "pick the baby up. You must or he won't be able to breathe. Put your finger in its mouth and clean it out. Hurry, now!"

But I could not move.

I didn't.

Mama cried now, screamed almost, the effort making her breathing as labored as the delivery. She begged me to pick up the baby but it wasn't a baby to me. It was foreign, carried with it red wounds and pain and mis-take. I could feel myself sweating and breathing, light-headed as though I'd soon faint. It wasn't a child; it was covered with down, raw and unfin-ished—a piglet? a kitten? They could take care of themselves. This would all be fine.

"Ivy, please!"

Mama pleaded and cried and I could see her struggling to sit up, to put herself on her elbows, then flop back, too weak, and then forcing herself up again to see where her child lay with no sound yet, no crying. Mama's hair stuck to her forehead and cheek. She sobbed as she begged me.

I could not move.

Then something oozed out of my mother, a sphere of purple and pink, the insides of my mother slipping out of her like a fish plucked from water, slipping and sliding and settling on top of the infant that lay there, unable to breathe.

"Mama! What is it?" It seemed to throb, and I pushed my hand in my mouth so I wouldn't scream.

"The placenta," Mama said. "It won't hurt you. Give me the baby, Ivy."

Why wouldn't it breathe? Why wouldn't it move? It should all be fine.

Papa found us like that: Mama sobbing, her head arched back on the bed, her eyes swollen and red. Me, hands clasped in my lap as I sat on my chair, dry-eyed, staring at the spongy oval that had rushed onto the baby with a flow of its own, unable to part from what it had once nourished.

Papa lifted the infant, his hand moving with one motion the placenta from the child's face. He washed my brother and laid him on my mother's belly. Her long fingers stroked the tiny head, the dark cap of hair. Tears ran down her cheeks. Then Papa washed her face and covered her legs that were shaking and trembling and listened while she cried, holding mother and son in the crook of his arms.

After she slept, he came to me.

I shivered with the wonder of what his rage might do, should do to a child so disobedient that she had caused a death. Instead, he lifted me from the chair that I was glued to, wanted to die on, and carried me into the next room where he set me gently on my bed. I heard him pour water into the pitcher, lift a rag and dip it, and then come to wash my face. He washed and washed while new tears came to take the old ones' place.

"I decided then I must never birth a child," I told Frank. "I must control myself and give in other ways or pay a great and lasting price."

"Forgiving yourself seems in order. You were so young." We were alone in the dining room now. Only a flash of lightning occasionally broke the afternoon darkness, accompanied by the rumble of thunder. "You didn't know."

"That's what my mother says. 'If I had had the strength, I would have done it myself,' she says. 'So you wouldn't have had to. Or if your father had been in from the fields, he could have. Or if the baby hadn't come early. There were so many 'ifs' we'd like to fill in, but that isn't our choice. Just accept it as part of a larger plan.' He's buried in Sumter County," I finished.

Frank picked up the white napkin and dabbed my cheek free of the tears that squeezed toward my ears.

"Did your best." He put his large hands over my clasped ones before me on the table. "Only a child. Something like that, it's been forgiven. Need to forgive yourself, Ivy. Too sweet a soul to have it clouded with old pain."

"I've often wondered, if the time came, a time when I truly needed to be strong to make the difference, would I? could I? It's a question that haunts me."

"None of us know for sure how we'll respond to challenge."

"You know. You came south, started a new life."

"The mill accident, yes. One challenge. One response. Each one's all new, Ivy. You give yourself to your students. A way of redemption, maybe. Acceptance of God's sovereignty over our own."

"I've no desire to face this one again, Frank. It's not negotiable nor reversible. I'll take no chances. And I'll never change my mind."

I looked at him then, at the pain in his eyes, at whether he understood just what I meant and how he'd respond in the end.

"We all change, Ivy."

"Frank—"

He raised his hand to stop my protest. "You're a passionate woman, Ivy. I know that from the fire in your eyes and...your kisses."

"It will be directed, Frank. Directed passion."

He folded and unfolded the napkin, sat silent for a time. "If someone had said this could happen," he said, "I would have told them they were daft. Not what happened to you, Ivy. That was a tragedy for everyone, and tragedies happen. But when I worked in the steel mills, the problems I had with the arsenic, the doctors said that in all likelihood, I'd not only wheeze, asthmatic-like, but have other problems. Not be able to, ah..." He searched for words, couldn't find them. "They told me never to hope for a family," he said.

"What are you saying? That you're not able to have children?"

"Not certain. With the right person, I was willing to prove them wrong." A slight smile formed at the corner of his mouth. "Though through the years I'd say they knew their medicine." He shook his head, his hands folded, opening and closing against themselves. "Who would've thought I'd be led to love a woman who wouldn't be distressed by that uncertainty?"

"Love and devotion can be expressed in many ways," I said. "No one ever questioned the depth of love of the old saints nor what they accomplished through their directed passions."

"I will want to...hold you," he said. He reached for my hand, rubbed the half-moons hidden there. "To smell the scent of your hair, feel your skin. Can't promise I won't wish for more. But I promise to understand, to never make you feel that you have erred in being who you are. I'll remember this conversation, abide with you as you like."

At that moment, I felt truly known by another human being, known and accepted in a way I'd never been. Abide. He had stepped into the pain that marked mine to dwell there, and assured me he would not be consumed by its depth, would not abandon my need.

"Our two forks of past experience have been joined together in a rather remarkable river," I said. "Great things have been accomplished by those who took vows of celibacy, Frank."

"Don't know how much greatness will result," Frank said, "but think we'll learn the meaning of endurance."

We told no one, wanting to avoid all the fuss.

Pink's feverishness came back and for a time we thought to delay the marriage, but she came out of it as before. Frank, back at the post, made arrangements writing to clarify the way my name should appear on the license, conversing gently about the trips he made to the beach with friends, how he wished I were there to join them. He had purchased a new trunk for our traveling things.

Mama knew, of course, and she worried. Our ages were an issue; my decision about babies still concerned her. She knew, too, of my love of teaching and worried over whether I could leave it all so easily. I had not told her of our plan to challenge propriety in a lady's genteel way.

Frank wrote shortly after our discussion.

Mothers should know what is best for their daughters to do and give good advice. Many do not always agree but I hope you will be one of the fortunate ones. I remember well our last talk and have not changed any plans or way of thinking since then. I hope to get a day off the coming week and will surely endeavor to make it convenient to take the train again to see you.

Frank also shared my enthusiasm with Ed King's arrival and announcement that the board had extended me a contract again for the next year.

It's good you have friends here looking out for your interests, he wrote. *They like Miss Ivy on the New River, a fact that does not surprise me.*

Frank arrived in Lemon City by train on August 15. On August 16 at just around six o'clock in the morning, we were married by Rev. C. Fred Blackburn of the Miami Methodist Church South at my father's home. There were no refreshments. All my family attended, even Pink, who got up in time for the event and to see us off at the train station. We would be stopping briefly at Fort Lauderdale and then had another train to catch farther north, where our honeymoon to Asheville, North Carolina, began. Frank had placed a notice in the paper that the post would not be open this summer season so that we could travel until October.

First we had to resolve the issue of my contract, my teaching.

"I'll stand behind you," Frank said. "You've got time. We'll be back in October, probably well before classes would begin. Could wait until then."

"They need to know. I need to know what I'll do. Uncertainty doesn't wear well on these narrow shoulders."

"Susan Byran did pass her test," Frank said. His words were quiet, as though he'd known for a time but hadn't wanted to say.

"They wouldn't have to look far, then."

"Meant you had time to consider, decide later."

I had never had a time when I wasn't doing something. Working or teaching or helping Mama at home. I tried to organize my honeymoon time, structure our days. Frank resisted, said we were to "vacate" the routine.

"This vacation may be more stressful than diligent labor," I said.

"Until you've discovered how to rest, Mrs. Stranahan. It's a luxury you're unaccustomed to, I can see that."

"And you are?"

"Practicing—which I believe you always say makes for perfection."

"Permanence," I said. "Practice makes for permanence."

We traveled well together despite my attempts to control the schedule. We explored preferences in our "vacating" time, such as how he liked his wild turkey prepared or how many pillows I preferred piled beneath my head at night. We exchanged memories of childhood, happy ones and sad. And the gentle connecting and acceptance of our interests, what we read, what we noticed at the beach, which shells caught our eyes first, what memories the ships brought to mind, how people struck us, what we longed for in the future, all formed a mosaic that became our marriage.

After a week or two in North Carolina—which included a brief visit with my mother's parents, the one and only time I'd met them—we rode on to Ohio to meet Frank's parents. His stepmother wore an apron of invitation; his father, the gentle philosopher Frank had alluded to, was a kindly man who nevertheless kept people alert during his sermons at the Presbyterian church.

We took the train on to Canada and Niagara Falls, where we felt the mist on our face, the wetness spray onto the silk of the umbrella we huddled under. We wandered into old bookstores, the scent of musty pages and leather like a salve to Frank's eyes. He met with buyers of the baby alligators and cloth and hides he'd be sending up. We commented on women's fashions, the alligator bags and plumed hats that swept across their faces as we sat at sidewalk tables.

"I don't like plumes except on birds," I said.

"Business," Frank said, even more now a man of few words. It appeared that if nothing had changed from his previous expression of information or devotion, he felt no great need to restate it.

Still, our communion felt both strong and sweet. I found a fabric chair on a frame that looked somewhat like a hammock, which I was sure my husband would like. I bought it with the small amount of teaching money

I had left and had it shipped back to the post. And this man, who watched me brush my tawny hair one hundred times on our wedding night, gave me a silver mirror and comb set the next morning.

We watched lawn bowling on a gentle slope of green. Beyond dipped and draped a golf course flowing as if to the sea. A black-and-white-striped lighthouse stood as a symbol of endurance and safe harbor along the Carolina coast. The birds and sea sounds surrounding brought us closer. But more than anything, I relished the meeting of our minds formed from stimu-lating, passionate conversations.

I'm not sure what it was that finally made me change my thinking.

"Cause some tongue wagging, but most people would settle in without a fuss."

"Hiram Frost would protest, but that isn't a worry, really. I don't think people take him seriously."

"What is then?"

"Just a sense I have, when I say my prayers, read the Scriptures. I'd been so sure I was to teach, but now, I don't know. It isn't as compelling as it once was. It's so strange."

"Maybe you've been given time to explore another stream."

"Explore another stream. Yes. That could be it. But what? I don't like not having a clear path worked out in my mind."

"Lauderdale will become as popular as Asheville," Frank said.

"You think so?"

"People will come for the beach," he continued.

"On their vacating trips."

He nodded. "For the climate. I imagine thousands in Lauderdale. Not that it pleases me, but I can see it."

"That kind of growth needs good planning, for what happens to trees and the land. Those shanty houses popping out like pox wherever they want need more careful thinking or people could destroy what everyone loves about the New River."

"Could," he agreed.

On the train back, Frank talked of business and contracts.

"The post, too, will have to expand. It may be the first store but it won't be the only one before long."

"Much to Frost's delight."

"Have to keep up. I could use help handling the produce side now," he said. "Will's time is more taken up with the bookkeeping and his wish to travel hither and yon." Irritation entered his voice with the mention of Will. "The demand for Seminole products should only increase."

I didn't know if he thought I might meet that need at the post. It wasn't anything I'd considered before, though I thought I could manage numbers with a bit of practice. The day-to-day activities of stocking and recording and ordering weren't something I thought would long hold my interest. I liked getting things finished and then moving on. But if I wasn't teaching, what would I do with my time?

"Maybe we should ask Bloxham," I said.

"Or DeWitt. Your papa could spare him more easily."

"I'd love having family with us on the river. Maybe even Pink? We could bring all of them up, Frank. That would be grand."

"Think Pink's your mama's saving grace just as Bloxham is your father's."

"Begin with DeWitt, then. I'll send a letter off as soon as we get back."

That's probably when the seeds of change began in me, the letting go of my dream to have my own little schoolhouse, to teach and touch little minds. Perhaps listening to Frank's father did it, hearing him speak of the challenges God presents to each of us and the creative ways He meets our needs if we but listen to Him and let Him lead. Certainly Frank and I coming together proved an example of that.

Frank talked of our little village growing but I knew that would happen only if there were permanent homes, places people could become attached to and call their own, so their children could go to school each day. Then they'd invest in the village, want schools and churches and government to civilize it, structure it, and keep it whole. Perhaps that was where I'd make my mark, encouraging good, enduring south Florida homes.

Or perhaps getting my family here, safe and protected away from the fevers and where I could look after them, Mama especially, perhaps that was God's plan for my days.

I told Ed King I intended to resign my contract.

"We'll appoint Susan, then," Ed said. "If you're sure, if I can't talk you into it. I know there might be a fracas about your continuing since you're married, but the support for you's there. Despite Hiram Frost. He's sour about most things so folks don't take note. That's not why you're quitting, is it?"

I hadn't thought of myself as a quitter.

"I changed my mind, Ed. For the good of the community. Susan'll be a fine teacher. And I can be of help to my husband."

Ed looked at me, those bushy eyebrows raising and lowering.

"Your confidence in me means a great deal, but I think this will be best," I said. "In an odd sort of way, this isn't the battle I think I'm meant to wage, allowing married women to teach, not that I have any doubt that it's a worthy fight. It's just that others *will* fight it, when the time comes. It's something more, something I can't place exactly, but I feel sure of it. As sure as I did before that I was supposed to teach."

"Frank approving of this?"

"Frank approves. I wouldn't have decided without Mr. Stranahan's agreement. I do appreciate your understanding, Ed," I said. "It's just the strangest thing for me not to complete a commitment made."

"Made a new one. With Frank. He's probably pleased to see you came just for him and not for all those kids. Besides, you'll be having your own before long, young woman that you are."

He coughed into the silence.

"Anyway," Ed said, "we have you here in our little community and that will make a great many of us happy. Time and change will take care of the rest."

Frank and I settled into our small cottage set behind the post and greeted guests arriving with congratulations. DeWitt came on the train not long after. His presence pleased me, with his wry sense of humor, his unassuming ways.

"Don't you miss teaching, then?" he asked one evening, chewing on the chicken I'd fixed. Outside the window, we watched a primary child skipping rocks into the river. "Thought teaching ran through your blood." He held his fork in the air while he thoroughly chewed each mouthful. His digestion must have been perfect.

"It's strange, isn't it? Teaching was what I'd longed for, lived for, was destined for. I'm still sure of that. And yet marrying Frank seemed destined too."

"Imagine you'll keep busy," DeWitt said.

Busy, yes, but where?

I resisted talking of my struggle, not with Pink nor Mama nor even Ada, especially not Ada. I knew my decision had disappointed. Frank knew, but who could really understand about an uncertain place, a not knowing, except the person going through it?

At times, strange as it often seemed, I'd experience a peace, a thought that warmed me so completely and made me believe that someday I might do something valuable, perform an act of meaning that would touch others. I had never expressed it to another living soul, hadn't even written it down. But being on the New River heightened the sense it would happen.

I began saving things, correspondence, notes and newspaper notices, small shells, signs of my Stranahan beginning. I laughed to myself as I tied up the letters Frank had written to me while I was back in Lemon City. He would have thrown out mine to him. Most would. It was both pretentious and pompous to think of anything noteworthy being done by me, one who had failed to act and cost a brother his life. Me, a being exiled, destined to remain with my own generation, no legacy to pass on. How could I possibly think something remarkable had been laid out just for me that I needed to then write down?

Our New River friends still acted surprised at our marriage.

"Didn't even know you were sparking," Cap Valentine said. He pouted the words out as though we'd deliberately deprived him of a great event.

"Cap was too busy checking out Zapf's to notice," Ed King said when I told him of the former postmaster's words.

"You were a bit surprised yourself; now admit it," Susan King said to her husband. We had decided to take the train to Palm Beach with the Kings and ride the Afromobiles, two-person carts driven by Africans bicycling around the city. Later we stopped for chocolate milk drinks at one of the sidewalk cafés.

"I was, sure enough. But happy we are for you both."

"Is that the infamous Zapf's?" I asked as we pedaled later down Banyon Street past an establishment that featured music and men stumbling precariously out the door.

"One and the same," Frank said.

Indians—men and women—sat on the boardwalk too, just outside. And something more horrifying appeared as well: an adult tipped a flask to the mouth of a child. Three or four other children slept like a litter of puppies on the boardwalk beside them.

"Doesn't seem right," I said.

"Just part of life, Miss Ivy. Guess I can't call you that now," Ed said and cackled.

"You can call me that your whole life," I said. "You were the first, I think."

We celebrated the first community-wide Christmas party, not just for those with children in school. I knew this would become an annual event if we could arrange a place large enough to accommodate the growing we were doing. Our holiday tree was a small pine seedling decorated with paper rings and stars. We sang carols and ate biscuits with my own home-made marmalade. I was at peace, not wondering what I should be doing, not planning or organizing, just enjoying the season of joy and new hope.

I stepped outside the post to see if I could hear the manatees and when my eyes adjusted to the twilight, I saw rather than heard them. Standing near the trading post, looking in the window, stood at least a hundred Seminoles.

I stepped backward inside and located Frank stomping his feet to the music.

"We've visitors," I said. He followed me out. "Are they here to trade?"

Frank shook his head, put his hands on my shoulder. "Quiet as butter-flies."

"Should we invite them in? Would they come?"

Frank looked past me. He waved at someone he knew who waved back.

"Offer food later. Curious is all they are," he said. "The music and frolic. Like their Green Corn Dance events. Don't think they have any idea what we celebrate."

"It's like a Christmas gift, their coming here," I said. "Will they stay around until morning?"

"Never know. Just take it as it comes."

"I need to make up sandwiches. Is there anything I shouldn't serve? What would they like to drink, do you think? Can we make sofkee quick?"

He turned me around to him then, that rare light of joy crossing his face. "Shhh," he said. "Nothing to organize now. Just be. You're the draw this year, dear Ivy. You're the special light that's come to this section of south Florida and even they seem to know it."

After the New River guests left, I listened to the settling sounds under the porch roof of the post; the Osceolas and Tommies and a dozen others and their families were nestled in beneath thatch chickees. Cap Valentine called them "seekees" and maybe they were that, places of comfort and shelter sought by the people. Dogs barked at guests leaving, the sounds of harness and pop boats, at flickering lights on the river. A baby cried then gurgled. Insects hummed.

Frank, DeWitt, Will, and I set out baskets of food covered with red-checkered cloths. "I can't believe this will be enough," I said.

"Loaves and fishes," Frank said.

"Means we'll have some of them biscuits in the morning, then," DeWitt said. "Share breakfast with a Seminole. Won't Gussie and Albert envy me that!"

But in the morning by the time we arose, people and food were all gone. Only empty baskets with folded cloths remained.

I wrote in my journal of firsts about my first Christmas as a Stranahan, my first gathering with guests. And I wrote of the river and the land, not because it was the first time I had considered them, but because the gathering of the Seminoles inspired me to write of them in a new way.

It's said that the southern half of Florida is truly just a giant river that flows so slowly south its inhabitants fail to notice as it shifts from freshwater to salt, from solid ground to marsh. We've come to call it the Everglades with its two seasons of winter and summer, wet and dry. But it could describe our lives as well, the inexplicable, almost imperceptible, movement and change. The times of fullness and moisture when our thirsts are quenched, followed by dryness when our souls feel cracked open and empty. Each is needed in the cycle of life. Each promises the return of the other. Lessons and guidance come packaged within. Each is recognized as part of our lives, though not awaited with the same songs of expectance.

CHAPTER SEVEN

Bustling energy described my outward life those first years on the New River. Tourists arrived more often, the FEC providing the tracks and—Frank noted—the economy providing their tickets. Seminoles poled in from their Big Cypress camps and those near the headwaters of the New River. They came with amazing predictability, keeping Frank's contracts intact. With Frank's help, I began to recognize different family groupings, who had their dogs under control, who made the trip to Zapf's, who offered sofkee to a small, curious woman who watched and waited.

But into the rainy season, with lightning spattering the night skies and flashing brilliance onto dark days, my soul often felt dry and brittle. I wandered through a maze of wondering: Had I left teaching for my own purposes? Had God found me wanting in a way and taken the opportunity to release the passion I'd been given to instruct, to provide tools to unlock a small child's mind? Had I mistaken an excuse for a calling?

In passing, I mentioned my malaise to Susan King.

"When your family comes," she said, "you'll wonder why you ever wondered."

"That's where satisfaction lives, then?"

"Don't you think?"

I didn't. Perhaps in my grown family, making things happen for them, perhaps satisfaction lay there, but I was sure that wasn't Susan King's meaning.

So I listened to the rain on the tin roof like a clatter of horses and pushed the treadle harder on the White sewing machine to have something to show at the end of my darker days. I felt a grieving, not unlike a stream of feeling that had flooded me after Mama's baby died. I'd been young then but Mama assured me I'd been forgiven for my folly, my failure to act.

Papa's thinkin movin. Bloxy redy, he says. Mama feelin beter.
Think I come to see you soon.

Pink's letter encouraged. Now might be the time they'd all come north, settle here, and finally stay, so Albert at least could finish his school years without a break. Gussie too. Maybe I could get Pink to think of her lessons. Her letters piqued a place inside me that caused an awful ache.

I wrote to Papa, suggesting again the New River and its cool breezes for Pink's sake and maybe Mama's too. My words fell on empty ears. Perhaps my malaise lay there, in not being able to make a thing happen when I was sure that it should.

"Can't control other people's lives, Ivy," Frank told me. He looked up over his glasses as I tidied the papers on his desk, inhaled the scent of leather-bound books as I dusted. The shelf clock slowed. I found the key to wind it.

"I know, I know," I said.

"Take your walk. You feel better when you do."

Routine became a tyrant at times, throbbing like a headache; but striding out did usually lift my spirits. I could watch the birds and butterflies swipe color on the canvas of cypress and sea. Maybe the landscape was my calling, my place for passion?

I'd followed the debate about a law against the egret plume trade. The papers arriving weekly by train carried news of the governor's wife, May Mann Jennings, who refused to wear hats with plumes; that was her way to protest until women could vote. She'd been quite outspoken during the campaign of her husband.

"Women should come out of both the kitchen and the schoolroom," she'd admonished, "to thrust their will and wisdom onto Florida's economic and social development." Her vision had been an inspiration. I could see passion in the words she spoke and in the fire in her eyes from the photograph printed in the paper.

"Enforcement of the egret trade could consume me," I told Frank one afternoon after a stuffy gathering at the school to hear campaign speeches and fan flies. He docked the boat under its roof. I waited for his head to appear from the cave of the boathouse.

"You push it."

"What?"

"Your…passions," Frank said, wiping his forehead with the back of his arm. He replaced his hat. "Your paths. Make things happen, all right. Get into a thing just to be moving and you may miss the real opportunity. Maybe you're to be the nail rather than the hammer."

"I don't understand that, Frank."

"Letting go. See how you might be used instead of deciding on your own what you should do."

"Do I do that?" He nodded his head. "But what if I wait and then miss what it is I'm to do?"

"Need to pause to find out," he said. "Take the plume trade. If the bill passes, it will change things, more than just for birds or how it's enforced. Bigger picture than just fashion."

Frank flicked at his ears and looked away.

"You can disagree with me, Frank. I can listen to opposing opinion."

"Trouble accepting, though," he said. "When it isn't your idea. Feathers for hats today." He pulled a linen from his vest pocket, polished his eyeglass lens long after it needed it. "Might be alligator shoes next. Maybe even deer hides will go."

"It's unlikely to go that far."

He raised one eyebrow.

"Well, I don't see how."

"Law would affect our friends," he said.

"What could we do to help them?"

He paused. "Imagine you'd have a plan."

He didn't sound upset, but I often couldn't tell with Frank; his face almost always stayed the same, all serious and solemn. He was self-conscious about the yellowing of his teeth and often put his hand over his mouth when he might be smiling.

"It's usually wise to."

"Sometimes, dear wife of mine, you pluck the chicken long after it's cooked."

With the population of our village growing, Frank decided we should expand the post; and as soon as the season warranted it, we had lumber shipped up from Miami. It would be good to have a sturdy building made of termite-proof pine, one that could house the variety of goods local farmers and settlers found wanting but didn't want to have to wait to have them ordered in. Ed King did the building design; I had one of my own.

"He can pound nails and send the money back to Papa," I said when I realized how large a building Frank had planned. "Or Bloxham could help in the store, free you up to oversee construction. Give DeWitt a little chance at his lessons in between working for you and Ed King."

Frank grinned and slowly shook his head.

"Bloxy can," I said.

"Oh, I know."

Frank chuckled deep and I thought then that while he protested my "chummy meddling," as he called it, he also admired it, my commitment to a worthy cause.

Bloxham and DeWitt chided each other while they dove into constructing. They were careful not to disturb Frank's plantings of royal and coconut palms he'd purchased from Mrs. Brickell—the very first resident of the area. Frank's purple bougainvillea grew undisturbed as well.

It was to be a somewhat unusual building. The main floor would house the post and provide storage and stocks. The second floor, entered only through an outside stairwell on the west side—where the Seminoles docked their dugouts—would serve as a community center for dances and meetings and additional space for sleeping.

Both levels of the post would be surrounded on three sides with covered porches. The verandas were to serve the Seminoles, providing places to sleep out of the rain, off the ground, away from poisonous snakes.

"Want the post and porches to be there for them. Always," Frank told me.

I understood. He wanted a place predictable, out of the wild. A place of refuge, I called it, in a sheltered, inviting setting.

We'd continue to live in our simple cottage built back behind the post; resources from the business went first into the expansion. Bloxham and DeWitt shared another thatched cottage and took their meals with us. My face ached with the grin of it, watching my brothers spar and laugh together, nod slowly with words from my husband, then shuffle lumber, stand walls, and settle poles to support the wide, planked porch.

Frank and I planted a live oak tree in honor of the construction.

"Aren't you disappointed, sister?"

Pink's visit in the season of 1902 came as both welcome and troublesome.

"About what?"

"That you're neither teachin'," she said, "nor gettin' ready to birth a baby."

"More to life than either of those," I said. I folded the tucks of my waist, smoothing them flat.

She cocked her head to the right side in that way she had, her straight, small nose lifted just enough to tell me she had a wonder in her mind.

"No need to pull the screen down," she said. "I'm not meanin' to pry."

"Now, Pink."

She reached up with her soft palm to fold the finger I'd lifted to the air. "That chastisin' finger needn't wag at me." She smiled, the long lashes lounging just a moment on her cheeks.

I dropped my eyes and pulled my finger from hers. I'd never shared the moment of my deepest failure with my sister; I didn't think I ever could or should, though it might explain to her my reasoning over babies.

Pink leaned back in the rattan chair, letting her long blond hair dry in the air. A breeze lifted and sifted the honey strands reaching almost to the porch floor. She stroked a white rat she called Vanilla in her lap. The rat must have been sleeping because it failed to squirm as it had when I tried to hold it.

Pink's eyes stayed closed and she spoke with a dreamy tone in her alto voice. "Just know how much you loved teachin' and little ones. Sort of sad to see you without."

"I still see children." I threaded a needle with white thread and continued stitching the tiny ruffles on the blouse I sewed. It would be a gift for Pink. "A couple stopped by here just last week. Byrd's filled out. Tenley is…still struggling. They talked about Miss Byran. They like her fine. I've been out to the school, helped out once or twice."

"Mama and I thought sure you'd fight it, you being so strong-willed and all."

"That rule'll be changed once women vote. That's the real fight, I suspect. More children moving in every day, staying, homes being built. We'll need upper grades soon. Then they'll open the door to married women. How do you keep that rat from running off?"

Vanilla moved up her arm and she brought her back, holding her like a sausage. Her tail laced around her finger then lay flat as the rat relaxed.

"Her stomach directs her. I keep the vittles," she said and grinned. She rubbed her hair between her fingers then, drying out the wet lengths. "So that's your plan. Be available for a growin' school."

"That is not what I have in mind at all," I said.

"Are you hoping for a baby, then?"

"Honest to truth, Pink, I don't think I'll ever teach again in the same way I did before. It was the strangest thing, but after Frank and I married and we traveled north, I felt as though my life was destined for, well, different things."

"Must be strange to be so sure of somethin' and then have it slip away. You always like knowin' which road you're travelin', unlike me. Or Bloxy. He just does loll his way through life, isn't that a fact?"

We watched Bloxham at that very moment, lifting a heavy barrel of fertilizer onto a wagon. He had a cowlick that swirled like grass around a fence post at the back of his head. Another young man carried a barrel out of the post on his shoulder, his muscles straining beneath the thin cotton shirt. DeWitt lugged a sack behind them.

I loved having both Bloxham and DeWitt close by. Every morning I took a guava with them or a grapefruit juice and with Pink here for a week, it had been a sweet reunion.

Bloxham acted perfectly content to just take what life gave in its own pace and space. DeWitt understood my joy of "firm plans."

"I do envy him that at times," I said. "Bloxham."

"He may lose his love if he doesn't act before long, though. Lollin' in that department can be disastrous."

"Bloxham has a love?"

"Louise," she said.

"Ah, Louise. I'm surprised she'd confide in you."

"Bloxy did. He knows I won't be goin' anywhere with it on my own. At least not far."

"Well, waiting does have rewards."

"You didn't," Pink laughed. "Except now with this baby thing. You're hopin' for a family, aren't you?" The rat lay curled in the lap of her lingerie dress, its alert pink eyes staring out from beneath her hand. Pink's almond eyes held mine. "I'm wantin' a niece to spoil." She pulled her hair over her shoulder and started to braid it. "Louise and Bloxham might just honor me first if you don't hurry on. Wouldn't it be fine to have a weddin' between a Cromartie and—what's her last name?—a King?"

Pink smiled and lifted a blue ribbon from the bowl of her upturned hat next to the chair.

"They'd have a Methodist to marry them at least," I said, though it galled me that such an opportunity came about by Hiram Frost's sour-faced efforts. "Better than a justice of the peace. Blessed by faith."

"Why, I think that Cap Valentine is just a sweet old man."

"A real pastor and a real church promise to make our little village all that more civilized," I said.

"You sound like Frank," Pink said. "Families make a place worth stayin' in, sister. You could surely help with that."

She wove the blue satin among the thick blond of her braid. Finished, she lifted the rat and snuggled it against her neck. She still watched Bloxham and she still pursued a subject I'd tried to step over.

"Mama's pregnant," Pink said after a pause. It was spoken to Vanilla rather than me. "Guess you knew."

"I didn't. I thought Papa wanted to move."

"She's hopin' I won't fall in love and leave."

"There's time for that, for you, just turning eighteen. A whole world waits out there for young women, and becoming more so. Mrs. Munroe and Mrs. Jennings and others all say it's just a matter of months before women'll contribute in greater ways than just the schoolroom or the kitchen."

"Or in Mama's case, the bedroom," Pink said and laughed.

"Pink!"

"I was only funnin'. Have to find humor in it. Always did think that was the best way to deal with fear and trepidation." She twisted the braid like a crown around her head. She was beautiful.

"Are you worried? For Mama?"

She nodded. "She's awful run-down. Think that's why Papa isn't pushin' on the move. Why I'll stay 'round, too."

"Bless your heart, Pink. I'm glad. Mama must be, too."

"Why, if you and Frank were to have a youngun before Mama, he'd be older than his aunt. Or uncle."

"That's highly unlikely since Mama is with child and I'm not."

"Never know what the Lord will bring your way," she sang in a child's voice as she stood. Vanilla started as Pink lifted her limber form and eased her through her palms, hand over hand. Pink stretched then headed off to talk with Bloxham. The rat rode up on her neck inviting a pat from the man beside Bloxy, who stopped what he was doing as soon as Pink approached.

The three of them engaged in chatter. Frank had decided he could use Bloxham's help well past the building of the post. DeWitt remained, too. The boys' presence should have given me all I needed. But something still left me in a state I thought of as protected purgatory.

I felt a twinge of envy for their youth. They seemed so fresh, so full of ideas. I believed I had always been thirty or more though at my birthday just passed I had officially turned twenty-two. Somehow, being older, I'd thought I wouldn't waste time in trying things, walking down roads that turned out to be trails ending nowhere. Ada had said that every trail had a lesson to teach, that none were dead ends. They only look that way when you're on them. Later, you'd learn the lesson you were too busy to get, but this time by failing.

Frank began making loans to new people trying to buy up muck land to farm. He accepted credit at the store as well, something I discovered when I helped out with the numbers from time to time while Will traveled. Even a few of the Seminoles had a credit sheet. On one Frank had written "Charley's other wife," so he must have had two.

"Is that common? More than one wife?" I asked Frank. We were alone inside the post, the Seminoles having finished their trades for the day.

"'Spect it was in the old days. Not so much now. If a man dies, his brother might assume his place, take care of that family like the Israelites did. They're committed in that way."

"Not so sure I'd like Will looking after me," I said.

"Don't think I'd care for the condition that would bring it about either." Frank grinned.

He took his glasses off and held them up to the light just as a Seminole man and his wife entered.

"We're closing soon, Squirrel," Frank told him, replacing his glasses.

"Need kettle. For Sarah."

"I'll take care of them," I said and came out around the counter to show the woman the enamel pots and pans we'd just gotten in. She must have been an old grandmother, judging from her slow shuffle behind me and the raspy breathing I heard. She turned the pot I handed her upside down, checked its weight in her gnarled hands, and knocked on the side, listening to the sound. She nodded, a smile on her toothless face, and held the pan up for Squirrel to see. He hadn't moved from Frank's side. He pointed then to Frank's ledger book, which was closer to me than to them.

"I can see what's on your account," I offered.

"No!" He held up his hand to stop me. "Frank know."

"Oh, yes, Frank carries those figures in his head," I told Sarah and reached for the ledger. Frank shook his head and took the book from me. "I can carry it out for you if you like, Sarah. They'll let women do that." She smiled and nodded.

The men determined the price and exchange of the kettle, and finished, Sarah turned to leave. I was following, carrying the pot, when she stopped abruptly. I nearly stumbled over her at the door. "What is it?" I asked.

She clutched at the beads at her throat. A strange clattering sound rushed out and she sank, her head falling onto the wooden walk outside, her bare feet lying still in the store.

"Frank!"

Frank dropped the ledger, and with quick steps matched by Squirrel, dropped to the floor beside us. "What's wrong? Has she fainted?"

I lifted her head onto my lap while Frank felt beneath the rows of beads to feel a throb at her throat. I'd never seen someone so still. "Will she be all right?"

Frank shook his head. "She's dead."

I felt the worst fire sear the outside of my skin, and inside, bile rose up. I swallowed, felt shivery and cold.

"Just like that? With no warning?"

Others gathered around us, their hands on Squirrel as he squatted. "How could it happen so quickly, Frank? Had she been ill?"

"Old," Squirrel said. "What happens."

"But without being able to say anything to her, to comfort her... Let's bring her back inside," I said. My legs felt numb and my hands, clammy.

"No!" Squirrel pressed his fingers against my shoulder. "No move."

"But we can't leave her like this, half in and half out. Frank?"

"We'll leave the door open, Squirrel, all night. Just bring her in where she'll be out of the weather."

Squirrel hesitated, looked up at some of the others, then nodded and helped to move his wife toward a pallet Frank had already begun to roll bins of molasses from. They laid Sarah on the wooden pallet and I opened a Hudson Bay blanket I took from the shelf and spread it over her. A dozen women entered and surrounded Sarah, singing a mournful chant as Squirrel picked up the kettle his wife had purchased and walked out into the night.

The door to the trading post stayed open, and the chanting and singing voices drifted back to our cottage behind the post.

"How did you know the open door would comfort him?" I asked Frank in our bedroom that night.

"Something I've noticed."

"What do they believe about it, Frank? Do they think they'll see each other again? Do they have that to comfort them?"

"Don't know. Just know they grieve as we do."

"It was so sudden, no time to say good-bye or tell how he felt about her or settle any old grievance, or...anything."

"Happens that way in the flick of a fawn's tail. Best have said what you want when you want. Never know."

We lay quietly together side by side, the frogs and turtle shell rattles background to the music of their voices.

"You're not worried about...losing anything? With the door open?"

"Never gave it a thought."

"You know them. They accept you so easily. I wonder if they'll ever see me that way, as someone they can trust."

"Just takes time, willing to learn. Can't judge 'em just because we don't understand. Just be honest and yourself."

In the morning the blanket I'd placed on Sarah's body was covered with several yards of skirt material, all the deep dark shades of the rainbow. Women surrounded her and I could see beneath the cloth that now she lay dressed in her finest, wore strands and strands of beautiful beads.

Frank hitched up his wagon and Squirrel and several other men moved Sarah's body into the back.

"Want to go along?" Frank asked as he checked the mule's harness.

"No. You go. I've never liked funerals all that much, especially when I don't know what to do."

"Be yourself," Frank said. "Willing to let yourself be led."

"I don't do that well, do I, Frank?"

He didn't respond and when I didn't move, he accepted where I was and drove off with Squirrel at his side, rows of family mourners walking behind.

Life went on. *The Tropical Sun,* a paper that came out when it wanted, ran a column called "Fort Lauderdale Laconics" that covered our little village's activities, of how A. D. Marshall from Macon, Georgia, had come to cultivate the "Salk Creek Muck" or how the Braddock brothers set out their eggplants five days before Christmas and they were doing well. A tram road built to ease transport of tomatoes from muck land to the tidewater progressed, and a fish house rose on the river for collection for northern markets.

"Both the Olivers and Marshalls have carloads of fertilizer coming in," Frank told me. He'd spent the day helping Bloxham and Will unload lumber for a wheelbarrow line that H. Powers was building to reach his farm far up in the muck.

Business boomed. My spirit didn't. I thought about Sarah's death, the quickness of it, how we never know the day that we'll be called. Time had run out for Sarah. I worried it might do that for me before I found my path.

I posed this dilemma through my prayers, carrying on a conversation out loud on my walks that if any had been close enough might have warranted me a referral to that hospital near Miami for "addled" souls.

"What is it I'm supposed to do?" I asked.

A covey of quail fluttered up in front of me, their wings making the slightest drumming as they settled among the sea grapes and ferns. "I believe that I've confessed the things I've been troubled with. I've asked You to tap me on the shoulder about those I'd rather not admit to and I haven't felt a single nudge I haven't said I'm sorry for. So what is it that's in my way?"

Only silence answered, broken by a turkey gobbling.

I decided doing daily, mundane things would keep me disciplined. I glued pictures into scrapbooks, securing all the photographs Frank had made of us. I pulled weeds every day. Seeds I'd ordered from the T. C. Woods catalog arrived down from Richmond. The smell of moist earth as I knelt, shaded by my wide palmetto hat, gave me momentary peace. I sewed, made all Frank's clothes and mine, read books, classics and some legal tomes Frank had boxed. Cap Valentine still loaned us books. He'd taken to imbibing more and so I didn't relish as much our conversations, strong drink changing the character of a man.

I spent hours in reading Scripture, expecting intervention to come my way as it had to John Wesley at Aldersgate. But no white light appeared, no brightness pierced with clear direction. Once I felt more than heard words that said, *Do what no one else can do,* but nothing to say what that might be.

At times I felt like Tenley: "Every day searching/Yesterday's light." It was difficult to do what I'd told him worked for self-encouragement when I didn't know what to keep my eye on. I still trusted that I'd been given the tools to do it—if I lived long enough to know my assignment.

They came in, as predictable as the afternoon rains in the winter season. Their presence always intrigued me, the color and movement of their days during the week to ten days they stayed. Confidence filled their faces, a fearlessness and sureness, leaving only when they'd come back from Zapf's and then only for the time it took for the liquid spirits and sleep to wear off.

I was curious about their lives in the swamps. Frank had been to their camps, where clusters of families lived in the cypress on the fertile hammocks. He described their thatched homes, different chickees for cooking, eating, and sleeping, each with raised floors—except the cooking one, which held a central fire—and storage areas of twine hung from the ceiling thatch.

"Fire in the cooking chickee burns all the time: oak at night; pine during the day."

"That's that sweet smell pushing up through the palmetto roofs."

"Fights off the bugs and snakes who like to harbor in the thatch. They've good gardens, lush, well tended. Grow sweet potatoes and peas, stalks of corn and purple potatoes, even bananas and sugar cane. Pigs're fenced, too," he said.

Canoes were docked and one could see the flattened trails they made as they moved out through the saw grass. Beyond the camps would be fruit trees of sour oranges, limes, and coarse skin oranges raised and then brought in for trade.

"Seen them wrestle alligators," Frank said. "Quite a sight straddling their backs. Do it for fun, too. Keep alligator pens. So they can bring in the eggs to hatch."

"Such a strange habit, people buying little alligators to take back north," I commented one afternoon as we wrapped leaves around the eggs to keep them warm until they hatched.

"Vagaries of fashion," Frank said. "What we depend on."

Frank had participated in the annual Green Corn Dance—or at least been invited to it and watched. Clan groups met at the annual festival from all over, Frank said. People played games, flirted, and married. Courts of justice met, too. "Sentences carried out by cutting. Use sharp pins, wrapped together like on a comb, then rake them across a defendant's legs or back. Draws blood sometimes."

I shivered at the thought.

"Lined kids up, too, and talked about old infractions. Least that's what Charley told me. All in their language so I didn't get all of it," Frank said. "Didn't even make the kids cry. Ten, I'd say."

"Ten scratches?" I asked.

He nodded toward the river. "Manatees."

"That's what those scars are from? On the backs of their legs? Oh, Frank, that seems so cruel!"

"Wondered about it," Frank said. "Like a whipping I knew some schoolmates got from their fathers. But not as vicious, I'd say, with everyone getting the same treatment and only once a year. Kids acted like they'd been bitten by a turtle, just a little pinch."

But I remembered the first Seminoles I'd ever seen at Cohen's store. Their legs had lines of scars like mango roots raised across their calves. I told him so.

"Suppose crimes must warrant greater discipline," Frank said.

"Isn't that what happened to Crop-eared Charlie for helping the Cooleys? Oh, look, two more just blew. I think we have fifteen tonight." We counted five more, fifteen total that came in to do their dance.

"Take their rules seriously."

"And do they have a religion, Frank?" We walked back in, arm in arm, and closed the screen door on the cottage. The breezes felt balmy and soothing after a hot, humid day. "What gives them their strength?"

"They believe in a creator who rules over us all. And tradition, their place in the glades, the Green Corn Dance, and the rituals of examining the medicine bundle that they believe carries strength and power. And families, I suspect. They still have clans to speak of, at least, despite the army's greatest efforts."

"They've never wanted a safe place to be? Like a reserve?"

"Prefer the swamps, I suppose. Without a treaty, they've no relationship with the government except warring. 'Spect they'd rather wrestle alligators than the United States government one more time but 'spect they would."

And yet the Seminoles came in to Lauderdale, moved among us, made our post possible with their quality and consistent trade. All through the winter they came, buying up pots and cloth, ammunition and traps, their pine logs burning and scenting the air. When they left, taking the activity and color with them, I felt an emptiness, as though a part of me left with them.

I wish I could have understood my attraction, what about them made me think of their lives when they were gone, dream about them on hot nights. Perhaps it was the impossibility of our communing at all. Why, their very name *Seminole* came from an old Muskogee word meaning "wild," used when the English and later Spanish ruled our state. That's what Cap Valentine told me one day when we sat at the seawall and watched the children fish for catfish.

"Indians escaping the north come south they called 'sim-in-oli,' wild. It was that 'wild' group that got attacked by the young United States back in 1817. Hit 'em for harboring black slaves making it to another country: our Florida. And it was that wild group got attacked again in '35. Joined their northern neighbors the Muskogees—that began the second Seminole War. Lasted seven years."

"Lost thousands of government troops. My father spoke often of that."

"Weren't successful in deporting to Oklahoma what was left of the wild ones. Had been 1800 but after that third war, only 100 or so survived. Just dwindled away with no treaty."

"But they were peaceable, that's what Frank said."

"Never knew a one to raise a hand against a white in my time," Cap said.

"The government's done nothing but hunt and kill them," Frank said, dropping down beside me by the water. "No reason they should trust anything it says."

"But we're the government, Frank."

Cap laughed. "She's got you there, Frank."

"They don't see it that way."

"So is there any other group they dislike?" I asked Frank later as the two of us sat under the porch watching rain splatter and pock the New River. Frank had gone for a dip after the children and Cap left, and I hung his striped suit on the clothesline strung across the porch. "Since they hate teachers and strangers and the government, categories I seem to fit in with so well—though I think I'm changing the stranger part. Anyone else they're wary of?"

He sat thoughtfully, holding his nail file and tapping it on his finger while he thought. "One more. Guess you should know about that group, too, being who you are."

I raised my eyebrow, after Frank's fashion.

"Christians," he said. "They've no time for missionaries or Bible pushers or people who say they come to bring them new life."

"That isn't me, is it?"

"Have a way of walking with your faith out like a drum, some."

"I'd prefer to draw people to it," I said. "For its safety and strength. I don't want to be a thumper or a trumpet."

Frank took the clothespins from my hand and kissed my fingers. "I know. I know." He handed back the pins. "Been here going on ten years," he said. "Know most by name but few I'd call my friend. Good business relationships. Honest trade, my not acting one way with them and another with others. I accept them as they are—what's noble and what's not. Can't have trust without that. Same as for you and me and anyone else you want to commune with, I 'spect."

"You accept them. I guess I hold them in some mystery."

"Just people, with beliefs different than my own, but mine being no better. I don't condone the cutting, mind you. Or the drinking and heading off to Zapf's. But I don't like pain nor what spirits do to any race. They're more like us than not, Ivy. Just people with good streaks and bad. Don't want to change them. Think they know that."

I couldn't describe how something that he said differed with what I felt but I didn't know how exactly.

"Wouldn't put my interest there, Ivy, at least not with an eye toward change. Unless, of course, you've both the patience and the passion of a Job."

He left then and returned with a sweater he settled on my shoulders. He rubbed my arms and back with his long fingers for a time after that, both of us sinking into the intimacy of our own thoughts.

When they came in that next winter, I watched with new eyes, wanting to know them as Frank did. The children acted more aware of me this time. I'd become a regular thing to see, I suspected, my brown hair piled high though I still stood barely taller than many of the children. They offered a tentative wave in return to mine when their parents first poled in. They let me pet a dog or two, the tails wagging against my long skirts. I was a staple now they could count on being at the post each time, something reliable—that first, deep part of trust.

When they built their fires, I'd make my own scents: baking cookies, making marmalade and jellies. When Della, the African day lady we employed, came to help me with the washing, I'd hear the children rustling in the palmettos and imagined them watching us boiling water on hot days, swirling the linens with the paddle then rinsing and twisting before hanging the white sheets out to dry.

They began to be unique to me.

I could tell each child apart, and at night, I'd tell Frank which families had come in. Jumpers. Tommies. Tigertails. Osceolas. I recognized canoes and the family groups in them, their dogs and the items they brought in for trade, who had good sweet potatoes, who brought in frogs, and what they were likely to leave with. I recognized Squirrel and the enamel pot that always rode now in his canoe.

Most had stopped bringing their pigs with them after several had gotten out of the enclosed area Frank had for them. The animals had rooted through our own garden and new plantings of trees, and Frank actually turned red when he surveyed the damage.

They were terribly apologetic, the pigs' owners. I don't know what was said, but the next time the Seminoles came in, their canoes were minus swine.

Frank's view of them wasn't totally correct: they did change, these Seminole people, though in slow and subtle ways and for very charitable reasons.

I stood on the porch of our little cottage behind the post. I'd almost feel them there, the children, making their way through the vines and palmetto, half hidden by foliage, seeking entertainment, maybe refuge from the heat. They watched me as I opened the screen door.

"This is such a lovely day," I said out loud.

I spoke the words to the wind, fanning myself with my big hat.

"I wonder if anyone would like a cookie?" I set a platter out on the steps, brushing bugs away with my hands. "Who might come to take chocolate and cookies with me today?"

I heard giggles beneath the shrubs. I knew they understood me. They knew quite a little English and the combination of what I showed them and my words made it clear enough what I intended.

Our communion went no further that day. My cookie platter stayed piled high. They remained in the palmettos.

Later, I recognized the child with the high forehead who wore a faded dress ending just above her callused knees. I'd seen her at the post, a girl with a younger child on her hip helping her family bring in pumpkins and corn for sale by holding one end of the canvas bag while an older brother strained against the other side. Another lifted slabs of otter pelts and deer hides to the steps. The little girls with their straight bangs helped carry out yards of cloth their mothers bought, burrowing them into the bases of the canoes. One skirt, Frank said, could take up to eighteen yards. It was time-consuming, creative work.

Frank, and Will, when he was there, helped DeWitt and Bloxham load crates of salt pork and flour into their canoes, replacing supplies of alligator eggs they'd brought in for Frank.

"Look at all those eggs," Frank told Billy Osceola on one trip in. My husband's eyes grinned when he saw the supply.

"Many wear north?" Billy asked. A large man, he scratched at his belly as he talked.

"I suppose," Frank said. "Oddest custom, pinning those little alligators to dresses. Can't imagine where the joy is, watching little green legs walk across a woman's chest."

"Strange," Billy answered him.

Billy stood taller than Frank's five feet seven inches. His face had high cheekbones and a wide nose whose nostrils flared when he laughed as he did now, talking about alligator pins.

It was a disgusting fashion practice as far as I was concerned. Perhaps even more vile than the plume hunting.

"Not all of the eggs end up that way," Frank defended when I commented. "Most become pets in Mystic, Connecticut, or Minneapolis and Philadelphia."

"Just so hurtful," I said. "To have a pin stuck right through their little hides. As a decoration. They can't live long."

"Your fair sex promotes the practice," Frank said. "Billy and I just help supply a demand already there. Isn't that right, Billy?"

"I speak no more," Billy said, lifting his hands in protest. His belly jiggled beneath the colorful shirt he wore tucked into his jeans.

The men purchased necessities at Frank's post, but doodads as well, and usually those had color. Lots and lots of bright colors.

They brought no feathers in as Frank had told them of the new law finally passing. "Don't think they aren't selling to smugglers," Frank told me. "Prices just went up, is all."

We heard through the grapevine of regional gossip that the trade continued almost unabated with white hunters wiping out whole rookeries of snowy egrets then smuggling the feathers north.

I thought it odd and far-reaching that New York fashion could invade the lives of these distant people—and ours, too. We did purchase those eggs that became living fashion and at times I found it difficult to distinguish trade critical for our mutual survival and what was habit, based on fashion or whim.

One season I suggested to Frank that he ask for more of their craft items for the next time they came in. Dolls and carvings of birds and canoes would sell well and not place pressure on alligators or birds.

"I heard near Miami that tourists have been going out to swamp camps and offering money to the Seminoles directly to buy plumes they might have. They let them look at their chickees and pigs."

"Like spectators at a freak show," Frank said.

"I hope it's temporary. Families don't deserve such an invasion. They need protection, Frank, don't you think?"

"I suppose," Frank said, but he didn't change his order for the eggs.

The porches became Seminole bedrooms. It was a sight that never failed to fascinate me, their stretching out beneath the shingled, slanting roofs. Often nights were cool, the moon casting white light over ripples of the river. They'd wrap themselves in their unfurled turbans or a Hudson Bay blanket or simply sleep knees pulled up beneath their lovely skirts.

I think my being there in the early mornings, striding out for my walks along the New River toward the beach, gave me a place in their lives.

When three small children accepted my offer of cookies served from a china plate, things changed. I ought to have been prepared; I'd dreamed of a rushing river the night before.

CHAPTER EIGHT

The children appeared out of the foliage like blooms against green and stepped onto our little lawn. The thick-bladed grass felt as though one walked on sponge during the wet season and the children's feet sunk in as they huddled together, encouraging each other on. The sun burned hot though filtered through the palms and pines. I'd brought the cookies out onto the lawn and sat next to the plate, eating one, oohing and aahing about their fine taste, hoping to repeat my success of the day before.

A short, stubby girl with a flash of purple ribbon in the cape that draped from her shoulders came first. Like stars in a dark sky, three or four others looked from behind her, staring at the white plate piled high, their eyes longing for the taste. Squirrels chattered and chased each other next to our cottage and a couple of younger children turned, distracted by the noise. One brave girl actually lifted a cookie then sat down beside me to eat it. Another made his way next to her and the first handed a cookie to him, watching me with teasing eyes.

I took my big, merry widow hat off then and placed it on her head.

She turned to face her friends and they stared. One or two giggled. Another reached out to touch the brim but the brave one who wore it jerked back. She spoke in their language and shook her head, one hand gripping the straw palmetto, another finger shaking at them, something I'd seen myself do. Another child reached and I could see an argument ensuing.

"I have more." I stood up. "Come on inside."

I motioned for them, then stepped through the screen door and offered another hat left hanging on the coat tree with a long black ribbon draped down the back.

They stood on the bottom step and peered inside. They didn't cross the threshold but stepped up on the porch of our cottage. A girl with wide feet pointed to a pair of my shoes set next to Frank's chair where he'd left them after rubbing white polish over the scuffed toes.

"Oh, put them on!" I picked them up and handed them to her, motioning toward her bare, brown feet.

Giggles followed as one from behind pushed forward and three stumbled inside. There were five children in all and their laughter spilled into the space like a wind chime breaking up a still day.

Now joyous chatter began, as though having broken past the doorway, they had permission to truly indulge. Hands reached for hats and shoes. I hustled into our bedroom and brought out a shawl or two, another hat with a narrower brim, and a pair of Frank's boots. The items were snatched up like guavas from a basket.

"Come look in the mirror," I urged. "Look how beautiful you are."

The girl wearing my hat peeked first. The others crowded around her boldness. She grinned, showing even white teeth, and then just as quickly she brought her forearm to her eyes to cover them.

"But you're beautiful," I said. "You look lovely."

She kept her eyes covered.

She backed away from the mirror, then turned before sliding her arm from her eyes, as cautious as a summer dawn.

"I wonder what your name is?" I said, not really expecting an answer.

"Me Esther," she said.

"You're beautiful, Esther," I said, my heart pounding with connection.

I wanted to feel the smoothness of her cheek, to bend and brush the dirt from her knees, touch her thick, black hair that peeked out from beneath my hat, to fold her into my arms. I didn't, and still it was sweet, an almost mystical communion. One that thrilled me to my toes.

Esther stared then turned back to the mirror. She held her skirt out, cocking her head side to side the way I'd seen my sister do at that same age, maybe six or seven, maybe eight or nine. I'd done it myself in front of a mirror with a frilly new frock. I smiled, recognizing in Esther the twins of discovery and delight.

With her forearm back at her side, Esther slowly lifted her gaze to mine. I'd seen those eyes before in children seeking, thirsting, making new discoveries: a wish to be challenged, exposed to different things and thus to see the world through new and tutored eyes, to forge her own tools to make a difference in her life.

The dream I'd had the night before, of carrying children through the New River, struggling and pushing against water and wanting to be useful, flooded back in my head. A thought, a calling of sorts, churned inside me, like the flow beneath the saw grass. Was this the answer I'd been waiting for?

It would have to be incessant, unquestionable in its endurance, composed of clear and unpolluted care. Predictable. I must be honest and accepting of her, her strengths and values, but true with her, as true to who I was within my soul as the being they'd see when they looked at me with those full and wondering eyes. It was the only way I could see to protect them and make a lasting, sheltering change.

Esther dropped her gaze and fingered the shawl she pulled around her narrow shoulders. One of the boys spoke to her. He laughed and pointed at his chubby feet pudging out of my shoes. Esther laughed too.

The children easily chewed on the cookies, almost comfortable now. Having once decided to enter this unknown world, they took it in with ease. They moved around the room, fingered the lamp, and sniffed the begonia blooming near the window. Until an adult's voice in the distance halted everything.

They stood as still as a Key deer at twilight.

Esther's eyes flashed a quick look to me, then back to her friends. The children spoke low among themselves. Esther ripped the hat and shawl from her head and dropped them like hot rocks on the arm of the divan. She gathered up the others like a mother hen in motion, shooing them like chickens out the door. In seconds they had slipped out of the clothes and left a trail of ruffled edges across the cottage and down the steps as they disappeared into vines past Esther, who gave one last look around the house and then stared at me for just a moment.

I smiled but she did not return it.

Instead her gaze felt hot, bold, and I could almost hear her speaking. Her eyes held questions; could I lead but not control?

"We'll do this together, Esther," I said.

I had no idea if she understood me or if what I read inside her steady eyes was the message she intended. But I did know without a doubt that a burden had been exchanged between us.

"Do what must be done for the children." The phrase formed inside my head, speaking of commitment and direction, speaking to my soul.

Esther did not come back again that season. But after Christmas, when the families came in to trade, my heart pounded, scanning the faces for her. I'd hear a chattering beneath the wide elephant ear leaves and push them and palmetto fans aside to see if Esther hid and teased. Instead squirrels rushed out, startled me, then disappeared. The longer she stayed away, the more I wondered if someone had discovered that Esther and the other children came into the house with me and had punished them for their curiosity.

I asked casually about the alleged Seminole fierceness.

"They didn't outlive soldiers by licking honey," Frank told me.

"I know they were once great warriors, but I mean now. Look at Shirt-tail Charley. He sort of mopes around, doesn't appear to have much self-respect. Why, Edna Zeigler even started a rumor that he took his first bath in the New River just last week."

"No rumor," Will said, striding over.

"Well, is he more representative of them now than the others? Do we really have to worry about them causing a fracas over something? Being harmful, I mean?"

Frank stopped working on his books and looked up at me over the top of his glasses.

"Want an orange?" I asked, offering him a slice.

"Why the sudden interest over punishment?"

"I just want to know about them. I see their children. They're curious about me. A few will eat my cookies."

"Wouldn't be concerned about an uprising unless someone's been stirring things up," Will said.

"Can't imagine who'd do that," I said.

"Hmm," Will said. I noticed he wore a gold pin on his collar. An eagle stood over a shield, the word *tote* engraved on it.

Frank went back to his books, moving his finger down columns of numbers, checking on names, making notations.

"Interesting pin," I said to Will.

Will grabbed at his collar as though stung by a bee. "Just a lodge I belong to," he said. He put the pin in his pocket and pulled at the narrow end of his handlebar mustache.

"Their judging system with children. Tell me about that."

Frank took off his glasses and rubbed the spot on either side of his nose where the lenses perched. He started to tell me but Will interrupted.

"Children always get fresh water for guests," Will said. "They wait to eat until their elders are finished. They keep the pigs out and the vegetables in. Their jobs as children are to do what they need to to become adults. Including playing; something adults don't do enough of in my opinion."

"It's the discipline part of child-rearing that interests me."

"Need to know men and women, then," Will said. "Women head the clans, but fathers and uncles, aunts, all end up disciplining the children for little things. Teach them their ways, too."

Frank replaced his glasses and his eye caught the law books on the top of the glass bookshelf. "Rules are set. Everyone knows. If they choose to break them, well, they know the consequences. They've a good life, Ivy."

"One that doesn't need to change, judging from the tone of your voice."

"Amen to that," Will said.

When the next trading families came in, a few children appeared through the palmettos behind the post, moving as one to sit at the steps of our cottage. I'd cut up a young cabbage palm, swamp cabbage we called it, and boiled it for lunch. The children's presence eased my growing sense of guilt. Surely there could be nothing too harmful happening to Esther or these children would not present themselves so easily on my porch.

Billy and Rebecca were two new ones who came, their hair worn cropped around their round faces. They sat beside me on the lawn, watching as I drew an ivory comb through my hair, spreading it across my shoulders to dry in the sun. Their small, dark fingers threaded themselves through my sand-colored hair when I nodded for them to touch it.

They watched what I did when I worked in the garden, showed me how they did it differently. Often they just stood and gazed, as though writing down all my movements that might be different from their own. Memorizing with their eyes, that's what they were doing.

I sang little songs to them, and once, even though their eyes grew large as turtle eggs, they listened to Frank's Victrola as a band beat out a marching tune. Frank told me the first time one of the Indians had heard it they'd run from the room yelling, "No like man in box!"

Sometimes we tossed balls between us. They were very good at that, with their strong arms and accurate aim.

And once or twice, they—usually girls—would come into the house. Nodding their heads at my hats and my shoes, the dress-up play would begin. Giggling, they'd droop the merry widows askew over an eye while swirling themselves around the room. I'd watch as they shuffled their way to stand before the oval mirror. I was but a helper in their discovery, a strange adult who asked, "Would you like to try this?" or "What can I get you next?" They designed their own instruction. I simply provided materials.

Their presence highlighted my days, though I was careful not to sound too enthusiastic about my time with the children when I spoke with Frank. His support of my actions felt restricted by pragmatics. I had no one, not really, to share it with.

Then Pink wrote to say that Mama felt poorly and was sure she'd lose the baby. I took the train south immediately, both to see Mama and to confide in Pink, a sister who was also my friend.

I was irritated in a strange way with my mother, a feeling that became wrapped in guilt when I found out upon arrival that she had indeed lost the child.

"Susanna Wesley had twelve children, and look what she gave the world," my mother said. Her voice was breathy as I sat beside her on the bed. Eyelet lace had been embroidered onto the white sheets, giving the bed a festive look that did not fit the occasion. "John founding a whole denomination and Charles composing all those wonderful hymns. Think what the world would have missed if she hadn't persisted in fulfilling God's plan for her life."

"Perhaps she might have found a cure for the plague if she hadn't had to help care for so large a family," I said.

"You always did have a ready answer for everything." Mama sighed. "No, if God wants us to have twelve, that's what He'll give. If not, not. You can't change what God wants for your life, Ivy."

"I'm not resisting anything." I leaned to kiss her cool forehead.

"I know that tone," she said. "'Subject's closed.'"

I spent a few days longer with my family, wishing I'd done it more often. No reason not to. It was good to see Gussie and Papa and Albert, who no longer waddled when he ran but instead jumped easily over the puddles the rains left in the white-rock roads. He coughed, Mama said. Especially in the winter season.

I needed to pay more attention to Pink, too. She was a beautiful young woman with an undisciplined spirit that attracted total strangers when she twirled her umbrella over our heads as we walked down the street in the sun.

"Do you have plans, Pink?"

She shook her head. "I'm like Mama in that. Just trustin' to whatever comes my way."

"We're born driven," I said. "First to breathe then stand upright. With purpose. We've been given gifts to use."

Pink lowered her eyes and fluttered the lashes at a well-dressed Cuban seated at a sidewalk table across from us. Smoke drifted around him as he watched her lazily over the length of his cigar.

"He's a perfect stranger!" I shook my head. "I'm fearful you'll get distracted," I said, giving the man a stern look. It just caused him to smile when he noticed me, his eyes only for a moment drawn away from my sister. "End up wasting your talents."

I swirled what was left of the melting ice in my lime drink. "Perhaps you should come spend time up north with Frank and me. Stay longer than a week or two."

"Expose me to quiet village life?" she said. She seemed unaware of the effect she had on the Cuban. "Bloxy says it's all work and no play there. Seems an accurate description if I recall."

"Much of life is that. Doing what must be done."

"I'm just a leaf makin' its way down the stream, sister." She moved the fan back and forth in front of her face, barely moving the breeze. "Must be close to ninety degrees." She sighed. "Never know where it'll take me. Maybe north to Lauderdale. Maybe not." She laughed, a warm and friendly laugh but one that said she might just visit me once again, but her remaining there would be unlikely.

When I returned, I told Frank about Mama's sunken eyes, how the veins stood out on the backs of her hands, and how she looked so strained and pale.

"I find myself irritated at Papa, too," I said. "Putting her through that time after time."

I unpacked my camisoles and underdrawers from the valise and placed them in tight piles in my bureau drawer. The scent of vanilla rose up from the sachets buried within the folds of my clothes.

"All relationships have an element of risk attached to them," Frank said. "Can't protect people from pain."

"You're not proposing we risk..." I stopped, my hands tensed at the drawer.

"Nothing like that."

I nodded my head. I felt guilty about that too, my physical relationship with Frank, my commitment to managing my fear. "You do understand," I said. "Mama's condition just confirms it."

"I understand," he said and leaned to kiss me, his lips leaving a whisper of fondness on my forehead.

Captain Valentine died. He'd been drinking grog, *wyomee*, the Indians called it. He wouldn't sit down in the boat. He toppled overboard. His less inebriated friends hauled him back in once but he toppled over again and couldn't be found in the dark night waters of the New River. The mockingbirds sang beneath the full moon, a serenade to the passing of one of our own.

"You should have spoken with him, Frank. Maybe he would have stopped."

"You're the talker," Frank said. "Did you?"

"No, I did not. But I think I will take a stronger stand on that. Prohibit the sales, that's what we need."

Frank just shook his head.

I waited for Esther with each visiting group but didn't see her. A bold young woman people called Mary Gopher came with one group. She was in her teens, and when she reached up for something on the post's shelf, her cape lifted up too, exposing her bare midriff as the style allowed. Mary exposed more than her skin; she looked pregnant.

"Deliver them alone," Frank told me when I asked. "Maybe a medicine woman, though those are rare. Mostly men. They wouldn't help with a birthing."

Frank stocked simple medicines for toothaches and stomach ailments. Once I asked Dr. Kennedy—who was actually a doctor now—about Seminole health problems.

"Intestinal problems mostly. Worms and such. Poor teeth that makes 'em sick. They lose a lot of babies, too. I can't do anything for 'em. Own people act as doctors to 'em, not any of us."

While I watched for Esther and others, I began paying attention to more of the women, what they might be needing to make their lives easier. I noticed they preferred certain enamel cooking pans, dark blue with white flecks that reminded me of the night sky, and I urged Frank to keep more of those in stock.

Over the next season or two, I realized that several Seminole families came in not just when the large number of dugout canoes arrived. I'd recognize them standing where the men worked on the Andrews Avenue bridge, creating an arch over the New River. There watched a boy with a lazy right eye; a girl with ears that split her thick hair. Mary Gopher had her baby and brought it along when no other Seminoles traded. Sometimes a man—probably the baby's grandfather—would unwrap his turban and fold the lengths of cloth around the infant, then tie it around Mary's neck, making a carrier for it so the girl's hands were free to help bring in alligator eggs.

Mary, I decided, must live in one of the permanent camps close by to be in the village so often. The Jumpers and Tom Tiger and Robert Osceola also came in to trade when no others were about.

I should have realized earlier that there were two groups: those families who lived deep in the swamps, who traded with us and probably several other posts around Lake Okeechobee and farther south once or twice a season; and a group more acclimated to our ways who came in almost weekly. Both groups knew to mix themselves into the anonymity of a crowd. But Esther must have belonged to the interior group whom I decided was the more traditional and thus standoffish.

The families living close to non-Indians told me that some were willing to risk in new and different ways. They would go out with white fishermen, guiding them to places where they could bring in trophy catches and sharing with them the ritual of the unusual manatee hunt.

Books had been written about our area, and many northerners arrived with leatherbound editions in hand asking to meet "Tom Tiger" or telling us they wanted a certain Indian to be their guide. I discovered that Frank would often take them out to the nearby camps, driving them in his wagon with his white mule already knowing the way.

Children lived in these permanent camps, too.

"You'd think they'd come around more, the children," I told Frank. "Not just when the Big Cypress groups come in to trade."

"Surprised you've gotten them this far," he said. "Not that you aren't fruit to a fly."

Esther returned the next season, and I was surprised at the degree of my delight—and yes, I admit it, relief. She was close to ten now, I decided. Her dark hair still hung thickly down her back so she was still considered a child, not yet of marrying age. She didn't sneak back through the palmettos and sable palms as so many other children did. Instead, her stride resembled mine when I stepped out to walk, arms swinging, eyes forward and sure. Her fingers fluttered, though. Was that new or hadn't I noticed before? She did not seem to be fearful and she came alone.

As she approached I noticed another change in her, a change in the side of her face. Her hair partially covered her left cheek, but standing before me I could see the skin puckered, like a healed hot-water scald.

"I've been worried over you, Esther," I said. I fluttered about her like a fussy aunt.

She didn't smile.

I reached to touch her face but stopped myself. "What happened?"

She shook her head.

"Was it hot water that spilled? Did you stumble into a fire?"

She looked almost sullen. Insects buzzed around us and she swatted at the fearless flies that kept returning to the space above her lip.

"How I wish you could tell me, Esther, could say what you're thinking."

I offered her lime juice and we sat on the porch steps drinking it, her dark fingers gripping the glass.

It could have been an accident. It most likely was. No one could have known of her interest in the stories and songs. And they wouldn't have harmed her that way if they had; I was sure of it even if Frank wasn't.

Esther pointed then to the book I had lying beside the wicker chair, what I'd been reading when I saw her walk through the green.

"Book," I said.

"Book, um, book," she said.

"Yes, that's what it is! A book! It has words inside, see?" I set my glass down and ran my fingers under the letters.

"Book," she repeated in a whisper. "Book."

She watched my mouth and silently said the word.

She stayed that day two or three hours. Mostly she watched my mouth as I read and looked at the black marks. A few line drawings were scattered throughout, covered by tissue paper, and Esther stared at them the longest. I wished I had something with color.

Esther's taste went to bright things: a book of blue fabric folded near the White sewing machine caught her eye when I saw her the next day at the post. I held it up to her face. "Blue becomes you," I said. "I wish I knew what else might encourage you."

I considered learning her language, more than just a few words. But I didn't know who could teach me, and honest to truth, I believed it would be a better tool for her if she could learn mine.

"Perhaps I should talk with your parents, Esther. To see if they mind the time you spend with me."

She opened her eyes wide with my words.

"No? It's not necessary."

I'd seen Esther's parents once quickly board the train after they finished their trades. They wore tight faces, eyes set deep with sleepy looks. Esther stood beneath the post's porch facing the New River staring somewhere into the future, while her parents and others walked off toward the station anticipating a time to forget. I wondered about Esther's parents leaving her unattended for so long.

Esther, I decided, must be an only child. Unusual, but it would explain her hours of freedom with me, with no claims of younger children or adult voice lifting over the green to call for her return.

Alone with me later in the store, she said, "Blue, um, blue," and nodded to the cloth. Then she pointed to a copper pot. "Orange," I said. "And Esther. See your pretty face reflected there?"

We walked back toward the cottage where I found a picture of a parrot with its orange and green in a book Frank's mother had sent us. Esther grinned up at me as I showed her orange again. She seemed to love the colors in the books. I vowed to look for more.

That night, Esther slept on the porch. She'd stood for a long time looking toward the train station, the evening breeze lifting her dark bangs from her wide forehead. She ignored the calls of other children that urged her to come and play in their stick game. Frank lit fat smudge pots to ward off the insects, and several families curled up to sleep. Esther still stood. Finally, as the moon came up, I saw her sit and lean against the wall where she could see anyone coming from the train.

"I'll be back in a minute," I told Frank as I slipped from my bed, then brought a light blanket out and stepped among sleeping people to hand it to Esther. "There's a chill in the air."

She looked up at me, a movement I felt more than saw. I squatted to wrap the cotton quilt around her shoulder and when I did she leaned into me. I felt a wetness against my breast, a gentle shaking. I sat beside her then, nestled her into my arms, and sang softly to her until she stopped her quivering and fell into a jerking, restless sleep.

Her parents returned near sunrise. They slumped down onto the porch barely aware we were there. I slipped out from under Esther's arms as she slept. I stretched then went inside to dress and take my walk.

When I returned, I touched Esther's shoulder to get her attention and motioned for her to follow. She came, her eyes looking back toward her parents snoring beyond us.

She showed no interest in the book when we sat on the porch drinking juice. I'd brought it with me. She finished her drink then stood and walked back to the chickee, where families were gathering things up, making plans to leave.

Esther's father stood at the helm now, her mother already in the center of their canoe. Esther lifted her skirts to climb in. That's when I saw them: red lines like raised welts on the backs of her legs. They were healing scars, older ones, but scars nonetheless.

After she left, I felt an emptiness. I cared for her, for all of them, wanted so to communicate that to them. Wasn't that what compassion was, upholding from deep within? How was I to do it?

The parrot book lay beside my chair when I went back inside. Esther's earlier interest in the book gave me an idea. I mixed a batch of glue with wheat flour, salt, and water and began attaching pieces of paper below familiar objects such as the book, the copper pot, and the umbrella in its brass stand. I wrote each name on a piece of paper. They looked just fine. I removed them then and placed them between the pages of a *Ladies' Home Journal*.

The next time Esther came, bringing three or four others who were as quiet as turtles, I hung the words again and pointed to the letters to let the children "see" the object's name. It was all I knew to do: provide the tools for change.

"Hat," I said months later. "This is a hat. Bowl. This is a bowl."

Esther mouthed the words but also stared at the letters written beneath them; and I could tell by the way she turned her head, tipping it to the right and then the left, that she was both troubled and intrigued by the relationship.

I quickly grabbed another piece of paper and wrote the letters E-S-T-H-E-R on it, then moved the mirror so she saw herself. I held the word beneath her chin. "Esther," I said. "That's your name. Esther." Then I turned her to look at her image.

She shuddered, put her hand to her face.

"You're beautiful, Esther," I said. "Don't look at the scar, look at what's here."

I touched her hand to her chest.

"Esther," she repeated, this time out loud while she reached back for the paper.

"Yes, you're Esther and I'm Miss Ivy."

"*Watchie-esta hutrie,*" Esther said, pointing at me.

"What? I'm sorry, dear, I have no idea what that means."

Esther shook her head. The wide-eyed others, standing in a semicircle beyond her, had understood. A trace of fear formed in their eyes while Esther's look was tender.

All of them left shortly after that, and I couldn't even remember what Esther had said to repeat it to Frank or Will.

A few days later, one of the forgotten pieces of paper drifted with the morning breeze to rest between Frank's blackened boots.

"*Hat tree?* Forgetting in your old age? Need to write it down?"

"Just a little something I'm working on," I said. I took the paper from him and slipped it into the pocket of my skirt.

He stood quiet a time, his eyes bulleted and stern as they could be when he experienced displeasure. His dark brows laced with spiderwebs of gray met in a furrow just above his nose.

"No simple undertaking you're about, Ivy," he said. A little gray found its way into hair at his temples, too. "If parents find out, object..." He flicked at his ear.

"Who's to tell them? The children barely even whisper the words. And who's to say they picked them up here? Their parents speak enough English to get by, so they could learn the language anywhere."

"If they point to 'barrel' written down..." He shook his head. "Walking in muck, here, Mrs. Stranahan, and it's a danger. We need them, Ivy. To fill contracts I have up north."

"I thought you'd be pleased."

"Don't you blink those blues at me," he said.

"They're so bright, Frank. And they want to learn new things."

"Teach them sewing then. I'll get machines they can take back with them into the swamps. Teach them cooking. That's how you can fix them."

"It's not about change because I don't like them as they are," I protested. "It's to protect them from all that's going to happen to them if they don't have other ways."

"Trying to make them like us, then, and that's wrong."

"I don't want them like us, Frank! Truly I don't. I just want them to have tools to be the best at who they are. That's what reading English is, a tool, no different than the newer guns you sell them. Or the sewing machines. But more far-reaching."

He stared at me for a long time. His dark eyes could be fierce at times, and they took on that look now, as though he could chisel into my thinking and pull out the plug of passion that I kept from him yet placed before these children; a passion I could see he feared might someday bring harm.

He took in a deep breath through his nose. The air came out in a long sigh. He neither shouted nor protested.

"Broward'll pursue this Everglades draining if he's elected," I said, my voice full of neutral fact and calm. "All of us are facing alterations whether we want them or not. I'm only offering their children another option, another trail through the saw grass. That's all it is, Frank. Honest to truth."

"Maybe you need other interests," he said, burying his head in the paper, closing me out. "Without quite the same risk."

It struck me as odd that Frank would suggest other interests since I felt I already had a dozen. I'd gone to West Palm Beach with Louise and her mother to hear Carrie Nation speak. She'd inspired us all with her words against the demon rum, and I was pleased the Methodists felt so strongly against drink, too. It was the one thing I thought I had in common with Hiram Frost. I regretted not speaking more firmly with Captain Valentine about the danger of it. Perhaps I might have saved his life, or someone could have, if we'd had a dry community instead of what we had.

A woman's club interested me, too. Clubs like that could cut through political tape faster than ice melting on a south Florida day. They could influence people, bring on a dry vote, or even have a say about political problems. We needed a garden club to beautify our village. And there were statewide challenges not the least of which was women's suffrage, a cause even Frank supported. And then there was the egret trade enforcement.

Bloxham overheard things. He could be so unassuming, people forgot he was present—unlike me. I acted ladylike; indeed, I never raised my voice to make my point. But Bloxham was an observer, a historian of sorts, who could accurately account without need to intervene.

While Bloxham leaned over a crate or stocked shelves or carried baskets of vegetables to the hunters' camps, he listened, eavesdropped without notice. Sometimes what he heard he disagreed with but had no need to respond, allowing others to have their opinions without having to address it. But I didn't. I counted it as weak if I did not respond to an opinion, a wrong, an injustice of any kind. There being so many in the world, I had no lack for interests.

"Now don't you go scratching around where you oughtn't," Bloxham told me. "These white hunters know what they're about. They've good equipment, they've invested heavily in their guns and ammunition, and they don't want anyone getting in the way, least of all a lady."

"I won't as long as it's wild boars or turkeys or raccoons, legal things they're hunting."

"Some of 'em do mention curlews and such."

"But no one's supposed to be shooting them! Audubon has wardens out now, at least in the Keys. They're making arrests."

Bloxham nodded. "Remember the Smiths and the Bradleys in Lantana? Papa taught one of the boys music. Tom, I think it was. They've all moved south now and word has it that the Smiths are plumers and Guy Bradley's the Audubon warden there. Protecting the Cuthbert rookery. Almost wiped out."

"We wouldn't need the law at all if the market dried up." For a moment a horrible thought occurred to me. "Frank isn't..."

"'Course not. He's a law-abiding man. A little too serious." Bloxy snapped at his suspenders. "Never takes a rest and expects no one else will either. He can always find something for a man to do, big sister. Your husband has an unending reserve of work. Good thing you have as many activities as him or he'd be keeping you busy too." He laughed, his eyes dropping discreetly to my flat stomach.

"You haven't actually seen stocks of feathers, have you?"

"They're not all plumers," he said. "Come to fish too."

"They don't bring contraband into the camps?"

"Oh now, they're much too clever for that. But they'll talk of killing hundreds of birds. Killing them before the Indians do, they tell themselves, like it was a competition."

"They wouldn't."

"Take the Indians much longer."

"The Seminoles want to supply their families' needs, that's the only reason they'd kill. These northerners don't seem to care that all the birds could be gone."

"It'll all work out. Besides, what can you do about it? If women want feathers on their hats, they'll get them one way or another. If not here, Central America. No sense fretting."

He hung the broom and brushed dust from the front of his long leather apron. Scanning the room, he left me to help a customer reach a new kerosene lamp hanging from the center rafter.

An ounce of feathers now brought thirty-two dollars, and I'd heard that the milliners in New York earned profits in the millions. Florida was still the only state that had outlawed pluming, though it certainly had not stopped it.

I had no idea how to touch the trade, how to make a difference in a larger way. I didn't think I could do what my women's club friend Mary Munroe did, wife of the novelist Kirk. She charged up to beautifully coiffed women in Miami hotels or as they strode along the beach, her tight corset cinched at the waist, making her chest appear abnormally large. And her shoulders, heightened by the mutton-chop sleeve style, gave the impression when she thundered toward them of a moving train whose track was built right through their eyes.

"You have a feather in your hat," she'd shout. "Its presence is both morally deplorable and illegal. You must take it off immediately."

Then she'd wait, her hands clasped at her waist, elbows akimbo; and if they did not move, she would, pulling their hats. Hair and pearl-handled pins would rip causing startled shouts and shrieks of pain. The surprise of it and the violence caught even onlookers like me by surprise.

While a woman's escort might object, he had little experience in responding, having rarely been accosted by such a formidable and respectable-looking woman. So he'd pull back, creating even more distress while feathers fluttered against felt and straw until someone from the hotel intervened or the hat lay flat on the floor. A dozen other women watching at the sidelines at least considered their hats and immoral acts before Mary Munroe was escorted out.

I couldn't do what she did, though I admired it immensely.

"Of course you could," Mary told me following a concert she and I attended in Miami. "We women have been told we're weak and insignificant, which is both imprecise and controlling. Not descriptive of me. Nor you either."

During the intermission she'd verbally attacked three women wearing feathers. She must have targeted them during the symphony's prelude.

"I'm not comfortable confronting people like that. It's, well, it doesn't seem to fit me," I said. My cheeks were hot and I was aware before the lights went down that others spoke about us behind their fluttering fans.

"I wasn't always exactly like this," Mary told me as we rode home in the covered carriage. I'd expressed my inadequacy in objecting to injustice as she did. She had a New Jersey kind of accent, talking through her nose, emphasizing some words over others. "It's taken me *years* to believe I had a contribution. My mother always said a woman's *place* was with her children. She had fifteen," she said, leaning toward me. "Yes, fifteen." Mary was a tall woman and I felt fragile beside her.

"My mother is the novelist Amelia Barr. Yes, surprising, isn't it? She writes books that *appeal* to everyone, especially children. I enjoy children."

"Are you planning on any?"

"Not exactly. Kirk's quite a bit older than I. I want to start a club for young girls, call it *Pine Needles*. Children will be nurtured and grow into mighty trees. And I run a little Sunday school up north. Maybe start one down here."

"I have four brothers and a sister. Living," I said.

Mary removed her own straw hat so she could lean back against the leather cushions of the buggy. "My mother claims only *children* can keep a woman young and that if women get involved in business or worldly affairs, that we'll grow old and coarse. I think fervor can keep women vibrant, and passion and intensity, too, don't you?"

"When it's for something that can make a difference, I don't think age or coarseness matters."

"Exactly. You're as strident and service oriented as the rest of us. I intend to protect those beautiful plumed creatures any way I can. I have my sights set on Flagler's Model Land Company, all that *luscious* land the state just gave him for promising to bring his railroad into the Keys. That's perfect country for a park or conservancy. And I'll do whatever I must to stop the desire for plumes. I'm absolutely *passionate* about it."

She pounded the handle of her umbrella so firmly the driver turned back to see what we wanted.

I tried to imagine myself taking on a cause the way Mary Munroe did, full bore, at the risk of others disliking her, including even her mother, it seemed.

"You just don't have your marching orders yet," she said. "When you do, you'll be unforgettable, do historic things. Mark my words on that. Exactly."

Unforgettable? Historic? I doubted that now.

I did want to make a difference, but I saw it happening in gentler ways, by persevering like the flow of the Everglades, relentlessly easing toward the sea.

One thing I did agree with Mary Munroe about, though, as I thought of Esther, the egret plumes, Mama's poor health, and Pink's wandering ways: stewing and fretting did not belong to my family; I claimed only action and protection as my kin.

CHAPTER NINE

After Broward's election as governor in 1905, one of his first acts let the bid for building two dredges that would help to drain the Florida Everglades.

Reed Byran became the supervisor over several local men at the shipyards on the New River. Progress arrived along with land speculators who could envision drained swamp as winter homes, orchards, and farms.

Frank built the seawall that year. A big storm had raised the river level and gouged out a huge section of the bank, dropping the pilings and the boat dock and shed into precarious positions.

The high water brought another phenomenon: clusters of mesmerized cottonmouths, drifting and twisting and floating, catching on cypress roots exposed in the banks. Some even pushed up against the boat dock, a dozen or more.

"Happened one other time," Frank said as he handed Bloxham a shovel. They struck at the snakes; the thud of metal against reptile and mud vibrated my feet. I jumped back when blood spattered up onto my skirts.

"What makes them just lie there?" I said.

"Maybe they drowned," Bloxham offered. "Got all bloated up with water and died."

"They're still alive, though."

I watched a snake Bloxham's shovel had tossed up onto the bank. It pulled itself into an S but didn't advance, just slithered back and forth. It did what was familiar but failed to make progress.

"Carried away with the current," Frank said. He stood and leaned against the shovel all red with blood. "Caught up in it. Probably didn't even know what was happening until it was too late. Couldn't swim out to safety."

✦

Bloxham became one of the workers on the seawall and still helped Frank at the store. DeWitt had returned to Miami to work with Papa. He proved to be a better letter writer than Pink so I heard news more often, of how our little community was perceived as progressive, what with the Byran vegetable-packing plant being built, along with a new and larger school, and for the first time, a real Methodist church, made of brick.

Pink arrived in May, the morning after a horrendous thunderstorm, early for the summer season. Rain surged off the roof in such force a section of the gutter broke, allowing a deep hole to wash near the front steps.

"Have to put a grate there," I said.

We jumped to avoid the hole, but no matter where we set our feet the water soaked up high and into the upper laces of our shoes.

Pink shook off her umbrella, the black French fringe sending sprays of water onto the railing. I lifted my hair with my fingers while we waited for the storm to pass. Almost as quickly as it began, it stopped, leaving a heavy, damp smell. The sun came out with a beastly heat.

"I feel like a sweet potato steamin' in the pot," Pink said. She waved her hands to move air across her bodice.

"The high color on your cheeks at least becomes you. Is that a fever or just the jumping to avoid the puddle?"

"Better, sister," she said. "I'm twenty-one and in love. Need I say more about my high color?"

"Are you? Is he from Miami? What does Mama think about him? And Papa? When did this happen?"

"Happened faster than a good hound trees a coon," she said, her eyes sparkling like sun on the sea. "Papa and Mama just think he's fine." She squeezed the wetness from the bottom of her hem. "He's a grower, like Papa. A fine size grove. He's tall and blond with baby blue eyes. His people come from that Danish settlement south of here. Dania."

"He's a Methodist?" I asked. "Probably a Lutheran."

"Haven't talked about any of that," she said. "Just lettin' the love roll over my shoulders like the sweet smell of jasmine." She shimmied her shoulders, leaned her head back. "He says I have such pretty shoulders," she said and bumped my hip with her own.

The new store that Frank had decided to build on Brickell Avenue, closer to what Flagler said would become the heart of Fort Lauderdale, was well on its way. But at the existing post near our cottage, there were men pounding and others moving stocks, and Pink thoroughly enjoyed herself while she visited. She accepted the workmen's compliments as she brought the water jug to them or carried out cookies and fresh-squeezed lemonade. I hadn't realized how vivacious good health made her. The high color on her cheeks gave her a vitality not shadowed by the wide brim of her hat. I wondered how serious her new love was.

"Louise and I think you should go with us to Palm Beach," Pink said.

The two women had been sitting on the porch chatting while I filled my spice drawers with a new shipment of cardamom and cinnamon, nutmeg and mace.

"Married women do not usually promenade," I said.

"Think of it as exercise," Pink said. "To shop and stroll along the walks. Or as a time to concentrate on noble thoughts. You could confer with someone about their plumed hats." I scowled at her and she grinned.

Pink lifted her wrist into the air and gave it a little twist, with her index finger catching the breeze.

"Thus sayeth Ivy," she said. Her eyes twinkled in their tease.

"You two have a nice time. Take your rat with you."

"Wish you'd join us, Ivy, honey," Louise said. She'd developed a beguiling voice that northern boys mistook as a southern drawl. "So Bloxham won't be jealous." She blushed.

Pink said. "We're just wantin' you to play. Always so occupied with your causes, never have any time for just fun."

"I'm not sure I learned how," I said. "Too busy looking after you."

"All the more reason to come now."

"And your new beau, what's his name?"

"Jan."

"Yes. Jan. Would he approve of your promenade in Palm Beach?"

"He loves seein' me happy," Pink said.

I sent them off, excusing myself that I had yet to write my two letters and wouldn't know when I'd do it if I rode off on the train with them. Besides, I expected the children later.

They'd been coming in little clusters at a time. Several had learned finger songs, the kind I'd taught DeWitt and Gussie when they were that age.

They sang the words out after only a few times and even though it might be weeks before a certain child returned, they remembered. I imagined they practiced them. Their parents must have allowed it.

They came that day, too, the day Pink and Louise went to Palm Beach. Esther moved among them, her hair twisted high on her head, her bangs cut straight across. She'd brought me a pineapple and four chicken eggs, the latter especially a treasure. Her fingers fluttered against mine as though scratching at dirt.

"Let's bake a cake," I suggested, holding one egg in each hand. Esther and her four companions all smiled and walked past me toward the cottage.

"You understand everything I say, don't you?" I asked Esther as I followed her into the separate cottage where I cooked to keep the heat from building up where we slept. She smiled and glanced around the room.

"So what do we need?" I said. "For a cake?"

The shortest of the five stood on tiptoe, pointing to the shelf. They all understood me! Esther began to lift the tin of canned milk, one of the luxuries preserved for rare dishes.

"Oh, I think we'll save that for a really special occasion," I said. "We can make this cake with water and soda and flour."

A look of disappointment flashed across Esther's face.

"All right. We'll do it, and save a piece for Mr. Stranahan as well."

She built up the fire in the oven and the others took turns stirring and sifting and waving a palmetto fan over the bowl to ward off the bugs. I made a big production out of cracking the eggs and pouring a stream of milk from high over my head into the bowl. We popped the batter into the oven. While it baked, we sat on the steps and sang.

"Tasty," Frank said when he ate his piece that evening. "Like it's got dairy."

"A little," I said. "One of the Seminole children brought chicken eggs and we decided to make an occasion of it. Used up the last tin of milk. You'll have to order more in."

"Hmm," he said. "Didn't think I'd married such an extravagant woman."

"I wish cows could survive here," I said.

"Saw one or two tough ones at one of the camps," Frank said. "Squirrel keeps one for his family."

"Whatever do they do about the bugs?"

"Suppose they live shrouded by smoke," he said. "Must have some way of keeping them from clogging their noses."

"Milk would certainly be a blessing to them," I said.

"Fresh beef wouldn't be bad either."

I wrinkled my nose at him.

The morning after, Pink and I had a long talk about how the boys were doing. I stitched a pair of Frank's pants that needed mending. Pink doodled on the back of an envelope.

"Fine, I think. Papa's not working the fields so hard, workin' 'em less. He's lookin' better too. Teachin' more music, not wantin' to move as much."

"Finally ready to settle," I said.

"He's around the house and Mama likes that. It's good, too, now she's...oh, look at those gators! Don't go swimming over that way later."

"She's what, Pink?"

"Now, don't you fret, sister. My mouth tumbled over my mind. Mama don't want you knowin' just yet."

"About?"

She sighed. "She's havin' another baby. Just found out last month."

"Ouch!" I said. "Grab me a cloth, will you, Pink? I've drawn blood with my needle."

"Maybe if she eats better she'll carry it," I told Frank later. "I didn't notice if she ate her greens when I was there. We need to make sure she has milk. Mary Munroe says that's the hardest thing to give up when she winters in Miami, fresh dairy. Has that worked then, putting fertilizer bags on the mules' legs?"

"I doubt anyone pays as much attention to diet as you do," Frank said.

"Must have had other thoughts pushing in when you were there last."

"You've said yourself how much you've improved with my cooking, using spices instead of all that salt. And you're not coughing as much. Maybe strange reaction to foods causes your wheezing."

"Could think about staying there with her, make sure she eats right."

"Do it right this time? Is that what you mean?"

"Not what I said." He looked wounded. "Thought you might like to give to her in that way, you having such a generous spirit."

"I didn't mean to snap like a turtle."

"The best way to overcome fear sometimes is to face it head on," Frank said as he lifted my chin with his fingers.

I had little time to lament or worry, face old fears or not. I had no time to implement a plan to take better care of my mother, look after her, see her through this delivery and perhaps avenge an old unworthiness I still carried deep inside. I could do nothing more than pray and cry with Frank, because the following morning, May 10, 1905, a telegram arrived telling us my mother, age forty-six and born on Christmas Day in Suwanee County, Florida, had succumbed to "paralysis of the heart" and died.

Albert held Papa together after Mama passed on. The needs of a child kept my father from sinking into a pit of endless grief. That, and Papa's having been with her when she passed over, so he heard her confession, he said—that she was ready to leave this earth, held no regrets, and sought her Savior's face.

She'd been out tugging weeds in the vegetable garden and had then cut a calla lily to slope into the vase for the table. As she'd come inside, she told Papa she had "a catch in her back" and that her arm ached. She rubbed at it as she talked to him. She'd been tired, Papa said, but had been resting more, wanting to have good strength through the summer and fall until the birth of this next baby.

By early evening, the pain had worsened and Papa'd gone for the doctor, who listened to her heart then shook his head.

"Just worn out," the doctor told him, pulling at his earlobe all the while he spoke. "Probably congenital. Your other children might have the condition, too."

"She talked about dying then," Papa said. His eyes were puffed and red and he kept a handkerchief balled up in his fist, lifting it to his eyes while he talked. "About what a good life she'd had and how sad she was about not being able to leave this last baby here on earth. 'Selfishly taking it with me,' she said. Didn't have a selfish bone in her body, your mother didn't." He stopped to blow his nose. "She gave that gift to each of you."

Bloxham sat hunched over in a corner chair, his arms on his knees, his nose red and eyes pinched narrow. Albert leaned into his big brother's chest. Both sat dazed and distant. Gus, as we now called him, stood near me wiping his shoes off on the back of his pants, shifting legs, leaning into me, his eyes straight forward, away from Papa. Pink blinked back tears, leaned against the doorjamb, long bare arms clasped behind her, eyes piercing the ceiling. Outside, DeWitt tossed coconuts into a basket. I could hear them clunking over and over again and wondered if the sound felt soothing to his soul.

"She wasn't afraid of death," Papa said. "She said she was ready. Had her own wishes for each one of you, worries, too. But mostly grateful for being blessed with such a fine family. Said for you to know especially, Ivy—" his voice raised to be sure my mind hadn't wandered to someplace with less pain—"that she was pleased she had children of hers gone on ahead. 'Heaven can't be strange when you have someone you love waiting to greet you.' That's what she said."

"She'll hear a chorus on her arrival," I said.

Later, my father and I sorted through my mother's lingerie dresses, her keepsakes and such, to be given to the church or needy neighbors, and the special pieces to her children. The scent of her perfume rose up from the clothes. I thought I'd take a shawl of hers to keep with me. And for a brief moment I sensed a wash of guilt press across my father's face and settle with weight on his shoulders.

"There was no other way," he said in the middle of his sorting.

"What?" I said.

"She wanted the babies, Ivy. She truly did. Said it was no duty to her, but a gift. Her gift, that she felt needed to be given to the world. As Susanna Wesley had. She mentioned her especially."

One of my mother's many crosses lay in the palm of my hand. It had been her wish that both Pink and I each receive one.

"It's how love gets expressed between a husband and wife. You know that, Ivy. You understand about marriage, the passion and…all."

"Love and companionship and service, that's what I know marriage to be. And with passion, yes."

"Companionship," he said, nodding. "'Course that. Your mother and I were friends."

"Perhaps she could have lived…longer, if she hadn't had…so many." I'd said it out loud, the thought I had carried for years.

"But it was her, being pregnant was." He sounded surprised. "Always looking forward, always planning for those little ones. Seems like she forgot the misery of the last. Said that was God's plan too, to help her forget so she could keep going on with what He'd planned for her. What was I to do?"

He lifted both palms upward in surrender.

While it wasn't the best circumstance under which to meet him, Pink's beau came for both the funeral and the gathering afterward at the house. Frank took the train down, too, and he acted as though he liked the young Dane. At least they stood together beneath the coconut palms, wordless it appeared, as they looked toward the Keys.

I thought later that it was the grieving and the unreality that surrounds those times, the blurring of important lines and schedules, that caused me to find fault.

"I am pleased to meet with you," Pink's friend said. He towered over me, big and broad-shouldered and blond. He wore small round glasses he took off and on, polishing with a blue handkerchief he stuffed into his white suit pocket. "Pink, she tells me much about you, her big sister. It is all good news, I assure you of that."

"Pink has a vivid imagination," I said.

"Ya, she does that." He grinned at her and reached his hand out to hers.

Pink lifted her fingers to him as though pulling them up through deep water. He turned her palm over in both of his and kissed it. His nails were chipped but scrubbed clean of any orchard dirt.

Only family and a few neighbors remained following the service. A shower threatened then made good on it before the sun chased it away.

"How many acres of citrus do you work?" I asked, cooling myself with the round funeral fan. I wished the house closer to the cooling sea.

"Nearly twenty," he said.

He answered without turning to look at me and inhaled Pink, his eyes sinking into hers. His palpable affection felt out of place.

"Twenty," I said, fanning faster. I felt so hot. "I'm amazed you found time to join us with so much responsibility."

"Sister!" Pink said.

She'd been watching him while I spoke and her eyes flashed to me now, her jaws clenched. "I hope you're funnin' 'cause otherwise you're bein' unladylike rude."

"Perhaps we can talk another time, Mr....what did you say your name—"

"Nordstrom," Pink said, not letting me finish. "It's Jan Nordstrom. And don't you be forgettin' it." She took his arm and headed outside. He looked over his shoulder, wearing puzzlement on his face.

"You don't like him, do you?" Pink asked me later as we lay side by side in our childhood bed, each of us staring at the whitewashed boards of the ceiling. Frank and Bloxham shared quarters down the hall. Pink lowered the bar as I blew out the kerosene light then sank into the five pillows I'd gathered to hold me at an angle for the night.

"I never said that. He's fine."

She didn't respond for a moment. "That's what you do when you're caught in the truth: deny, then say, 'It's just fine.' Bloxy likes him. And Papa, too. He and Frank had things to talk about."

Bullfrogs growled outside. A firefly drifted in through a crack in the shutters, a flickering dot of light in the night.

"I don't dislike him," I said. "It's just that you're young and I hoped you'd finish school and even go—"

"We've had this conversation. For all I know, I'll only live to be as old as Mama, maybe only twenty years more. Shouldn't I enjoy them as I can?" She waited then added, "Schoolin' never meant the same to me as you."

"You didn't take it seriously enough," I said.

"You can be sharp as saw grass, sister. Sometimes I don't even know you."

I turned over to face her. The pillows made me slightly higher than she. She smelled warm and I reached to stroke the silk of her hair, push it back behind her ear in the dark.

"I don't think infatuation is the answer to loneliness, Pink. And that's what I see you seeking."

"I'm not afraid to be alone!" I felt her body tense beside me.

"What do you want, then?"

She lay quiet a long time and I realized then what a difficult question I had asked. I wasn't sure if I could answer it for myself.

"What anyone wants," she said after a time. "To love and be loved. To be hungerin' for life, eat, and be satisfied."

"A life that just drifts carries pain with it."

"Pain's a part of feelin'. The risk's worth it, I'm thinkin'. Till you find what you're seekin'. You have everythin' all planned out."

"And you think Jan's worth it? Pain?"

"I don't think he isn't."

"That's a half answer, Pink."

"It don't really matter who I'm with."

"Doesn't. And it does, Pink."

She turned her back to me but I could tell by her breathing that she lay awake.

"I hate it that you know everythin' there is to know," she said finally. "Who's to say that Mama's not right, that it's a waste to be tryin' to control things like you do. Or the opposite, pretendin' you're following a 'plan' and trustin' when you're really doin' things your way, makin' stuff happen as you want. We get back what we give, I'm thinkin'. I don't see your life as so full and rich, because you didn't want to fight to teach when all those years you said that's what you'd do, why you left us all."

"Pink, I…" I didn't know what to say.

She lay still so long after that I was sure she'd fallen asleep. Then she spoke into the night, her dusky voice as plaintive as a mourning dove. "I'm not like you, sister. I'm not strong. I don't know what God intends for me the way you seem to. I'm just ready to take what He gives me, give some away, and hope He don't forget I'm here."

Kin could be a trial. Frank was having his trials too. I don't know what happened between Will and Frank. One day Will worked at the new store, made trips to Palm Beach and beyond; the next day he didn't. Frank's inflexibility might have caused it. He could refuse to change a thing because he thought it worked just fine the way it was, even though a shift might please another and not lessen effectiveness either. Will traveled and corresponded, and I'd thought his absence meant buying trips to fill contracts. But when he failed to return, I guessed he had found a way to work without the daily routine of the New River.

Frank didn't comment on his absence except to say Will had decided to move on.

"Do you know where or why?"

"Not privy to Will's thinking."

After the corrugated tin roof covered the two stories of the new store downtown, Frank officially incorporated the business. Frank Oliver, Bloxham, W. O. Berryhill, and Frank became stockholders. They employed two other Oliver brothers and DeWitt as well, along with two Africans who helped stock the shelves. Bloxham remained as the assistant postmaster, Frank still being in charge, but I was pleased my brother had saved enough money over the years to invest in the business.

"Maybe he'll marry Louise now," Frank commented after the grand opening.

"Do you think that a good match?"

"Think it might help him get a little inspired," was all my husband said.

I missed the post office being close. It was a few blocks away at the new store now on New River Avenue. Picking up the mail had brought people to me, popping by in their boats or riding in from the north. The river was a natural highway. I hoped people traveling it would still stop a moment to talk and keep me from stumbling on the news well after it had been tossed out. I warned Frank that as soon as those automobiles became available I wanted one so I could drive down to see Mary Munroe and check on Papa, Pink, Gus, and Albert. With Mama gone, there was no reason they couldn't move north.

"Never replace the mule," Frank said. "Roads alone would kill us in taxes, keeping them up. Trains and boats and mules'll last me for a lifetime."

"Oh, you dear boy," I said. "Automobiles won't get eaten alive by the bugs. I can't believe how selective you are about progress. A new store is fine; stabling the mule isn't. How did I ever convince you that women should get the vote?"

"Value in that and no harm. And it hasn't happened yet." He scratched at his ankle, pulled at the garter holding his sock. "If I could see benefit in those horseless carriages, might feel differently. But from what I read about their use in Europe, they're a self-indulgent man's toy, not of much good to the commoner."

"If the drainage affects things the way folks say, we'll have need for roads and vehicles, rich and commoner alike," I said. "The glades'll be farmed, not saw grass rivers. People will live far away from water."

"Won't alter things that much," Frank said, then put one of his choral recordings on the Victrola and cranked it, a sign he'd heard enough.

Sometimes I thought he could delude himself quite well. Already much had changed. Flagler planned to take his railroad south, this time across the Keys, bringing in Italians and Spaniards and hundreds from New York and Pennsylvania as laborers. Even the Greeks had come to change the way the Conchs of Key West did their sponging, wiping out in one season a lifetime of experience and history.

Word had come too, about the killing in the Keys. Fronie Bradley had sent her husband off to bring in a plumer, once a family friend they'd shared music with. Walter Smith and his son Tom had been sighted shooting in the Cuthbert rookery south of Miami. It was a famous place, birds of the most beautiful foliage living there in a tropical arch of greenery and light. Guy Bradley, the Audubon warden, tried to arrest his old neighbor's son and the war veteran had killed him. "To protect his son," he said.

Captain Smith gave himself up after the shooting. But with his connections he never served a day, pleading self-defense.

Mary Munroe was outraged when I saw her next.

"They are brazen, these men," she said. "Nothing will change until every law in every state forbids the use of plumes." We had gathered at

Cape Sable to place a plaque on the grave of Guy Bradley. "It'll become a platform for women's clubs everywhere. We must protect what we hold dear or we'll lose it. We must preserve it as it is. It's as uncomplicated as that."

I didn't think "protect" and "uncomplicated" belonged in the same thought. Much as I disliked it, everything changed.

After the stocks filled the new store, Frank decided we should remake the old trading post into our own, permanent home.

It would take some doing, turning that sturdily built square designed for trading into a residence whose pine sides would reflect the flicker of a reading light on a dark winter night. I was surprised that Frank initiated the idea—or that he'd even decided to build a new store at all, though Flagler had encouraged that. But to convert the post into a home on the river, well, that was lovely if not extravagant.

A kitchen soon formed out of the back of the house, and a living room, dining room, parlor, and office for Frank finished the main floor. A master bedroom and a tub room made up part of the open upstairs, leaving a still sizeable place for meetings and parties. Each door had a transom to permit the natural ventilation to continue moving from the shaded verandas through trap doors and attic windows reached by steep, twisty steps.

Downstairs, we added bay windows that offered views of the river. Frank's office overlooked the New River as did the master bedroom, upstairs. Best of all, the plate border in the dining room alcove held the Bavarian porcelain fish plates we'd received at our marriage, their gold scalloped rims gleaming warmly against the fine Dade County pine. It was a home, my home, the first wood structure I could call my own.

"Think we needed a setting for entertaining men like Flagler. In a quiet place without crowds," Frank said. It was after the first dinner in our new home, planned for just the two of us.

"I prefer hospitality this way, in a family setting rather than gatherings with smoke and fans and no time to truly be with others. I didn't realize how small our cottage was until I feel all this space around me." I swirled around the living room. Frank held one of my hands but kept his dancing feet still.

"We can put them up upstairs," I said, serving Frank after-dinner chocolate. "Bunk them in the meeting room."

"'Spect they'll be content to still sleep in their yachts and river boats."

The influential docked at our seawall and wrote notes in the trading post's log about the length of an alligator killed or the size of a catch. Frank often sat out with them under the chickee's thatch while the men smoked, and they listened to violin recordings lifting over the palmettos to the river.

They did often speak of investments, too, and the future, though they came south mostly to forget the stresses of deals. Instead they whiled away the hours watching the sun set, helping me count manatees at dusk.

Besides Henry Flagler of the railroad and Standard Oil, we served greats like Charles Corey, author and member of the British Ornithologists Union and curator of a museum in Chicago; and even former President Cleveland, who often brought along his friend that actor, Joseph Jefferson (I think for the latter's houseboat, the *Wanderer*). He'd re-outfitted an old Mississippi River sternwheeler, adding fine guns and servants rushing and bowing about. Its size always surprised me when I'd awake and see it there on the New River, water lapping against its fine sides.

"A smoky sternwheeler's no place for a lady," Frank said when he came in late one evening. "Just talked finance."

"A soft word spoken over a hot chocolate could make a difference in protecting birds, advancing Indian relations, and urging suffrage," I said. "Let's always have politicians to dinner in the dining room."

"Few at a time? Agreed," Frank said.

It troubled me a bit about the trading post being moved to the downtown area while we still lived at the river. It wasn't as well hidden as the cottage had been.

"Think the Seminoles will still come by here?" I asked Frank. "Suppose they won't need to. Get all their things near the train now, except for the egg contracts. There are always the porches."

"Ah, the porches."

But I wondered if the children would still peer out through the growing royal palms Frank and I had planted just two years before, scatter the squirrels and geckos? Would Esther stride up, swing her arms, and bring others with her to sit on the porch of our home now while their parents traded downriver?

I decided that if the children came to our home after the trading post business moved, it would be because they wanted to. If they came, then it was a confirmation that I was doing what I should be, trusting in a larger plan.

In April, when Governor Broward, his wife, and six daughters arrived on the New River for the launching of the first of Reed's dredges, we served a sit-down dinner not in the dining room, but upstairs in the part of our "remodeled" post home that would remain available for public gatherings. It wasn't in the style I would have liked—it lacked the intimacy I wanted— but no one complained. And the memories of the occasion, the Broward girls' laughter, the scents of perfume, and their long beaded dresses, lingered long after.

In the morning, Constance Byran launched *The Everglades* (though she might have used something besides champagne, I told Frank), and the 180-foot craft eased out of its berth at the shipyards near Sailboat Bend, set to dredge the south.

"Nothing will ever be the same again," I told Frank when everyone had gone and we sat wrapped in the comfort of our new home.

"Change is the only constant, my father used to say."

"Did he offer any advice on surviving it?"

"Old seaman, Dad is. 'Keep your eyes on the heading. Don't get hung up on the rocks.'"

I kept my eyes on the children.

They arrived in the same patchy patterns as they had before, barely noticing the hammering and lumber scraps that announced renovation. After we'd moved into the post, they wasted no time in sitting on the steps, eventually coming up the wide boards to try on my shoes and my hats. Our home sometimes felt like a rookery with children like colorful birds perched on the second-story porch or at the seawall, dotting the greenery of the garden or settled among the palms while I talked and waited for their giggles of recognition.

I still used my little papers with the names on them. But on our trips north, when Frank prowled around bookstores looking for old history books in Tallahassee or Jacksonville, I sought discarded children's books for large printed letters with pictures. Most were dark and dank, all the vivid imagination and color coming through the meanings of words instead of the black-and-white drawings. When we visited Frank's parents we found an artist's book. I thought of drawing pictures to illustrate the stories and songs.

"I can't even draw stick figures," I told Frank, who watched me with a puzzled look as I put the book back on the shelf.

That night I dreamed of the Ohio River.

A hundred boats of various sizes dotted the dark waters. Each was painted a vibrant color, like the feathers of a parrot, and they fluttered in formation toward some common goal that I realized when I awoke appeared to be upstream.

In the morning, Frank and I attended church with his parents and that's when I saw it: Presbyterian Sunday school material that struck me as perfect for my own teaching.

The teacher used large cards, as tall as a toddler and beautifully painted with bright colors, that told simple Bible stories: Joseph with his coat of many colors being sold into slavery; Mary and the birth of the Christ child; David mastering Goliath and his own fears. Three or four cards made up a story set. Beneath each picture, in large print, were words. English words, in thick, black letters. "Joseph's coat." "David slays the giant." "Mary and Joseph travel for the government's census."

But the card that spoke the loudest to me, the one that made me write the Presbyterians to purchase cards of my own, held the picture of Esther. Esther, seated at the table of the king. Esther, in a foreign land. Esther as she prepared to rescue her people.

I ordered the cards before we left Ohio and they arrived by train from Philadelphia packaged in brown wrappers tied with string. "The Methodist children will love them," I told Frank.

"Don't suppose you'll limit the pictures to just them," he said. He flicked at his ear.

"Why, Frank, I learned early on the importance of sharing."

The Seminole children delighted in them when they joined me later beneath the hanging porch. The colors drew them as I knew they would. They repeated the words after me, learned to recognize them by sight. As I could, I pointed out the alphabet and all the sounds, and they would laugh as they sang them out: "A-a-a-a-y," "B-e-e-e-e," "C-e-e-e," and on and on.

I'd attempt their language too. Good teaching is always a process of learning from one's students. How they'd laugh as my tongue stuck to my teeth or as the throaty sounds clogged in the back. But always, they'd point to the pictures and the English words and the richness of the stories.

I'm not sure who realized it first, the children or me, but I began to understand that they grasped the ideas behind the pictures as well as the words. When Billy Tiger sang out "Je-e-e-e-s-u-u-s" and Esther and Nancy Osceola extended "E-s-t-h-e-r" and their eyes lit up and their faces smiled, I knew another kind of learning had occurred.

"I want them to know English well enough to express their ideas to outsiders," I told Frank as we ate our chicken and fresh greens. "So they can talk well enough to solve their problems, negotiate through all this modifying going on with the land."

"You're pushing far as any'd dare now, Ivy."

"But the potential, Frank. Think of the potential."

I began with the children but I knew they would teach others, their mothers and their fathers, maybe even their grandparents. Will had said that children were expected to do the work needed to become adults. In a changing world of dredges and drainage, empty rookeries and *wyomee*, their work had to include learning the language of negotiation, to read and to write.

"I want them to have schools someday, run by their people and with their children in them, taught by Seminole men and women."

"Never hurts a soul to want," Frank said, looking at me over the top of his glasses. "Guess I'm living proof of that."

"That's how they could tame the government, Frank. It wouldn't have to be a fearsome thing."

"Don't think it's fear holds them back." He folded his newspaper to look at me as I talked.

"What then?"

"Hanging on to what they value. Don't want to lose their traditions."

"They already are, Frank, unless they begin to see it another way. The government has a special obligation to them, or should have, even without that treaty business. They need to see them through these transformations of their ways, at least offer them the tools so they survive. The government has so many things to think about, it'll forget if someone doesn't keep harping."

"Seminoles haven't harped well, that's true."

"Until they learn, others'll have to do it for them."

"They've survived all these years, Ivy, left alone."

"But they won't be, now. And they never really were once they made contact with people like us. You gave them sewing machines, Frank, to help them out before. They need new equipment this time." I could hear my voice rising with intensity. "In the process of the learning, they'll discover that outsiders, especially enemies, are disarmed by knowledge."

"Calm down. I hear you. No need to strain that soft voice. I'm not deaf."

"The way I see it," I said with less force, "is that these Seminole children, in their skirts and shirts and shoeless feet, will have to change a generation's thinking if they're to survive. And with these cards, Frank, these Bible stories, they'll be exposed to the greatest lessons ever. It's… almost…divine!"

Oh, I suppose it was a fanciful, outrageous plan, something no one else might even think of doing. But there is power in the saying of a thing, the passionate commitment to a cause however strange and dreamlike it might be or sound to others, that must be done before the wheels of faith and providence can move. So I said it to myself, my little three-legged stool plan I called it: I wished to teach their children to read and write English; to teach them that the government could be their friend; and to share with them the love of Christ. On that foundation, they would have the tools to stand, be the best at who they were.

It was my commitment—my passion, Frank called it—which served not only as a beacon in a sometimes dark and dreary world but as encouragement, too, to keep enduring when unworthiness and defeat came calling with their cards.

Part Two

CHAPTER TEN

I sure do admire your husband, Mrs. Stranahan."

The speaker, Randall Moss, "hailed" from the garden state of New Jersey, he said.

"Benjamin Franklin wrote once that admiration was 'the daughter of ignorance,'" I said.

He laughed, a pleasant enough sound. "I suspect, dear woman, that if I knew him better, I would only admire him more. Almost singlehandedly developed this area of the south. That's what I hear about your husband. Sure need to listen to a man who's accomplished that if one's planning to build on such success."

"As you are."

"Oh, yes. Bought up a goodly portion of the muck the state offered at two hundred dollars a tract. Expect it'll sell well. 'Course, it'll sure sell better if it's already drained. Don't know too many New Jersians who'd want to invest in swamp water. Know I wouldn't." When he smiled, two dimples formed on his cheeks. His lips, even when he held them still while listening attentively, moved up at the ends, as though expecting any moment that life would make him smile.

I hoped he might be one of the honest ones the four years of dredging and draining had unsurfaced. Speculators had turned up like hungry alligators coming out of the swamp with the word of Broward's "success." I debated that word. Already the changes to the landscape had left me feeling scraped and bare.

"Frank'll be home shortly. You're welcome to sit and take limeade. Mr. Stranahan and I don't serve alcohol."

"Noble gesture, Mrs. Stranahan. Don't imbibe myself." He lifted a shock of blond hair that fell across his left eye.

"Shall I get us some, sister?"

I turned to see Pink ease out onto the veranda, sweet and quiet, like night-blooming jasmine. She'd decided against her Jan Nordstrom, and against William Base, a vegetable grower near Lantana. She'd told a musician who brought her flowers and wrote her sweet poems that he was too old for her and the vaudevillian he was too flighty. It had been four years since Mama's death and in that time, Pink had courted three times that many suitors. I'd had three times that many children learning English at my steps.

I learned of her "paramours," she called them, from her letters, and Papa's, too, and my heart ached. I hated seeing anyone's life written in pain and Pink's was surely being scripted with afflicted ink.

"Yes, please, Mr., ah…Moss, I believe you said? This is my sister, Pink Elizabeth Cromartie. Of Lemon City."

"Miami, now," Pink corrected. She wore an ivory pleated lace dress with pink satin bows at the waist. Her fingers lingered at her throat, swaddled with the palest peach.

"What a fascinating name," Mr. Moss said. "Pink. Don't believe I've ever heard of it."

"It's just a flower variety. As Ivy—Mrs. Stranahan—is a vine. It's really quite prophetic to my way of thinkin'."

"How's that?" he asked with a tone of genuine interest. "That flowers are composed of colorful petals, as you surely exemplify?"

"No, sir. I was thinkin' more that an ivy is sturdy and far reachin' while a flower blooms and then just fades away."

"Let's gather refreshments, shall we?" I said. "You'll excuse us, Mr. Moss?"

"Sure will." He clicked his heels and bowed slightly, and I watched a smile as gentle as a sigh spread across his slightly opened lips. I touched Pink's elbow and moved her inside.

"What are you talking about?" I said it in a whisper as the screen door slammed behind us. "Prophetic, my foot!"

"Just a conversation starter," Pink said, "though I do think myself clever to have come up with it on the spot."

"Clever, yes."

We brought the drinks back as Frank arrived, his jacket, neatly folded, draped over his arm. The men introduced themselves and shook hands, then Frank went upstairs to brush out his coat and hang it up. I had followed him upstairs. He removed his collar and settled it around the holder in the collar box Pink had painted with a wild turkey scene and given him for Christmas. He put on his everyday vest over his white pinstriped shirt. It was his casual look.

I could hear Pink and Mr. Moss's muted voices rise up to the upstairs porch I stood on just above them, but I couldn't distinguish their words.

"Who is he?" Frank asked, his words pulling me back into our bedroom. "One of Pink's?"

"A land speculator," I said. "From New Jersey. Wants to talk with you about development. Reed Oliver, at the Keystone, gave him your name. Seems pleasant enough."

By the time we returned, Pink and Randall Moss were sharing in open laughter, and I watched that fine, high blush pushing against Pink's cheeks.

"Your sister-in-law is quite the wit," Randall said. He'd removed his jacket and rolled his sleeves above his elbows.

"Is she?" Frank said. He patted his shirt pockets.

"They're on your desk, Frank. I'll get them." I stepped out and returned with his eyeglasses. While Frank perched them on his nose and straightened the papers the New Jersey man handed him, I studied Randall Moss.

He had tiny lines leading to his hazel eyes that were clear and sparkling with interest. I guessed him to be in his late twenties or early thirties, and while he apparently enjoyed Pink's company, he paid attention to Frank's review of the papers he'd handed him.

"Know this tract," Frank said. "Sound piece. Little far inland, which'll mean mosquito problems most of the season. 'Specially in the evenings."

"Screened porches?"

"Definitely, though I've seen the screens so black with bugs you can't see out, but at least they aren't on you."

"A vivid picture that might not have to be mentioned in the brochures," Randall said.

"Folks actually miss the beauty when they wait to come till winter," I said. "All the blooms appear after the May rains. So many are gone by winter."

"I have noticed a kind of grayness. Oak leaves falling off and the moss looking like cobwebs. Sure didn't expect that the first time I came down. Thought only the north and midwest really had that dormant season."

"Planning to sell up north mostly?" Frank asked.

"There are sure a lot of northerners here already. Dredging the New River to Lake Okeechobee seems to have brought people from all over."

"So it seems," Frank said. "Flagler's railroads've brought the most."

Randall sipped his limeade, then said, "Lots of those folks already know about bugs and snakes and sand, but they sure want to stay for the sunshine and the growing seasons. If they can raise money and buy."

"That what's really brought you here, then. To this porch," Frank said.

Mr. Moss grinned again, a look that made him appear both wise and wily at the same time. "Now, I did hear, from more than one source, that you are a bit of a landholder yourself and that you have, on occasion, made personal loans to folks that you know. At reasonable rates."

Frank's finger gently tapped the papers lying in his lap. "Never regretted that. Didn't seem like much of a risk when you know folks, their people, where they work and all. Usually pay back, and my money has earned for me and mine as well."

"Absolutely. No usury at all," Mr. Moss insisted. "These are changing times, though. And there's no bank in these parts and sometimes lending institutions in other regions of the state are reluctant to loan against land they haven't seen."

"Lending institution," Frank said. "Quite a term for a man."

Mr. Moss nodded gravely, to honor the significance, I thought. "Lent for progress, if I read you right, Mr. Stranahan. What I heard was that when you came here sixteen years ago there were four people, and now there are almost 170. That's sure good growth, thanks to you."

"We'll need a planning board soon," I said. "There are so few services. Garbage builds up. Dogs and pigs digging up the Sables. No library. No decent parks. No decent roads. Trails, yes, but...Frank, you know what I mean."

He lifted his eyebrow and I put my hand down, resting it in my lap.

"Sure want to be a part of the growth," Randall Moss continued. He leaned forward, elbows on his flannel-clad thighs. He sat at the edge of the Sears-Roebuck rattan. "But to do it wisely. I don't have the lending ability myself. I'd like to know if there are...possibilities here."

Frank shook his head. "I'm a practical man. Lend to those I'm familiar with. Couldn't say I'd do that for someone else. Not sure that anyone should, really. There are, after all, biblical prohibitions against making loans."

"'Neither a borrower nor a lender be,'" Pink quipped.

"That's Ben Franklin," I said.

"Ah, yes, so it is," she said and actually winked at Randall Moss. Moss acknowledged her with a nod, then moved his whole body to face Frank.

"I believe interest was not to have been taken from those one knew. Foreigners, however, were candidates for loans and permitted to have interest charged, as well. Leviticus and Deuteronomy."

"Quite right, Mr. Moss. Quite right," Frank said. He had one eyebrow raised in interest.

"And if the truth were surely spoken, Mr. Stranahan, no self-respecting Israelite would have loaned money for business purposes at all, but only to help the struggling poor. Anything else would have been, how would you say it, a question of character. What I'm proposing would indeed help those less fortunate folks get a foothold on prosperity, and more importantly, a home. A place to call their own. To be a part of a community, send their kids to school. Go to church, meet their dreams." His arm arched out toward the river and the homes on the south side. "That's what you'd be promoting. Not really a business venture, but a way of service to others."

"That's what Frank believes in," I said. "He's given so much of himself to this town."

"Sure shows. Contributions like Mr. Stranahan's live on after a man. A woman's, too, not wanting to crowd you out. Heard you're a leader in looking after Indian affairs and saving birds and such."

"Oh, what I've done is little compared to Mr. Stranahan's efforts." I centered the silk jabot at my throat, wondering why they didn't just call it a bow. "I just spend a little time teaching the children songs and stories and such, serving on committees to educate lawmakers. Mr. Stranahan makes sure they have goods to care for their families; that's the real contribution."

"A fine matched team you are, then," Mr. Moss said. "And I'd be pleased to hitch up with you. Things're going to boom here. Life'll change in big and important ways, and I'm going to be a part of that...passion, if you will, that energy and spirit that marks a time we all look back on and say, this was when it happened, when Providence moved forward a commitment men had made."

He sounded so right, so sure, so familiar. I liked him and decided enthusiasm and youth lit his face more than his disarming, charming grin.

Randall Moss stayed to escort Pink to Bloxy and Louise's wedding in October of 1909. It was the first wedding in the Methodist Church, and it came at the end of a year that had begun with the death of Frank's stepmother, a sad time for him especially because business kept him from traveling north for the funeral.

"It's just the finest time to celebrate a union," Pink said. She wore a lovely straw hat with a cluster of little papier-mâché apples painted green around the band. The rest of her was dressed in yellow, including her shoes dotted with beads the color of birds of paradise you could buy up north. An orange boa draped across her arm and an umbrella the color of mango leaned against the railing.

A rainstorm had passed over, leaving a chill. The silk lining of my dress felt cool against my skin. Within the hour, Bloxham and Louise would finalize what the rest of us had known for years.

"Isn't that right, sister?"

"I wish they'd have a place of their own to go to," I said, stepping out on the porch. "I think it's hard to start out under the feet of your in-laws."

Ed and Susan King were fine people, that much I knew having lived with them myself the year I taught, and we counted them both as friends. Ed had just rebuilt after a fire, and their two-year-old home had been installed with both indoor plumbing and acetylene lighting, the first home with both, so Bloxy would at least be living in Lauderdale luxury.

"He's lived close to family his whole life. I'm thinkin' he knows how to avoid bein' stepped on," Pink said. She leaned out over the railing looking west and south, across the river, her hands unconsciously slipping the boa through them.

"Time to go," I said. "Wouldn't want to be late for our first church wedding."

A lovely crowd attended. There is something confirming, something solid and sturdy about two families of an area joining their histories together in matrimony. That we all knew them—knew stories of their growing and courtship—made each of us feel as though we'd had a part in this union. There existed among the communicants witnessing the wedding vows a community commitment, to uphold their marriage and do what we could to ensure they remained a happy, growing couple. Vows said between those we know less well are no less sacred, but the community's responsibility seems diminished, a value of village life I hated to see passing as the growth of Lauderdale continued and new faces appeared, like Randall's, filling the New River Inn.

People liked Louise for the most part, and Bloxham as well. She'd certainly been faithful waiting for my brother. Louise glowed, her arm strung through Bloxy's, holding tight as they nodded to well-wishers fanning themselves at the reception tables beneath the oak trees. I was glad for her, for them, and for their new life together.

Lovely music and tables of food kept people on the lawn long after the vows. Bloxy wore his usual grin and had greased his cowlick down but as the afternoon wore on, both began to droop. I wondered how long he'd wait to escort his new wife out.

"Gathering your chicks in Lauderdale," Frank said as I fanned myself beneath the coconut palms. "Looks like this one at least will stay. Seen DeWitt or your dad? Bloxy's asking for them. DeWitt said he'd take photographs of you all."

"I'll go find them," I said.

Only one brief encounter marred the occasion, an event we eavesdropped on initially. But then, Brother Hiram Frost commented more loudly than needed so it wouldn't haven't mattered how far away we'd stood.

"Government's failed its people when they brought that tourist owner near Fort Myers up on charges," he said.

"A lot of fussing over a bunch o' old Indian bones," agreed another.

"Waste of taxpayer money doing anything for heathens and spirit worshipers," Hiram repeated as murmurs of approval arose.

"The Cow Creeks up that way are ministered to by the Baptists," I said.

"With invitation from their leaders."

Hiram Frost jerked his head to see us standing beside him, scowled, and returned to his more receptive audience. "Bet it hasn't changed their lazy ways," he said. "Don't take care of themselves. Live out there in the swamps using up good, God-given space that could be sold for solid citizens to build on. Coming right into our town now. Drinking on the streets." Brother Frost shook his head in disgust.

"I believe a grave had been disturbed," I said. "A Captain Tiger's, with the bones removed by the tourist camp owner for his own profit. Think how we'd feel if our cemeteries were ransacked."

"They returned 'em," Hiram said. "Just lucky the heathens didn't make good on their death threats."

"I suppose that's the reason the government brought the charges against the tourist park operator," Frank said. "They sought legal redress rather than violence."

"Isn't it amazing what can happen when the church and government work hand in hand?" I said.

"It is distressing that even the little ones act uppity," Reverend Basil Holding said, joining the group in his black suit, squeezing his palms together as he talked. "You'd think they'd been to school, the way they hold themselves."

Several heads nodded in agreement.

"Yup. Government got too darn much money to waste now with them thinking the sixteenth'll be ratified," continued Hiram. "Income tax! Then comes the Federal Reserve banks, they say. Run by the government. Can't run itself, let alone a bank. You know it'll be a group of rich'uns forming that. Bankers and Indian lovers sleeping in the same chair." Hiram grinned at Frank and me then. "Well, hit two stones with one fat turkey, didn't I?" he said.

"If you're throwing things, I believe it's 'two birds with one stone,' Brother Frost," I corrected. "Though I'd be wary fussing with a child's slingshot. It just might be a boomerang."

"She's got you there, Hiram," Ed King said, slapping him on the back to ease the tension. "Time to celebrate now or Louise'll have all our hides."

Frank had resisted the bank. Frank Oliver had come to him with the plan for a charter and he'd said he wanted no part in it. But Tom Byran had sat an evening or two on the porch waving at folks as they popped by in their boats, the evening breeze ruffling the few thin hairs on his wide head, and slowly, he talked Frank's objections down.

Frank didn't believe in debt, not even to buy homes, and it bothered him that the very purpose of the bank Tom proposed built on the idea of money making money at the expense of those without any in the first place.

"Exactly why you need to be involved, to make sure loans aren't granted that overload people." That's what Frank Oliver had used to convince Frank. Frank Oliver had marble black eyes and wore a cookie-duster mustache. He combed at it with his fingers as he talked. His pinkie finger had a gold nugget ring that flashed in the sun. "Banks are investments, Frank. In communities, the same way Stranahan and Company is. We've done well in that together. Fort Lauderdale Bank will just be an extension."

"How much will my part of the, ah, extension be?"

"Whatever you feel comfortable with, Frank. H. G.'s going to put in $20,000 along with me and Tom. We'd like to keep the principals to a few. Make it be a place that invites folks to put their savings into. Encourage frugality that way. Your name would lend much to the respectability."

"Little strange to have a Fort Lauderdale Bank chartered before we've even settled on a town name nor incorporated it, either," Frank said.

"By the time the state grants the charter, we'll be a real village. Just got to settle on the name, is all. I can count you in, then?"

He lifted his limeade in salute to my husband's almost imperceptible nod.

My husband didn't talk about finances with me directly. I overheard most of what I learned, as did most women that I knew. So I liked hearing the discussion directly on the other side of the screen door. I found it difficult to plan and prevent problems without adequate information.

They were reasonable objections, I thought, given Frank's financial history that had seemed to come in and out like the tide. Almost penniless when he first arrived on the New River, Frank became indebted more deeply by a shipment of goods sunk at sea. He worked double those next years to recover the loss.

Will had gone through Stranahan and Company's money, too, the way sand flies bite through stockings. Will always had a good reason for wanting more: "Takes resources, brother, to secure contracts for the Seminole pelts and hides. Market's declining. Takes risk and money to make money."

When Frank got a little ahead, he invested the money mostly in land and solid structures, for our own security so we'd always have a home and a place to call our own. We seemed to have enough to meet our needs and he spoke of our resources as bounty we were blessed with, that we were to be good stewards of God's provision. I shared that view. I liked living with a man who was honest to a fault and who had a reputation that others held in high regard.

So I was surprised by what Louise had to tell me later the next week.

"Your husband, Ivy, honey, can be a difficult man sometimes," she said.

"In what way?"

I filled the tins with kerosene at the base of the table legs to keep the fleas and bugs from climbing up the legs. The work kept my head down so I couldn't see Louise, just heard her words, each one spoken precisely wrapped in whine.

"Bloxham says he deputizes people in name only, not in responsibility. Says there's really no need for an assistant postmaster if Frank persists in sorting letters, posting them, and preparing them for departure. Let me fill that for you, honey."

She took the kerosene tipper from me, filled it, then handed it back. Her eyes checked the turpentine levels at the pie cupboard's legs as she turned.

"Honest to truth, Louise, it's a large responsibility, being the postmaster in a growing community. The appointment is from the government itself."

"Yes, honey, I know it is that. But it diminishes a man to be nothing more than sent to the train to pick up the post. Why, that colored man Tom Reed could do that easy enough and he gets paid much less than Bloxham."

She picked at the tucks of her shirtwaist, bloused over her belt.

"Bloxham earns a good living under Frank."

"Well, yes, he does. But a man has to feel good about the living he's earning. Bloxham doesn't always. He wonders if Frank will ever see him as more than just your little brother he lent a helping hand to years ago."

"Perhaps if Bloxham were more decisive Frank would view him differently," I said.

"Well, I think he has been just that this past week, wouldn't you say?"

"How would that be?" I said, looking at her straight this time, the tone of her voice telling me I ought to.

"Why, bless your heart, honey. You didn't know? Well," she said, patting my hand, "I'm sure Frank'll be telling you any day now. When he thinks you're able to hear the news." Her eyes glanced away. "Oh my, it must be one hundred degrees outside!" She reached for her bleached and braided palmetto hat and fanned herself. "I best be heading home, honey. You all have a nice day."

"Bloxham's decided to sell his shares of Stranahan and Company back to me," Frank told me when I pressed him about Louise's conversation. "Berryhill did the same."

"Both of them? But why?"

He shrugged his shoulders. "Maybe they want the money to invest in something else."

"They wouldn't compete with Stranahan and Company?"

"Plenty of business for more than one mercantile in a growing town." Frank's voice had an edge to it, like a man sliced by a familiar knife.

The *Miami Metropolis* lay open on his lap but he wasn't reading it. I stood behind him, my fingers circling on his shoulders. The flannel of his shirt felt warm.

"Why didn't you tell me?" I said.

He reached up with one hand to hold mine. "Not things for women to worry over, money and such."

"Louise knew."

He tensed. "Sort of thing a man should manage and not bother his family about. We've worked it out, Bloxham and I. There're no hard feelings."

"Then you've seen merit in his ideas? In what he has to offer?"

"Wants to expand too quickly. Just because there's a land boom doesn't mean we should extend ourselves. I've already committed to the bank, put my name into that. And I've bought land to farm."

"Louise said something about him not being taken seriously, your not giving him enough responsibility."

He exhaled a burst of air through his nose. "Sounds like Will. Quoted Ambrose Bierce to me when I suggested he behave with more responsibility. 'A detachable burden easily shifted to the shoulders of God, Fate, Fortune, Luck, or one's neighbor,' he said." Frank shook his head in wonder.

"Where is Will these days? Have you heard from him?"

"Easy to blame others for your troubles," Frank said. "Bloxham could have taken more responsibility instead of laying the lack of it on me."

Frank patted my hand then released it, returning to pick up his paper. I cupped my fingers over his right ear and he leaned into my palm, our connection both tender and close.

Bloxham and W. O. did assume responsibility for their destiny. They formed Cromartie and Berryhill and began building a large new store on New River Drive and Andrews Avenue a few blocks down from Frank's.

I noticed an almost imperceptible difference in my relationship with my brother and his wife after that. They stopped by less often; and on Sunday, after church, when we women stood and fanned ourselves by the cistern of rainwater while the men smoked cigars in the shade, I always asked Louise what day during the week would be good for me to stop by, no longer feeling fine about just dropping in unannounced.

Frank never mentioned their store. It marked a rigidness in my husband's character I had failed to notice in the first ten years of our marriage.

Our little village incorporated in 1911, and William Marshall became the first mayor. He'd already been cited as the first licensed real estate broker. He had married just the year before, he and his new bride stepping off the train ten minutes before midnight, December 31, 1909. They walked beneath the full moon toward our home where Charlie Root played his accordion and almost the whole town had gathered up to dance. Even Frank, though he only clapped his hands. I danced with everyone, including Bloxham and DeWitt, the Byrans and Ed King. It was one of the few entertainments besides swimming I allowed myself.

The group celebrated anew with Mr. Marshall's announcement and introduction of his wife. Mrs. Marshall proved to be the prettiest little thing and became a fine addition to our town, joining with me to form the Women's Independent Civic Club in 1911.

For all Frank's contributions through the years, he did not receive the votes to be elected our first mayor, nor did they place him on the city council. His colleagues and partners made it: Ed King, Tom Byran, Will D. Kyle, W. H. Covington, and W. O. Berryhill, to be exact.

The results both surprised and pained me.

I'm not sure when I knew that Pink and Randall Moss would marry, but I was pleased to have played my part. I saw him as stable, someone who adored Pink and, honest to truth, someone whom I thought I might convince to stay in Lauderdale.

When I commented on his kindness and obvious admiration of Frank, Pink had cocked her head to the side the way she did with a new thought and then concurred. "He seems respectable enough," she said.

I laughed. "Now, that is a stretch of the imagination, that his respectability should be at the top of what you notice first in a man."

"Didn't say it was what I noticed first, just what I mentioned."

"I should've known."

"Maybe I'm seekin' finer things now that I've turned twenty-six, sister. Time I should be settlin' in."

We were picking Key limes, dressed in long-sleeved dresses and thick dark stockings to discourage mosquitoes and flies. The temperature steamed at ninety-five. We had taken *Jennie,* Frank's pop boat, to the property Frank had begun irrigating as our new little "farm" up the middle river. Pink had done the honors, starting and steering and mooring us to the flutter of spoonbills lifting from the water's edge. In no time we'd filled one of two baskets with the fruit.

"Randall's actually older than he appears. Did you know that?" Pink asked. "He's twelve years my senior but he has that love-of-livin' look that appeals to my spirit. We bolster each other's weaknesses and enhance our strengths. That's how he describes it."

She appeared to be blushing but it was difficult to tell through the netting draped over her hat and tucked in at her neck.

"Is he still in Philadelphia?"

"Yes. He writes often, but he's makin' good contacts there and should be comin' back to Miami this winter. He's not a part of that land lottery that Boles and Chambers are promotin'."

"He stands alone, then," I said. "Just about everyone else is."

"He doesn't believe in women being involved in land and all, like Mrs. Brickell or Mary Lily."

"Mrs. Flagler can afford to indulge herself," I said, "which I'm sure she does in that marble mansion of hers."

"He thinks a woman belongs at home. With her children." She stopped picking. "Look at me, sister. I want to see your face when you tell me what you think of that."

"He doesn't stand alone in that, either," I said. "Are you wanting a family?"

"I believe I'm ready. If I can. Seems like we Cromarties have little luck in reproducin' ourselves. Louise has none. And neither do you."

"If you're asking for advice on birth control—once you marry—there are devices, you know."

"You've been using 'em?"

"Having a child is a grave responsibility. Not one to be taken lightly."

We picked quietly for a time, the scent of moist earth filling my head. Mosquitoes buzzed and lit like old pains, brief yet threatening to sting if they stayed.

"I'll be likin' a family, sister. I'm sorry you haven't one."

"You know I love children, Pink."

"S'pose that's so, though I've wondered..." She left an opening I didn't take. I did so wonder why I couldn't share that side with Pink.

"If Randall makes you happy it doesn't matter how much he may disagree with my views about things. I imagine he doesn't approve of women voting either."

Pink's straight white teeth broke into a grin I could see beneath her netting.

"He seems to be a man of his word, and if he loves you, what more could I want for you? Except maybe to live in Lauderdale instead of just visiting. The air's so good for you here."

"We're settin' the date for—What was that?"

"Sounded like crying," I said. "Way off in the distance."

We stood quietly, then heard it again.

"Could it be a panther?"

"I hardly think so." I lowered my voice to a whisper just the same. "They rarely come around where people are."

"I heard once about a child swingin' in a tree right overhead of one. He thought it a funny-lookin' dog and brought his feet closer and closer, tryin' to make it run away."

"That story's as old as statehood," I said. "Probably no truth to it. No, it's something different."

"Let's go see."

I looked around for a weapon, something for defense if it was a panther. Spied the oar, then put it down, my heart knowing before my head that I wouldn't need that kind of a shield.

We made our way beneath the lime trees, pushing past the leafy branches, walking deeper into vegetation.

"I still get disoriented in these palmettos and palms," Pink said, her voice kept low. "Can't tell if I'm goin' north or south."

"Just keep your eyes on that smoke," I said, pointing to a tiny strand of gray rising through the shrub, "but don't forget to watch your feet."

A splash off to the side startled both of us and we hesitated.

"Likely just a gator," Pink said and pushed forward until we heard the cry again.

CHAPTER ELEVEN

ot an alligator's length in front of us, we stumbled upon a woman giving birth in the palmettos. She was dark skinned, a Seminole woman who looked to be in her thirties. Hanks of beads like those Frank stocked at the post coiled around her neck, heavy and colorful. She had twisted her skirt of a dozen colors so that it was fluffed like a pillow in front of her.

"Can we be helpin'?" Pink asked me while staring at her.

My mouth turned dry.

"We should be doin' somethin'. Sister?"

"I'm so sorry, we must be intruding. We'll leave, Pink…" I swallowed.

My heart pounded and I could feel an acrid taste forming in my mouth. I started to back away from the squatting woman, who gave me only the barest glance then hugged her knees again, her skirts hiked up around her hands. She grasped the material in her fist, and the look of it and the smells and the sounds ripped me backward to a day so long ago I gasped, short panting breaths, swallowing hard, no air. I couldn't get air and I ripped the veil from my hat. Gasping and swallowing, I tried to keep from retching; and when I knew I couldn't, I turned away, shaming myself again.

"Are you sick, sister? Faintin'?" Pink put her arms around me and placed her warm hand against my forehead. My stomach lurched again. "Come on fast."

My mouth tasted of bile and bits of the tomato I'd eaten for lunch. Insects swarmed against my ears. My heart pounded and my head throbbed. Embarrassment snatched my breath; fright swiped at my control. My hand shook as I wiped the back of it against my mouth.

"Let's leave her, Pink, in her privacy."

"You're better now? You've never left a needin' person."

"She's fine, Pink. Just fine. I know these people. They're strong." My head felt tight and full, a bullet of remorse ready to explode.

"But who was cryin' then? Not her, it seems like."

"It's not our business. She's fine. She's doing fine. Just fine."

"Listen," Pink said, turning from me toward a whimper. "We can't leave. She's just now havin' the baby!"

My stomach lurched again. I felt ten years old. The world smelled of disaster laced with death. Terror scraped like prickly pins from my neck to the bottoms of my feet, but I kept what remained of my stomach inside.

"Look, sister. Look now. Oh, just see!"

As if weighted by rocks, I turned to watch an infant slip into the world, wet and willing, without voice.

"Oh please, God," I heard myself say, old anguish mixed with fresh unworthiness tightening my throat. "Please let this one live."

"She's birthin' two!"

Pink left me, moved closer to the palmetto, and squatted. To the woman, she motioned her willingness to pick up the first child.

"It's like a little Moses!" Pink said. "All lyin' there in reeds."

The twist of thick hair at the top of the woman's head shone in the sun. Sweat beaded on her forehead as she watched Pink reach for the firstborn infant. The sight of it wiggling, arms and legs in unison kicking, helped me hold my fear. The baby in the woman's arms began to move, too. I heard a cry from her lap and then my own breathing steadied.

"You'll be a wreck at your own birthin'," Pink told me over her shoulder, her face close to the baby's.

"Most mothers are, I'm told." I sat and dabbed at my wet forehead with the back of my wrist.

"I'll have mine first, so you can practice. But you better not retch on me."

She stood rocking the newborn, dark and squirming against her white dress. The netting of her hat made it difficult to see her face but I could tell Pink smiled, then made kissing sounds to the child, as natural as water.

The woman, still squatting, lifted the newest infant to her breast. It began to root, its mouth opening and closing like a gasping fish.

I spied the scratch well the mother must have dug in the soft earth to ensure herself fresh water close at hand. I tore a section of the base of my slip off and dipped it in the smooth, clear water. Dark palmettos arched over it, and it reflected a very white face that was mine. I wiped the woman's forehead with the water then noticed the cup she'd brought with her, prepared for everything—except two babies. I filled it and lifted it to her lips.

"Do I know you?"

She shook her head. She leaned now against a mangrove root, one baby still sucking. Discomfort crossed her face for a moment. The placenta would not affect these babies. The cords should be cut. I mentioned it but she shook her head.

"I take care," she said. "You drink. I go back soon."

She motioned behind me with a nod of her chin toward the smoke.

"Isn't this just the sweetest li'l thing?" Pink said.

The chubby infant Pink held squirmed; the one in the woman's arms shifted but without will, its wail weak.

"I'll go get someone," I said.

The woman nodded and closed her eyes.

A trail of sorts made its way through vines. I stepped through elephant ear plants near the edge of what appeared to be a cultivated garden. Birds called out. Dogs barked now, and pigs grunted above their smell. Dirt-smudged children turned in my direction. A couple of them recognized me and came running over, leading me in with their gritty hands slipped into my fingers and pockets.

"There's a woman out there," I said to the first adult I saw, a woman wearing a dress with the cape over her arms and a long, faded skirt. "She's just had her baby. Two," I said, holding up my fingers and motioning a rocked child with my arms.

An older woman grunted, showed a mouth of broken teeth. "Twin," she said in English, then made her way past me, disappearing in the direction I'd come. The dogs sniffed at my heels.

Esther called them off.

"Is this your camp?" I said. "I thought you lived farther into the swamp. It's been so long!"

"*Watchie-esta hutrie,*" she said. "Little white, white mother." It was the first time I had heard her put English words together. They carried a lilt to them, a hesitant dance I wished to remember, to write down in my book. Her fingers fluttered in that way she had, even when she turned to the others who were gathering about. If she lived so close, why had it been so long since I'd seen her?

Several adults lounged on chickee platforms. Their eyes showed no invitation, only fatigue. One older man came from behind a thatched shack and at Esther's voice he scowled, said something in Mikasuki. Esther's eyes dropped.

"Your grandfather?"

Esther shook her head and kept her eyes down, then backed away from me, disappearing inside a distant chickee. Others made room for the man dressed the best of the men present. His long shirt with pleats to his waist stopped above his knees. He had tanned skins on his legs and leather moccasins that fringed beneath his knees. He must have come walking through saw grass. He wore a turban wrapped loosely around his head. Wrinkles rained down his face.

"No need white mother here," he said, looking past me.

I'd seen him in the post a time or two. I couldn't think of his name but he had a daughter named Annie, who Frank said was around my age.

"You go."

"Of course. I didn't mean to intrude. I…"

He didn't wait for my response but turned his back and followed one or two women who scurried out toward the cypress grove where I'd left Pink and the new mother.

"I'll just be off then."

Esther reappeared as if from nowhere. She stood in the open area surrounded by chickees and motioned for me to sit on one of the salt pork boxes used as a chair; I realized I was shaky.

"I really should go," I said.

A few adults moved back in a circle from me, their eyes cast down, but they stayed within sight.

Evidence of our white trading post—and other posts too—was everywhere. Cans and pots and pans and the trappings of white culture were shoehorned into the Everglades, an uneasy, miserable fit. Brown pelicans hopped and pecked at fish carcasses farther from the camp. The smell of carrion, old bones, and smoke was stronger than that of the gardenias. The lumber on the walkways above the swamp looked rough, and the railings showed a need for repair. The scratch wells had chips of wood and matted grass floating in them in an area not far from the pigpens.

"Well. Here we are." I folded my hands in my lap. "That's lovely cane you've got growing there, Esther," I said, nodding toward a fenced-in patch. "And just look at that corn. My, my."

Esther motioned to a younger child, who fetched a cup of water for me, and I remembered something Will had said so long ago about children serving guests, about their jobs being to prepare for adulthood. The grown-up world that awaited them carried questionable promise. I didn't like acknowledging my own part in the change.

The water smelled brackish but it looked clear and tasted good in the steamy heat. I smiled at Esther over the cup, and as I handed it back to her she pointed to a box next to me that looked just like the one I sat on.

"Salt, salt. Pork." Her finger outlined the words on the box.

A prickling worked at the back of my neck. "You just read that, didn't you?"

Esther nodded and buried a smile behind her fingers. The burned side of her face had grown tighter through the years and pulled the side of her mouth so it twisted slightly. Her dark eyes sparkled.

"Are you pleased?" I asked her.

She nodded.

"I don't think we ever even talked about those words. You sounded them out. Oh, Esther, you can read! You can."

The forehead of one or two adults pinched; someone spoke in their language. Esther turned quickly, her eyes darting about. "Salt pork," she said, turning back. "Read good."

I felt a stew of feelings: joy and guilt, satisfaction and anguish, responsibility and fright.

"Kinda lost, ain't you?"

Both Esther and I turned to the man's voice, sounding from a distance.

A woman who'd been serving at a chickee stepped aside. Behind her, a man dressed in buckskins and a raccoon hat sat cross-legged at an eating platform. He untangled himself, stood up, stretched, and started toward me, kicking an empty peach tin out of his way with his foot, tipping over a mason jar containing clear liquid. As he came out of the shadows, I thought I recognized him.

"Will?" I said. "Is that you?"

"No. I ain't your kin, Mrs. Stran-a-han. He finds himself hanging at this camp some. Not been here for a coon's age, though. Stretch Johnson, that be me."

He had the characteristic of speech with satisfied yawns, spoken like a Cracker, a native of the Keys.

"Surprised, you here. Old Johnny," he said, nodding toward the man who had asked me to leave, "he kinda partial to who he lets stay in this camp."

"Johnny Jumper. Yes. I couldn't remember his name."

He stared at me, then. "Your kin hangs with a kind of rough bunch."

"Will?"

"Hear him tell. Times in Colorado and California. Lucky he be still living." He spit then, and a dark stream of tobacco juice disappeared in a gray patch of old palmetto. The sunlight flickered and reflected against something gold on his hat.

"What's that pin?"

He snatched at it and pulled it off. "Nothin'. Ain't nothing." He picked at his tooth with what looked like a gopher's leg bone. Meat still clung to the thin sheaf the color of cashews.

"Will had one like that. He said it was for the Order of the Redman. Some secret Masonic group."

"Do tell."

"We'd know if something had happened to Will," I said.

"Know everything, do ya?" He spit again. "Like most white folks think."

Esther frowned. People had stopped tending to various tasks with sugar cane and sweet potatoes, penned pigs and chickens. They leaned on hoes now, laid their whittling knives down. The tired ones appeared to revive.

"Patetic," he said, mispronouncing the word. "What you're thinking, ain't it?" His eyes moved around the camp as though seeing it for the first time as I did.

Children's clothes were unmended and worn thin. A portable sewing machine gathered dust beneath one of the chickees with no evidence of bright-colored books of material. No one smiled, least of all Stretch. Even the pigs were thin along their backstraps.

Where were the colorful turbans and proud stature the Seminoles wore when they poled in to trade?

"Hides're scarce," Stretch said. "'Course, no more plumes."

"I should hope not."

"Make demands, then change. Like you white women to do that."

"I never wore a feather, not ever," I said.

He snorted. "Trash the lot. Look at what you done to their trade."

"I've tried to protect these people, to ensure trade, avoid swindlers. As I can." My heart pounded and Stretch looked through such narrow eyes I wondered if I might be in danger.

"Raccoon hats're in now," he said after a pause.

"That'll start another trade that won't help them."

"Know all about helping, do you, Mrs. Stran-a-han? Keep yer hands clean, though, let others do yer dirt work. You put little girls up to things. What d' you think happens when they come back here and speak your words? And read 'em? Think they hold a party then?"

"Maybe they need a place of their own." I nodded toward the chickee Esther had entered. "Where they can live and learn without disruption."

"On one of your reserves, I suppose," Stretch said and snorted again. "Will Stranahan say, out west, reserves're pens of disease and degradation. That's where you'd put 'em? For safekeepin'?"

"Where others can't intrude on them, yes. And they could farm their land without fear that someone would take it from them when the harvest looks good."

"You livin' in fairyland, Mrs. Stran-a-han. Reserves'll kill 'em. Besides, they got no government guarantees of anything without no treaty."

"Judging by these conditions, we may be witnessing that happening anyway, Mr. Johnson. Stretch."

"We?"

"You. Me. All of south Florida, unless we—"

"Sister!" Pink came through the foliage then and motioned for me to come.

"Please tell Esther good-bye for me, would you? And that I miss her when she's gone."

Stretch snorted again as I turned my back to him and headed out. I'd seen a reflection of my intervention, the consequences of my teaching. The results felt mixed, like the pinch of new shoes at the beginning of a long walk toward shade.

Pink and I picked our way through the palmettos back toward the *Jennie*. "Don't want to be in that boat come dark," Pink said. "They had a regular celebration over those babies. Thought you'd come back."

"I ran into a young girl back there. One I used to read to at the post."

"Did you know she lived there?"

I shook my head.

"Imagine, all those goin's-on, just right under your nose! Babies born, gardens tended. Even them dogs greeted us with happy tongues hangin' out."

"Those dogs."

"The woman's name is Josie. Has a cousin named Annie. That old man? He's a medicine man. Just grunted at our success but I could tell he smiled inside."

"You certainly got a bucketful of information."

"Just listenin' and askin' gentle," Pink said. "People like talkin' of themselves."

"So what's this Stretch Johnson man doing there, living with them? Did you discuss that?"

She shrugged her shoulders.

"They looked so...diminished," I said. "Careful of that low branch there. Could poke your eye out."

"I think they're just the poor cousins. The plumper ones live someplace else, I'll wager."

"Not sure there are more prosperous kin. These might be the harbingers of the future," I said.

"The mama acted hopeful, if you want my opinion, nursin' two babies at once. Can't imagine someone that hopeful bein' beaten long into ground. How come you've never been out here? Seems like you would've."

"Oh, I wasn't sure where the camp was. And I didn't want to intrude."

She laughed. "Not intrude?"

"I didn't!"

"Oh, don't get fussed up. Just meant with you teachin' and swappin' things the way you do, helpin' 'em sew and all, that I can't see how you think it ain't meddlin. Sister, I'd say you didn't want to be known outside your own kitchen, that's what I'd say. Got nothin' to do with intrudin'. Don't like having anyone see you where you're not whole, not really."

"I don't think that's fair, Pink. I've always been honest with them. And caring." I'd never heard her use the tone she'd chosen nor the insinuations of her words.

"Do their parents know you teach 'em?"

"I only want to prevent them from being destroyed by all the changes that're coming. They survived wars but they might not defeat the enemies of ignorance and being unschooled in the ways of a swamp without water. I just want to be of...service."

"Long as you're...in control, I'd say, sister. That'd be the word I'd use to describe your service."

Pink stepped into *Jennie* over the baskets of limes and twisted to start the engine. She turned back without doing so, stared at me before speaking. I swatted at insects with the back of my hand, remembering too late where I'd left my hat.

"What was that about? Your gettin' sick back there?"

"Just the heat. Honest to truth."

I felt more than heard her sigh. "Why don't you be honest to truth with me? You've never said a thing since we've been grown that might shed a light on you. Never been yourself with me. Just your carin' self, your prayin' self, like I wasn't trusted to be told or confided in, like you were some kind of saint or somethin' and the rest of us not good enough to see more'n the outside of Ivy."

I wiped my face with my handkerchief. "Some kind of saint. If you only knew."

"I want to!" Her eyes watered. "It was more than heat, wasn't it, sister? Somethin' about the birthin' bothered you mighty."

"More than the heat," I said. My face felt hot.

"So you won't be tellin' me then?"

"Watching that baby be born reminded me of *how* unqualified for sainthood a soul can be, how terrible the mistakes a person can make and still live, still hope for better for tomorrow."

"You bein' the dramatic one now."

I swished my linen hankie into the water and wiped the back of my neck. The starch of my high collar scraped against my skin when I did, and it felt good; gritty with just the edge of ache.

"You had a little brother once," I said and felt the sigh of it, the old grief still fresh enough to step right up and strike my face. "Tiny and perfectly formed he was, too. He died, Pink. Didn't need to, but he did. Because I failed to act. Because I didn't do the simplest of things: pick him up and hold him. Pick him up and meet that tiny little need. That's all I had to do and I didn't so he died. I live with it every day." My skin itched beneath my long sleeves. The hum of mosquitoes drummed beside my ears. "And I'm doubly sorry that my not talking of it has made you feel...unsuitable, because you're not. I'm the unworthy one. And nothing I can do can take that back."

Pink picked up the oars as though to push us out from the bank. "You did what needed doin' back there," she said. The wood broke into the dark water.

"You helped with the baby, Pink, not me."

"Had to a'been pretty young."

"The baby before Albert. Five years to the day earlier, ironic as that seems."

"Just a baby yourself, then."

"But I *could* have acted and I don't know why I didn't. Haunts me, not knowing."

"Seems to me things happen that God holds. He does the controllin'. All we get to do is ask, 'What next? How do you want me to move on?' Or maybe, 'What's the lesson you're teachin'?' That's what Mama always said."

"I try to let Him be in control, be obedient. That's why my club work is so important."

She nodded, her arms straining against the water. Out from the hammock far enough, she balanced the oars on her knees and started the engine.

It popped into the overhanging silence.

"So brave 'bout so much, but not birthin'. Seems strange your faith wouldn't show up for that." She eased the boat out into the river. "With a little practicin', bet you could deliver one," she shouted above the pop. "Maybe even your own if you had a mind to. Might believe then you're forgiven, loved no matter what you did. Stop tryin' to make it up."

That evening, we chanted psalms chorales at the house. I'd newly organized the group of fifteen or so. I loved the blend of voice and Scripture that led us in worship. Tonight I needed it more than ever. The sounds brushed me with a strange kind of unity where one voice could cover for the breathing of another, so it always sounded as one. I had heard that monks and sisters chanted the psalms and had for generations, morning, noon, and night, a pause in each day, a worshipful moment. Sharing that with them gave me a sense of gathering, of joining in a strange and mystic way with people who had chosen differently than others, put their passion into service and to love not in the physical, but in a celibate way. The music told me their union was deeply meaningful and perhaps even stronger than those who chose the noncelibate life.

My decision, which had become our decision—Frank's and mine—was unexplainable to others, I suppose, in many ways. Certainly to Pink. I loved Frank no less. In fact, as I looked and listened to the women speak of their husbands while at the women's club or as I watched for evidence of tenderness between husbands and wives, I often felt dismayed, shocked by the lack of tenderness I saw there; and I was amazed at the abundance of what I felt existed within my own union. Children would not have added to that abundance, I didn't think. And their presence would have made it difficult for me to reach out to so many others.

Sharing these chants proved an abundance beyond measure. The tones washed over me throughout the week when I walked, sewed, cooked, and yes, even when I continued to watch the children appear like stars in the night sky through the dark greenery surrounding my porch, continued to share Bible stories with them, watch them feed my soul while I hoped I nurtured theirs.

Frank's favorite chant came from Psalm 91: "He that dwelleth in the secret place of the most High shall abide under the shadow of the Almighty." That was the first verse in a psalm that spoke of protection through knowledge and surrender.

I loved the twenty-third psalm, but as with many great prayers, blending it into a sung choral rendition was a challenge. As a chant, it filled my soul and I found myself rested with it that night, rested from the encounter with a birth that day, with Stretch's accusations and sharing my shame with my sister. Had Pink described me best? Was I afraid to know the Seminole people better, expose myself to them? The Baptists were living among the Cow Creeks. Was I willing to do that? Or was I volunteering to share their burdens but only on my terms, under my control?

Pink was right about one thing: I felt exposed when I let others stand too close. I preferred to live unattached.

The words and chanting rhythms soothed me like a long-awaited prayer.

No, my motives with the Seminoles were pure. I was even hopeful, almost, what with Esther's self-taught lesson. And this day I had summoned help, stood firm against a challenge and exposed a sin to Pink. My sister still spoke to me seemingly able to bathe the past with forgiveness.

I would strive for that within myself.

Pink and Randall chanted with us when they were in Lauderdale. That didn't happen much after they were married in the spring of 1912.

Pink wrote to tell me of their wedding from Arkansas. She'd gone back to Miami after our encounter at the camp and had promised to consider moving to Lauderdale. I worked on Randall, too, before he headed north for one of his interminable business meetings.

"Lauderdale sure is a nice place," he said, "but I'm not sure this is where I want to set my main office. Might need to be farther west."

"Best land and water anywhere, Randall," I assured him. "Breezes would be good for Pink. We'd be close by when you have your family."

"Sure will think about it," he said.

I waited to hear of wedding news. DeWitt stopped over for an evening and we speculated about the dates. He had offered to take photographs at the ceremony, his new hobby giving him many happy hours of pleasure after pounding on houses all day. I even considered buying one of those new sheath dresses for the event, with a yellow-dotted veil for my wide-brimmed hat.

"Next we'll see you in those fishnet stockings," DeWitt said. "What-taya know about that? Pretty classy, I'd say, with those legs of yours."

"I'm amazed at how easily those slang words slip into our language."

"Which? 'Classy' or 'whattaya know about that?' 'Spose you don't like 'peeved' then, either?"

"I'll be peeved, indeed, if Pink and Randall don't have a classy wedding, get married soon, and move right here for sure. Whattaya know about that?"

DeWitt laughed.

Then I received Pink's letter.

Be Mrs Moss, Sister. Justice of peace marry us fine. Plan to live in Arkansaw a time. Randall buys and sells mor land. Come see me in yur new Ford car if you learnt to drive it. Randall travels north and fusses over me. Hope he move me back to Daddy, bugs and you soon.

Randall had disappointed me, depriving us of a lovely event and a chance to woo them to remain. But Pink sounded happy enough. I'd written that I'd love to visit, but there were changes happening here and I felt a need to be present, at least for a time.

Randall had done well in our area selling tracts of land. I was pleased he hadn't become involved in the land lottery set up by Boles and Chambers as soon as the north canal to Lake Okeechobee was finished. The men had been indicted for misrepresentation and illegal financing schemes. Dredging and draining had made thousands of acres available for sale and people from the north turned daft buying up chances at "waterfront property."

The frenzy affected all of us. Talk grew about Flagler putting currency into a big hotel if he could match investors.

"Even our mayor pitched money into that effort," DeWitt told me. I believed that Frank did too but he spoke little of it, busier dealing with the newly formed board of trade he served as treasurer.

I looked at my schedule, trying to decide if I could take a month to spend with Pink. Then she wrote to say she hoped I'd come visit before *this baby mak me big as a hors troff*. It took me a while to decipher exactly what she meant.

"Maybe I could piggyback a trip to Arkansas with that women's club meeting in Tallahassee. Just go on from there," I told Frank.

"Schedule what you need. A rest from suffrage discussions would surely be relaxing."

"Time with Pink is rarely restful," I said. "Interesting. Intriguing. Unpredictable, maybe. I don't know how far along she is."

"Not sure you'd recognize relaxing, Ivy," Frank said. He looked up over his glasses.

"Is that a criticism?"

"Observation."

"I don't think that's true, Frank. I have my causes, issues I work for, but I always make my Christmas marmalade. My staghorn ferns and flowers win prizes from their tending. And I take fresh bread to friends."

"I suppose," he said.

All the changes in south Florida consumed both Frank and me. At gatherings we both listened attentively when talk turned to draining more swamp, of using the sludge and muck to actually build spits of land that looked like combs, with little rows of water between the teeth. People built cottages on the tines of land and told their northern friends they had "frontage."

"How things'll change," Frank said as we stood at the seawall at dusk one evening, waiting for the manatees. None had come in.

"Maybe they're calving later this year," I said.

"Maybe they won't come at all," Frank said.

"Surely the dredging won't affect everything."

"Everything that moves on the river," Frank said, a sigh high in his throat.

Including proud people in dugout canoes, I thought, but didn't say.

✦

"Change isn't always for the better," Frank said. He finished his Key lime pie I'd served as the Oliver brothers, James and Dave, chased flaky crusts around the Spode with silver forks. Vests were unbuttoned and the men leaned back in their chairs, expressions of satisfaction blessing their well-fed faces.

"Know that's so," Frank Oliver agreed. "But you'll have much free time to consider how, now."

"I hope he won't regret this," I said.

I cleared dishes, waving the Oliver women to remain seated. "I'll just get us chocolate," I said.

"Don't you worry about that, Ivy," Frank Oliver answered as I slipped out through the dining alcove into the kitchen. I missed the rest of the conversation, picking up bits and pieces when I returned.

"Going to run for city council again, though, aren't you?"

"If they have need of me," Frank said.

"Always so modest," Dave's wife said. "Thank you, dear." She accepted the art nouveau china cup and sipped at the chocolate I handed her, the liquid as dark as her eyes. She looked so tiny compared to her husband and spoke with a tinkling voice, gentle as a delivery bell. They'd only recently been married. Grace Dunlop, Frank's cousin from up north, had held a party for them upstairs to honor their nuptials.

"How do you like the produce-growing business?" James Oliver asked. "Is that drained swamp really as rich as they say?"

"Just a stockholder in that one," Frank said. "I'm just a stockholder."

"'Spect we'll hear more about that as time goes by. Well, I propose a chocolate toast, then," James Oliver offered as he stood. "To the new owners of Stranahan Mercantile. May we do as well with it as the founder did twenty years ago."

"Hear, hear!" the other two Oliver brothers said. We women raised our voices as well, lifting the dainty cups of chocolate in celebration of change.

Only Frank stayed silent.

"If you didn't want to sell, why did you?" I asked him later in the evening. We were upstairs looking out at the river through the bougainvillea that trailed its way in both directions along the porch roof, dipping down to the crisscross in the railing. His suspenders hung on either side of his narrow hips, and he stood almost stiffly next to me. My toes were aware of the slant to the porch that allowed rainwater to run naturally toward the gutters and into the cistern. A breeze moved the windmill, creaking and cranking a little east of the house.

"Sold because it seemed the best thing to do right now." He sighed. "Trade is going to dry up, Ivy. Literally go the way of the swamps. I've kept a few of the contracts. The alligator eggs. Like to give the Seminoles that business. They'll bring those in. We'll hatch them here and ship them north. Maybe the dolls. Don't know what else they'll have that folks need or want. Sad."

He stepped to lean over the railing a bit and the floor creaked, a loose board. I reached for his arm and slipped mine through his.

"Hide market is almost gone; business in general is shifting. I don't know. I have an eerie feeling about the future. Kind of tangles in my stomach like a knot of snakes sometimes." He shook his head as though brushing off the strangled thoughts.

"Remember those mesmerized ones?" I shuddered at the thought.

"Land's our future," he continued. "Tourism, too, much as I have mixed feelings about it. Gone into it with both feet with the bank and all. Sixteenth'll be ratified; I'm sure of it. Income tax then. Can't afford distractions. I'm not getting any younger."

"Perhaps there'll be less weight on you then, with the store under new management. Will you resign as postmaster?" I tentatively offered the next advice. "Might be a good time for Bloxham to move into that position. He's covered for you well when you've been out of town."

Frank stood quietly for a time. He picked a bougainvillea blossom and turned to stick it into my hair. "Not just yet," he said. "Need to keep my pulse on the happenings at the store. Coming in to sort the mail won't arouse suspicions. Besides, I need to know the gossip in town."

He smiled at me, pulled me closer to him. The scent of laundry soap against his shirt drifted to my nose. "What better way than managing mail. Look what it brought me all those years ago."

He put his arm around my waist and I held him the same as he moved me back in through the bedroom door.

For some reason, as we stepped into the room, I became aware that our two beds appeared more separated than before. Goose-down pillows piled high on mine kept me almost at a sitting position when I slept, an angle I'd read proved good for people with potentially poor hearts. Since Mama's death, I'd been conscious of frailty, though I did not speak of it to Frank or anyone else. With Pink not around, I found few to confide in.

Frank's pillow lay thin, almost flat, and the coverlet I'd sewn for it looked too frilly all at once.

"Come to bed with me," he said, his arm tightening ever so slightly against my waist.

"You need a good linen coverlet," I said, bending to brush down the border ruffle. "This one is much too feminine. Don't know what I was thinking when I sewed it up for you."

"Hadn't noticed."

"I will, if you'd like."

Though he rarely asked, I readily curled beside Frank in either his bed or mine. I'm not sure how it would occur, what or who initiated the connection. Wrapped together in the safety of affection and care, we did not talk there so much as commune, each with thoughts making their way through the channels of the human mind, twisting and turning together. For hours it might be, I'd lie there beside my husband, my mind racing to a Seminole camp or a conversation with a woman at a garden club, a Scripture I had read whose meaning troubled me, or creating a list of things I must finish in the morning. Often the sounds of the chants would appear with the pounding of his heart so close to mine. My thoughts returned to him, then, moved toward attachment and communion.

He seldom spoke though I knew he did not sleep. We'd had more intimate conversations when we'd been on beach trips the year before we married than in the twelve years since. It was as though once he'd shared with me his inner feelings, he had no need to repeat them. So my mind wandered.

Sometimes the touch of his arm over my shoulder would bring me from the things I planned to say at the suffrage gathering, the recalling of an interchange with Mary Munroe over plumes. His touch, the warmth, would be so sweet, so gentle, and so tender that tears would rise unbidden to my eyes and I would wonder at the fullness I felt, and still the distance I allowed between us.

We were there now, the night we celebrated the sale of the store, lying spooned together. I could feel his breath on my cheek, the gentle stroke of his fingers moving my hair behind my ear.

"You are the most competent, capable, beautiful woman I know."

"I know you think that," I said, "though what brought that on is beyond me." The pillow felt cool and soft against my cheek.

"It's true. You do anything you set your mind to."

"I've been fortunate that way."

"Things I try, they don't always turn out the way I plan."

I felt a catch in my stomach, wondering what worries were operating on him. I should have just listened to him, reflected back what he said, but instead I had to talk, to convince him he was wrong.

"Seems to me you've done quite well, beginning with very little and now being able to sell and put your time into other interests. Not very many men who could do what you've done."

"Will's the real tycoon," he said.

"Will does seem to have the temperament for risk."

"He does."

"He fails to put himself into the cloak of success so he won't have to wear failure, though. Tries new things without risking himself."

"How you see it, is it?"

"I think risk may have a better press agent than caution," I said. "But a venture without faith has little value, if you know what I mean."

"I pray about that," Frank said. "About what I'm supposed to do, how I'm to use what I've been given to manage. How I'm supposed to demonstrate my faith, as it were. No answers come. A lot of empty sound. Reminds me of water lapping up against the seawall, going nowhere, just wearing down."

His words brought a loon to mind, quiet and distant and alone. I turned to him, the moonlight pouring in through the window through the eyelet curtains. I had a full view of his face, the tiny smudge of wetness reflecting like glass at the corner of his eyes now lined deep enough to be seen even in reflected light.

"Oh, Frank," I whispered. "Your life's been a wonderful statement of stewardship. So much you've given!" I tugged at his nightshirt, centering the seam along his shoulder. "You've been a good friend to your neighbors. Honest. Far-thinking." My hand looked so small resting against his chest. "You're leaving things behind for others to appreciate, helping this place grow with a semblance of orderliness. Very few people could do that. Or would have. Your brother certainly never has. He'll probably never settle down."

"Doesn't seem enough," Frank said.

"Nonsense. Why, this home alone is a legacy fit for a king. Look at what you've carved out of nothing. Just lie here and let the magnitude of it wash over you."

"Means more to you than to me," he said after a time of quiet. "The house does."

"A home's the most important thing I can think of, outside of faith and love and service," I said. "I don't know of a man anywhere who doesn't feel it's the most essential act of manhood to ensure a roof over the head of his family. In his blood, I'd guess, like repeating the act of creation when God made a sheltered place of protection for those He loved."

"Be all the worse, then, if he did something to destroy that," Frank said. "Wasn't a good steward."

"Now stop this, Frank. It's a wonderful night for you. Of celebration, that you can retire in comfort and continue to serve. What a treasure that is."

"Never know what snakes lay in the grass ahead, Ivy," he said.

"Eve ate the apple." I leaned to kiss his forehead, hoping to lighten his burden. "So you can stop worrying about that."

CHAPTER TWELVE

The fire of 1912 took the entire downtown. Fresh-cut lumber of the store the Oliver brothers had just expanded burned as hot and fast as the old boards that once marked the beginnings of our village. Fire wagons clanged their bells, and bucket brigades set up faster than a tent on a rainy day, but Frank's old store and several others along the railroad were consumed by the pitch-fed flames. Cromartie and Berryhill's store still stood.

Smoke and ashes lingered over the town, brushing away bugs and mosquitoes, causing coughing and watery eyes for weeks.

No one knew for sure what started it. Lightning, most likely, said the men who gathered at the sidewalk café under the striped awning later in the week. Fueled by the lumber and the dried palms and the oil of the glossy lantana leaves, the fire had taken hold quickly and might have taken the whole town except for the efforts of so many.

Frank acted despondent, the way a horse in training will sometimes stop its resistance, tired and waiting. His silence felt almost frightening in its depth of distance.

"It wasn't your fault," I said. I stood behind him, rubbing his shoulders in that familiar way we shared. "How could you possibly have known the downtown would burn? You ought to be pleased Providence gave you the foresight to sell when you did."

"Can't rejoice at another man's misfortune."

"I'm not even close to suggesting that. We have control over very few things, Frank. Our response to life events seems to be where we have the most, how we think about a thing when it's been given. That may be our greatest place to demonstrate our confidence in the future, maybe even our faith."

"Are you listening to your words?" he asked.

"If you take everything that happens and use it against yourself, you'll pull back inside a shell."

"I remind you of a turtle, then."

"Of course not, though no turtle ever made progress until he stuck his neck out a bit. What good would that hard shell do him if he just hovered beneath it? Protection and exposure go together."

Frank grunted then patted my hand on his shoulder, holding my fingers in his.

"You've made progress because you took chances, Frank. Then Providence steps in and we're allowed to demonstrate something new about our faith. I think that's where we are now."

I didn't think to ask him until later how the fire would affect our finances. I didn't see how it could, really, since we'd sold the store. I let the question slip my mind. Instead, I looked for ways to encourage him.

"Maybe new interests are what you need now, take your mind from blame. What about learning how to drive, with me?" I sat across from him on the rattan chair, my face close to his.

Frank shook his head. "Not interested."

"Ed said he'd show me how to crank it though I think I have the hang of it pretty well. I might even drive it to Arkansas."

"Best he show you how to dig out of mud. You'll be doing more of that than steering or cranking. And certainly not cross-country."

"I heard that an Illinois family drove down. Camped out and had quite the adventure. And Kettering has invented an electric self-starter that will be standard before long."

"I'll take the train. Or a mule."

As if it heard its name, the mule stomped in its corral and called out. It stood not far from the windmill and Frank turned to look. "Don't you worry, Blue," he told her.

"Have you noticed the children stopping by to look at the Ford?" I said. "They like to sit on the running board. So cute."

"Because you're reading them stories. Aren't those cards the ones from church?"

"Your father introduced me to them. All around, I'm rather impressed with the Presbyterians. They send them to me free now. And they've adopted some new statement about the 'great ends of the church.'"

"Likely written in government words." Frank laughed. "A foundation Presbyterians gave our government it could have done without."

"The government's lasted quite a time, so perhaps the foundation's a good one."

Frank coughed. We watched the butterflies flirting with the orange blossoms of the lantana bush.

"They sent a copy with the last set of cards. Seems pretty straightforward. The first is about proclaiming the gospel for the salvation of humankind."

"Sounds profound."

"Until I imagine 'proclamation' as 'telling' or 'showing,' and 'salvation' as the rescue from being separated from God. The second's about 'shelter, nurture, and spiritual fellowship of the children of God.' A mission statement if I've ever read one."

I leaned back in my chair, hands folded in my lap. Frank signaled me to lift my legs. He untied my shoes and removed them, then cradled my feet in his palms. His hands always felt warm.

"There's one about social righteousness, too," I said as he massaged the flesh around my toes. "About helping to right the world's wrongs. They're for all of us, I think, brown and white and every other color of human skin. Goodness, that feels fine!" I said.

Frank smiled and pressed firmer with his thumbs.

"I haven't been able to get Brother Holding or the Methodists into ecumenical thinking. They don't seem interested in teaching materials nor the Seminole children who just love those stories and who have certainly been wronged in their time. Their parents aren't worried that they're government-like, with the pictures and all. They stop by and watch. I think they're proud their children can sing the songs with me."

"Just so long as they aren't reading, Ivy," Frank said. "Wouldn't want you to arouse trouble among them."

"Oh, they just love the music. So do Della's children. I think her Baptist church teaches them the same songs. It would be such a pleasure to have them all come to Sunday school, wouldn't it, Frank?"

"Suppose."

My husband massaged each individual toe, even my third one that grew oddly longer than the second. He didn't lift his eyes to answer me.

"I don't see how it's possible to bring the message of Christian love to other people without stirring up a little dust," I said.

"How d' you feel about having your papa and Albert and Gus move to Lauderdale?"

"What?" I lifted my feet from his hands. "Oh, Frank, could you do that? Maybe Pink and Randall would come too, then."

"Not sure about them. But DeWitt says Gus's a good carpenter. We'll be needing those with the fire and Albert could finish school here. You have great calves, Mrs. Stranahan," he said and motioned me to lift my legs to his lap again.

"Here I thought to lighten your mood and you've found a way to raise mine higher than it deserves."

"They'd be closer to their 'mama,'" Frank said.

"You understand better than any. I love you so."

I had a dozen thoughts about how soon and where they might live, how good it would be for them all to be gathered here, how much safer if we were all close together. Papa had written that Albert had grown tall and thin and coughed much as Pink had in the winters.

"Getting them out of Miami'll be so good," I said. "It makes me wonder what's there to make Cromarties take on that cough."

"Suppose changes here, drainages and dredging, could affect things farther south." Frank's fingers circled my ankles, pressed and released.

"I have wondered over that. Every time a new building request comes before the planning commission I think about the trees that'll die for it, all the lumbering going on, whether there'll be enough for all the people, not to mention the birds and alligators and even the snakes. Everything is so interconnected. I hadn't realized how changing one thing affects everything else."

"Doubt people see that."

"How could we not see that making waterways and canals and cutting trees would transform us as well as the swamp?"

"'Be fruitful and multiply' and have 'dominion over all,'" Frank said.

"It appears we've attended to the first while ignoring the latter. Dominion does imply responsibility."

"Control." He patted my feet as he finished.

"Control. Yes. It feels as though we've lost control, Frank, of growth and all the consequences."

"Never had it," he said. His eyes followed me as I stood.

"You must admit," I said, "that your White sewing machine transformed things and you had control over that. And you're going to bring Albert and Papa and Gus here. So there are things we get to do and hope we're acting wisely."

"Have to trust we are."

"And that a sovereign God who sees all we don't see loves us and does reign. Otherwise, it would be too frightening, hopeless almost. If I didn't believe that God loves this earth I'd feel...hopeless and...abandoned."

"Loved it every day, even before man arrived," Frank said. "We're here to take care of things."

"Exactly. And He provides us with what we need to adapt. Like your White sewing machine and my teaching. One stitches cloth and the other stitches souls. Isn't that so, Frank?"

He didn't respond, but his eyes looked to the river.

I snuggled up beneath his arm and stared with him, daydreaming about his generosity in bringing my family around me again. The thought of it felt completing. I was sure that then Pink would join us too, if I could just find out what Randall needed and make a way to meet it.

Never mind comin', sister. Baby ain't. Doin' alright. Don't worry none.

Her second letter came not long after the first. I tried calling, but there was no Randall Moss listed in Hot Springs. So I wrote and asked her to call.

"It's all right," she said. "I'm doin' good."

"Honest to truth?"

"Randall says the waters here are...curative."

"So he's being good to you."

"We'll try again," she said. "Still could use your company if you've time."

I drove alone and stayed a month, most of which was time without Randall around. Pink and I laughed and shopped and looked at store-bought clothes and ate chocolate and read *Ladies' Home Journal*s and rested.

"What we both needed," Pink said as we sat drinking limeade beneath an awning that lifted and sighed in the breeze.

"Frank says I don't vacation well."

"Easier for me," Pink said. "My mind's always vacatin'."

"Oh, Pink. You demean yourself for no reason."

"Can't say I agree, sister," she said and wouldn't elaborate no matter how much I persisted.

"I wish Randall were here," I said. "So he could see how well you look."

"Like having you around," Pink said.

"And would all the time if you came back and lived in Lauderdale. If he's here so little, why don't you come back with me alone? You're an independent woman."

"Ain't what I signed on for, sister. I'll be a waitin' wife, right here."

In 1913 we remodeled our home, the old trading post, once again. We added an inside stairwell that led up to the bedroom and created a few smaller rooms, for guests who arrived more regularly now from up north and for whom the little cottages out back didn't seem enough. The stairwell had two landings, and at the base, Frank had installed a safe kept hidden behind my tall china cabinet. East-facing doors were cut in to transform the entrance. All the traffic came from the streets and the rebuilding town now, not from the river. More Seminoles walked rather than poled in to take the train north and south.

We'd painted the window and door frames a vibrant green against the white-painted pine. If you hadn't known it had once been a trading post, a place that marked the splicing of a people and their past, of invitation and transformation, you could not tell it of our home by looking at it now. It seemed that all but the shape and the hanging porches had changed.

"Maybe we should have Della come twice a week," Frank said. "Looks like spiderwebs grow overnight." He pointed to the ceiling above the fireplace.

"I can take care of my home. Don't you think I do?"

"Do fine," Frank said. "Just wishing to ease it a bit."

"Putting that brick fireplace in is what did it," I said. "Wood burning does bring on the spiders."

"Extra day of help for you wouldn't hurt."

"You're sweet, Frank, but Della's got four other homes she cares for. I'll be fine with what time I have of hers."

Without children, I should have been able to perform the cleaning and washing needed by myself and I would have, except for my interests—my "causes," as Louise called them. That Frank wanted me to have more of Della's time warmed me. He understood.

Della had been my day lady for years, walking from the part of town where her people liked to live. She "craved" the money, she said, for her six children, to supplement their father's long hours at the livery.

"Tomorrow's wash day. She'll come early. We can take care of those cobwebs then."

"What would you say about one of those wringers?" Frank said.

"With all those stories of arms getting sucked into the rollers? We'd still have to heat tubs of water, Frank."

I asked Della, a short and wiry woman with python arms that could squeeze and twist sheets as though they were napkins.

"Las' thing I need is a squatty contraption replacin' me," she said. "You best 'member that gettin' those wrinkles outta them machine-washed clothes'll take twice the ironin'. I don' do ironin'."

"I'd still do that. I like ironing. Very soothing."

"Way we do it now, you get outside, chile," Della chided as she poked at the fire. "Never will get rid a those plum circles under your eyeballs if we don' take in outside air. New-fangled thing'll have us sweatin' inside and no smoke 'round to scare the no-see-ems, neither."

"Well, if Papa and Albert and Gus move here, and Pink and Randall, too, I'll have Frank get us a wringer. But we'll still need you, Della, for all our homes."

"Miz Ivy, your family be a-multiplyin' faster than rabbits. And you still with the flattest belly in town!"

Frank stayed home more now. He worked mostly in his office, though he had meetings at the bank and the trade commission and the Deep Water Harbor Company he'd invested in. I sometimes thought he lingered at the dining room table over his eggs and herbs as a way to avoid the rumors and tensions surrounding some of his transactions.

I didn't really grasp it all, but I knew the Alexanders were distressed. D. C. Alexander was a Stanford graduate who had bought land and an old hunting lodge built near the sea. The lodge had ambled into thirty-seven rooms by the time Frank and I were married. That piece of property had a history of dissension. Arguments over the lodge had eventually broken up the two Chicago partners. Then Frank's Deep Water Harbor Company had become involved. There'd been rumors claiming Frank had been "underhanded" in some way, locking D. C. Alexander outside. But D. C. had his hotel and a fine site; and Louise had been my source of information.

"There are rumblings, Ivy, honey, over Frank's involvement in Las Olas by-the-Sea. That's what D. C. Alexander calls his place now. It'll be a fine hotel one day."

"People just don't always understand high finance," I said. "Business takes on strange ways and Frank's known for his, but 'underhanded' isn't one of them."

"I'm just saying what I've heard, honey," she said. "Just sharing information so people can know what might affect them later on."

"There's a fine thread between helpful information and common gossip, Louise."

"Oh, honey, don't I know it!"

After breakfasts, Frank often worked outside with me in the garden, digging where I asked him. We still kept a few chickens and he'd throw corn to them, feed the mule. He often took the *Jennie* down to check the farm, and those days he'd be gone most of the afternoon.

The city had done its part to occupy Frank's interests. He'd been elected to the council, and this time he had the responsibility of auditing a city bond sale as well. I would have thought the duties would keep him occupied, but he remained at the dining room table in the mornings, as though unsure of what to do with his time without the structure of the store.

He no longer had the postal service to look after, either. After the fire, the government moved the post office down the street and Frank decided it would be a good time to resign, let others take his place. He'd lost that daily routine as well.

I had high hopes for my brother's advancement with Frank's resignation, but Mrs. Susan Craig replaced my husband as the postmistress. It was a government decision. Bloxham stayed on as her assistant.

"I don't think your Frank gave him the most noble recommendation he might have, Ivy, honey," Louise said. She had the most perfect fingernails, hard and long and tapered with fine, high moons. She fussed with them now.

"I'm sure he would have," I said. "Frank has the highest regard for Bloxham. He always covered so well whenever we traveled."

The two of us were wiping off books that had been donated to the new library, the first project of the women's club after forming the Civic Improvement Foundation. I'd been elected president and gotten the candy store owner to set aside shelves for the 120 books we'd begin with. "We'll lure those children in with candy, then feed them with books," I'd said and convinced the owner.

Outside the window, the blue scrub jays chattered and flitted back and forth, arguing over the peanuts I'd set out for them on the porch rail.

"Seems a man who has served for as long as my husband would be naturally promoted," she said. A film of perspiration formed above her lip. I felt the same moisture against my skin. June could be so hot and humid. I'd left the door open even though the new, wider screen we'd ordered from Sears and Roebuck had not yet arrived.

"I'm sure it is disappointing for you," I said. "How does Bloxham feel, if I might ask?"

"Oh, honey, he never says an unkind word, not one, about your Frank." She picked up *Anne of Green Gables,* furrowed her thick, dark brows, showed me the book, then stacked it in the fiction pile when I nodded.

"I meant about not being the postmaster."

"Oh, he's a very patient man, takes his time."

"A sound Cromartie trait," I said, pushing against my knees to stand.

"Waiting and working toward what you believe in and want is never a waste of time."

"I suppose so. DeWitt's asked Frances to marry him but they've set no date. You knew they'd been courting? Of course, we waited a time, too. Anything less is so, common, don't you think?" She swiped at a leather-bound book, releasing the scent. "When it comes to Bloxham and his occupation, I think of it as more his having learned how to live in the shadows, honey, without the benefit of so much light as others."

"Frank doesn't cast a very large shadow over others. He's such a modest, unassuming man."

There was a pause before she spoke again.

"But Bloxham does have to live with the sun rising and setting on a strong-willed older sister. That's the shadow I was speaking of."

I stopped my book-stacking.

"Is that how Bloxham sees me, as a kind of competition to him?"

"It's my observation, not his." Her voice pinched out in its whine.

"Strong-willed," I repeated.

"People won't ever say it directly," Louise said, warming to her subject. "You're so...so formidable, staggering almost, making the rest of us feel tiny and insignificant."

"I can't make anyone feel anything," I said. "No one can. We're responsible for our own feelings. Only you can make yourself a victim."

"That takes you out of it nicely then, doesn't it?" she said. "Permits you to do just as you please without even having to see your part in an action."

Her words struck me like icy water to the face when I'd been expecting warm.

"We always have a choice about our attitude." I heard the defense in my voice, calmed, then asked, "Others feel the way you do?"

"No one would say, of course." She examined her hands, pushed against the cuticles. She had oil-paint stains on her fingertips and I remembered it had been a long time since she'd shown me any of her designs. "You do so much good for the town, honey." She chewed on her lower lip. "It's just, you never seem to notice when you've pruned someone back."

I watched her heart beating in a blood vessel in her slender neck. "That's really how you see me, with a shears, cutting away at people?"

"Bloxy sees only your soft side. Lots do think of you as generous and giving. I suppose I did too when I was in school. Mama thinks you're just the finest fruit. But bless your heart, honey, you're so parsimonious about sharing that refreshing side, some of us get, well, bruised just waiting to see."

I shook my head and sat, fanned at my face. "I have a purpose, yes, but I think we all do, if we listen to our hearts. I always felt I'd been told to do things that others couldn't, not because I was better but because I was, well, called to it. Had my own penance to pay." Louise lifted her eyebrows. "I don't think I need to be blabbing that all over the river. Suffice it to say that I try not to worry about what people think, but I don't want a distance with my brother."

"Don't tell Bloxham about what I've said." She avoided my gaze.

"You have every right to your opinion, Louise," I said. "Is all that yours?"

She nodded once, like a chastised child caught with the remains of hard candy.

"I've something to think about then," I said. "And for that I'm grateful, for your courage in bringing me the subject."

"Why, honey, I do believe you've paid me a compliment about something I never thought of myself as having. My, my. I'll come back later to help stack the books on the shelves," she said, bending at her waist to pat my hand. "Don't you sit and fret the day away now, you hear?"

Relief came in when she slipped out the open door.

Formidable? Staggering? Making others feel tiny and insignificant? I didn't think it possible I could "make" others feel anything. I hadn't assumed any glory when a student captured an idea or created something wonderful from within, as Tenley had with his "Every day searching/Yesterday's light." So why did I have to assume detrimental weight when the opposite occurred?

Louise had spoken out of spite, I thought, but at times treasures come wrapped in tatty paper.

I turned to close the door. Something moved slowly along the floor, a darkness within my peripheral vision. Sleek and black, it slithered in among the books before I could intercept it. I looked around for the broom, found it leaned behind the kitchen door, made enough noise to raise the dead while rustling books around. When the snake's head stuck out between two fat volumes, I struck at it, stunning it enough to turn the broom around and lift the three-foot form to drape over the wooden handle. Walking rapidly to the river, I tossed the snake, heard a splash, and looked upriver. Children swam, crossing to the pond apple tree perched on a far little island. They were safe enough, I decided. When the snake revived, it would be far downstream.

I couldn't let Louise's criticism keep me from my passions, from carrying out the purposes I'd been given, working out my faith within the everyday. A prayer lifted from me as I stood and watched the snake drift and float downriver: "I know I have tasks, Lord. Please forgive me when others are caught in the vortex of my efforts. Show me other ways. I only want to serve, with endurance, but learn new lessons, too, and gain wisdom while I teach."

Orange blossoms have the most fragrant of scents, and south Floridians come alive with them, inhaling their depth and freshness like well-fed cats that lift and sift and roll around in ivory lushness. The climate, steamy and moist, stirred us but not too swiftly, the way a lady moves melting ice around in her glass. Perhaps our climate made us lethargic, never having to worry, truly, over cold weather or coats. Year-round residents found themselves surrounded by those who came south for their health or to play, and it gave a hopeful mind-set to us, I think, that no obstacle toward a goal was too troublesome. The sun would shine soon and any rain promised to dry away. Challenges might detour but not thwart. They were part of life's adventure, like golfers learning to skirt alligators sunning themselves on fairways of new courses.

Albert, Papa, and Gus moved north to Fort Lauderdale at last, thanks to Frank's efforts and generosity in helping them find a place to live and work. Papa actually rested some after the move.

We gathered for a catfish fry at the seawall one evening. Gus herded an alligator out of the way.

"I see tourists tossing rocks and food at them," Bloxy said, nodding toward the gator. "Splash things in the water and they head right for it, thinking it's food."

"Best we not go swimming there, then," Albert said.

"Just don't splash," Frank told him. "Otherwise, it's fine. I take my laps most every day. Need to watch for the currents, though. Can be tricky."

"Sounds exciting," Albert said and coughed.

"Not before you get rid of that cough," I said, handing him a plate of catfish and fresh sliced tomatoes.

"Yes, sir, I mean, ma'am," he said and smiled as he gave me a military salute.

Frances, DeWitt's intended, fanned herself and spoke to Louise and Bloxy. DeWitt fiddled with his new camera while Frank refilled everyone's glasses with ice and limeade. I loved having family close. Only Pink was missing.

"She's expecting again," Papa said.

"Is she?"

"Said she was going to write you to come for another restful visit."

"I'll just do that," I said. "As soon as things settle down here."

I told myself I had plenty of time to see Pink, more than enough years to nurture and continue a sisterly relationship, find ways to get her from there to here.

But when I got the telegram, I took the fastest way to Arkansas and went by train.

Randall stood beside her holding her hand as I came in, setting my bags down on the flowered carpet. I'd hired a cab at the station, knowing when I received the telegram what I faced.

"When did it happen?" I said.

"Early yesterday. Doctor says there was sure nothing he could do. Probably four months. A girl," Randall said.

His eyes were puffy and red as he sat beside her on the bed. Pink's fingers stroked his head as though he needed comforting instead of her. Her lacy bed jacket hung on her shoulders, limp as line-hung laundry in July. A large cat the color of smoke curled beside her, and slender strands of its fur drifted in the air.

"It's the third I've lost, sister," Pink said. "Didn't tell you 'bout the first, happened so fast. Thought surely this one would be fine. I didn't do any-thin'," she said, "at least not I knew would cause a problem."

"You sure didn't," Randall said. "We thought the hot springs would be good for her. But I should've been here. Traveling so much." He ran a hand through his blond hair. He had little bags beneath his eyes.

"Now's the time to move back to Lauderdale," I said.

Pink nodded and stroked the cat. To Randall she said, "That way if you're gone, I'd have Ivy or Louise close by. Or we could move to Philadel-phia, be near your people and—"

"No, no. Not a good climate for you. You're so…fragile, Pink, you sure are. No, a lush southern clime, that's what you need." His thumb made circles on the back of her hand. "Let's think seriously about moving closer to Ivy here."

"All the Cromarties except you are in Lauderdale now," I said. "DeWitt and Gussie have more work to do than they can handle, building houses. They're logging the swamps and the pines and cypress are coming down so fast I actually wonder where the birds'll roost. Worse than the plume poachers. It'd be wonderful to have your gentleness nearby." I pat-ted Pink's shoulder, felt her warm forehead. "I'd keep her safe and sound, Randall. Feed her good food, make her stronger."

I brought a small oak chair up beside the bed and sat on it, pulling the gloves from my fingers as I talked. I laid my hand against Pink's forehead.

"You've a fever," I said. "Did the doctor leave you lobelia tincture? No? Let me fix you hyssop and yarrow tea, then. Maybe you should put the cat down. I've heard they can be bad for pregnant women."

"Not pregnant now." A tear made its way to her ear.

I reached for her then and held her in my arms, feeling helpless and use-less as she wept. "I just wish I could take it from you, Pink. I do."

"Not yours to have," she said. "My grieving to do."

I dabbed at her eyes with a fragrant hankie. "Come, Randall. Let's let her be still. We'll be right next door, Pink."

She nodded and closed her eyes. Her hand stroked the cat as I closed the door.

Randall and I sat in high-back chairs across the dining room table of their furnished apartment. A crocheted doily marked the table center. Pink hadn't put out many of her personal things, which surprised me. I commented on it.

"She hopes we won't be staying here," he said. "Wants a home of our own somewhere besides Hot Springs." I noticed the slightest nasal quality to his words I hadn't heard before. Maybe New England? "But there sure are some classy real estate options developing. I'd hoped to get us a house before the baby came. Don't like children to begin in rentals myself. I simply didn't move fast enough." He ran his hands through his hair again and I noticed a small thinning patch that he made sure to comb over, even with his fingers.

His hands stopped in midair. "You don't think that contributed...?"

"Not likely," I said, "though tension doesn't help. But it would be good for her to be closer to family, even a doctor she knows, before the next one."

He sat quietly, staring out the window. Spanish moss hung like long hummingbirds' nests from the oaks. Sparrows chirped loudly in the bushes beside the house, answered by a dove.

"Frank has a number of contacts, Randall. I'm sure if you spoke with him, or Will Kyle, there'd be something. He has land investments he shares with Frank. There's the Everglades Growing Field and the lumber company. Frank wants to build a roller-skating rink, which could turn into a steady income, year-round. You wouldn't have to leave at all. You'd do well with tourists and families. Personable."

"You're sure kind, Ivy. Frank, too. But a man wants to do it himself, of course. On his own. Without charity."

"Never considered what a family gave as charity," I said.

"'Doing good for good-for-nothing people,' that's what Elizabeth Barrett Browning said charity was."

"I didn't know you read the poets, Randall."

"Write a bit, too," he said.

"You never cease to surprise me."

"Distract me," Pink said the next morning when I helped her sit up on the side of the bed. "Tell me about your meetin' in Tallahassee. Will all Florida go dry? Are we women going to get the vote then?"

"Yes to both, eventually, especially if May Mann Jennings has anything to say about it. I do like her, Pink. Do you want to try to walk?"

Pink nodded, and with my hand under her elbow, she took a few guarded steps. "Don't step on Mazy," she said.

"Whatever happened to your rat? What was her name?"

"Vanilla. Eloped." Pink laughed.

"She's the head of the Women's Federation now, you know."

"Vanilla?"

"Oh, you. May Jennings. There's a committee on Indian Affairs as well as women's suffrage and preserving the beauty of Florida and having decent places for people to live. She's even in favor of a statewide library, and, almost too good to be true, compulsory education for all children, regardless of color. It's as though my whole life's interests are right there under her direction!"

"It is such a pleasure havin' you here." Pink squeezed me as I turned her around to head back to the bed. "I just feel like fresh juice when you're around. So comforted and safe."

"Feeling safe. Well, I'm pleased you do. That Randall needs to be more on hand. It's important for a man to feel he's provided well for his wife, given her shelter."

"It's funny, sister," she said. "I think some, that Randall…" She was breathless with the effort to walk and talk at the same time.

"Here, let's get you back into bed." I tucked her feet in, fluffed up her pillows, and brought a cool glass of lemonade I set next to the bed. "Now, let's talk about what you think with regard to Randall."

"It's nothin'." She looked away. "Put Mazy up here, will you?"

"Come on, now. That Randall what? Travels too much? Doesn't want children? Go ahead." I lifted the cat. It's ash-colored body and whiskers reminded me of the manatees I so loved.

"Did he say that?" She looked alarmed.

"No, he didn't, and I don't know why I even said that."

She sank back into the bed. "He adores children. You should see him when we're on the street walkin'. Little people just run right up to him, they know he's so loving."

"What, then?"

"I don't know." She shrugged her shoulders. "Just somethin'."

"Postpartum blues," I said, patting her hand. "That's what it is. Randall adores you. Even I can see that."

"Maybe I'm too old for this." She sighed. "Twenty-nine, Randall keeps remindin' me."

"It isn't...necessary, you know." I reached for the cat's tail and ran it through my palm. It let me.

Pink's eyes held a question.

"To have children. For a woman to be fulfilled."

"But I want them!" Her words wore an ache, desire wrapped in sorrow.

"And I want that for you. I just wanted you to know there were other choices, other ways to see a thing. Frank and I have a rich life, one blessed despite our not having a family." I pulled at a thread on her wedding-ring quilt. I'd made it myself and stitched each tiny strand that held it together, comforting and warming my sister.

"But don't you feel...incomplete?"

"Not in the least. Why, I barely have time to sew Frank's shirts. I actually bought one for him in a ready-made store when I visited Tallahassee last and it was quite well manufactured—which is good, since I expect suffrage and prohibition will take much of my time and free more women to do things other than stitch and clean."

"Sounds like a speech you've heard, sister."

"Does it? Mary Munroe might have said a word or two like that. She's a great crusader for important causes, too. I've got to get my sewing scissors to snip that thread."

Pink pointed to her dresser drawer where I found a basket tucked beneath embroidered linen. My distraction proved insufficient.

"How is it you and Frank don't have children?" Pink asked. When I didn't answer she continued. "Or have you been with child and never told me? You haven't lost one?"

I focused intently on the thread, snipping it and looking for others frayed and difficult to see against the white background. Cat hair camouflaged. Louise's admonition of my "formidability" still rang in my ears. Protection and exposure battled in my head.

"We made a choice, early on," I said, "to put our energies into other facets of conjugal life. Into service, really." She raised her eyebrows. "Does that sound pretentious? I don't mean it to be. Not having a family has freed us, I'd say, to put our passion and devotion into civic things. Frank's work with the city, his trading contracts, the banks; mine with the Women's Federation, education, and city planning. It could affect many people, even your children someday, Pink. We can give to others that way, without our having to feel torn between family and future."

"I suppose it's how Catholic sisters and Tibetan monks justify hoverin' inside convents," Pink said.

"I hadn't thought of it as hovering or hiding or even similar." I heard the stiffness in my own words and softened. "Most such celibates are quite active in the world, Pink, doing work that needs doing."

"Celibate sounds so…distant."

"Married women without children by their choice doesn't mean we're cold or distant or hiding either."

"Didn't mean to criticize, sister. Just makin' an observation."

"How did we get on this subject, anyway? My fault," I said, raising my finger to the air. "Wanting to offer a way to look at loss that didn't fit you. I'm sorry. Weren't we speaking of you and Randall and maybe a welcome move to Lauderdale?"

Pink nodded.

"I'd just like to see him take a position more permanent that requires less traveling."

"That would be nice, wouldn't it?"

"I'll talk with Frank, see what I can do, if you'd like."

When she didn't answer, I thought she probably hadn't heard.

Randall returned to his trips back and forth from north to west and the only concession he made moved Pink back to south Florida, but not to Lauderdale. He wouldn't even consider letting me talk with Frank, and while I admired his independence, I thought him naively selfish as well. I also felt, well, unsuccessful—not able to give to my family, who mattered to me most of all.

They chose Miami where there were "more diversions."

"But I thought you wanted to be with the rest of us." We sat together in their rented cottage without even a view of the sea.

"You'll be travelin' almost as much as Randall, what with the Federation and all," she said.

"You get that awful cough here in winter," I said.

"Folks say the cough's related to the red tides. They're comin' up the New River, too," she said.

"Frank thinks the tides might be affecting the manatees," I said, "but I've never heard anyone associate their declining numbers with illness. They're damaged mostly from the shipping, I think. Sometimes I see long scars on their backs from the blades. Doesn't seem logical tides could cause coughs."

Pink shrugged her shoulders. She stood, placed a piece of catfish onto a china plate, and set it on the floor. Mazy and two kittens came forth, their tails twisting between her legs as they dove for the food.

"You can drive your Ford this way, visit Mary Munroe and me. When you and Randall are gone, I'll have familiar sights to occupy my time. 'Member those Cuban places?" She grinned at me and I loved the joy in her face, the way she could move away from disaster, soak up what she needed from everyday things to strengthen her spirit.

"Now, don't you go flirting," I said. "Remember, if you don't want the garden you'd best not plant the seed."

"I'm faithful as a goose." She laughed. "I just like pleasurin' my eyes. Takin' up paintin', did I tell you? Louise's idea, but I doubt she knows about the naked models our instructor has us drawin'. Such fine bodies. Paint flowers, too," she added when I raised my eyebrows. "Somethin' beautiful and soothin' to think on'll surely bring Randall's next child to full term."

CHAPTER THIRTEEN

Did you visit some camps?" I asked Frank. He'd put the *Jennie* away so late in the day.

He nodded and his eyes told me he'd been brooding, saddened by something.

"The town's almost growing around them, isn't it? Do you think they'll be forced out?"

"Possible."

"Could we give them our land near there? Sell it to them?"

"Farm's not very big. Might hold things off for a time. We've donated land for parks and other things in town, guess we could think about it. Might try to buy the land beyond, sell it to Jumpers or Osceolas on time payments, maybe."

"Why don't you pursue that," I said. "You know, I haven't seen Esther since a day ages ago, when a set of twins were born."

"Could visit her."

"Oh, I wouldn't want to—"

"Intrude."

Women's suffrage, the Women's Federation, and the Indian Affairs Committee all consumed me in 1915. There were rallies in Washington, D.C., and New York, where I shared rooms with women whose influence went far beyond a little village on the New River. These women knew politicians and financiers and at least a dozen ways around a problem. I wanted to reassure Frank that my involvement with the cause would only come to good, especially when he sent the letter to the Hotel Netherlands in New York.

It arrived with the themes of Reverend Holding's latest sermon: women belonged at home, beside their husbands and guiding their children. That was the first part of Frank's distress. Hiram Frost's complaints about Frank's involvement in commerce with the Indians, selling land to them in the "guise of protection," and cheating others from the purchase, that came next.

Frank's letter carried distress; mine back to him fired off just plain mad.

I'm sorry that Bro. Frost has had his plans so upset but you know that ridiculing people publicly from the platform is a preacher's privilege and he has long considered himself such without the benefit of study or certificate. As for harm to me is concerned, that is utterly impossible, for he and a dozen Holdings cannot prove that I ever did any harm to my family or home and have stood only for the cause and against the wrongs that need resistance. As for what Holding says regarding any graft, just let him have all the rope needed and he will hang himself. Just as surely as he and Frost are doing these things, they will have to reckon for them. They are both good church members as is usual, you know. However, if Holding goes too far with this graft I would make him swallow some of it but keep your head. You and I have seen many attacking us go down in defeat, and we scarcely notice it. I should just like Frost to keep my name out of his mouth. I am sure what you told him was plenty.

When I returned home, Frank gave me more detail.

"He took on quite a number of the Federation's pets," Frank said. "Fears government-run libraries will bring sinful books into the hands of innocents."

"Holding said that? From the pulpit?"

"My summary. Didn't comment on the plume trade. Only thing he left out. Reserved greatest invective for women voting. 'That's how Eve changed all the world for all mankind, pushing beyond her limits and pushing Adam beyond his, pressing to change laws given by God Himself.'"

"Rubbish," I told Frank. "Pure rubbish. Don't you even think that anti-suffragists have merit," I said. "It bothers me greatly that the minister proclaims negative things from the pulpit, with others having to hear it from the voice of 'ecclesiastical authority.' Makes it sound like God has said it Himself."

I'd had plenty of time to work up a steam on the train heading home. Frank picked me up at the station in the *Jennie,* tossed my carpetbag into the bow of the boat, then helped me step down off the dock. His hands felt warm against mine, almost a little damp.

"Suppose I shouldn't have written to you of the situation. Got agitated."

"Bully pulpit to speak their minds, that's what they all have; and their parishioners just have to sit there and take it." I smoothed my skirts as though my hands held heavy irons.

A slight grin eased onto Frank's face. "Never would have tried it with you sitting there in front of him."

"The coward!"

"As for Brother Frost..."

"He wanted the property, didn't he? The part of the land you bought then sold to Johnny Jumper and a few of the others?"

He nodded.

"I knew it!"

"Didn't know until everything was signed. Claiming Seminoles can't own property. Supposed to live where the government puts them, if they ever do. Like at Dania."

"You practically gave them the land. That's not graft. If you had, Frost would have claimed it an unfair transaction that way, too. Just because it's good land and close in. That's why they wanted it."

"Suppose the commercial potential of it, too."

"But that's where they've lived, Frank. This is what they wanted. It was a good thing to do."

"Hmm. But Frost might be right. People will keep crowding in on them, even if they own the land. There'll be legal challenges, too. Frost surely will, and Seminoles won't fight the squatters. Never do. May have given them more time but not a solution."

Frank turned the boat toward the ocean instead of our house. "Had Della pack a lunch," he said to my questioning eyes. "Thought we'd have a picnic like we used to, out at the beach, try to forget all this folderol."

"Wonderful," I said.

I felt my shoulders drop, the steam of my fury fade away in his presence. We putted and waved at familiar people who noticed us and lifted their hands to their hats and waved back. "Apparently not everyone thinks we need chastising."

Sea grapes and ferns dropped over the water. Yellow orchids dotted the oak trees with clusters of color. Wild hibiscus bloomed orange and shot up through the grasses on undeveloped land along the water. The New River was still a restorative place for me, welcoming in my return.

We ate fried chicken, slices of orange and mango and tomato, and soft rolls, the latter one of the things Della was famous for. Frank leaned back and put his hat over his eyes, crossed his fingers over his stomach, and in the shade of a palm, fell asleep. I couldn't.

"I'm going for a walk," I said to Frank's grunt. He turned on his side and slept on. I set the umbrella to shade him.

In the distance I saw people moving, their parasols floating like lily pads above their heads. I slipped off my shoes and strode out along the sandy beach. Soft lines of foam formed far out toward the horizon and moved in toward shore to sigh onto the sand. After fast walking, I slowed. With my foot, I lifted at strings from the palmettos and broken chunks of palm bark littering the beach.

I bent to pick up tiny periwinkle shells as small and perfect as a baby's fingernail and marveled at their perfection. Fans of multicolored shells dotted the beach in a high tide line. An occasional bougainvillea petal brought bright pink to the mark, a flash of color in an otherwise shell-crushed line. Such abundance from the sea and communion with the land never failed to humble me, never ceased to bring ease.

The walk and the view settled my anger, though the accusations from the pulpit distressed me still. I stared out at the water and the fluffy clouds billowed in the distance. Reverend Holding had no right to use religion as a weapon to whip people into his view of morality, no right to tell one whole facet of humanity that they were the enemy, causing great social harm unless they stayed quarantined in their own homes, out of the voting sites, as though inflicted with a social disease. Women were his main target, but his words attacked anyone who wanted to right injustices, anyone who longed for more for their children than they'd had for themselves. He wanted us to feel isolated, sequestered, set apart from the world and alone. It was not the sweet communion I knew Christianity was meant to be.

Confronting an adversary directly did not appeal to me. I feared it, the strong feelings, the pounding of my heart; but I feared not standing for a cause much more. That sense of rightness overcoming fear had come on early in me.

It happened after the baby died. I must have been around ten, maybe eleven. Despite feeling great relief at Papa's response to my actions, I'd felt burdened, too, thick and sluggish for months. I know I cried often for no reason, at least none I could see. The slightest raised voice caused me to shiver and scurry and huddle in a corner. I didn't often have the luxury. Too much to do with Mama down, too many children with noses to wipe, diapers to change and then wash.

Cries of a seagull, cats that wailed, the screech of a windmill at work, all sounded like Mama crying the day I let her baby die. The sounds could turn me into a shivering ball. Sometimes I'd just sit on the sand and rock. Some days pinched with the painful distractions; others carried a heavy, foggy loss. I couldn't control when the fear would seize me. It rose up like a shark out of water: swift, sure, and bent on destruction. I started imagining terrible things, seeing fear in the faces of once-friendly people, and watching for pain in the benign every day.

There'd been no one, not an aunt or neighbor, no one who had seen me disappear inside myself, no one willing to stand beside my brothers and sister to help while Mama healed. Perhaps because we'd moved so much, few knew us; perhaps because we set ourselves as independent folk who, as I'd heard Papa say, "can handle things ourselves," perhaps that's why no one offered a hand.

One day I took an early morning walk alone. Almost as soon as I arrived on the beach, I wondered if I should even be there. Bad things could happen to children alone: panthers spring out of palms; wild boars rip and tear; snakes loop down from trees. Even sand was a danger: the poisonous man-of-war could lurch from it, unsuspecting.

But that day, I encountered peace.

It wasn't an audible voice, not a vision—nothing as dramatic as that.

But a presence, a sensation that washed over me. It began at the warm sand at my feet and moved through me until I felt tears press against my nose and pool at my eyes.

"You are my child, Ivy. I will give you strength and protection. I know the plans I have for you and they are plans to give you a future and a hope. Do what no one else can do."

The words sounded like familiar Scripture; but it was the use of my name that astounded me.

I actually turned around to see if Papa walked on the sand, but I was alone, the sound of the waves all I could hear. A line of brown pelicans floated just inches above the water, scanning then lifting to slice the sky.

The Presence promised safety and that I had work to do, but there would always be a way to make a choice that moved me closer to God's will. I need never be paralyzed with fear even though I might feel it; never have to cower in shame or humiliation if I did His work. I'd been given all the power I needed to do what He'd set before me. I need only trust in Him.

It had been the first time I felt peace and power braided together as one.

Those twin emotions stirred now inside of me as I thought of Reverend Holding and Brother Frost. Frank slept off in the distance. A town we cared about and had helped build bustled beyond sight. But people who mattered—perhaps whom only God knew by name—needed sheltering.

I did not believe I acted outside of God's will. I'd made prayerful choices, learned to discipline myself so I was usable, or so I hoped. Still, almost everything I believed in appeared to be directly opposed to Holding and his partner Frost. They were religious leaders, spiritual counselors who also followed God's divine plan for *their* lives.

Was it my place to challenge ecclesiastical practice? Tiny prickles poked at the base of my neck with that question. I sank into the sand to my ankles. I would have to hold a conversation.

June marked the season of storms.

The Sunday I chose to "confer" with Frost and Holding, the humidity made our skin scream for rain, to get it over with, drench us fair and square so fresh breezes could blow in and offer cooling. I suppose that described my wish to deal with Reverend Holding and Brother Frost as well.

Brother Frost came first. He smiled as we stood fanning ourselves waiting to walk into church. I knew he'd be there and felt certain it was the place to talk.

"Will you help us serve Communion this morning, Brother Stranahan?" Hiram asked, reaching out to shake Frank's hand.

"Suppose so."

"Well, good. Don't want no pridefulness over last week to come between good Christians. Mrs. Stranahan." He removed his hat for me and nodded. "Glad to see you've revived."

"Arrived. Yes, Friday last," I said.

His pocked cheeks turned pink.

"Arrived, yes. Heard you were in New York—" he emphasized the *New*— "at one of those women's gatherings." He shook his head at a fly. Strands of hair stayed plastered across his balding spot. "That's a worry, you working on those Indian and suffrage things. Not good for a woman to leave a man's side to involve herself with such, though I know you don't agree, do you, Frank?"

"I believe the Bible gives women both the authority and the ability to get things done," I said. "Takes a strong and faithful man to recognize that."

"Believe Mordecai did so with Esther," Frank offered. He flicked at an imaginary fly by his ear.

"Why, thank you, Frank. I hadn't thought of that, but yes, he did. He knew that risk was necessary for God to work out a great result and helped Esther see it, too."

Frost sniffed, reached for his handkerchief, put his hat beneath his arm, then blew his nose.

"Two of you like peas in a cob," he said. "Won't change the facts, though: the heathens have no treaty, so no rights. Ought not have land. End up being squatted on, bringing sewage and poor sanitation practically downtown—and you say you love this place. Have a strange way of showing it."

"I'm sorry you see it that way, Brother Frost. I fear we walk on different trails."

"You're being led down yours," he said, "and not by any force for good."

"Now, wait—"

"No, Frank, let me." I took a breath. "Brother Frost, I believe God gave women and men the power to influence others for good. That's really all I've tried to do."

"Eve wanted to sway things, too," he sneered. I noticed several others moving closer in, fanning themselves as they sought something of interest in our threesome. "See where Eve took us."

"Ah, yes, Eve. Well, she was a woman made of bone, after all. She gave us that legacy, too. Strength, so we can stand against wrongs. Have the backbone to do what must be done, despite resistance, and not grow weary and whine. Be like the woman in Luke who kept demanding justice until the judge gave it, mostly because she persisted. That's me," I said. "Wanting to stand against disgrace and shame and injustice until all are changed."

"Got a lot of standing ahead o' ya then," Brother Frost said. He put his hat back on his head and looked over mine as though seeking support or an easy escape. It pleased me that he received neither.

Then the church bell clanged, calling us in.

"What I want, Brother Frost, before we step in to worship," I said, touching his arm, "is to accomplish what God wants me to, even though I'm a woman, even though I may make enemies, even though it may take my whole life, even when I'm misunderstood."

"Even though you descended from Eve?"

"Even though I descended from Eve, which you did too, Brother Frost, which you surely did, too."

I don't remember much of Reverend Holding's sermon that day. My mind desperately wished just to worship, to have that sense that I had come to give my all and praise Him for the place and grace to do it.

I did until the offertory. Then I disconnected from the order of worship as my mind composed a speech to Holding. I revised it during the hymn we sang—"The Church's One Foundation" (though it was one of my favorites)—going over each point in my head: the role of women and how I wasn't damaging my family because I worked for justice and education and the right to vote; how I wanted the church to seek after those things too, to proclaim the gospel through our actions to shelter others. I gasped just in the thinking of it. I wasn't sure when I'd give my speech to Holding, but I was sure I would.

Then during the sacrament of Communion, it happened. The day had stayed so hot, so sweltering hot. All the windows stood open so we could watch the greenery droop in the heat, hear the birds muted by the dense air, and long for any breeze at all that flirted by. We fanned ourselves without stopping but not even a ribbon on Mary Jo Dunlop's pigtail stirred in the pew before me.

Frank left my side to assist with the Communion trays and cups. We had partaken of the grape juice and broken bread together and remembered why we did. The whole congregation waited to be dismissed, to find a cooling place outside. Reverend Holding held a tray of cups in each hand. His eyes scanned the congregation and then he said the words that changed it all for me: he asked, loud enough for all inside to hear: "Has everyone been served?"

I know he meant it for the sacraments we'd just celebrated, to make sure none had been turned away from the Communion table, but the question clanged against my mind like the call-to-worship bell. We'd completed our Communion, accepted forgiveness for our sins, and now the important question remained: "Has everyone been served?"

Wasn't that just what Christ had said to Peter when he told him, "Feed my sheep" from the Gospel of John? Jesus asked if his disciples, his students, loved him, then said that if they did, they must serve. "Feed my sheep"; protect and shelter them, nurture; that's what He'd commanded.

There were sheep in need: men, women, and children, people of color, people I didn't even know but who were part of my family. Even the landscape had needs. This church might not reach out to them, but I would.

"Has everyone been served?" No, I decided, they had not.

I thought of standing, of answering Holding with the clarity I had inside my head, but didn't. Not out of fear but out of love, for Frank, for my own family, who might have sunk inside their pews to hear me speak my piece right there, right then.

I had my confirmation and that was enough. I was to serve in whatever way I could even if that meant I must find another congregation who could shelter and serve others, nurture and protect; who would shelter and serve me, too.

"Can I go with you to the camp?" I asked Frank. I helped him with his jacket, securing the button of his collar at the back of his neck, smoothing out the seams along the shoulders.

"Never wanted to before," he said, looking at me in the mirror as I came around from behind him. The gas lights glowed in the early evening.

"I know."

"Always been welcome. In fifteen years, you've never wanted to come. Might not be the best time. It'll be all night, likely."

"I thought that if I went with you today, when Sam fetched you and saw me here, too, that my presence wouldn't be, oh...you know."

"Get your wagon clothes on then," he said. "We're not going in your car."

Frank hitched the high-sided wagon to the mule, loaded it with a shovel and linen sheets, then stopped at the storage shed and piled in a bag of flour and salt pork. He signaled the Osceola man that we would follow, then stepped on the foothold, picked up the reins with one hand, and reached with his other to pull me up. His eyes held mine in the shadow of my straw hat for a moment before he stepped back to give me more room to sit.

"Seems strange, you coming along. But nice." His lips eased into a grin in a straight slice across his face.

Frank let loose the brake and set his booted foot up on the edge, smacked his lips to the mule and flicked the reins. We headed out. Frank wore hand-cobbled boots. I remembered the pair that had been damaged in the steel trap when he'd come courting and how much the replacement must have cost him. In recent months I'd tried to buy him a pair of ready-made, but his high arch made him nearly impossible to fit. Only his toes slipped inside the boots I'd bought him. We'd given them to Albert, who had entered his teen years preceded by his large feet.

The wagon rumbled over dried palm fans blown from the trees. Puffs of dust rose up from the mule and the wheels, and our noise scattered wild turkeys roosting in the overhanging trees.

"Did he say why he wanted you?"

"Said bring the wagon. Usually means a death."

I hadn't realized such an often-used road had been cut into the swamp. I supposed that with the drainage, walking served their purpose better than poling.

We rode in silence. It was dusk and I bent over to check the lantern. As always, Frank had filled it so we'd have a light to mark the way home. My fan chased away the night bugs from our faces though they settled on Frank's hands without disturbance.

I smelled the smoke of cooking fires before I could see the camp. A wall of palmetto fronds circled the area like the security fences around European castles I'd seen in photographs. We drove in through a narrow gate.

Chickees draped in tropical shadow sat orderly around a central gathering area that was filled now with solemn-faced people. Sam directed us toward a certain thatched section where people hovered. The wind lifted the tips of the roof fronds the Seminoles called pom poms, and I could hear the turtle rattles and the men's rhythmic chanting coming from inside. The group parted, and Frank stopped before the palmettos that were brown now, had lost all the green brightness that marks a freshly built home.

"Wait here," he said. He stepped down and bent toward the chickee. I could only see the backs of people hovering around the platform.

The sense of loss lingered everywhere: in the silence of the palms, the distant barking of dogs kept away, the stooped posture of people. Family members, I assumed, stood quietly near the opening of the home. I felt a rising discomfort at not knowing what to do. I didn't need to know any of them personally to feel the sense of loss; their faces invited the sharing of burdens. I just didn't know what to do.

Frank backed away. He motioned me in toward the platform and I passed in front of him. Walking past a wooden box labeled "salt pork," my eyes adjusted to the darker shadows of the palm thatch and fell onto the raised platform used for sleeping. That was when I saw her, the body lying wrapped, the face exposed and still. A child.

Esther leaned over her, her eyes raising to mine as I knelt beside her. I put my arms around her. She leaned into me and wept.

Must have been a little sister, I thought. I hadn't realized she had one.

There are no words sufficient to the loss of a sister, the pain of a child's death.

Esther sat back, her eyes sunken inside hollow caves, wet and dark. The scarred portion of her face, her left cheek and ear, looked rippled in the dusky light.

Stretch Johnson appeared through the darkness. I felt more than saw his presence, bold and wild. His being there seemed more foreign than mine until I saw him place his nail-chipped hands on Esther's shoulders. She leaned her face into his fingers, not unlike the way Frank would to mine.

Esther was just a child, for heaven's sake! What was this man thinking of? I looked at his face and answered my own question. It was their child we'd come to bury.

Esther patted his hand at her shoulder. The act censored my thoughts and I bit back the stinging words I thought to say.

"What happened?" I said before I saw Frank shake his head.

None of the natives spoke but Stretch did, his words spit out.

"Died," he said. "Don't know what of. In her gut. Couldn't keep anything inside, not even water or teas. Just kept screaming."

"I do nothing wrong, not wrong," Esther said. She looked at me then, her eyes seeking confirmation. She fidgeted on the rough platform she sat on.

"'Course it ain't from nothing you done," Stretch said. "Don't let no outsider say it so." He dropped down on one knee in front of her to touch her face with his hands. "You're a good mama. We'll have others."

Esther stared at me. Everything I thought to say sounded hollow, and I knew it wouldn't take the terrible emptiness from her eyes.

Frank motioned for me to sit off to the side. He sat too. Mary Gopher, the wife of Johnny Jumper, entered then, followed by a girl about ten or twelve years old. Taller than the other women and with a handsome beauty, Mary had a presence that said she was in charge. I thought she might object to my being there, but she didn't seem to see me at all. Mary had a mission and she set about it, taking the child from its mother, washing it, then dressing the baby. Twin boys played quietly in a corner as the women wrapped the infant with a soft leather hide followed by a colorful block of material draped across the form. Then people came and went and stood about while Esther rocked over the baby. Smudge lamps lit the night, giving faces of the chanters and the workers a ghostly look full of shadows and light.

They sang accompanied by the rattles, swishing like a steady rain against tin. The chants, though unfamiliar, were as soothing as a psalm, and I found myself drifting to another place.

Not long before dawn, Frank tapped me on my shoulder. I'd fallen asleep, my hat askew as I huddled in the corner.

"We'll be going soon," he said. "Almost dawn."

Mary Gopher came to take the child and she walked out with her in her arms.

Esther stood to leave. Other women walked on either side of her, helping her stand, holding her in her grief. The men joined Stretch, and I thought it kind that the parents weren't left to be the sole support of each other, the whole camp becoming a family to share their grief. Frank and I followed.

Esther and Stretch with two or three others climbed onto the back of the wagon, where the tiny form was held by Mary. Others planned to walk behind. Frank swung himself up onto the wagon and reached for my hand.

"I want to walk behind, with the mourners. Do you think that will be all right?"

"Be fine," he said.

Frank started off. I pulled my cape tighter against the dawn air. A small child, a boy, came from nowhere to take my hand, and that was how we made our way, following other mourners.

Frank drove without direction, and I realized he'd been a part of many burials deep within the swamps. Just at dawn, the wrapped form was laid within a shallow grave. Already the seepage of water formed a darkness around it, a watery grave that would hold the infant's form only. Its spirit had gone on.

I said my own prayer over Esther's baby, not unlike all the other prayers I'd offered when a child had died or a baby was not allowed to see a sunrise melt across the sea. Not a chastisement or an angry prayer, but one of question, trying to understand the purpose in a tiny birth and single shortened life.

Esther moved beside me then, and I reached my arm around her shoulders and we stood together. "The right word spoken at the right time is as beautiful as gold apples in a silver bowl." It was a Proverb that came to mind, but I did not say it to her. Instead I thought the words, prayed them silently as I held her to me: that I would give her words of wisdom, offered to open her clear and perceptive mind; give her words of comfort so she could feel the love I had for her that might lift and buoy her in the swirling waters of her loss. I prayed for words of joy, spoken to make her spirit laugh and see the brightness of a future filled with those who cared for her. And I wished to give her words of endurance, words to inspire her and support her and yet to let her know of my great confidence in her own courage to continue on. I wanted to nourish her soul, place apples in her silver bowl.

I spoke none of it, but I believe I was a hollow reed that allowed the prayer to flow through me to her, for I felt her relax against me, a girl who was taller than me now and who had survived what no one ever plans for, the loss of one's child.

We stood, the scent of wet and dried palmettos, of cypress trees, mangoes, and swamp swirling around us. A screech owl hooted into the silence. The deep throatiness of bullfrogs barked in the distance.

I wished that I could know what moved inside Esther's heart, that she could speak words—or I could—that held mutual understanding. But we couldn't. We didn't. And so I hoped that what I sent to her in prayer would tell her, that she'd feel the strength I left behind for her, within the Comforter's care.

Frank and I drove back in silence. I stayed awake when we arrived home, fixed steamed chocolate, wondering about them, what I held back from those I loved and why.

Sometime later, when the sun was high over the bougainvillea and I'd swept old purple blossoms and dried leaves from the porch, I asked Frank about the illnesses and sicknesses in the camps.

"Stomach worms. Whooping cough. Things all babies get without access to proper treatment. That's what they die of."

"But there are medicines that would help. And hygiene practices that could make a difference. There's a new pharmacist, that Alfred Beck, who seems easy to talk with. He might have a suggestion."

"Has a nice young wife, too."

"Does he?"

With a towel, I dried a handful of raisins I kept in a water jar in the ice-box, then plopped them into the oatmeal and sliced the banana, preparing our regular morning meal.

"Didn't I hear that Mary Gopher treats people with medicines?" I asked, setting Frank's bowl in front of him. "It seems a crime for us to have such supplies and not them."

"If it looks like it comes from us, from white people or the government, they won't touch it. Don't trust it. Hard not to blame them."

"Children shouldn't suffer because of old wounds. They're blameless. It's why I'm pushing for the government to hang on to the land for them. It ought not to go on forever."

"The sins of the fathers, and all that," Frank said. "No?" he said, responding to my scowl. "There's no changing that, Ivy. Don't even try."

But I did, of course. It was something within me that would not settle.

I began going out to the camp whenever Frank did, pushing him a bit to check with the Tigertail men about the egg contracts or some such excuse.

We occasionally met others on the road, tourists. The Seminoles had set themselves up as a sight to be seen and like those in Miami and out at the Big Cypress swamp, were now charging twenty-five cents for the privilege. They'd spilled over onto more lands now and paid fees to those owners, Frank said, for allowing them to remain.

They didn't charge us to come through the gate. We drove Frank's buggy into the camp and pulled up beside Esther and Stretch's home. Our wheels drove into the impression they'd left on visits before. Stretch usually grunted when he saw me and left without speaking.

At first I came along just to visit with Esther. I brought material for her to sew and new colored threads. Children would peek around the beige sides of the chickee and eventually smile. With the nod of a parent's permission, I gave them sweets and guavas in season, pulling the fruit from the car trunk.

Away from the impending war, from the arguments Reverend Holding might advance, from worrying over Randall and Pink, I gained a kind of sustenance beneath Esther's chickee, and my presence appeared to take nothing from them.

Some days I watched men carving egrets and alligators out of the soft cypress wood, and a line of them stood on a table near the gate for tourists to buy. I'd overhear their conversations, those tourists who had found their way to this camp.

"Why do they live this way, so dirty and primitive?"

This from a New Englander spoken in front of a grandfather carving a small canoe. She spoke as though he weren't there.

"Just filthy, that's all. Look at the cans and things tossed about. They must live on lard. Papers folded there. No wonder they're overweight. Disgusting." This from a midwestern matron who knew nothing of the staples survival required.

Women sat in the shade of a long chickee, making dolls, twisting the rust-colored palmetto fibers into faces.

"They're really quite inventive," her friend commented. The midwesterner put gloves on before picking up the toy to examine its construction.

Annie Tommie, a tall Seminole woman, stood off to the side. I could tell she understood what was being said and her eyes looked across the heads of the women into mine.

I wanted to confront the women's bias and ignorance, to be Mary Munroe charging up to people she felt were unjust, but I didn't. The way Annie Tommie looked at me said she understood, approved, in fact, in not wasting passion on people who would not be convinced with one encounter to change their minds.

During my visits, I sewed with Esther and the friends she occasionally invited to her chickee. Annie Tommie came by often. I liked that woman, the way she looked after Esther and other young women, treated them with dignity and respect regardless of their clan affiliation or their age, at least as far as I could tell.

Sometimes I brought along parts for the portable sewing machines. Esther always made sure those who needed the small screws got them. She sorted through the material too, and I noticed each woman received something and Annie Tommie took whatever was left over. I saw her later distributing it to others.

When Frank asked what I'd been doing there, I told him, "Making alterations, tugging gently at threads that hold seams together, considering a newer, stronger stitch."

"Hmm," he said, staring through his round glasses.

America would go to war, at least that's what the newspapers implied. It was all people wanted to talk about at the city zoning and planning committee meetings. By my presence there, I hoped to clarify the garbage collection problems and responsibilities. A part of me chuckled, remembering the tourists' chastisement of the Indian camps. If only they'd walked down Broward Avenue they'd have seen "civilized" trash. It was one more civic obligation I felt must be addressed, and no one seemed to have much interest in doing it. Even less now with the war looming.

Grace Dunlap, a sister-in law of the Olivers, suggested after one of the zoning meetings that I was "involved in a few too many things, perhaps, dear, don't you think?"

"I will happily bow out when others come to take my place," I said. "But until then, every city needs proper planning, proper zoning, and street maintenance, or we'll look like a hodgepodge town of blocks put together by lazy children. No one will want to come here to raise their families. Clean cities, solid homes, predictability for a community are all essential for safe growth, Grace."

"Are you campaigning?" she asked, dropping the -ing the way so many south Florida women did in their speech.

"Just clarifying why I feel the zoning board is so important," I said.

"Perhaps it's more a man's place to worry over such things than a woman's," she said. She stood with her back to me, as straight as a wagon tongue, gazing at a photograph. We'd walked back to our home and stood in the parlor. I was deciding whether to make chocolate or to ungraciously finish the conversation and get Grace moved on her way. She slid the pictures in the photo frame back and forth to change the images. Frank's photo of me taken at the beach one summer showed first. One of early Fort Lauderdale spread out along the New River slipped over it next. Behind it was one of a child watching Seminoles cut up manatee steaks in front of the trading post following a successful hunt. So long ago, that was.

"Well, Grace, I believe we've each been given tasks to do on behalf of others. I try to do my best. If you can find a man willing to take on garbage and beautifying streets, then lead him—or should I say send him—forward."

"No need to take offense, Ivy," she said, turning to me, photo frame still in hand. "I'm just sharing what the talk is."

"What else, then? You have that look in your eye."

"Folks say you drive a wee bit fast. Not to mention your involvements. Your poor Frank must rarely ever see you." She moistened her pouting lips.

"I work for women's advancement much less than I'd like. Having so many 'other obligations' keeps me from it."

I did find the work had to be accomplished around the subject of war, though. South Florida had had its share of military discussions over the years, of course, what with the three Seminole Wars, the War between the States, and the Spanish War. It was a daunting terrain in which to battle. A Captain Harney had come to conquer Indians, taken one look at the swamps, and left for a place called Oregon where Indians could be seen for miles and captured among sagebrush. I'd heard they'd named a fort for him there and even a county. He must have thought himself a wise military man to have left for more hospitable warring climates.

Our town, too, was named for a military man, commander of the Tennessee volunteers who had come to "capture the savages." He hadn't, of course, but had left behind three forts named for him, the last one being the only one insect-free enough to inhabit. It was built on the beach.

So in our little town the talk of war was not new, but speaking of places like Sarajevo and Austria with overtones of assassinations did consume new interest. Even Flagler's death and the speculation about his incomplete projects and hotel investments in south Florida didn't take people's talk from foreign battles.

Selling Liberty Loans to fund American's involvement, should it come, became an occupation allowed women, and much to Grace's chagrin, I imagined, I became the coordinator of that effort in Broward County, too.

I did worry about Albert, though. He was the right age for soldiering. He'd finished school, and he, Gus, and Papa lived in a small cottage just down the avenue from us, often taking meals with Frank and me. Della and I did their laundry with a new wringer machine.

Even after the move, Albert hadn't looked healthy to me. I worried out loud about that.

"He mentions night sweats and chest pains," I told Frank. "I thought the climate here would improve that."

"Maybe it's all that meat he eats."

"You're teasing. That could contribute, though. And now Papa's talking about getting back into farming again, while Albert's still at home and could help. Looks too weak to me."

"Might keep him from the war," Frank said.

"He doesn't want that. Wants to go." DeWitt and Gus, strong and healthy, felt prepared to go too. They talked of it when they hammered on the new houses they framed in Lauderdale.

"Albert's still a boy," I said, though he hammered on houses too.

"It's what I'll have to do," Albert said. His voice had changed and it was deep, so that I could sometimes not tell if he or Papa spoke when I was in another room listening. "If the time comes, big sister, don't be angry at me for volunteering."

"I always support what the government thinks best," I said. "Why would you think I wouldn't?"

"Papa says you're a suffragette, and they don't believe in war." He had Papa's dark eyebrows and Mama's pale complexion, dark, deep-set eyes in a slender, handsome face. He coughed. Was he losing weight?

"We just think there are more civilized ways to solve problems than shooting at each other. And with women voting, we'd see that diplomacy prevailed. Women have the power to subdue, you know."

Albert laughed. When he did, he showed straight white teeth. "Is that how you ladies get marriage proposals?"

I punched his shoulder in play. "I wish it were an option now, so that none of you would have to think about going. Are you feeling well, Albert?"

"Just fine," he said, dragging out the word *fine*. "Diplomacy only buys you time needed to find a big stick. That's what Roosevelt says: 'Walk softly but carry a big stick.'"

"You'd quote a Republican in Papa's house? Now, that is warring potential. And you're worried about my wild ways!"

Albert laughed and reached a long arm around me while I sliced the tomatoes we'd be serving with supper. I hugged him back. I could feel his ribs.

"You'll have to put on weight before they'll take you," I said.

"Papa wants me to go to Lake Okeechobee to farm. But I'd rather go to Europe."

"Put my hot water out, would you, Albert? It always helps digestion. Want some for yourself?"

He shook his head. "Can we go for a ride later in your automobile? Think you'll stay with Fords?"

"I'll *stay* with whoever brings out the first automatic transmission. So I don't have to endure the shifting. Automobiles aren't built for my short little legs and all that maneuvering. But I do love that little thing."

My Ford was black with a wide windshield and single wiper for when it rained. The Model T put-putted me along not unlike Frank once had when he courted me in his pop boat. I only got mired in the mud a few times, and I quickly learned how to use the hand pedal to back up and ease over tree roots and to move around puddles.

"Take a run to Pink and Randall's?" I said.

A strangled look crossed Albert's face.

"What is it?"

"Nothing," Albert said, looking away. "Wish they'd move here with the rest of us, is all."

"You want that too?"

He nodded and inhaled deeply.

"You'd best not think about farming or war," I said. "Just getting you well should be our task. That could be the very reason why you're living here in Lauderdale. Yes, I surely think that is."

CHAPTER FOURTEEN

"I'm fit as a fiddle," Pink told us. "Healthier than you, Albert, from the sound of that hackin'. And I'm lackin' those purple thumbs under sister's eyes."

"Family trait," Albert said.

He and I had made a day of it, driving down early in the morning, past the old neighborhood where Albert had grown up, from which I'd launched my teaching career. The house looked smaller and in need of care. I drove us along the palm-shaded streets, the sun flickering through the split leaves, past Cohen's old post on the Miami River where I'd first seen a Seminole with an umbrella. I told Albert of that day as we drove away from the bay and arrived at the Mosses' new rental. Their cottage was built up high with a view of the sea.

We'd had fruit for breakfast, and Pink had shown us the plantings she'd placed in window boxes outside and a few charcoal drawings she'd purchased and hung.

Pink's color looked good, and her eyes had a sparkle to them. Her waist stayed tiny, cinched in by a wide, beaded belt. Her skirts were rising, showing the tops of her high-buttoned shoes. She wore her hair pulled back into a bun at the back of her neck but one's eye went automatically to the widow's peak at the center of her high forehead, then that peach complexion and on to her sensuous smile.

"You're looking dandy, I admit," Albert said.

"I can wrestle you to the ground, big feet and all."

"Only because I taught you those pugilistic moves and twists." Albert held his fists up like a young boxer, then stuck his foot out as though to trip her. She squealed and slipped away, barely missing the cats who stretched and arched near my car.

"You two look ready for adventure," I said. "Want to drive out with me to the camp?"

"Whatever for?" Albert stopped his artful pursuit of attack.

"In Miami?" Pink asked.

"I've cards I want to show them. The children at home love them, and I'd like to see how they're received away from my porch."

"Cards? What kind of cards, sister?"

"Come with me and see."

It was perhaps foolhardy, and I'm not at all sure what made me think of it. Maybe my meandering through the past with Albert earlier in the day; maybe that insight about service.

"We'll go in as tourists. Pay our money, wander around, and then sit on the running board and see who comes by."

The day felt sultry and rain threatened, so few tourists pawed through crates of dolls or squealed at newly hatched alligators. We felt no pressure admiring items for sale. I bought a striped cloth men used as turbans, telling Pink and Albert how they wrapped things inside and carried them in a hammock on their backs.

"I once saw a crippled boy carted by his father that way. His family seemed very protective of him. I wonder what became of him."

"Probably died young. Maimed often do," Pink said.

By late afternoon, all the tourists had left except Pink, Albert, and me. Pink fanned herself, her narrow white skirt and pleated blouse making her look both fragile and seductive. She lifted and set her patent leather shoes like tiny, pale stones dropped on a bank of grass.

Pink held up dolls in her tanned hand and admired the beads draped around an old woman's neck. With a smile, the woman pulled them from her neck and offered them to her. Pink turned, surprise in her eyes. Even strangers could see her kind and open spirit. Such a shame she hadn't a child with whom to share it.

Albert walked with his hands behind him, leaning over, peering at the cooking pots steaming, and I noticed he hummed without being aware of it. He accepted the offer of a taste and nodded his head, marking it as *ojus*.

We were an innocent family just out for an afternoon, taking in the peace and pace of life between chickees.

Then with a beating heart, I got out the cards and set them along the running board, the tall backs leaning against the black paint beneath the

Ford's windows. The pictures stood out with their bright colors against the dark background. Even the adults stopped, then stooped to stare. They pointed and spoke to each other.

I looked for signs of wariness, an indication of who the medicine men or women might be and if they'd tell me to gather up the cards and leave. The writing in black letters looked more prominent than I remembered, and I felt my heart pound rapidly with the risk.

A broad-faced man commented to another dressed in traditional clothes using words I didn't know, then saying something I did.

"Big man." He pointed at the picture of Goliath.

I nodded, took a deep breath, then told the stories of David and Goliath, about Joseph and his coat of many colors, of Esther and her rescue and of Jesus and his life; stories, rich with warriors and winning, family stress and sorrow, love and loss, betrayal and sweet reunion.

A small crowd gathered. Children sat on sawdust walkways, watching. A few with fingers in their mouths lounged in the laps of their parents, mesmerized. I wasn't sure they really understood. And yet I knew: it was the stories that would reach them. It was the stories—not the teller—that would truly touch their hearts.

When finished, I started to pack the cards up, circle them with hemp rope. As I bent over the car's trunk, I heard the words, spoken with authority.

"You leave."

"Yes," I said, "we'll be on our way."

Albert had one foot in the passenger side of the front; Pink had settled in the back.

I turned to face the speaker.

His was a twisted body, the back bent like the gnarled knees of cypress trees, his legs short and bowed. A stick stabilized him but he bore his own weight. I recognized his eyes. They were the eyes of a boy I'd seen carried and protected by his father all those years before.

"Leave stories," he repeated.

He pointed to the cards. One eye wept, I noticed now, and he wore a bright-colored shirt with diagonal stripes of blue and black and red divided by tiny ribbons of white. His good eye held mine with challenge.

"I need to take them with me," I said. "So others can hear the stories."

He glanced around. Except for my family, we stood alone. He could easily have grabbed the cards. I had, after all, intruded. He could lift his stick and scatter them, calling to the children to retrieve them.

But he didn't.

"I could come again if you'd like, when I'm here. Get a set to leave."

"You teach stories," the man said.

"I teach," I said. "You could learn them, too. Then you could teach the children."

He grunted. "You come back."

"I will," I said. "Or someone will. Thank you for asking."

My words were polite and said quietly but inside I soared. If they could accept these stories from a total stranger, then surely the camp nearer Lauderdale would allow me to do just what I'd done this afternoon, just casually teach, right there in the camp.

"I'll start a Ford Running Board School," I told Pink and Albert as we bounced along the road back to Pink's. "They were perfectly accepting. I've got to get someone to start coming in, spending time with them. We could introduce other ways. Talk about sanitation and medicine and nutrition. Think how that would serve them!"

"They don't know you," Albert said.

"That's the point. And yet they had no trouble with my telling the stories. I've been too cautious. You were right, Pink."

"Me?"

"You said I should be riskier, expose more, be out of control and trust in God's dominion."

"Those ain't soundin' like my words," she said.

"I summarize," I said. "Maybe the Presbyterians would come in and help. I haven't asked them for a while."

"Her way of 'bein' out of control,'" Pink said, holding her face in her hands as she leaned between us from the backseat.

I felt alive, full with the rush of the possibilities. "Why don't you move to Lauderdale with us, Pink? You could wait for Randall there. We could do it together, like we did when DeWitt and Gus were little. Play school but for real this time. You're the last holdout."

"We all have our own ways of waitin'," she said.

"I could use your help, honest to truth."

"Maybe you should stay here," Albert suggested to me. "Frank would survive. You could come right back to that camp and teach yourself."

I did let the thought linger for a moment.

"No, my place is there beside Frank, at home. But now I can see a way to branch out. They're ready for new thinking. They can see the world changing and them not much a part of it. Maybe they just don't see how they can change within it and yet still keep who they are. I want them to be who they are, just have tools to make the most of it."

We arrived back at Pink's, the house just as we'd left it. "I was hopin' Randall'd be back."

"We planned to spend the night," I said, "to keep you company."

We ate a light supper and after laughter and talking, Albert stretched out on the divan while Pink and I prepared to share her and Randall's bed.

"Look what Randall brought back from New York." Pink lifted her arm so I could see the side seam while we were undressing. A metal strip was sewn there.

"It's a zipper. They've been around for years but just now bein' used in garments. It's the newest rage. Go ahead. Pull on it."

I pulled on it.

"Now back up. Isn't it just too fine?"

"Do they think there'll be much market for these?" I asked.

"Randall says so. He's taken an interest in a company to make them and sell them to ready-made stores. He's got very big plans. I'll be modelin' clothes and wearin' them in photographs. He thinks I might be travelin' with him some."

"Wouldn't that be fun?"

She shrugged her shoulders. "It's something besides the land sales. I'll get you zippers if you like."

"Not necessary," I said, then looked at her face. "On the other hand, it might do well on a skirt instead of those tiny snaps. I would like to try one, Pink." I patted her hand.

"I'll write Randall and tell him."

"Where is he now?"

I undid the knot at the top of my head and began brushing my hair. It had never been cut and I could almost sit on it. My face looked so round with my hair down around my narrow shoulders.

"Travelin' up north for a time, workin' too. That's what he does."

"I'm sorry he decided against the roller rink. Frank says it's doing well and the children just squeal there, so happy."

"I think he likes wanderin'." Pink slipped out of her dress, rezipped the zipper, and laid it across the round ottoman covered with material of yellow chrysanthemums and spring green leaves splashed across white. "It's in some people's blood."

"Like Papa's," I said. "I hated going from school to school, didn't you?"

"It was always interestin' to me, the newness, the surprises. Will's a wanderer too," she added.

"Our Will? Have you seen him?"

"He did try to court me once, did you know that? Said he thought it would be a fine thing for sisters to marry brothers and was I interested. It was that day Louise and I went to Palm Beach to shop and you just wouldn't come along. Will did. Carried Vanilla all afternoon. Knew everyone. Especially the Indians who wandered out of Zapf's. Life would have been a surprise with Will."

A cream-colored nightdress fell like a whisper over her shoulders and graced the floor. She picked up her ivory brush and with the other hand took out the pins that had held the knot at her neck. While she brushed her hair, she walked around the room, always fluid.

"Will was a funnin' man," she said then. "Loved takin' risks. Goin' west to gold mines and gamblin' halls and all that. Said I could easily work in one of those. Liked the hot springs of Arkansas, too."

"Was?" I said. "You said he *was* a funning man."

She pulled back on the mosquito bar and slipped beneath the sheet, then finished with a tone I couldn't quite decipher. "Didn't mean to use imprecise English, sister. 'Fraid I can't help you with your wonderin'. I ain't seen Will for years."

The road to the camp near Lauderdale became familiar. Once or twice I caught the swift drift of a panther startled by the auto's engine as I eased by. Occasionally a wild hog darted out and stood its ground, staring at me with its beady eyes momentarily before flicking its short tail and disappearing into the mangroves and cypress. Usually I could drive without even seeing what surrounded me, my thoughts were so given over to the camps.

My visiting there had not stopped the steady visits of Seminoles to our home. That pleased me. Frank continued to meet the alligator egg contracts for buyers in Tallahassee and I think he liked the arrival, unannounced, of Johnny Jumper or the Osceolas, the gentle setting on the porch that followed, talking softly, eating catfish I fried in olive oil. It brought back the early days to Frank, I think, a time when things were simple and what he did each day made a difference he could see. Such influence seemed easier for him than days spent in managing property and evaluating loans, buying acreage and watching investments change.

He occasionally rode with me in the Ford. Those times I behaved with more discretion, which was difficult since the children scampered out to sit on the running board and called for "Stories! Stories!" and pressed their faces against the back window seeking the cards and special treats I usually brought.

"Every place is a school, Frank," I said. "A place for learning. My visits here are just that for them. And the camp is a school for me, too. I learn new things every day."

I often brought out herbs I'd found useful in treating coughs and fevers, and talked to a few women about sanitation, to cut down on the flies carrying disease. Prevention was the key. But blocking disease meant even greater change—water handling, sewage, nutrition, and dealing with the change all began with knowledge.

"It actually starts before education—with trust," I told Frank as I drove through the palmetto gate into the camp. Chickens scattered before us. "They need to trust that I'll just accept them as they are before they'll be willing to try new things."

"Contradictory," Frank said; "accepting just so you can change them." He wiped the perspiration from his face with a freshly ironed handkerchief, folded it, and returned it to his pocket.

"It's not *so that* I can change them, Frank, but what must happen before they'll hear what I have to say so they can decide for themselves." I switched off the engine and turned to look at him. "It's like baking powder in flour. I don't add it to actually change the flour—the grain still remains what we know it as, lovely ground wheat. But the baking powder becomes a catalyst, something to make the flour perform in ways it otherwise couldn't. It begins as flour and ends up as...cake."

"Takes a heap of heat to make that happen," he said.

"Oh, south Florida's used to heat."

"Suppose."

"They can't go on like this or they'll die, Frank." I picked up his hand in mine. "That's the truth of it. Seems terribly tragic that they could survive three wars and then be killed off by squatters and disease and lack of knowledge for how to conquer this century."

"My little revolutionary," he said and squeezed my hand. It felt oddly cool.

I opened the door and eased back the children, who'd attached themselves to the running board as soon as the engine stopped. Annie Tommie came out to greet us. She'd become a medicine woman herself now, called out to look after the ill. At least Esther told me that's where she went. And I noticed she took some of the herbs and medicines I brought and offered advice in English whenever Esther and I attempted to exchange information. She'd brought in a syrup or two to treat a child while I'd been there once and at my next visit, his bare feet spit up the dirt as he ran out to play.

I rarely ran into Stretch. He trapped coons at night so sleeping during the day made sense. It never would have been permitted if he were a Seminole, though. None of them did that.

I could almost see the flame set in his hat flickering against the swamp night as he poled just beyond the mangrove roots until his light caught the eyes of the animal. He'd lift his shotgun and shoot, bringing the animals back for Esther to skin and salt while the men sat and oiled their guns later with lard-stained papers or strips of bacon if needed.

Eventually, stacks of coon hides would grow and be enough for shipment north to the ever-demanding garment industry to meet the needs of fashion. The killing saddened me, though it brought fresh protein to the chickees, food for the children's bellies. And remained one of the few ways they had left to trade for lard, canned milk, and salt pork.

Stretch scowled if he saw me and once or twice I noticed him leave and speak at the edge of the camp with other men, non-Indians. I asked Esther about them, motioning with my head to the boats where white men stood leaning against the poles that would ease them into difficult swampy places.

"They new, new," she said. She fidgeted, switching her legs back and forth. Movement seemed to be necessary when she talked. "Live at edge of camp, at the edge there, outside."

"Are they trappers?" I made a motion with my arms as though I opened up a trap. "Or farmers?"

She shook her head and made a shooting motion.

"Plume hunters?"

With her fingers, she signaled me to be quiet. "Stretch say they hunt for place to live," she said. "Just live, like live here."

"Squatters," Annie Tommie said. "Knew they'd come."

I didn't feel pity. I grieved for them, for the passing of their way of life, but what kept me talking of their needs to the Women's Federation was the hope I saw within them, the possibilities. If only they had a place protected by the government where no squatters could intrude. I ached for ways to touch their lives without shattering who they were.

I'd written several letters, reports actually, for the Federation, about the conditions of the camps and their needs. I'd included mention of seeing a half-eaten turtle, greenish with decay, and being appalled by a child's grab to eat it; of gopher skeletons scattered about and sparsely planted gardens. I wanted the Federation to take up the Seminoles' cause, bring awareness to lawmakers about their degraded state. The reports had been sent on to the main committee headed by May Mann Jennings, who had the influence of her husband, the former governor, and his cronies in the legislature.

I suppose in the back of my mind I imagined Annie Tommie's camp someday going to the land at Dania where they could start fresh. They could be provided for there, protected from the prying eyes of tourists and raise their children in established homes and yes, even have schools and churches, places to feed their minds as well as their bellies. But they needed some kind of formal relationship with the government.

My notes grew after each visit.

"They have so many illnesses," I told Alfred and Annie Beck, the pharmacist and his young wife, who had invited us to supper. "Oozing sores. Babies born small and weakened from malnutrition."

"Would you like pie?" Annie Beck asked. She stood two inches taller than me with intense brown eyes. She handed me a piece of Key lime pie. "I don't eat pie if it's ever been refrigerated," she said. "It just is not fresh."

"My sentiments exactly," I said, lifting the plate from her fingers.

"What about housing?" Alfred asked.

"Chickees mostly, but exposure isn't really a problem. I think the greatest threat to their survival is the encroachment of others. And their having no voice with the government."

"You'll have to put your efforts there, then," Annie Beck said.

"Addressing sanitation might be easier," Alfred offered. "And I could get some medicines perhaps, if they'd use them."

"Almost anything'd be easier than connecting them to the government," Frank said.

"What's a day without challenge?" Annie Beck said, and I knew I'd found a friend.

Esther signaled me that she wanted to talk in private. It happened on a day when Frank came with me to the camps. He stood off talking with one of the Tigertail men, overlooking an alligator pen. A slap of water and Frank's jumping back told me it was occupied by more than just eggs.

"Boy want go to school, in to school," she said as we sat on the edge of the eating platform inside her chickee, our legs dangling over the side. A couple of children "played school," one holding my cards while seated on the running board in front of three or four others. "In the town school, that school."

"Someone wishes to attend the Lauderdale school?" My heart skipped a beat. Had I heard her right? "From here?"

She nodded her head. "He comes talk with you."

She stepped outside and motioned toward a young boy, who looked to be ten or twelve but was probably older. He'd been standing off to the side, waiting for a signal.

"How does he know about the school?" I asked.

"I teach him," she said. "Salt pork. Lard. Words from boxes, the boxes. He watches school in town."

"Bring him over," I said. "We'll see what we can do."

His name was Tony Tommie. He might have been a relative of Annie, a distant cousin. She had such a large family. He had bright eyes and wore his hair cropped short and straight across his forehead. He had jeans on his slender legs, and he wore the blouse-shirt of his people with the colorful diagonal stripes. I could see he'd dressed for the occasion of our talk.

"How do you know about the school?" I asked.

"You teach Esther. Come here teach. Not many times enough. Want to read books and write," he said. "Need go school do that."

"You need to go to school to read and write," I said. "That's right, you do."

My heart pounded now, my hands slippery with the excitement of this request, the power in it and the risk.

"And will your mother let you? Does she know?"

He nodded his head once. "She know. Go school in town tomorrow?" he persisted.

"If that's what you want, you will go to school, but you'll have to give me a little time," I said, laughing. "So it won't be tomorrow."

A shadow cast across his face.

"You absolutely will go to school," I said. "Tell him, Esther. Nothing will separate him from his dream. I will leave right now, tell him, and begin the work. And be back as soon as I can, so summarize it. I mean, tell him. He's going to school. Oh, Esther, see what you gave him? Just see!"

I fumbled around gathering up the cards, shooing children from the side of the car. I started the engine, forgetting Frank had come with me. He walked quickly toward the car when he heard the engine start.

"Something wrong?"

"No, no," I said. "Get in. It's the most wonderful news!"

I filled him in as we drove back. I wished the roads would let me drive the full thirty miles per hour the salesman said the car would go.

"He actually wants to go to school in Lauderdale?"

"Yes! Isn't it wonderful? Oh, Frank, this is what I've dreamed about, that what I did those years ago would open up doors for them."

"You'll be doing the door-opening. Think they'll let him in?"

"And why not? He's of age. He speaks a little English. If he can get there each day, why not? The tribe must have approved it."

"Think he's motivated enough?"

"If you could have seen the look in his eyes, Frank, the fire in them. The spirit. He wants this. He's hungry for it. And it may open the door to dozens of others. Oh, Frank." I reached across to squeeze his hand. "It's what I've prayed for."

"Keep your hands on the wheel, woman," Frank said, though his voice held the lilt of encouragement. "Don't want to be rubbing bellies with a gator."

Dr. Ashmore, the superintendent of the Fort Lauderdale schools, was less enthusiastic when I raised the subject with him.

"Have you considered a Negro school?" he asked.

"They aren't interested," I said. "And neither is he. He wants to live at home, too, not be sent away to some boarding school. This is the place, and while I know it is much to ask of you, I think it would mark your leadership, statewide, to let him in."

"He'd have to enter the primary grades, Mrs. Stranahan," he said, looking through his smudged oval glasses at me. His white suit jacket hung over the back of his chair, giving me full view of his blue-and-white-striped shirt and black bow tie. Children played outside the window, rolling balls with sticks.

"I do love the color blue," I said, nodding to his shirt.

"What? Oh, yes. Lovely color, blue."

"Did Marjorie buy it?"

"Yes. Yes, she did. Now—"

"We share that love of color, your wife and I. We've spoken of it often at the Civic Club."

"Have you. Mrs. Stranahan—"

"Please, call me Ivy. We're practically neighbors. Don't you live on Stranahan Avenue? The zoning board just approved widening it. Kitteredge and Hall and my husband'll be doing that work next year, for the city. I truly hope the dust won't be bothering you and Marjorie. It will make your property so much more inviting, don't you think?"

"Should improve its worth, yes. We were much pleased the board approved our request."

"Yes. Now, you were asking about Tony's being able to manage the elementary students, being as how he's older and all. He's a small child. Doesn't look like he's fifteen, though that's what he says he is. Very personable and quite gentle around the younger children at the camps. I've seen him with twins and they're quite a handful. He redirects them without any rancor. Does quite a nice job with them. He speaks enough English to convey his needs. I don't think he'll cause the slightest problem. And he wants this, Jerome. So much. You know that look in a bright child's eyes. Well, Tony has that. It would be a crime, sinful almost, to deprive him of expanding it."

"So he's motivated, you say?"

"And I'll be happy to encourage that in whatever way I can."

"Not sure how the other families will accept this." Jerome said.

"The Women's Club will support you. It's one of our goals, education and other improvements for the Seminoles. Statewide, that's part of the platform. This will be a first for our new Broward County and perhaps pave the way for leadership across the state."

"You think so?"

"I do, Jerome. We can't deprive him."

Jerome coughed and took his glasses off, looked my way and sighed, and I knew I had my answer.

I took the word myself to Tony Tommie. His eyes lit up just the way I'd imagined.

We arranged for me to pick him up the first few days or so; and then one of the Women's Club members located a mule and soon Tony was off and riding on his own.

A Seminole child, attending school in a schoolhouse near his home. He would not even have been born when I first came to the New River. Maybe it was his spirit that had moved across my eyes that day I'd stood in my schoolhouse alone, amazed that I was there at all. I remember that shadow. I'd thought it eerie and worrisome, but it might have been only the passing of a cloud, giving time for Tony to grow up.

Blue jays argued outside the window, scolding and chattering in the early morning. Squirrels rustled about beneath the arelias. I eased onto my side, though I knew that sleeping that way was bad for my heart. That's what all the latest medical information said, and I'd responded by almost sitting up now, the eight to ten fluffs of down perched like white feathers stacked in a pile. Turned, I could see the even breathing of Frank's back as he slept. He snored a bit, but even that was both discreet and unobtrusive.

I wanted to be next to him, to seek the shelter of his presence; and I pulled the covers back and slipped over to his bed. He moaned slightly in his sleep and adjusted himself to make room for me without even waking. It was like him, I thought, and smiled. He accommodated.

I slipped my arm over his hip and invited his body's warmth, taking in the care it offered. I felt vulnerable, alone except for Frank. He was such a comfort, this man, so willing to be where I was in my life, to express his opinion but never push it on me. The warmth from his back pressed into my breasts and I wondered if I'd erred those years before. Maybe we could have conceived; maybe I could have endured a pregnancy; maybe we could have survived the fear and the torture, of wondering if I could have delivered a chubby, live child. Maybe Frank and I should have had our own children racing about, scampering onto the bed in the morning, making demands we found it a joy to fulfill. Maybe Holding was right, that I was in violation of all that God planned. Maybe I hadn't let God truly be in control.

I pulled Frank closer to me and felt the tears press against my nose.

Word of Tony's presence in the school reached Reverend Holding, and things promised to get messy. Something about who I was and how I lived out the passion of my beliefs threatened some people. Powerful people. It wasn't that I wanted to be disruptive. I didn't. I'd have been perfectly content just to quietly follow my path, my vision of what I'd been asked to do.

Yes, I'd been elected chairman of the Women's Suffrage League in Broward County. I was glad not for the position but for the influence it could bring, to change the hard lives of women, to permit their grace and wisdom to influence cities and school boards, to even serve in Congress where they could legislate change for the Seminoles and perhaps vote against international wars.

My election as chair of the Indian Affairs Committee of the Women's Club granted me a wonderful forum from which to champion the need for change. Tony had been living proof I'd been on track.

"Too ecumenical, too universal," Holding had said.

The pattern proved familiar: while I met with women out of town, Holding hit. Once again, Frank had to sit in the hard pew and take it, testing his ability to remain calm and accommodate.

Following the hymn singing—at which Bloxham had played his guitar for accompaniment, Papa the piano, and DeWitt, Albert, and Gus had lent their voices in song—Reverend Holding expounded on the role of women and Paul's admonition of their need for quietness and submission. Frank said the murmured "amens" and "yes, indeed, Lord," inspiring Holding to discuss what submission was, as he saw it: the need to follow men, to always listen to one's husband, and to never challenge what he had to say.

To me, it simply meant sometimes we didn't get our own way and it applied to all humans, not just those who wore corsets.

"Summarize for me, Frank," I said when I returned.

"No need for meddling with the downcast. The Lord'll take care of those folks on His own. The poor will always be with us."

"That's a favorite excuse," I said. "Go ahead."

"Lord doesn't need the fairer sex trying to fix what God's placed as His way. Women's clubs are a challenge to Scripture."

"He actually said that?"

"I think he remembered several communicants are members, so he qualified it. Said, 'When they go beyond the care and support of what their men have set as goals in a community or church,' that's when they violate God's law."

"I should have taken him on before this."

"There's more." Frank used a monotone to report. "Single women must obey their fathers and upstanding male citizens as their spiritual advisers. Not challenge, for that is surely folly and borders on sin."

"Oh, Frank. There are hardly any single women in church, except for young girls kicking their feet beneath the pews or making finger plays with fans."

"Joan of Arc was unmarried," Frank said.

"But not a Methodist. I don't imagine Holding mentioned that or commented on the church's role in her death, either. A celibate woman who saved France and they still burned her. More threatening than married women, that's certain."

"Now, Ivy," Frank said.

"Go ahead. Tell me the rest. I may as well hear it all."

Frank coughed. I do believe his asthma bothered him more when he was nervous. "Spoke of holiness…" Frank struggled. "Of women who bore children. Said those who're barren, who're so busy meddling—his words, Ivy, not mine—beyond their backyards, had no time to perform wifely duties and comply with scriptural demands." Frank wiped his forehead with his palm. "Said having even two children was no multiplication of a man and woman. Three's his bare minimum."

Frank's ears turned red just with the retelling. I could imagine what they'd done there in the pew.

"How could you sit through it?" I put my hands over my ears. "I can't hear any more."

I felt my anger more for what people like Bloxham and Louise had endured listening to that sermon than for Holding's insults to my person. I made my way upstairs, ran my hand along the banister, checked on the ixoria spread out like welcoming fans.

"My brother so desperately wants a family. What a detestable thing to lay against them."

Frank had followed me upstairs. "Didn't want to give him the satisfaction of believing he'd got to me," he said. "Why I stayed. He almost did."

"Coward, that's what he is, choosing to shout about me while I'm not there. Well, it won't stop me, Frank. It's important work I do. You believe that, don't you?"

He nodded, though I thought a bit slowly. "I do. We're partners in it, women's suffrage, efforts at Lauderdale's future. Wish you didn't have to be gone so much to do it. Not that I mind Della's cooking. Just miss you, is all."

"I wouldn't go if I didn't think it was necessary. I work for women like Della and Esther and Annie Tommie and women of the future, who are so bright in their minds but who don't have the choices. It's for all women, Frank, and their children."

"'Me thinks thou dost protest too much,'" he said.

His words silenced me into introspection.

That had been last night. I'd lain awake during the night, feeling guilty over the disruption I brought to Frank's predictable life, guilty and strangely distant. He didn't complain, but I could see in the drop of his eyes that he might have wished for a wife who bore him children, washed their little faces with spit before walking through the door on Sunday morning and who massaged his feet before he slept at night. The latter was all he'd gotten of the traditional wife, that and my sewing for him, cooking for him. I never even shared the meat I fixed him.

I curled myself beside him, wondering if maybe I had sinned, had erred in this journey of my life. And yet I'd felt so led, so sure that God had closed doors and then opened new ones. Hadn't He said, *Do what no one else can do*? And hadn't Tony Tommie done well in school? Hadn't my response to Esther made that happen? Hadn't I overcome a great tragedy and turned it to good?

I'd read about the McWhirter Sanctification group, women who were in business as men were, who ran restaurants and bakeries to survive but who lived separately from men, abstaining from any demonstration of affection. They'd begun in Texas and moved to Washington, D.C. "The seat of power," Papa called that city. Maybe Frank would be happier if I went somewhere like that, where he wouldn't have to explain me; he could simply say I was daft.

Frank turned over.

"Thought I felt you here," he said. His eyes were soft as a fawn's behind the sleepiness. "Thinking heavy thoughts, are you?" His hands stroked the hair from my forehead, then gently outlined my cheek and my jaw, skipping across my lips to the other side.

"I'm sorry, Frank. For any disappointments that I've brought you."

He frowned.

"I never intended to hurt you."

"Haven't," he said. "Where's that coming from?"

"This thing with Holding."

"Ah. Well, each entitled to our opinions. I don't share his."

"Do you feel deprived, though, Frank? Have I let you down? Maybe by not giving you a legacy, someone to carry on the family name? We might have taken in children."

"Expect Will'll take care of that part of the legacy," he said, "though I wish he'd tell us. I wonder about him. As for the name, you've done noth-ing but make it shine, Ivy. It stands for doing good things, right things. No need to apologize for that."

I continued to watch him, to stare at his face and the dark eyebrows, the clear though sometimes troubled eyes, that straight, patrician nose above a sober mouth that could be so soft when he kissed me before bed-time, so hard when he was upset. My mind began to wander.

"Where are you?"

"Just away."

"Stay. As for the other...I'm a man of my word, Ivy. It was what you wanted and needed in order to be with me for life and I accepted that. It was you I wanted, being with you, sharing breakfast with you, sitting beside you while we read the paper. Even watching you plump up the pillows at night. Never thought to possess you. Admired your spunk and independent spirit. Nothing's changed about that."

"But a family?"

"Don't deny I would've liked the trying," he said, his words barely audible. "The look of you in the morning with that nightgown falling over your hips, that thick hair, your warmth, makes me want to forget the steel mills of Ohio and what they gave me." He cleared his throat and coughed. His words sounded as though they preceded a cold. "Would've had to share you with any child we took. Haven't had to." He lay quietly for a time. The scent of jasmine drifted in through the screens. "I made a decision, Ivy; to love you in the way you needed, not the way I might have wanted. And if I'm nothing else, I'm a man whose word means something."

He continued to stroke the side of my face.

I considered the wonder of the man, his lavish unselfishness to love me as I needed. "You dear boy. You have such integrity. I marvel at it and am so grateful for it and for you."

He said my name softly then, over and over.

"Please don't leave me, Frank. Don't ever leave me," I said, surprised and embarrassed by my need of his care.

"Why would you say that?"

I lay quiet but present. "I don't know. Sometimes, when I feel very close to you, that phrase comes into my head."

He pulled me to his chest.

"It's not a worry you need carry," he said. "I'll stay for as long as you want."

His love was an eagle's wing folded around me. He cradled my head on his breast and I slept.

CHAPTER FIFTEEN

I'd arranged the meeting with Holding for a Wednesday, my thinking being that he'd be wound down from his Sunday service but not yet wound up for the next.

"Glad you could come, Sister Stranahan. Always a pleasure."

The Reverend Holding showed me to a chair across from a shiny table that served as his desk in his home office. It held only a photograph of his family and a Bible with a long red satin ribbon as a bookmark.

"You may not think it a pleasure today, Basil," I said, settling my knees beneath the table. I looked up at him even though the chair stood high enough that my short feet did not touch the floor.

His toothy smile became a single, strained line.

"Now, Mrs. Stranahan, let's be reasonable. I'm called to serve the Lord and preach His word as He reveals it."

"As are all saints."

"Yes...with very certain roles and limitations, especially for wom—"

"We are all saints, I'm sure you'd agree? With gifts differing?"

"Yes. Where is this going, Sister Stranahan?" he said. His fingers tapped together above elbows perched like talons on the table.

"Bear with me. Priscilla worked with her husband to teach and influence a man who became a great preacher in the first century."

"Apollos. Yes, Acts 18:26, but Paul—"

"And as mothers, we are asked to prepare our children. Women are told to train and serve through our beliefs and actions, to model to others, to help prevent disasters that could affect individual spiritual lives. We're told to be envoys, ambassadors, subject to our leaders—"

"Pastoral leaders. I'm pleased you understand." His bushy white eyebrows raised high and he leaned back, his fingers folded as in prayer. "Now then, Ivy, your suffrage work—"

"Leadership lives in God, Basil," I said, and before he could interrupt again put my hand up to silence him. "As His emissary, I can count on His refuge, His safekeeping, His response to my prayers as long as I live as an example to His Word and way. And I believe that He has sent me to bring that example of His love and commandments to those you don't approve of, such as women without children, women without a voice, to Indians, others of color, to outcasts."

We were interrupted then by a day lady bringing in a tray that held tall glasses of limeade and a dish of pecan cookies. Lula Marshall's soprano voice filtered in from the church across the street, where she rehearsed for Sunday service. I passed on the cookies but lifted the glass when offered, catching the eye of the dark-faced woman before she served the reverend.

"And often," I said as she backed out the door, "ambassadors are asked to present their credentials, to convey the authority from which they act. That's what I'm doing here today. And then, regardless of your acknowledgment or not, to bring messages from their Leader, messages meant for His good, to teach, I believe, not just behind a schoolhouse door, but where He places us. To teach and train and model faith." I took a sip. "Today He placed me here. But it's in His hands if I've taught or not. And next Sunday, I believe He wants me somewhere else. I just wanted you to know so you wouldn't misunderstand my actions. You did not drive me out, Basil. The Lord has simply moved me as I've been moved by a father a dozen times before. And though I behave differently than you, we share the same sovereign Leader. We're both ambassadors in this foreign land."

I sipped and watched him over the top of the glass.

His mouth opened and closed, but Reverend Holding held his tongue.

Pink and Randall had at last moved to Lauderdale! It had taken another miscarriage, this one early on, and none of us being close to her again, to finally convince Randall that living in Lauderdale would be good, not a Cromartie intrusion.

We could see each other every day, laugh and lounge and love. It was a treasured gift of satisfaction.

Pink had driven in her own Ford down Las Olas Boulevard and stepped out wearing the latest candy-and-white-striped narrow-skirt dress with a hat that swept so low over her face its brim almost touched her shoulders. Dried flowers adorned the straw along with beaded white strands that gave it elegance. We talked about her settling in after their move. Then we spoke of mine.

"I've left the church," I said.

"Can't believe it. It's your lifeblood, sister. You've always gained your strength there." She pulled the hat from her head, replaced the hat pins, then puffed her hair with her fingers. She wore tiny pearl earrings and looked refreshingly young.

"I've said it wrong. I'm not leaving *the* church, just the Reverend Holding's. The Methodists have shown no interest in reaching out to the camps anyway, and they have no support for women's suffrage."

"But where will you go? Will Frank go, too?"

"I'm becoming a Seventh-Day Adventist," I said.

Her eyes still reminded me of a child's, curious yet gentle.

"They're Bible-based, just like the Methodists, and they believe in grace, not works.

"I hear they have scads of rules. That should be suitin' you, sister."

"They're committed to reaching out to others in very specific ways, that's all, Pink. They send missionaries to a number of countries. They almost always begin with a school, whether they've gone to Egypt or a needy city here. Why, they opened their first Sabbath school in 1872. I've even thought of going to their college at Oakwood, in Alabama. They're not afraid of the spiritual and intellectual work of women. They see them as having value beyond motherhood. Ellen White—who was, by the way, both a wife and mother—was deemed both wise and spiritually guided until the day she died. Just this year."

"You've done some studyin'," Pink said. She twirled the long string of pearls that hung almost to her waist.

"They're health sensible, too. Most don't eat meat, for religious reasons I haven't grasped yet. Just makes me sluggish. Fruits and vegetables and fish and chicken are more than enough to keep a soul healthy, I've found. And if we ever find a way to be rid of the insects, we'll have dairy here, too, and our bones'll be strong enough without red meat."

"What does Frank say?"

"I haven't told him yet." I fanned my face. "The Adventists don't have a place to meet except in homes, but that's fine. I'm sure he'll not stand in my way. He's always so supportive."

"Leavin' the church," she said. She stared out the window. Yellow orchids bloomed in the oak tree. "Methodist thinkin's been your whole life. Won't you miss teachin' Sunday school and sittin' with Papa and hearin' Bloxy play guitar and all?"

"Methodists introduced me to the foundation. But I truly hope that Christ has been my life, Pink," I said. "Oh, I'll miss the familyness on Sunday. But that Holding had no right to whip Louise and other childless women or single ones when what he wanted to do was harness me."

"I suppose the denomination don't really matter," she said.

"It's about the life of Christ. That's what the word *gospel* in Greek means, 'good news.' And if it's the good news we're to live by and share with the world, the roof under which we do it really isn't important. What matters is what's holding it up, the foundation. I don't believe that Holding is."

"Wish I had your faith, sister," Pink said. "Reflect it like you do."

"I'll best reflect it surrounded by Seventh-Day Adventists, I think, than by the Holdings of the world. Now, enough about my changes. What about yours? Besides those candy red nails."

"Well," she said, fluttering her fingers before me, "I'm pregnant. Keep a-tryin'."

I stood and reached for the duster, brushed at the swags and tassels at the window coverings, my heart catching in my throat. "Is Randall going to be around?"

"Oh, yes, he's promised. He said to assure you that he'll be travelin' less. Acted more concerned what you'd say than even me. He's actually plannin' to sell land tracts here in Florida, so he promises to be at my side when this baby arrives."

"Which is when?"

"I'm only three months now, so, September."

"I'll be there with you," I said, "if you'd like."

"Hope so, sister, if you're not too busy. With all this ruckus with the Methodists and your recruitin' more Indians for school—"

"Nothing more important that being there with you. And I'm not recruiting. Tony Tommie might. He's doing well. But that was never my intent. I hope they'll build their own schools and teach their own children. Who knows, maybe Tony will become that first teacher. Frank received a letter from him—can you imagine that? Handwritten in English after less than a year of schooling!"

"What did he say?"

"Wants a loan." I laughed. "For alligator eggs, which I suppose he'll hatch to pay back the money and have enough left over to buy shoes—he spelled it s-h-o-s—and schoolbooks and a bicycle. It's for ten dollars."

"Of course Frank'll loan it to him," Pink said. Her words held a wistfulness that made me turn from the tassels to her.

"Tony wrote in the letter: 'I paid you back soon.' Still needs work on his future tenses because he meant, I'm sure, 'I will pay you back soon.'"

"Frank's so kind and reliable," Pink said with a sigh. "You chose such a harborin' man."

In May, Pink lost the baby. She carried not quite into the fifth month before the familiar aches and bleeding and the blending with loss began. She'd been in Lauderdale. She had a good doctor. She'd eaten well. Still, we had not protected her nor ourselves from another grieving loss.

Randall called me at the earliest signs, right after he'd fetched the physician, and I'd stayed with her day and night until it was clear that her body had once again failed to give her what she longed for most.

Randall's face was a tight canvas stretched across a rigid frame. He'd lost weight, and I could see a hollowness now when he grimaced, a feature of his face I hadn't noticed before.

"I'm sure it's not her fault," he said.

I shook my head at him. His face lacked the usual tan of Floridians, and now Pink's condition appeared to make him pale as a New Yorker at the beginning of the season.

"Why am I being punished?" Pink said. I sat against the pillows of her bed, holding her, rocking her, stroking the side of her face. "What have I done wrong? Why doesn't God want me to have children?"

"We'll try again, Pink. When you've recovered," Randall said.

"But the doctors said my body wasn't—"

"I can't believe God doesn't want your happiness, Pink," I said, my eyes silencing Randall. "I just can't. But it might not be in this way. Maybe your body isn't strong enough to bear children, because we're all different. Maybe it's something in Randall. Maybe we just can't know."

Randall shook his head and walked out the door.

"Don't go," Pink called to him.

"I'm just getting some air," he yelled back.

We heard the screen door slam and the barking of their hounds as he must have neared the animals' pens.

"He's angry with me," she said. "What could be more important than havin' babies, raisin' them into lovin' children?" Pink caught quick breaths in between sobs. "Oh, I know you've found other ways. I didn't mean that."

"It's all right, Pink, honest to truth. You needn't worry about my feelings, not at a time like this." I patted her shoulder. "Try to get sleep now, honey. Get your strength back. Life always looks better when we're rested. Then all this grief can actually change us. It may be the only value in loss we really ever find."

"How'm I supposed to change, sister? This is just who I am."

I stroked her hair, rubbed her shoulders, felt her sink into me. I talked softly as to a child until she slowly drifted off to sleep. I stayed there with her for an hour or more, staring out the window at the varieties of green, the staghorn ferns and palmettos, arelia and lantana. I heard squirrels rusting beneath the holly trees then the screen door shut and imagined Randall had come back. When Pink's breathing changed to sleep, I slipped away.

"How do you do it?" he asked me when I eased the bedroom door shut and turned to face him in their living room. His eyes followed me. He held a cigar in a hand hung over the arm of their sand-colored stuffed chair. Smoke drifted up around his now thinning hair.

"Do what? Give to her? I love her."

He shook his head. "Keep from pregnancy."

My eyebrows raised before I could censor them. "There are devices," I decided to say then, uncomfortable to be discussing this intimacy with a man not my husband. "Clinics that offer advice. For both men and women."

I poured myself limeade from the pitcher on the tray at the sideboard, brushed the smoke away from my face.

"That's what you do?"

I walked back to sit in front of him. His eyes were dark marbles set in bleached concrete.

"Actually, no, it isn't, though I've heard they work well. We, Frank and I, have an understanding. That love and passion need not be expressed in…those terms. They can be conveyed in the care we have, what we give to each other. Even beyond, in the love we share for our family and neighbors."

Randall snorted.

"We don't force our views on anyone, Randall."

I sipped at the tart taste of liquid. The glass straw clinked against the side of the glass, felt cool against my fingers. "It is a way we've chosen. We are as joined together as any couple, perhaps more so as we see each other not through lust-filled eyes nor even procreative ones. But through love, equally given and received, not one sex dominated by the power of the other."

"That's how you see it? I 'dominate' Pink?"

"Poor choice of words. I only meant that some women want so much to have children that they risk their very lives for it. It's as though they're held captive by their desire. They can't see that they have value and worth without them."

"You've never wanted them? Never adopted or took one in?"

"I had my teaching," I said.

He didn't say anything, but his eyes narrowed, searching. I hadn't known him back in the early Lauderdale days.

"Our culture doesn't hold single women in high regard nor married women without children, either," I said. "Sometimes, and I'm not saying you do this, Randall, but sometimes the men in our lives tell us in subtle ways that having children is the only way we'll ever make them happy as husbands, that our existence bears fruit only when we make a man a father. Frank has never ever given me that message. He understands me completely and communes with me in a deeply profound way."

"Mystical, sounds like," Randall said. He wiped the back of his hand over his mouth.

"Pink says you love children."

"I've lived without hers all these years."

"Maybe Pink needs to know that you love her just for her, not for the family she so desperately wants to give you."

"Wouldn't change anything. We're both passionate people."

"You're both adults, too. It's a learned thing, Randall, your body's response. Education could do wonders. And if it meant the life of someone you loved, you could discover a myriad of ways to express that, ways that wouldn't endanger her. Another pregnancy and miscarriage could do that, you know."

He put the cigar in his mouth and looked at me through the curling smoke, his teeth straight and bared. "You're as tough as a Cracker, Ivy. As hard as those people who live on nothing and tell the world they're happy to do it."

"Those folks are survivors. Have to be in the Keys. They do what they must, so I'll take the comparison as a compliment."

"Not how it was intended," he said as he pushed himself up from the chair. "But then you always did see the world through rose-colored eyes. Excuse me while I check in on my wife. Think a trip back to the Hot Springs for her might well be in order."

March of 1917 brought an early spring, even in Ohio, where Frank let me drive him when his father became ill. After weeks of lingering, he died. It was a difficult time of loss though the service was lovely and Frank had a chance to see a half brother, but still not Will.

My husband said the strangest thing at the funeral. He said that he was now an orphan, which while true, seemed odd, to think of him as orphaned at his age. But the more I thought of it, as we stood beneath the maple trees at his father's home and watched the buds ready to bring forth new life, the more I saw its truth. We are all in first relation to our parents, first attached to them. Without them there's an emptiness, a missing linkage, with no time after they are gone to discover them: what our parents thought of when they fell in love or took on a new adventure. No time now to ask them, to see how we are like them or how different as we've moved inside the circles of our own making. No more time to tell them how we loved them.

I slipped my hand inside Frank's. "Annie Beck says in her Episcopal prayer book there's a verse about being 'protected from sudden death.' She says she always says a loud amen to that. Wants to always have a chance to say good-bye, and you did that, Frank."

"All just children, aren't we? Bigger children and older."

"And living with the wounds and lessons we acquired when small and vulnerable. What we learn first is so powerful."

I vowed to spend more time with my papa and to give Frank the extra attention he so deserved.

Broward State Bank opened, with Frank as a principal but with his good friend W. C. Kyle as the president. Bloxham mentioned in passing that Frank was probably worth close to a million dollars now.

"Good heavens, don't even think that!" I said.

"Probably on paper, land, and banking; those're his interests."

"That's just talk, and not good talk either." I dismissed the speculation.

"I overheard him and Mr. Erickson once," Bloxham continued. "He said something about Frank didn't need to live like a pauper, that Scripture didn't really mean a camel could pass through that needle easier than a wealthy man goes to heaven. I figured a man's lawyer would know his value."

"Have you ever, well, felt that you didn't receive all you could have, from Frank, I mean?"

My brother looked startled. "Where did that come from?"

"Just wondering," I said.

I kneaded coarse dark flour, my knuckles sinking into the dough pressing out the soothing scent of yeast. My brother sat with his hands folded, his forearms leaning onto the table so that I could see that cowlick swirled near the top of his crown.

"I have a good life, Ivy. Louise and I do. Some people aren't meant to be so much as others. No less blessed, though. That's how I see it. I don't have the weight of being the postmaster or the head of anything. Berryhill's the brains behind our venture. So Louise and I spend good time together, reading, traveling." He picked up a piece of dough and pressed it between his fingers.

"And serving at church."

"That too. Playing guitar. I don't worry much. Something to be said for that, a lesson your Frank is still learning."

Frank did struggle, with issues of money and worth. He always pointed out ways others might improve their lot or how we could assist, as though getting everyone raised a step or two would make him feel better about himself. Maybe it would make him feel less guilty, a thought that hadn't until then occurred to me.

"Running water had to cost him plenty," Bloxham said, as though to confirm his own observation. He leaned back and sat straight in the chair, then pulled open the screened cabinet for a chunk of cane sugar. He sucked on it.

"He still likes to dip rainwater from the barrel, as though he hasn't really accepted what he brought about." Bloxham smiled at that and I did too.

Frank's suggestion to add running water into the house had been a lovely idea. He mentioned it while watching me water all the staghorn ferns that flourished around the house.

"Won't have to carry rainwater if it comes through a faucet," he said. "For sure you'll win blue ribbons at the garden club exhibitions and you won't be so tired from doing it."

"You worry about me too much, Frank. I'm sturdy as a mule even if I don't weigh a hundred pounds."

"Strong wind would fly you like the flag."

We'd laughed together and I'd thought the luxury of running water not too extravagant. The Kings had it and so did several others not considered to flaunt their status.

Still, for Frank to be a millionaire, well, that was an unsettling thought, one that might cause consternation for him as he communed with the keeper of his soul.

When Frank donated land to the Women's Federation so we could build our own club in Lauderdale, I wondered if perhaps Bloxham had been correct about my husband's wealth. Still, Frank placed his worth in integrity and honesty, took his wages in action his money incited. He did talk about donating land for a hospital, possibly a school. He lived simply and quietly, the way that I loved, and his donations were not displays of his assets but a way to once again give to others.

I thought his gesture of donating a piece of land to the Women's Federation in downtown Lauderdale, right on Andrews Avenue and Broward Boulevard, the most wonderful statement that he approved of my decision to work toward suffrage and all the other causes I felt so strongly about. I became president of the Florida Women's Suffrage League that year.

The donation also confirmed for me his acceptance of my decision to leave the Methodists. There had a been some whispering and woeful gossip about my spiritual state, but when I didn't die from a lightning strike and didn't malign the Methodists, the roar died down.

Since the Seventh-Day Adventists didn't have a church, the few communicants met in homes, worship happening wherever hearts are turned from personal gain. Meanwhile, I liked the intimacy of the community, not unlike how I imagined the early church had met and gathered, quietly seeking guidance for service and protection through Scripture and shared learning. The nurture and support of the small gathering that shared Sabbath days fed my spirit.

"You have Sundays free now," Annie Beck said, watering her prize begonias, "what with your Friday and Saturday Sabbath."

"I do. So I can take my cards to the Seminole camps on Sunday afternoons."

"Land sakes! Doesn't God work in mysterious ways!"

There had been what I called a hiccup of activity about the Indian situation when a statewide group known as the Friends of the Florida Seminoles had gotten the legislature to set aside nearly 100,000 acres throughout Florida for reserves. Florida officials said the Indians were a source of embarrassment, appearing as they did out of the swamps, sometimes begging, being found drunk, often becoming victims of bootleggers and developers. There had been a few visits by Federal Indian Affairs agents back in 1909 and again in 1911 but they'd amounted to nothing. At least now firm land had been allocated, but Frank said it would come to nought.

"They'll never go," he said. "Who can blame them? A state reservation. No commitment for maintenance or housing. Nothing. They deserve to be left alone, where they can hang on to the past as long as they can."

"That is the heart of it, though, Frank," I said. I heated the iron on the stove, tested it with spit to my finger, then pressed it over his shirt. "I'm coming to see that hanging on to what's past is wasted effort. Carrying what we value from it into the future, that's where we need to place our vigor, I'd say."

He grunted and returned to his paper.

Construction began on the Women's Club that year, and the firm that employed both DeWitt and Augustus won the bid to build the facility. Both brothers worked together on the construction and we were the happiest family of Cromarties—until America entered the war.

It would be a short war, everyone said. At least our part in it. With America engaged now, we'd only have our boys there a year or so, said the official line. I wanted to support the government and I did, outwardly. But I agonized inwardly when, along with so many husbands and sons, my brothers joined up to head to France.

At the going-away party the afternoon before DeWitt and Gus boarded the train, Papa played the piano and we sang. Frances, DeWitt's wife, stood bravely at his side. I watched tears slide down Gus's face. Our voices carried out the windows, lifted over the cowhorn orchids blooming yellow against the old oak tree.

I sang but without the joy that singing and chanting often brought me. I felt defeated, watching Old Glory rise up the flagpoles Frank had set years before. All my efforts toward suffrage had changed nothing when it came to the very human quality of aggression and defense. And now here they were, the flesh that I loved going off to trenches to face foreign enemies and illness, too. Influenza killed almost as many as wounds, people said, and the thought of sending my brothers into that was a constant reminder of my inadequacy to foster any lasting social change.

Some Seminole boys had enlisted as well, along with Della's son. They hadn't joined us at this farewell gathering though they'd been invited. They were always included. A few of the Jumper and Osceola boys signed up, too. We wanted Lauderdale to take the lead in community relations. I imagined the races would be separate in the troops and thought it the strangest nation that asked its men to fight for freedom but under separate conditions.

The only bright spot was that I'd influenced Albert not to go. We'd convinced him that Papa needed him home, to help with the cropland—purchased with Frank's no-interest loan. I'd debated with myself and decided that Papa and Albert's leaving for other parts was preferable to my baby brother going off to war.

Albert was barely twenty-two, and if the war didn't last long, perhaps we could keep him out of harm's way permanently.

Papa had his eye on a larger piece of newly drained land near Lake Okeechobee.

"You and Papa can start clearing ground. Then when Gus comes back from Europe, he can join you. You'll be helping Papa a great deal, Albert. Gus, too."

"I told you not to try to talk me from it," Albert said.

"Well, I'm not. I just want you to see how needed you are. I only have your best interest at heart. You're looking so much healthier since you came here, finished school."

"Just don't want me to do something foolish for myself."

"You'd be serving either way, Albert. Helping family—and planting crops the government can use for troops—it's all important."

"Just not as interesting," Albert added.

The land Papa'd found wasn't far from Indiantown, an area near where the Cow Creek Seminoles lived, and with the inland waterway nearly complete, shipping crops to rail lines and markets north would be easy regardless of the distance.

The Bowers family, two brothers and a sister, farmed citrus in that area. The Bowers were friendly with the Indian people, we'd heard. It would be a lucrative piece of ground for my brothers and father to farm, a safe place. Albert finally came to that conclusion and stood beside me when we sent the two bugs off to war.

Frank continued to be busy with his council term. The city reelected him in April, and he received his registration certificate as a banker. He spent more time now in activities away from home, going in to the bank, talking with potential investors and encouraging them to place their funds in the Fort Lauderdale State Bank where he served as president. A flurry of effort to raise money to match a Massachusetts investor hoping to build a tourist hotel in Lauderdale after the war took Frank's time. The board of trade was involved along with the Lauderdale realtors and bankers, the city and private investors. "Business as usual," I called it.

It should have been a life held in a sheltering hand with letters arriving from DeWitt and Gus that they fought yet still lived.

And it was, until Albert became ill.

Almost overnight it happened, though looking back I could remember times when he was younger that he'd coughed and looked as pale as a raked beach.

He'd had a slight cough again that summer. We thought it might be from the dust and dirt of newly cleared ground. He liked the work, his long fingers pulling and tugging at palmettos and helping fell pines. He and Papa tended the land, the oldest and youngest Cromarties together, both singing and humming as they stacked and burned cuttings.

They'd decided to give the clearing a rest for a few days and came back to the house in Lauderdale.

Albert's cough became a fever. One minute he fanned himself at the kitchen table, eating marmalade on a slice of one of Della's fresh-baked biscuits, and the next he spoke strangely, about rivers rising and lettuce lakes being submerged by falls of water. We decided to move him to our home, closer to the evening breezes and the doctor, too. I've been forever grateful I hadn't been traveling.

Despite the cool packs and compresses, Albert's fever kept going higher. Nothing Pink or Papa and I did made a difference. He became delirious. He wrestled us and something else in his sleep, his eyes open and glazed. His breathing turned troubled. It wasn't like the yellow fever that had plagued the region just twenty years earlier but swifter and crueler, taking the healthy and young without warning.

"It isn't the flu, Ivy," Dr. Kennedy said. "Tuberculosis. He's probably had it for a time. His resistance is way down."

Even the medicine Alfred Beck sent over had no effect.

"He needs to be moved to the TB hospital in Miami."

"We can't care for him here?" I asked.

"Needs isolation. And twenty-four-hour care. Not realistic—even for you, Ivy, with your stamina. You're all exposed now, too. Even Pink. We'll stabilize him," Kennedy said. "I'll make the arrangements."

But during the first week in October, 1917, when the sky hung heavy with dark clouds threatening thunder and lightning, Dr. Kennedy said it was too late for any hospital. Between family and those of our churches, we'd had help to ensure that Albert stayed constantly attended, but Dr. Kennedy told us not to hope for recovery.

"There's always hope," I told him, "with prayer."

Next to Albert's bed, I wiped one of the dieffenbachia leaves of a plant Albert had given me years before. The white speckles appeared like stars against a sea of green. It seemed to me his breathing had quieted, that our prayers had been answered in the way that we hoped.

"Did I wake you?" Albert's eyes opened to look at mine. They were clear and moist and lacked the fever of the night before. He patted my hand, swallowed, and tried to speak.

"Thanks." He croaked the words.

"Nothing to thank me for," I said. "We all wanted to be here, to help you through this."

"For being strong. For everyone. When I'm gone."

"You're going to make it," I whispered to him. "Prove Tom Kennedy wrong. You'll put flowers on my grave someday."

He shook his head. "Will you miss me when I'm gone?"

"Oh, Albert. You said that to me as a baby, do you remember? When I left to take my test?" I felt tears press behind my nose.

"Didn't want you to go."

"But I came back. And you have, too. You're much more rested now."

"Time to live and a time to die," he said. He sounded so wise and mature, yet something in his voice sent fire bells to my head and I felt rather than thought my next words.

"Don't you want to live? Don't you want to keep fighting? You can make it, Albert. Don't talk like this."

He shifted then, his long fingers moving along the linen sheet as though playing an unseen piano. His breathing sounded like leaves scraping against the window.

"Are you uncomfortable? That's expected," I said in my teaching voice. Even I could hear it. "When you've been away from us for so long, fighting the fever. You're going to be fine, Albert. Just fine."

I lifted his hand. It felt cool. He squeezed my fingers and sighed.

"Let me go," Albert said.

"I'll not have this hopelessness, Albert."

He smiled. "Your way of being out of control."

"We're going to make you better. Don't you give up the fight now, brother." I heard my voice catch and turned away. He squeezed my hand, spoke to me without words. I turned back, giving him every ounce of will I had to make him want to heal.

His eyes moved toward the water glass.

"Just what you need. Water. We'll refresh you; and in no time, Albert, you'll be fully recovered."

I slipped my hand from under his, patted it, relieved that we had passed this crisis of will. I stood to pour the glass of water from the pitcher, settled the straw.

"You just think on the future now, brother, on getting your strength back for when DeWitt and Gus come home. Should I have Pink come in? Maybe read to you for a while? Albert?"

I looked for an affirmative nod, then saw that he couldn't. His eyes were closed. He had stopped breathing.

"I didn't even have a chance to say good-bye," Pink wailed instantly when I fled into the living room, my hand over my mouth to keep the awful taste there from spilling out. Papa stood, having just woken up. One look at me and he knew. He moved past me to the bed.

Frank put his arm around my shoulder and held me. "Take some deep breaths," he said.

"I thought he'd make it. That he'd be safe here, away from war."

"He came through the delirium," Louise said, coming in from the kitchen, assessing all quickly. "It was natural to assume."

Frances sobbed softly into her handkerchief, pressing the embroidery against her red and swollen eyes.

"We all thought he would," I said. "I was so sure he was better. But he knew, accepted it. I didn't want to hear him say he was dying. I wouldn't let him say it. As though not speaking of it could prevent it." I could hear the escalation of grief thicken my voice. Frank squeezed my shoulder.

"Suppose sick folks know when they're going," Frank said. "Can't be forestalled by avoiding the subject."

"I feel like I've been cheated," I said. "Lost him and the chance to tell him how much I loved him. To hear his last confessions, if he wanted. I didn't pay attention, just drove off full speed on my own little road."

"Don't be hard on yourself, Ivy," Frank said. He patted my shoulder. "Always so hard on yourself."

Papa cried quietly behind us, his forehead on the back of Albert's cool hand. Bloxham helped him from the death bed and we prepared to bury another of Papa's sons.

I missed Albert more than I had thought I would. Perhaps because he was the youngest, had been Mama's last. Perhaps because I'd thought to keep him safe and failed. Perhaps because I had not said good-bye to him, had not wished to let him go. I'd missed an opportunity to commune in a quiet and special way that can only happen once in anyone's brief life.

Annie Beck was seven years younger than I, loved plants and flowers and Lauderdale. But I suppose the greatest bond we shared was childlessness, for Annie Beck had no children and from what she said, did not intend to have them. Yet children filled her mind and hours as she raised funds to feed and clothe small frames regardless of their color.

Sometimes Annie Beck rode to the camps with me, although she preferred to drive. My time there—though not daily, not even weekly—gave me a sense of continuity to my life. Here were families who dealt with hardships and endured. Here were people who lost sons and brothers and didn't permit grief to steal their generosity. Here were children, small, smooth hands slipped into mine, bright, dark eyes sparkling as I told the stories, taught the words, and heard them sing the songs.

"What a fine thing to do, Ivy," Annie Beck said of our visits.

No other children came forth to go to school in Lauderdale. Tony had seen success from what I could discover and yet no one else had risked leaving the camps to make their way in town. I wasn't sure how he'd been received after he finished school. No word had come to us about his acceptance back or lack of it.

I had never attended a Green Corn ceremony so knew only secondhand about what could happen to a person who defied the tribal ways, which Tommie had, of course. Annie Tommie had invited me but I did not attend, in part because I could not accept their views of the medicine bundle's spirit and so felt that being there would be dishonest on my part.

Frank went.

"Believe we share the same Creator," Frank said.

"Oh, I agree," I told him. I sliced fresh pineapple to complement the green beans and fried chicken I served. "It's just that I think I'd be giving up a part of myself if I stood by and watched that bundle blessed."

I did agree we knew the same Creator. And it formed a natural path to me that they might find strength and comfort in knowledge of the Son sent to live among us, learn how He gave His life to rescue us and teach us about love. I wanted them to know, not to convert them to my thinking, but for them to have the choice. Education is always, after all, about modeling the choice.

My friendship with Annie Tommie at the camp continued, and I could see we were kindred spirits. She wanted something different for her people, too, something enduring wrapped in dignity. Once when Annie Beck and I were sipping Annie Tommie's sofkee in her chickee, I noticed in one of the hanging twine bags that held the family's precious things a Christian Bible pressed against the rope.

"Wherever did you get that?" I asked her, nodding toward the book.

"Joe Bowers," Annie Tommie said.

"From Cow Creek way?"

"He brings Indians from Oklahoma, talk about your Jesus person. Preacher Brown, they call him. I go hear. His family scared out during second war. Come back as Baptists." She grinned.

"But still a Seminole," I said, and she nodded.

"Always Seminole. Hear George Washington one time, too. He a Wewoka, Oklahoma man. Has Baptist mission at Bowers Grove."

"At Bowers Grove. Near Indiantown. So the Baptists are there permanently now. My father farms out that way, he and my brother. Well, not

Albert now. Maybe Gus when he gets back. Isn't it strange, the connections?"

Annie Tommie's granddaughter, Pocahontas, raced in, chasing after a dog with a cypress laundry stick. "You. Outside," Annie Tommie directed, and the girl giggled and disappeared through the opening. We sat quietly sipping, we three women, listening to the swamp sounds broken up by the distant hum of automobile engines and the beeps of impatient people's car horns.

"Squatters come," Annie Tommie said then.

"More trappers?" I asked.

She shook her head. She pushed the long sides of her cape up over her elbows and crossed her arms over her broad chest. "Come farm. Take fields cleared. We plant cane and corn. Many times again. Chop more trees first. No fight."

"Isn't it your land?" Annie Beck asked. She sat on the platform having her first taste of the ground-corn sofkee.

"They can't just come and take it from you," I said.

"Say don't belong to us. Their land, our land. Say we have other land, government gives."

"I'll bet that's Frost talking, or someone like him. But you've farmed this. Paid for it. You've cleared the trees and sold the firewood. There's no need for more clearing, I don't think, but you ought not to have to fight for your fields. I don't like the sound of this, Annie."

"Start at Indiantown. Say Cow Creeks must go to place set for them."

"They have 2,200 acres there, right where they've always lived. They don't have to move, and others aren't to bother them."

"Say may need move. Others want land. Happen here."

"This is different, Annie, because it's not a reserve. But you've worked it and I don't like the idea of squatters just taking it from you. We need to alert that federal agent, Spencer."

Annie Tommie snorted. "He want Cow Creeks off reserve, to sell good land. Shed no tears for this place. I speak no more."

"Land sakes, someone should speak about it," Annie Beck said.

"The Indian Affairs Committee or the Women's Federation," I said.

"Do what you do," Annie Tommie said. She sucked on her full lower lip as she did when deep in thought. She scratched at the soft spot inside her elbow and at last said, "More come though. Always do."

When the war was over, Gus and DeWitt returned to welcoming arms, and things in the nation began to boom again. DeWitt stayed in Lauderdale and Gus moved out to Lake Okeechobee to help Papa farm a little island he'd bought named Ritta; and even Gus heard of the problems in Indiantown and closer to the Cow Creeks.

"People say the agent, Spencer, up in Fort Myers, is starving the Cow Creeks off their reserve," Gus told me.

"That's the federal man assigned to the Seminoles near us," I said.

"Doesn't sound right, his attitude toward those he's supposed to be protecting."

"Is it safe for you out there?"

"Don't worry about us," Gus said. "Worry over the government's employ of a weasel like Spencer."

I began writing and recruited Annie Beck's flowery penmanship to write to legislators and the Women's Federation to do the same. We'd find a way to bring the needs to those of influence; we women had the power to educate and inform.

The Osceolas spoke of squatters, too, when they brought in their shipments of eggs and little alligators, recently hatched. Billy and Frank would talk about how hard it was to keep the alligator pens contained, that outsiders came and found the eggs.

"Sometimes kill gators."

"Destroying the very source." Frank shook his head.

He and Billy moved the palm-sized reptiles to boxes sectioned off for twenty-five or more for shipment north.

"Trouble, maybe like when old bones were moved," Billy said. He counted to make sure twenty-five were in each section.

"That was a long time ago, Billy, ten years or more. Maybe we've learned something through the years," I said. "The grandfather's bones were returned, remember? The Baptists and the government intervened."

"This trouble different. More people now," Billy said. "More wyomee." He wore a white scarf at his neck that hung down over the striped blouse. Billy pulled on the scarf and loosened it, tightened it again, a habit of his. "Not like time with you, Frank Stranahan. You good friend. Work out any troubles."

"Things change, don't they, Billy? Need to take more time, not less, to know each other when the world starts moving too fast."

"More time for change," Billy said as he began to hand Frank his supply of alligator eggs, wrapped in old newspapers.

CHAPTER SIXTEEN

Esther gave birth to another child, this one born lively with health the spring of '18. With motherly perfection, Esther looked after the little girl, Julia, named for Stretch's mother. Great tenderness and sweet, repeated words covered this baby, who at six months was chubby and babbled for her mother's breast.

Esther listened to Annie Tommie and my suggestions during the pregnancy and had eaten plenty of bananas, pumpkin seeds, and oranges, especially to reduce the leg cramps she complained about. I brought out blackstrap molasses, which I thought would keep her mood up, along with black-eyed peas. I made sure that millet became a staple in her diet and I gave her encouragement, the salve needed for every pregnant woman's soul. Annie Tommie was a staple, too.

Once the baby arrived, Esther used the washing detergent I brought out and boiled water to scald and sterilize her dishes. She kept the shallow scratch well dug by hand for fresh water covered with boards, and Stretch had fenced it off to keep the pigs out. To prevent the spread of germs, perhaps cut down on influenza deaths, that was our plan; though we still knew so little about what caused the deadly disease that had spread from Europe to Montana, from Canada and now south.

One day I'd come to the camp at dusk and could hear men's voices arguing in the distance.

Esther looked at me out of the corner of her eye. "You worry?"

"No. Do I look worried? Just wondering. About the squatters. And all the white trappers that come here."

"Stretch, he live here, Stretch does."

"Stretch is different. He has ties here, with you and the baby. The others don't. There are a number of new faces, Esther. All of them white. Someone needs to see how many there are, out in the farther camps, too."

Esther's eyes opened wide, even on the side with the puckered skin. I wondered if her face ever hurt.

"I need information, truths, to send to Agent Spencer and others, so we can protect your place here and your baby's future, too."

Esther stroked Julia's forehead as the baby nursed but held the child's arms tightly into her breast. "I fix you facts, fix," she said. "No bother Stretch. Come back five days, not sun, no sun time. Stop by alligator flags." She fidgeted on her seat, crossing the baby onto the other side and dismissing me with her focus on her infant.

The night turned cool. Frank had worked late on one of his projects. He sought a way to deed land for Stranahan Park to the city, but if he could sell it instead, the money could be used to help finance the hotel that everyone, including the city, wanted. Frank sat on the council and couldn't sell the land to the city directly. That would have been a conflict.

"So sell it for a dollar," I suggested, "and deed it to a private party. They can sell it to the city for that six thousand dollars and have the buyer donate the money to the building fund so the tourist hotel could be built."

"Might work," Frank said, his eyebrows raised. "Didn't know you had a high-finance kind of mind, Mrs. Stranahan."

"I have a 'get it done' kind of mind, even if it takes a convolution, which it seems to when development, tourism, and government wind together like rope."

I had my own convolution. I'd eased out the door, hoping to be back before Frank ever knew I'd been gone. Still, I left him a note so if he awoke he wouldn't worry. He had been rising more often in the night to relieve himself; and because he worried about waking me, he'd insisted I move across the hall to one of the bedrooms we'd set aside for northern guests. But he often looked in on me and I didn't want him to find an empty bed.

Annie Beck had wanted to come with me. She was an adventurer and sustained student of life.

"Not this time," I said.

"You come by or call me just as soon as you're back, you hear?"

"I hear and I will," I said.

Now here I sat, wood storks cackling loud enough that I heard them above the engine before I turned it off. The Model T backfired once when

I stopped well short of Annie Tommie's camp, near a patch of alligator flags, as Esther had instructed. I pulled the car off the road as far as I dared and shut down the lights and waited. It was close to 4:00 A.M. I hadn't wanted to be late.

The sounds of crickets and bullfrogs and screech owls filtered into the night. I smelled jasmine and the musty scent of washed roots and leaves. The swamp noises were soothing not interrupted by humans.

Though I listened with as intent an ear as I could turn, I still didn't hear anyone, not even when I felt the touch on my shoulder.

I jumped, hitting my arm on the steering wheel.

"You early," the man said.

"A lady is always on time!"

I cocked my head so I could see who it was from beneath the shadow of my hat and looked into the eyes of Tony Tommie.

"I thought you'd gone to Oklahoma when you finished school."

He signaled for silence with his hand and motioned for me to remove my hat and leave it, which I did. Then he lowered the handle and pulled open the door. The smell of whiskey drifted by my nose.

"Have you been drinking whiskey?"

"What you think?"

"I'm not sure this is wise, then, Tony. I cannot abide—"

"You safe," he said.

He led me a short distance, steady on his feet until I saw a low, flat boat on the lake of lettuce leaves. There'd be four to five feet of water beneath the leaves that were thick enough for long-necked limpkins to clutch while their sharp beaks snatched at snails.

Tony helped me into the boat, motioning for me to sit on the shoving seat, his wide hands holding a firm grip on mine until I sat. I felt my way more than saw. His form stepped into the boat. The small craft sunk lower. Tony reached for the pole, the familiar gator hook beaked out from the end. He pushed out into the center then toward an outlet, taking us deeper into the mangroves, moving easily through waterlogged leaves.

As familiar as skin these places were, I imagined, though the lettuce lakes had changed these past years as water had drained out beneath them. As Tony poled, I watched, still recovering my surprise at seeing him, my senses tuned up with the possibility of moonshiner influence.

Tony had inched up in height while attending the Lauderdale school and had a kind of presence about him now, of power and intent. He wore a skinning knife at his belt, and my foot had bumped a small-bore rifle against the side of the craft.

The smell of decay and roots reached my nose, and my skin felt wet with the night air. "When did you get back?"

He grunted, and something large splashed beside us and I started. Water gentled against the side of the wooden boat. Tony flipped the hook into the water and another splash broke the night. I knew that an alligator had thrashed momentarily beside us and been encouraged by Tony's hook to move along.

"Still early," Tony said. "Wait now." I felt him settle onto the seat, facing me.

"Will you be staying?"

"Show you what you want," he said after a pause. "When time comes, you remember who helped."

"Of course I'll remember," I said. "Would you like toasted pumpkin seeds? I brought a few along." I patted my pockets for the bag I'd brought.

"Make something happen."

"You must think I have much more influence than I have. If I can, if what I find out about the encroachers and squatters can be verified and believed, we'll get something good to come of it."

He grunted. Just the beginning of dawn, Tony stood to pole us out into a small stream that appeared to circle the area I thought housed the camp. He sat then and lifted two oars and sculled the boat sideways so we paralleled the cypress-bordered shoreline. We made our way, paddling and scootering the boat forward through narrow tangles.

Enough light filtered through the treetops and ferns to see the etched outlines of foliage. Blackness separated the smoky fires coming from the homes of Esther and Annie Tommie's people, and what I could see now were tiny flashes that looked like firelight, cooking fires of the camps.

Tony scootered the boat forward and we eased up onto solid ground.

"Stay low," he whispered. He reached for the rifle then led the way.

We didn't have far to go. I could see the mounds that must be sleeping people set like spokes of a wheel out from center fires. There were two or three fires with four to five people at each one. Custard apple trees and pines arched around the outside edge of the camp along with the forms of cut trees and slash piles.

As we moved around the perimeter, I watched two men tending copper tubing that disappeared like a snake into foliage. A fire burned beneath a barrel or tub, the heat sending the smells of mash and bootleg liquor into the morning.

Just the additional people so close to the Seminoles posed a problem. Of greater concern was the still. The whiskey would take all the money the Indians made selling their crafts and vegetables to tourists. What was left of their dignity would disappear into the pockets of bootleggers. Judging from the look on Tony's face as he watched, his hands squeezing and releasing on the rifle, the stills also sent invitations for violent retaliation.

Morning dusk filtered through the trees and Tony motioned for me to ease back. We crouched low, moving away from the fires but parallel to the water that had brought us. I watched each time I set my foot, hoping nothing would buzz or slither as I stepped.

I'd seen the land on the section maps but I hadn't realized how close to the Seminole families these lands were being developed. There couldn't help but be trouble if the Indians remained here; bootleggers joining squatters just fueled the fire.

Tony helped me into the boat. High above, wood stork parents circled in the air currents, their calls as distant as fog horns. Tony pushed the boat out and moved us back into the water, back toward my Model T. He paddled hard and quiet as we eased on by the squatters' camp, alive now with dogs barking and the smell of salt pork being parboiled.

A heavy dew had settled on my Model T when I reached it. At the car, I drew a small map on the back of butcher paper. Tony hadn't left. He stood, one foot up on the running board, watching me draw.

I looked up at him. "Why did you bring me, Tony?"

He shrugged.

I sniffed at the air. "It will hurt your own supply, won't it?"

He wiped his mouth with the back of his hand.

I thought of Cap Valentine, how he died without my ever speaking of his habit. "Everything you've worked for will be lost, Tony, if you drink it away. You've done so well."

Tony shrugged his shoulders again.

"There are hospitals for you. In Oklahoma and North Carolina. You could go there. And even stay and work there, with your education. You've come so far; you have so much to offer your people."

"You tell agents. Make something happen."

"I'll do my best," I said. "I truly will. For you, too, if you're asking for yourself."

He walked into the morning light with no further words.

I sent my letter off to Spencer, furiously writing of what I'd seen with my own eyes and imploring him to act. *The government is responsible for the conditions of the Seminoles even if they wish to ignore it*, I told him. There were squatters and bootleggers moving in and children exposed, and I wondered just what was it the government planned to do.

I received no response.

I wrote again, to him and to my congressmen and to others who might make a difference about the conditions and the violators. Commitment to this cause motivated my efforts, not whether anyone responded.

"Indian affairs," Frank said, "are low on the totem pole of influence with the government, I'm afraid." He drank the yarrow tea I'd fixed him.

"It's wrong, Frank. Liquor will be their death, it will, generation after generation unless the government works to prevent it. They have a special obligation. Americans tend to forget that, want to say 'what's done is done,' but it's true. Hope is the best defense against evil and the government owes them that hope."

"Don't need to convince me," he said, lifting his cup of tea. He wore thick glasses all the time now and the heat steamed them. "But without a treaty, the government *can* forget them. Never finished their wars. Poor ending, more ways than one. Legally, the government doesn't owe them anything."

"The government could actually sell that land, since they've no treaty, couldn't they, Frank? Then nothing would be left for them. They really have no protection at all!"

He was quiet for a long time before I heard, "Suppose." Then, "Think this is helping some." He showed me his empty cup.

"You ought to be able to sleep through the night, Frank. It can't be normal to be up so much, to flush out your system."

"Flush isn't exactly the word I'd use," he said with a sly smile.

"You dear boy."

"Herb tea's good, though."

"We'll try others and maybe increase the nuts and seeds. Brown rice and eggs; kelp, too, I think, would all help your blood. Good for kidneys. And I don't intend to stop writing to Spencer. Or anyone else until there's action. Hopefully before something violent happens."

"My little revolutionary," Frank said and lifted his cup in a gesture of respect. I did wonder about the Dania land. I'd called it a reserve for years but others might see it quite differently, as land available for claiming, the people intended to receive it left once again to drift and disappear.

Tony's comment, that I "made things happen," came to mind often, too. Did I? I hadn't seen much result over the years. Even he, the star pupil, obviously struggled now with the demon rum. And did we humans make things happen anyway? Or were the things we claimed as ours, the times we acknowledged "yes! I did that," were those moments merely gifts God gave us for not getting in His way?

Pink came by wearing a waist with a rose print on a sable background, a style popular years before but on her looking new and fresh. On the porch, she complimented me on my pearl earrings and the shine of my brown hair, commented on Annie Beck's straight skirt, then fingered the cameo at her neck before taking a deep breath and pulling a canvas from a cumbersome bag.

"It's my accountin' of the New River," she said. "The way it touched me when I came to visit that first time." Loose ringlets of her blond hair framed her face and anxious eyes.

"This is exceptional, Pink," I said. "The lighting is exquisite. I can almost...feel the wetness, the silence, and yet so full of life. I had no idea..."

Pink beamed.

"Land sakes, girl, you've quite a talent," Annie Beck said when I handed it to her. Pink started to intercept the canvas before I realized it, but I had already let Annie Beck take it from my fingers. "Would you draw homes?"

"Oh, with our windmill and live oak, the green screens and the white porch?" I said. "Maybe with the manatees coming in at twilight, the sea-wall, things like that?"

"Too many details," Pink said and laughed. Her fingers reached for the painting Annie Beck held, halted, pulled back. She clasped her hands behind her back.

"It's from your heart, isn't it?" I said. "Not really something you've seen?"

"Feel undressed," she said, "now I've shown it." She dropped her eyes and smoothed the straight skirt over her hips. She kicked at imaginary rocks on the porch boards.

"Do you have others?" Annie Beck asked as she handed it back.

"Dozens. Buried in the trunks. Randall says to paint over 'em. Might give the house and river a try."

"Land sakes, if they're like these, don't paint over them!"

"You could have a showing one day," I said. "At a gallery."

Pink looked up, startled. "Oh, no. That would be exposin', sister. Hung up for perfect strangers to be lookin' at 'em?" She shuddered.

"There aren't any perfect strangers, child," Annie Beck said. She fanned herself then pressed the sailor collar at her neck between two fingers. The act made me look at my own tucked dress and the ironing I'd be doing in the morning.

"Someone might be comforted by what you've drawn, Pink, by your willingness to share yourself. Gain insight, perhaps, learn some important lesson. All the great masters draw people into themselves through their art and make us feel things we never knew were there."

"The way you've captured the shimmering of leaves and the reflections, and the blues and greens, just fine," Annie Beck said, looking over Pink's shoulder. "Alfred knows gallery people up in Tallahassee. I could ask him about a showing. We'd have a fine time with that."

"You always did like taking risks, if I remember. Think what a return might be, that kind of exposure. Seems like you encouraged me to do that once or twice, let others take control."

"Hadn't thought of sharin' my work that way, as bein' somethin' someone else could gain from."

We looked silently at the painting, the morning light brought back as we stood on the porch in the afternoon.

"See what you find out, about a showin'," Pink said then. "I do like paintin' water mostly. Like to think of it as where life is, and keepin' my own healthy, for a baby, should we try again."

"That would give you just the greatest joy, wouldn't it?" I said, sitting on the rattan rocker. I motioned for my guests to take seats too.

"My lifelong prayer," Pink said. "What's yours?"

"Mine?" I leaned back and closed my eyes, listening to the squirrels chatter by the Surinam cherries. "To have you all here, safe and sound in Lauderdale. And for two years, I did. Then the war came and we lost Albert. Now Papa and Gus are gone. Maybe getting them back."

"Havin' everyone here didn't stop bad things from happenin'."

"It surely didn't."

"What about teachin'? Wasn't that what you always wanted more than anythin' in the world?"

"I'd love to see Seminole children in their own school in a place they can call home without fear of ever losing it. Finding ways to respond to change, I guess. Helping them and myself to adjust to all that's happened here."

"Must have been quite a sight before the drainage began," Annie Beck said then. "Wished I'd seen it before."

"Changed the people and this land, what we've done to the water...." Pink sighed.

"Was that a sad or tired sigh?" I said, opening my eyes.

"A waitin' one," Pink said. "Waitin's what I do best."

"I do that too, Pink."

"Don't seem the waitin' kind, sister."

"I'm trying to wait better, and be led."

The three of us sat and watched the river flowing smooth as a Della-shined mirror. Dusk drifted in and with it the wondering if the manatees would.

"I've heard them make chirping sounds," I said, walking to stand at the seawall. "When it's quiet, no breeze like tonight and I can barely see them, I've heard it above the bugs. There are so few now." The evening sat still as a sleeping turtle. Then the insect hum began.

"Guess none are coming in tonight," Annie Beck said. I watched her smooth her cream day dress in the twilight, pull the bow of her hair away from her neck as though to catch one last vestige of absent breeze.

"I guess my greatest prayer is to be faithful to the path I think God set me on, Pink, to take care of things, right wrongs. That I wouldn't let fear or my own willfulness get in His way. That's what I hope. It's a good question you've asked. A very good question, indeed."

Annie Beck drove with me to pick up Mary Munroe in Coconut Grove, and we motored on down the Dixie Highway south, crossing over from Homestead along the corduroy roads of cut pine poles into the Royal Palm State Park.

"Just stick your arm out there and point when you turn," Annie Beck told me from the backseat. "I can never remember those arm signals Alfred told me about."

"Just point?"

"Everyone just gets out of my way."

"They have signal features now," I said.

"Land sakes, who has time for those?"

"You must be *fearless* in traffic," Mary Munroe said turning to look at her.

We looked almost like three generations together: Mary twenty-nine years older than I and Annie Beck seven years younger. I was the middle sister. The years didn't matter: we shared the same spirit.

The Everglades were Mary's pet as Indian Affairs were mine. These monthly trips made sure proper care was being taken since she chaired the Federation's committee on conservation. The Federation practically single-handedly pushed through the park. Mary had taken photographs on a trip in 1916 and shown them about New York when she and Kirk returned there. The scenes of swaying trees and long-tailed birds draped through towering rookeries, double-crested cormorants with wings spread out against a golden sunset sea had been the talk of the General Federation's meeting that year. The imposing palms and water lilies inspired women everywhere about what joining together with a cause could accomplish.

Now, once a month we drove to the Everglades to find the peace of it and assess any legislative action needed to ensure its protection.

The wide vistas of saw grass as far as the eye could see never failed to inspire me. Panoramas dotted with hammocks of trees and vibrant colors and birds and sounds and smells that settled around a person like a comforting cape. More than its oceans, I think, the glades captured perfectly south Florida's personality: vibrance laced with languid; wonder buried inside believed-to-be-known scenes.

We drove to a rookery that had come back after the plume-hunting ceased, and it brought tears to my eyes to see the long egret plumes descend from the trees like a waterfall of alabaster and to hear the lively, lovely sounds of now flourishing life.

"You did something so important protecting this, Mary. You truly did."

"Even my mother noticed," she said. "Got more of her attention than my Sunday school classes."

Afterwards I insisted the two come with me to the Seminole camp near Miami, wanting to learn if encroachers were a threat in that area as well so I could add to my captured facts for the Bureau.

My two friends bought a few little dolls to take home for nieces and some carved boats for nephews.

While there, the man with the weeping eye, the one who walked with a stick and had asked me to leave the cards those years before with Albert, motioned me aside.

"I hope you got the cards," I said. "My sister's the one who brought them out."

His stick held him stable and when he didn't answer at first, I thought he must want to show me a carving he'd done or maybe he had a coon hide for sale.

"Did you get the stories?"

He nodded then, to that word. "Now have one for you."

"Did you make cards?"

He shook his head. "You come see. Early day. I keep safe for you see." His tone brought goose bumps to my neck.

"Why me?"

"You make happen," he said. A worried look eased onto his face, a visage as soft and free of lines as rising brown bread. "Come back. Alone." He reached up to touch my arm, his fingers callused but warm. "I hear you help."

Something in his tone, his words, the question in his eyes, all said that I should risk, should take a chance.

"What's your name?" I asked him.

"Dav-id," he said. "Who hurt Go-li-ath."

I didn't tell either Mary or Annie Beck. I simply said we needed to spend the night at a local hotel and I would need to leave for a while, then come back to pick Annie Beck up by three.

"So mysterious," Annie Beck teased. "Wish I'd have driven down myself."

"Is there another camp? As you found near Lauderdale?" Mary asked. She pulled the pins from her trademark palmetto hat, the brim rolled up at the back. Her short fingers lifted her hair.

"Nothing like that. Just something I wanted to follow up on."

"Look at you, the *fire* in those eyes. I *said* one day you'd be as strident as I."

"But I'm not, Mary, not really. I'm not even sure what it's all about. A little scary, actually."

My guide the next morning was more a man who knew the swamp well than one who walked with bowed legs and stood a foot shorter than me. That's what I saw as soon as he helped me into the swamp boat and we poled out. Dav-id didn't seem the slightest impaired with the poling despite his height and oddly shaped legs. He'd adapted.

"How far is it?" I asked.

He turned to signal silence.

"I'd feel better if I had an idea…" I whispered.

He shook his head.

We continued on for maybe thirty minutes, poling in silence deeper into the swamp, my anxiety rising with each sink of the pole. If something happened to Dav-id...I vowed to pay attention to the subtle signs that would get me back through the saw grass if I needed.

Wood stork babies squawked in the treetop nests. It was the season, and the birds were wild and noisy, never ceasing now, a sound almost deafening as we drew closer through overhanging emerald. We poled into the heart of an area that sounded not unlike a rookery, trees towering high, light screened; birds bobbing in tall branches and arched out like snowballs in a mound of green. Pink could have captured this on her canvas.

A vivid memory flashed quickly, of lying on my back once as a child, looking up through a canopy of trees playing with the sun. But within minutes it wasn't the sight nor the sound of birds calling that took my breath away. It was a growing sense of dread.

Makeshift chickees appeared, almost hidden beneath the trees. A putrid, sickening smell oozed from them.

My guide eased the boat closer and when we bottomed out, he stood to help me. I heard my heart pounding and my breath felt shallow and short. Beneath a canvas, Dav-id lifted a rifle and used the butt of it to balance, his hand gripping the steel of the barrel.

I'd placed a handkerchief over my nose but it did little. With my free hand, I pushed my hat firmly onto my head and followed his limping lead, glad my narrow skirt fell freely above my shoes should I have to bolt and run.

No smoke, no fires, thank goodness, just the chickees; and a strange low humming I couldn't place. The thickness of the tropics folded around us, filtering light and muting sound so the humming proved difficult to identify.

Then Dav-id pushed back one of the openings and I gasped.

Horrifying, vile, and evil is what I saw. Fury had come with me, but I hadn't expected to feel revulsion and compassion inside the same wrenching twist.

For there, stretching toward the ceiling, uneclipsed by any illegality, stacked the bodies of dead birds; hundreds and hundreds of blackened, decaying birds. Flies hummed like a growing thunderstorm, the blackness lifting and the sound increasing when Dav-id touched the stack with the rifle butt; then settling back down to consume.

I felt my stomach lurch; my skin crawled as though covered with a dozen spiders. The dense smell took my breath, and tears pressed against my eyes as I backed out, swallowing the liquid that gathered at the back of my throat, panting quickly to forestall the retching I was sure would follow.

"Come," Dav-id said, motioning me toward another chickee, set back beneath palms.

I felt myself shivering. I took a deep breath when he opened this chickee and held it, expecting another blast of black carcass.

Instead I gazed up at a hushed treasure of feathers. Like mountains of white, hundreds of illegal plumes lay silent. Egrets, herons, flamingos had all given their feathers, hundreds of graceful, living, beautiful birds.

"How did you find them?"

I couldn't help touching them, fingering them, so beautifully designed. I blinked away the blur before me. Sweat dribbled down my cheeks. The smell of salt grew stronger as I lifted one elegant plume, ran its softness across my face.

"Tell White Mother, she make things happen."

"They're worth thousands," I said.

We found two other chickees of feathers and one empty, either awaiting more dead birds or more stash. The shelters, thatched and tied well enough to ward off rain, sat camouflaged by surrounding foliage. Each held a treasure of egret plumes and heron feathers and even the thin slender feathers of flickers.

Dav-id looked around, signaled silence.

"What?"

He acted as though he heard something and I felt a rush of fear and anger, an outrage that perhaps I could confront these beasts who killed for fashion, who massacred and let meat spoil, who slaughtered for the cash and changed the landscape.

Dav-id stood silent as a sandhill crane at sunset and I held myself, did not speak, waiting for whatever danger entered the rookery, man or beast. I heard my heart pound, felt it in my throat.

But Dav-id's tension eased without any confrontation and he motioned me to move out.

Back in the boat I had a chance to think of how foolish I'd been to come here, with a man I didn't know, looking at contraband men would kill to protect, where no one had the slightest inkling where I was. Who said I didn't do things out of my control, I thought. Just let them speak at this.

Back at the camp I told Dav-id, "We'll have to proceed quickly. They could be shipped out soon."

Dav-id nodded.

This time I did make something happen. I called Hiram Byrd, president of Florida's Audubon Society, right there in Miami, told him of the stash and the way to get there. Hiram himself along with state troopers raided the site. They placed the value at $35,000 dollars and donated the feathers to the Smithsonian Institution so others could see the beauty of these creatures and know what part of eternity it was humans were willing to give up for fleeting fashion gain.

"That was terribly dangerous, Mrs. Stranahan," Mr. Byrd told me later. "And there could be repercussions if people find out. Your efforts have cut into significant profit."

"I could no more sit silent about this than drink whiskey," I said.

"Don't ever tell anyone how this came about," Frank said. "If I'd known what you were doing there..."

"What? You'd have tried to stop me?"

"Never that. You aim your own weapons. But I'd have spent a bit more time on my knees considering your safety."

"I just hope they find them," I said. "I'd like to spit right in their eyes." I never got that chance.

Frank was elected president of the city council and I think it was one of his finest terms, when people saw him for what he was: honest to a fault, sincere, selfless, and conscientious with an indomitable spirit, necessary ingredients for the development of a city, a community; for the nurturing of a marriage and a home.

These were good times. People acted happy again despite the gloom they saw from the possible passage of prohibition nationwide.

Frank had a dozen irons in his fire. He had oversight duties with the

Deep Water Harbor Company, which had capital stock of a half-million dollars. Fifteen men had been incorporators; Frank served as treasurer. His Las Olas Bridge Company had finished the road to the beach in 1915, making our sand as well known as Daytona's, even if we hadn't ever raced an auto over it. There'd been a little flack again with D. C. Alexander about the subdividing of the land back in '15. I'd thought that had blown over. But he snubbed Frank, even these years later, whenever the two met in the same room, and I knew dissension still lingered in that transaction. Frank's bank merged with the Broward County Bank and his friend W. C. Kyle became president while Frank stayed on as vice president of the Fort Lauderdale State Bank. I had to confess to him that I really didn't understand how this banking thing worked, what with most people I knew still stuffing any cash they had into mattresses and sugar bowls. The stock exchange proved even more confusing. Frank and W. C. engaged in those activities, too.

"Banking's built on the belief that making responsible loans to people can help everyone," Frank said. "People receiving advice from a good lawyer and a good banker are said to be secure."

"Something's missing there," I said.

Frank thought a bit. "A good bookkeeper's valuable too."

I laughed. "I'm sure that's true but I was thinking of the spiritual advice one needs, to direct all the others. I don't see anything in banking that relies on God."

"Bankers existed in biblical times," Frank reminded me.

"And didn't they get chased out of the temple?"

"Not for changing money, Ivy, just for where they did it."

I became a student again, taking a course on government from the University of Florida extension. As chairman of the Indian Affairs Committee for the state, I felt it essential I understand how the government really worked. Truthfully, I looked for the keys to the doors that would open for the Seminoles, so they could enter into everlasting.

Frank donated land for the Dillard School in 1920, a school where Della's grandchildren could be taught. It would serve Negro children and it gave me hope that perhaps we'd get one built for Indian children before I died.

The thought rose closer to the surface on a day when Tony Tommie stopped by the house. He had that furrowed look on a face that now had puffed, red lines arching across his flat, wide nose.

"Squatters," he said. "Bring cows. Build barn. On Indian land."

"The land around Fort Lauderdale isn't really 'Indian land,' Tony," I said. "It's private, you know, and—"

He raised his hand to stop me. "At Dania."

"On what's been set aside for the reserve? I'm sure they wouldn't allow that."

"Many cows there. Making milk. Sell in town."

"At Dania?"

He nodded his head.

"We've got to go out there, Frank, and see if what he says is true. That's the last place left for them."

"Didn't a Byran buy land out that way, some cousin or something of Reed's?"

"I don't see how he could have. It's all Indian land. They clarified that in 1911. There's only 360 acres. Such a little place."

"I think I remember something about a special grant from Congress Byran got."

"I didn't know about that. We'd best see what Tony's discovered."

We drove the nine miles to the area set aside for the Seminoles. Tony rode with us. It had once been swamp but had been drained, and we passed several prosperous-looking farms growing vegetables and orchards. *Nordstrom* was written on one of the orchard signs and I thought of Jan, of how Pink might have been settled in here, maybe surrounded by children, if she hadn't married Randall, if I had been less meddlesome.

The Indian land stood high and dry, covered with pines. It was prime land and meant to be. Davis Road marked the border. No signs of development or clearing should have shown.

But a fine, pine dairy barn sat there. Guernseys stood penned beside it, thin but chewing their cuds. Smoke lifted into the sunshine from a small house. Dogs barked.

"Many more cows there," Tony said. He pointed into the stand of pines and palmettos. "Many. Agent never come see. Take Indian land."

I insisted Frank stop, and I knocked on the door of the shack next to the board barn. No one came to the door, but it certainly looked like someone lived there, on the Indians' land.

I sent a letter off to Spencer telling him what I'd seen. I wrote to the Commissioner of Indian Affairs, an E. B. Meritt, deciding then and there that I would not cease writing until something happened. Congressman Sears got letters too, outraged ones about permitting special sales to private parties. I'd use my extension education to find out the truth of what Frank had heard about a Byran buying land.

Meritt wrote confirming that a man named Byran had indeed squatted on a portion of the reservation, then convinced the government that they hadn't known, had improved it with their clearing and building and since no Indians were there, gotten a piece broken off, by special order of Congress.

"That could happen again if we don't act," I told Frank. "How dare they? Back-room politics, that's what's operating here, where women aren't allowed."

The government had failed them! They'd permitted land be sold and now tolerated squatters on the pittance that remained. How could the Indians trust them? How could they expect fair treatment?

"I failed them, too," I told Frank. "I should have seen it coming. So busy checking on squatters at the camps that I never thought of Dania. I thought sure the government would keep that sound."

Spencer actually responded to the fourth letter I wrote. He said he had visited the site, had seen the squatters. There were two: King Solomon Branham and M. M. Williams. They had a large herd of cows, more than three hundred, which they assured him were grazing on private land though yes, the barns, house, and dairy sat on government land. "Indian land," I corrected as I read. Spencer noted they provided the first fresh milk to the region and had a number of supporters. He thought them quite surprised to know they were in trouble. "Ha!" I said. They'd been told they could get a lease with the government for the land and eventually buy it, as a Byran had done. While the letter sounded placating toward previous squatters, his final paragraph was not.

They will be evicted. I have begun the proceedings through the Justice

Department. I am most grateful to be made aware of the need.

Spencer sent me a copy of the letter forwarded to Commissioner Meritt and in it he underlined how important it was the government act. *These lands are valuable and must be retained for the use of these Indians. There are no other lands available in this part of the state.*

He had added something that I found distressing in its correctness and impossibility, too.

We must move one camp of Indians, at least, onto those lands very soon to preserve the lands. But of course they will not fight the whites and will not go if there is to be trouble. They would have settled on this tract long ago if it had not been for the splitting of the tract and they feared they would be run out of the tract as soon as they had made clearings.

Action must be at the utmost priority.

It was December 1922, and all should be well in a few months, Spencer assured me. *I should think we'll have it all settled in the new year. The government likes to move quickly in this sort of thing.*

I remember the early part of the twenties with fondness. I cling to them more than I should perhaps, but hope lived within them, within the harvest of my dreams. Women finally got the vote nationwide. Interest in creating an Everglades State Park grew. Fashion changed, and beads and straw flowers and bows replaced plumes and the deaths they required. Hemlines rose along with impulse; the fringe of lamp shades shimmied at undulating hips displayed during sweaty dances like the Charleston.

Frank was reelected every year to the council and served as president more than once. Florida boomed as it never had before. Even Prohibition at last encompassed all the land.

"I thought once we had Prohibition, things would stop spiraling," I told Frank.

"Just more change for Florida, all the coastline to watch. Too close to Cuba for smuggling rum."

"And all the islands in the Keys, so many stills. People don't seem to mind breaking the law over liquor."

"Too many folks willing to buy. Seminoles, too."

Special agents were said to be working to find out who sold to the Indians. The moonshine took food from children, made once noble people drop into stupors. I'd sent my speculations, to no avail.

No one appeared to mind about the morality of money; they were just happy to have some and liked it best when it was spent lavishly on them. We had a dozen northern developers who taught us how to do it. The success of John Collins creating Miami Beach from swamps and marshes and the pastel shades of Addison Mizner's Palm Beach Corporation and his lure of the wealthy to Boca Raton served as a massage. The strong fingers of Florida kneaded those tensed by the influx of wealth and speculation, eased out any worry they might have carried about rapid growth. We'd learned lessons from the schemes nearly twenty years before; we were wiser now, everyone said.

Papa and Gus still farmed near Lake Okeechobee on their Ritta Island. But Gus had found a nurse caring for a man on Torrey Island and rowed her way quite frequently until she promised she would marry him. They began their family quite quickly, almost catching up with DeWitt.

"So common," Louise had offered, her shoulders stiff and straight, "having children so close together."

"I'm just pleased the Cromarties are," Papa said, shaking his finger at me. "Thought for a while I'd be the last of them."

Ordinary people built homes during those years and went into debt to do it. A part of me felt edgy about that, but for a home, debt could make sense. Homes nurtured people, gave stability and permanence to families and children.

We all lulled ourselves into thinking that the twenties would be progressive for everyone. We'd been educated and wouldn't repeat our mistakes. We'd been well taught by our lessons.

Frank, of course, acted with frugality, always careful and conservative. One of his few indulgences was long vacations, mostly north to the mountains in Asheville or to Ohio, that I insisted he take.

I think he looked for a sign of Will when we traveled. No one had heard a thing from him. He'd not touched his bank account for more than a decade, and so in 1923, Frank began the legal proceedings to have Will declared dead.

As the judge read the final papers, I realized we'd witnessed another passing in our family. We'd told ourselves we'd see him anytime now but never had. Each of us had to think a bit about the last time we had seen ol' Will. When had he told that last joke, scratched those rubbery ears, or snapped his suspenders like a recalcitrant child? He'd disappeared without a moment's time to say good-bye. Lives could be like that, simply slip out of sight.

Frank's troubling health improved after that decision to declare Will dead. I hadn't realized he'd been carrying Will's loss around with him.

We had a small memorial service and invited several from the camps. Will had been such a good friend to the Indians. We'd found a certificate among his bank papers about his association with the Red Men group. Underground, he'd worked on their behalf. I wondered if Frank was a member but I'd never seen him wear any lapel pin.

Pink and all the rest of my family came to the service. My sister cried softly as people fanned themselves on chairs beneath the ferns and palms of our yard and told stories of Will's vibrant personality and his risky ways. The Jumper family brought turtle rattles and chanted a grieving song.

"I wonder when he actually died—if he did," I told Frank. He took down the flag from the pole that faced the New River. It was after the service and we worked alone.

"Didn't start thinking of him as gone until last year. Stopped imagining him coming through the door. That's when I knew he was probably dead."

"It's strange to me, his just going away one day and our thinking he'd be returning any minute. Careful with those ropes, Frank. They make terrible burns. It hasn't felt like waiting, not really, until now, until saying out loud that he is truly gone."

"Thought if I pushed the declaration he'd prove me wrong and show up," Frank said. "He could be so contrary at times." He handed me the flag and we began folding it into the triangular shape.

"I don't much like grieving."

"Can't prevent it, Ivy."

"But love is supposed to do that."

His hands had reached mine in the flag folding and he held his fingers over them, speaking words I would think on often in the years to come. "Love does as it can. But it can't prevent pain. The best we can hope for is to prepare people for the grieving that's a part of living so they have ways to make it through."

CHAPTER SEVENTEEN

rank's vigor and will flourished, fed a rich path to prosperity. He took on more tasks with a building company and stock in the Fort Lauderdale Securities Company, in an oil company, and in another construction venture. We often took drives toward Dania or the Hollywood area, as some called it, and ate out, an extravagance to be sure, at a quaint tearoom restaurant made of coral rock. We shared a lovely time together, just he and I sipping cool herb teas.

On one trip I drove him by the reserve to see where the dairy had been and stopped so short he had to brace himself on the dashboard. White dust drifted up around us.

"Whoa there, Nelly," he said, pushing his hat down. "What's the problem?"

"They're still there, Frank. Look. And there are more buildings, not fewer. They haven't moved them off, not one whit!"

"Told you government moves slow."

"But they said they'd move them in December. This is April."

"Three hundred cows won't herd easy, Ivy."

My eyes gazed out across the farm. A new chicken coop sat there. Someone had staked a boat next to the barn. Cows still grazed. Chickens and pigs flourished. It appeared an addition had been added onto the house.

"New commissioner," Frank said. "Best he be getting ready to have correspondence."

"Correspondence. Exactly that."

I started with another long and pointed letter to Lucien Spencer of the Fort Myers agency. I told him he needed to see the conditions of the Lauderdale camps, the encroachment, the bootleggers who were stealing the life from these people. Then I informed him of the changes at Dania. *Those men are still there, adding on to their holdings, clearing more ground for their cows. You simply must do something!*

"Remember when the agents wanted me to take them out to the camps?" Frank said, reading over my shoulder as I wrote. "In the early days? How they'd come back frightened of the dogs?"

"You never wanted to go out with them."

"Couldn't. Never believed that what the government had to offer them would ever help. Always thought being free, on their own, was what would keep them."

"Are you saying I shouldn't push this? Shouldn't take him out there to see what's happening, insist that he do his job of protecting them, getting rid of those squatters?"

"I'm saying I don't think anything has changed in all these years."

I put the fountain pen down, picked up my wreath. I twisted a twig, tied tiny dried flowers into the weaves. It would be a present for Annie Beck, for her thirty-sixth birthday, along with another begonia I'd discovered on a trip to New York. I squinted at the threads. My eyes weren't as good as they'd been.

"Just don't want you disappointed," Frank said. He bent to kiss my forehead then lowered himself into his stuffed chair. "I know you want what's best for them. I hope they'll know that too."

I waited for mail, some indication that now action would happen. I heard nothing and Spencer didn't come.

"Doesn't mean anything, them not answering," Frank said. "Except that you can't trust what they'll say when it comes to the Indians. It's what they've always known and now, after all these years, you're having to learn it too."

In early 1924, Spencer wrote telling me the matter had been referred to the attorney general, since the order from the commissioner to rid the squatters had been ignored. *They have a Miami lawyer, brother of the junior senator from Florida, who insists they can get the land deeded to them by special act of Congress. My hands are tied.*

"Tied hands. Wonder if they're as tied as with the Cow Creeks he pesters," I told Frank as I got out my pen and ink.

I wrote back, demanding that he see the conditions at the camps in Lauderdale, to experience the urgency of their needs for a better place, especially now that the land they bordered near Lauderdale had been put up for sale. *Where will they go if that land sells? They need access to good land at Dania.*

Spencer came once while I was in New York meeting with the Women's Federation and Frank took him not to the Lauderdale camp but to Dania, to see if anything had changed there. It irritated me that he had come with no announcement and then gone out with Frank. Still, he'd confirmed that the problem still existed.

"And only two years since I first informed him," I said and slammed the table with an ironstone bowl, a little harder than I'd planned. "I can't think of any way to push this. Even with Reverend Holding I at least could face him. I've never been so frustrated in my life."

"Suppose you could make a trip to Fort Myers."

"But he needs to see their conditions. Firsthand. I'll just keep this whole thing in my prayers."

In March 1924, Spencer did come. I met him face to face. He reminded me of an overripe summer squash, narrow and soft with a hard, crusty top turning rubbery. He spoke with a kind of high pitch and used words such as *should* and *shall* where most of us might say *would* or *will*.

"I should like to have you take me to the camps then, Mrs. Stranahan. So I shall see with my own eyes what the problems are. I am familiar, as you know, with the Cow Creek band. This is why I have not made greater effort to come here as I imagine I shall see nothing new." He swiped at his nose as though it itched and adjusted his round glasses. He was clean shaved and had hollow areas beneath both cheekbones. "And I am making every effort at Dania, as you see by my correspondence. They must go first."

"There are similarities, I'm sure," I said. "Just as each city is recognized as one. But one would never mistake Columbus, Ohio, for Columbus, Georgia, even though they share the same name."

"Quite right. And neither should they be taken for a Seminole city, I assure you." He pronounced *neither* to emphasize the *i*. "But the Indians resist moving. Until the attorney general enforces the squatters' removal order at Dania, the Indians shall not move, though they could, of course. That is where my emphasis is now, not in duplicating the list of conditions present at most camps."

I drove him out in Tillie, the Model T, talking as I went, about the terrain, the changes, the people and places that I knew so well, what my worries were for them, the poor foods, the illnesses, about how to help them survive these new times. He listened, didn't interrupt me, and I felt hopeful he might understand.

We drove through the palmetto opening, scattering chickens and a rooster or two. I stopped before Annie Tommie's grist mill. She lifted her head and waved, then turned back to her task. She ground corn, and her brother, Willie Jumper, caught the meal in a pan. Beyond them, Squirrel, dressed in a long blouse, bent over a pot of sofkee and poked at the fire. Smoke puffed up between the butterwood logs.

The path to the garden area was well marked, and I assumed the children must be working there since I saw so few, only a baby with two fingers in her mouth while she clutched close to her mother. Mary Gopher visited that day with her new toddler named Betty Mae, a child with quick, bright eyes. She waddled beside her mother picking up shelled corn, chewing on one or two, then tossing a few to the chickens, who were drawn to it like metal filings to a magnet. Betty Mae's father, a trapper, had been run off by her family, his drinking forcing the issue.

"I shall never understand how the Indian men have permitted themselves to become such *berdaches,*" Spencer said.

"Excuse me?"

He pointed with a notebook he'd just removed from his suit coat. "See. The men help with the cooking. I should imagine they help with child discipline as well, just as with the Cow Creeks. And the Big Cypress in Miami." He made notations with a short pencil.

"But that word, the one you used, that's a Plains Indian term. There are no such effeminate men among the Seminoles. These men are fathers and uncles, just helping."

"How would you rate the insects?" Spencer said, stepping over my correction.

"Is that a problem?" I asked.

"Everywhere," he said. "I should like to know how you deal with the insect devils here."

"No, that men assist the women."

He adjusted his glasses. "I'd forgotten your work with suffrage, Mrs. Stranahan. Forgive me, but it seems the men take no lead with their families, the Indian men. I shall apologize for my assumption about the berdache. I assumed all tribes had such persons. However, the Seminole men do fail to take responsibility for provision and for safety. And that is a problem."

"They haven't failed. They do and have provided, though differently. They hunt and fish as they can. And they've always gardened. Even Adam was manly enough for that, if I recall."

Spencer raised his thin eyebrows and made another note.

"Decisions are made together by men and the women, shared responsibility and influence, from what I've seen. They look at what's good for their children and the elderly, their future and their past, and have adapted as best they can."

"Exactly my point. The men have deferred to women, and now look at them. Permitting themselves to deteriorate."

"I'm not sure how much 'permission' they had," I said. I felt my cheeks warm. I adjusted my hat, cinched in my belt. "I think they've done quite well considering the circumstances they find themselves in. Drained swamps, meddling tourists, uninvolved government. It takes strength to share the strains of life and discover triumphs, especially when the latter tend to be well hidden."

He cleared his throat. "Now, about the insects."

"The flies literally clog up the noses of stock if we don't turpentine them or have heavy fires. A few families here have a Guernsey or two. If they keep them smoked and turpentined during those truly dreadful times, and avoid the horns, both man and beast survive. Milk has been critical for the children's survival, so that's optimistic, I think." I pushed the car door back to step out. "I need some fresh air."

"Yes."

"Would you like to meet some of the—?"

Like bandits in an ambush, we were swarmed by children who had hovered quietly beside the car while Spencer and I talked, waiting on the running board to then jump up and consume us.

There were giggles all around, except for Spencer who made notes, then wavered between holding his notebook high above his head and brushing at children who threatened the fresh crease of his pants. It looked a bit like a dance as he turned in the sand, and I had all I could do not to laugh.

We spent nearly two hours, children often leading the way. I showed him the deeper camps, ones clouded with flies over the food, with pigs and children playing in the same wallow not far from the eating areas, empty pint jars scummed with bootleg whiskey rolling nearby. He clucked his tongue.

"Tourists come even to these camps," I said. "It's unfortunate. They set up their tents at the edge of gardens, allow their children and dogs to drink from the rainwater supply, toss out trash, throwing money at the smaller children. They grab for it like roaches with crumbs." We drove to adjoining family camps so he could see the extent of the problem, then came back to Annie Tommie's, where I felt most at home.

"Bootleggers are a problem too," I said.

"Yes. I should think self-discipline problematic."

Ada stood with us next to the car. "Arguments. Many them," she said. "Take canoes."

"Anything that's left here unattended tourists assume is free for the taking," I added. A Tigertail and another named Billie and even Stretch spoke with Captain Spencer, and to his credit, he nodded politely, listened, and took interminable notes. For a time he even sat perched like a dog-surrounded cat on the Hercules Powder box brought out by one of the boys while the men talked.

"I shall not mislead you, Mrs. Stranahan," Spencer said as we drove back, a hot wind blowing in through the open windows. "These are difficult times, and the government is not much intrigued by the plight of the Seminoles. It is the same throughout Florida. Near Fort Pierce, Fort Myers, each site suffers its own plethora of Indian problems no less significant than yours at Fort Lauderdale." He fanned himself with his hat.

"Isn't it interesting that so many of the places you cite were once forts, occupied by a military that failed to conquer these people? If I recall my history, and I do."

"There was no military solution, no." He put his hat on his lap, freed a white handkerchief from his pocket, unfolded it, and wiped his forehead. "But there is a government solution, I should think. They could move now to Dania, even with the squatters there."

"Why can't the government get those Crackers off the land? Are you saying they won't?"

"No, no. I should keep hoping and I shall keep working on the Justice Department. They are to prosecute. The Bureau is actually, quite frankly, out of it now until something is legally decided. Unless your Indians were to just…move there."

"Your agency is responsible for the condition of these people," I said, aghast that he might simply allow them to be tossed back and forth between government claims. "And we are all the government!"

"Coordinating the Justice Department and the state attorney general and the Bureau and congressional interests, and private lawyers getting into it, it all takes time, Mrs. Stranahan."

"I've often wondered how I might have fared," I said, "learning to trade and live beside a people so totally foreign to me where I was dependent on them at the same time. I think they've done quite well as a people."

"That does describe you and your husband, in your early life along the New River, I should think, if I'm not being too presumptuous."

"They were a proud people then. But they accepted us, were good to us, and we've tried to honor that in exchange. What they face now is too difficult for them to adapt to without intervention. I feel that. We can't protect them so we have to prepare them. So many people have come. And so many more will. There is a disquieting about it all. I feel it in my bones."

I turned off the engine when we arrived back at the train station. I gazed out at the activity of people, of boats making their way up the New River, of the smell of prosperity.

I said, "I'm counting on the government, the very people they have no respect for, to earn that respect now. To do something, provide better housing materials or food and medical supplies, enforcement to rid them of whiskey so they can be safe in their camps. And get rid of the squatters at Dania, so they have that choice, to move there before it's too late and violence or disease takes everyone who calls himself a Seminole."

"I shall reply by post," he said, tipping his hat at me. "I shouldn't expect a rapid response."

"No, I surely shouldn't."

Sometimes I found Seminole children and their families on our porch on Saturday nights. They'd get off the train from Palm Beach and ask to stay, planning to make the long trek back by foot in the morning. They had great stamina and loved to walk, a feeling I knew well.

I never tired of their staying. Especially mornings. I'd fix a huge breakfast, my favorite meal for company.

"Little Stranahan, will you please run to the Becks' and invite them back for breakfast? Ask Annie Beck to bring some of her fresh-shucked shrimp. You understand?"

The child, named by a family for Frank, nodded and ran off, his white blouse-shirt barely moving above the long stride of his legs.

Children and their parents would sit on the porch or beneath the chickee we freshened every now and then for them and watch the river. On warm mornings they'd swim, their little feet leaving wet prints on the seawall. The men would talk with Frank and then we'd gather together for fresh fruit, potatoes, and eggs, and a mess of catfish and shrimp.

Later I'd drive a few of them back in Tillie if they wished, the older ones with a brave child or two to stand on the running board, hanging on to the door, hands out to the wind while I eased around puddles and potholes on the way back to camp.

I'd hold Sunday school there for the children, displaying my colorful cards. The parents always let me. And I realized one Sunday as I looked into their eyes that I had known them always, these fine, tall, and silent parents who stood behind their children. We shared a generation. Most had sat beside me once themselves, tried on my merry widow hats, nibbled on my cookies, then listened to the Bible stories and the songs.

We'd changed together, each reflecting new lines in our faces. I hoped we'd prepared each other for the challenges ahead.

Like an army of ants seeking picnic-filled beaches, 300,000 new people moved to Florida between 1923 and 1925. It was our own "Oregon Trail," our own "manifest destiny" I liked to think, with thousands drawn here by a promise of the future and hopeful dreams that Florida's sun-washed beaches and the hammocks of green would foster their new beginnings. Those were the ones who stayed, built homes, and planted flowers. "Binder Boys" appeared by the thousands to help them, binding up property for 10 percent down then inflating the prices and selling that piece to speculators who might raise and sell it again, several times, before any payment came due.

"Not like it was in the teens," Frank assured me. "Both national and state bank deposits're strong."

"But aren't some closing, too?" I asked.

"State banks. No federal ones. We're secure, Ivy. You know how conservative I am. I wouldn't be in this if I didn't see it as sound."

"I appreciate that, my dear boy," I said, plucking at lint from his jacket. I handed him his panama hat. "As do many others who are investing because they have confidence in you." I leaned my head back. "I've got to get glasses. I can hardly see if your button needs sewing on."

It was a natural next step, Frank and W. C. Kyle forming an equal partnership in 1925 to run a building company. Thirteen new counties had been created in Florida in the previous two years. Millions of tourists had funneled here, driving Fords and Oldsmobiles stuffed with children and dogs and plans to abandon routine. Shirt-sleeved northerners whose left elbows turned pink after quick hours in the sun joined others at tourist camps for the night. Someone had dubbed them the "tin-can tourists of the world" with their can openers and tents pitched into flattened splays of palmetto. Concrete roads were proposed and folks talked about building the Tamiami Trail designed to connect Fort Myers through the Seminoles' swamps, right into downtown Miami. *FLORIDA'S BOOMING!* the newspapers reported, despite the insects, hurricanes, and heat.

Frank and W. C.'s company began its first project, building an apartment house. I liked that. Apartments were homes, of a sort, that would enable families to put down roots and encourage them to stay, eventually buy their own structures with yards and send their children off to school. All Cromarties in the area would be employed working there, if they wished.

Gus and Papa had headed out to the accrued land near Lake Okeechobee and were doing well there. Gus had married his nurse lady, Vera Walker, who made him a strong, fine wife. No, they wouldn't likely be coming back. Vera was expecting her second child, a boy, they hoped, to join their young son, Billy. They planned to name the new one John if it was a boy.

DeWitt had advanced his family too, remaining in Lauderdale. Dale and Margaret played with the offspring of the Clarks, the local sheriff and now DeWitt's good friend. Dewitt occasionally did mechanic work for the city and helped out Ed King and a hardworking former student of mine, Tenley Bellamy, at the boat basin. DeWitt liked carpentry best, and Florida was the neediest place in the nation for that in the twenties, it most surely was. Pink and Randall still lived down the street, childless along with Bloxham and Louise. Pink changed her mind about the risk of a gallery showing, cutting her beautiful hair and electroperming it into rows of waves instead.

We had a photograph taken of Fort Lauderdale in May 1925. The vibrant skyline reflected against the New River on both sides of the water, and of course, well beyond now. The waterways showed, the inland rivers dredged to take people from one side of the state to the other on pop boats or canoes; even sailing ships. I tried not to think of all of the trees that had toppled to make room for the water and the buildings. I still served on the planning commission where I retained the reputation as the "tree mother," protector of anything tall and green, and I wished I'd worked a little harder when I saw how few palms and green space remained in that Lauderdale shot.

It wasn't all rosy, of course. Life never is.

"Keeps your back up good and straight," Frank said and smiled when I swatted his arm with Spencer's latest letter.

Unbelievably, squatters still squatted at Dania. Spencer had written that the men now *wanted to lease the land, since there were no Indians there, and be paid for the improvements they'd made.*

"Can you believe that, Frank? The gall."

The court had given them a stay, ninety days, to discuss the lease plan with the Bureau.

"Twisted ways of the government," Frank said.

"Meandering," I said. "Worse than an old river making its way to the sea."

Talk grew of a railroad workers' strike up north. Frank said he didn't think it would affect us. But then in October, when it happened, the shipments of building materials almost stopped as trains were diverted and sent else-where to cover for the strike.

"Prime building season," Frank said. He mopped at his forehead with his folded handkerchief. "Couldn't be a worse time."

"Maybe the government will intervene," I said.

"Always the optimist," Frank said and snorted.

"Can we bring material in any other way?"

"Hoping for a transport shipment, though a long time ago I counted on that and was deeply disappointed."

"That ship that sank, your first year. Remembering that?"

He nodded his head. "Still haunts me."

We inaugurated 1926 with the Becks serving imported chocolate and sev-eral more friends gathering for chorales and songs. Frank looked the healthiest he had in months. He had turned sixty the August before but still held himself like a much younger man.

That changed, I thought, looking back, shortly after word reached us that the ship carrying the lumber the area so desperately needed sank in the Miami harbor in late January 1926.

Frank did not sleep well for a week. He complained of stomach pain, and lower, but I knew it was the worry. The northern newspapers were full of the story of our problems, about how traveling to Florida this season might not be so wise what with train problems and supply complications.

So the wealthy that year went to Europe. And the tin-can tourists headed west.

Still, the lilt of progress drifted in the air so high and so fragrant that even the rains stayed, their cleansing promising blooms.

The squatters still squatted both at the Lauderdale camps and at Dania.

I kept writing that nothing had changed, and finally, in mid-May, Spencer wrote back that the original two squatters had "sold" the land to someone else; he thought the name might be Forst or Frost. Frost, or who-ever it was, hadn't been aware, Spencer said, and would surely not have "bought" it if he had known the land belonged to Indians.

"Ha," I said. "If it's the Brother Frost we know, he's been waiting a long time for this."

Apparently, it wasn't.

Spencer went on to say that when this man had been confronted with the facts that he now squatted, he said he'd need time to move. The original two squatters had gotten new lawyers asking to know who the "individual Indian" was who was supposed to get the land so they could meet him and buy it direct from him.

"Can you believe that, Frank?"

Finally the Justice Department had gotten its back up because they were being duped by these "supposedly ignorant Crackers," as even Spencer now called them, and they'd finally gone to court.

Because the squatters had cows, the court gave them more time to move.

Spencer said Tony Tommie had been with him on an earlier visit and had agreed they should have sixty more days to move all their things. Then Branham, one of the original cow-owning squatters, had come back and padlocked the gates, implying that he still owned the land, so it felt like we'd been moved backwards on the checker table.

Our Indians should get onto that land now, Spencer had written, *or others will.*

"'Our Indians,' he calls them, Frank, as though they could be owned. Honest to truth, that man does get on my nerves."

You must convince them, Spencer continued. *Not to wait until the sixty days is over. Do it now. This is so temporary, Mrs. Stranahan.*

You were right about the plan all along, Spencer continued in his tidy script. *They had planned to get the land by act of Congress. Should have, if you hadn't written to stop them. Still might if we don't get Indians out there to live.*

I drove again to Dania. It was May 1926. Nearly five years of haggling. I stopped Tillie and stepped out to see a cleared area and beyond, past the padlocked gate to where I could see no structures, just the land as it had been.

The soil, when I bent to run it through my fingers, was dark and granular, rich. They could grow things here, start a grove, perhaps, raise their corn and sugar cane, purple potatoes and tomatoes. Scratch wells would have good, fresh water. I thought I saw a huckleberry bush or two as well.

Each family would receive five acres to farm as they would, the same size as nearby groves doing well. Wild turkeys roosted here, maybe wild boars. Raccoons scampered about; they would be good for meat instead of the vile gophers so many had been forced to eat. Dogs could roam and lounge in the shade, unharassed by tourists. They might consider cattle, since their "predecessors" had such success. And all around, virgin stands of pine formed homes for curlews and hawks and with careful cutting, could be sold.

The pine meant something else I believed would be a gift: they could use some for the building of homes, permanent homes, structures they'd never have to leave, could not be forced out of. No one could take them away and maybe, just maybe, in their own camp of framed houses, they would want to create the dream I'd always had for them and build an Indian school.

"Think the government can be trusted to build them homes there, provide medical care, a school?" Frank asked me.

"Does seem a pretty big order, doesn't it?"

"Hate to see you disappointed."

"Maybe I give too much weight to this choice; maybe it's the first of many offers."

Frank looked up at me over his glasses.

"Five years of haggling added on to dozens. No, that land'll be taken by others if the Indians don't claim it."

That night I walked the floor, pacing and drinking water and praying. Oh, how I prayed, that I would know what to do, would know how to answer Spencer, would say the right things if I decided to convey his offer to Annie's people.

I was still a stranger to them, to their ways, to what their traditions were and what they valued. Perhaps I'd do them greater harm if I encouraged them to go now to Dania, a place so foreign with trouble still brewing there; greater harm if I didn't.

In the end, as the morning pink rose up over the royal palms outside our home, I handed the decision over. I would tell them what I thought might be the value and let them choose for themselves. It was the answer to my prayer. I couldn't make anything happen, not really: that power belonged to Someone else.

"I'm going out to the camp, Frank."

I sat on the corner of his bed and shook his shoulder gently. He turned over, sleep still fogged across his face.

"Hmmm?" he said.

"I'm taking Tillie out to the camp. To let them know about Spencer's offer."

He reached for my hand, held it and pressed his thumb against the back of my palm. "Don't be disappointed if they don't take him up on it. They don't change easily."

"Thank you for that. But I've decided it isn't my will that matters, so however they decide will be all right."

"You want them to go."

Did I? Was it the way to uphold them from deep within, to express compassion, to walk beside them as I wanted? I thought about what he said and I had to be honest, with him and myself.

"I want them to go. I can't protect them. I know that. Only prepare them for what lies ahead. With all that timber and good ground, there'll be others trying for it. It may as well be theirs."

"Could be right," he said. "But that's always been the case and it hasn't moved them, even before the ruckus with the squatters."

"Never do anything someone else can do, that's what I've always said, what I think I've been led to." I patted his hand. "There's no sense not trying."

I bent to kiss his cheek then pushed to stand. He reached and held me for a moment, pulling me to him. I sighed into the nurture of him, the shelter and the strength.

"Drive slowly," he said, releasing me.

I stopped at the back shed and loaded a few things into the trunk; then I headed out. At the camp I presented the terms of the letter and Spencer's offer of payment. They stood as silent as morning palms.

"If you want to go look at the land," I said, my eyes scanning their faces, "I'll take you. I've seen it. It's cropland and sheltered with pines.

Someone's tried to squat there already, but portions have been moved. Someone will have it. I think it should be you. But you decide."

I walked back to Tillie, stooping to look at a new puppy one of the children held up for me. I patted its soft, furry head and rubbed my fingers along its nose, around its ears, and scratched as it squirmed. It had a twine wrapped around its neck, and the boy set the dog down and pushed it, then tried to pull it toward the chickee. The puppy resisted both ways.

"You can't push him into something he doesn't want," I said, "nor drag him either. Let him get to know you. Then he'll do what you want because he'll know you only want the best for him." The boy sat down beside the dog, who licked his face, making the puppy happy where it sat.

I sat in the car and prayed. Not that they would come but that they would know I only wished the best for them; and that my being the messenger of Spencer's plan would not damage what we'd discovered about each other through the years that was good and long-lasting, that strengthened that tissue-thin layer of trust.

Bird sounds and insects buzzing filled my head. I slapped at a horsefly with my hat, pushing it out a door that stood open. How long would I wait? Would I be welcomed back?

I had walked beside them this long. What was another day?

I waited long enough that I thought I'd get out and stretch a while, look for some orchids in bloom. But it was not nearly as long as I was prepared to wait before I saw Annie Tommie, stern-faced, headed for the car, her striped skirt billowing out around her, the full width of her cape taking in air.

Instead of saying anything, she got in beside me, pulled the door shut, and stared forward. The sunlight glinted on her necklaces of beads. Her brother, Willie Jumper, came next, his hair already white with age though he couldn't have been much over fifty. He got in the back, pulled his shirt over his knees above brown, bare feet. Two younger people joined him next, the girl followed by the boy. Their small frames squeezed on either side of Willie. Jack and Pocahontas Huff were their names, and they were Annie's grandchildren.

The car being full, the children pulled their doors shut. I started the engine and we headed out, my heart pounding. My spirit soared with their presence. Just agreeing to see it was a momentous step and perhaps the greatest one, commitment being the first and best teacher, after all. But that Annie had come, a woman with respect and influence, and both an elder and youth had followed, said they would do this: they would take it, this land, and make a new life at Dania.

I hadn't known the road to be so bumpy nor so twisting and turning, that it took so long a time to go nine miles. Everything I saw along the way looked grimmer, more oppressive than it had the day before. Even the pines when we pulled onto the land looked spindly now, not promising of a future. If it had been me making the decision, I might well have turned around that day, pessimism often being more powerful than promise. But it was not my will, not me making things happen. I felt a great relief believing with all my fiber that I was not alone in my driving when I steered the car that day.

At the land, Annie eased her way out of Tillie. A big woman, her skirt must have used the full eighteen yards. It ballooned out over her feet. She had lost most of her teeth already and her mouth formed a puckered cave. Her gray hair piled high on her head wisped thin around her ears. The others stretched out of the car and walked about, eyes evaluating as they scanned the horizon.

"I've grub hoes and axes in the trunk," I said. "If you wish to clear the ground where you'd like, to build chickees to begin with, the government will pay you $1.50 a day. It's the going wage." I pulled at my waist jacket and then clasped my hands behind my back.

I wondered about the promise I'd made on behalf of the government. Why did I believe they'd come through with the pay in any timely fashion?

"The government can be your friend. Though it's made mistakes and you've had no one to tell them what they were doing wrong. I've tried to tell them. There is no promise of ease, no promise of complete safety if you take this land. There's a risk. But without it, where will your children be?"

Annie said nothing. But she walked to the back of the car, opened the trunk and took out a hoe. She handed it to Willie. Pocahontas handed one to Jack. They'd take it, the reservation. Once again, their lives would all change.

The men began grubbing. "I'll be back at quitting time," I said, and had all I could do not to sing it.

Annie and her granddaughter and I drove back to the Lauderdale camp, and she told the others and I drove out more men. At 5:00 P.M. I drove back, loaded them all up, and returned them to the swamp camp. The next two days I drove back and forth several times carrying different groups with hoes and axes. Esther and Julia came in one trip and helped thatch one of the chickees. "Need floor, the floor," she said.

"I know. We need lumber. As soon as you're ready with the thatch, I'll notify the agent to come and pay you all and then they'll build real homes if you'd like."

By the fourth day they were ready. I sent a telegram to Spencer at Fort Myers that the Indians were on the reservation. It was somewhat of an exaggeration with only a few families willing to be here, but they'd begun. And with them there, the threat of squatters had lessened.

We waited.

"What if he doesn't come, what if he doesn't pay?" Annie Beck said. We were walking out along Las Olas Boulevard, mottled shade marking our way.

"I can't worry about that," I said. "I've done what I can do. But I've never hoped for anything more."

Spencer arrived the next day in a truck, proof that prayer comes in unlikely packages wrapped with pale string. He paid all the workers as promised and then headed south to Miami. He took one of the Fewl brothers with him and when they returned, they had lumber. Good, solid, milled lumber, ready for chickee platforms and someday, to frame their new homes.

They'd done it. They'd taken the risk and with it, the land and the promise of permanence.

Pink's news in August that she was again expecting, I took as an omen of more good things to come. Her body had had time to heal from the last miscarriage; Randall stayed close and attentive. Perhaps prosperity would bubble over onto her baby, due the next April.

She drove out with me to the reservation a few months after more of the camp had moved. After the initial rush to clear space for chickees, there hadn't been much activity. The day we visited, it looked like houses were finally being framed.

Tins of white paint waited in the shade.

"Looks like they're makin' rows of corn with those chickees," Pink noticed.

"It is odd they aren't putting the houses around a central circle. I thought that plan so...embracing."

Annie Tommie had planted a garden, and fences propped up along its border kept the dogs out. Chickens bobbed their heads about. People looked healthier. Only pine needles and tramped palmetto flattened the tidy ground.

A padlock still held the gate closed to the squatters' site.

"Lookin' kinda small, the houses, sister."

"Yes. And with no windows in the designs."

"That the agent house?" Pink asked. She pointed to a two-story building going up. "It's got windows aplenty."

"So it does. I must keep writing to Spencer," I said. "I never imagined my life of 'service' would require such strong fingers."

I didn't want the government to forget the people here and that still, they lacked clear title to the land and important survival tools: the formal education of their children.

"Difficult to teach that the government's their friend," I told Pink, "when it keeps acting like it'd rather just be a boss."

Frank and I stopped over in Pittsburgh. We'd been trying to get to Ohio, one of Frank's uncles suggesting they might have information about Will.

"Would be amazing," Frank said as we rode the train north. "After all this time."

"Did your cousin say what information, exactly, that she had?"

"Hmmm, no." His wheeze and hesitation seemed worse when we were up north. Perhaps the cool September nights brought it on. "Just that someone claims to have seen him in Wisconsin a few years back."

"Well, that would be wonderful, if we could track that down."

"Don't want to get my hopes up too high."

"No, you never want to do that." I patted his hand.

He smiled at me. "Am I such a coot? Always finding fault?"

"I wouldn't say fault-finding, exactly. It's just that if there's a quarter-inch of caution buried beside three-quarters of possibility, you'll spend more time measuring the former even though you can tell by looking that it's shorter."

"Just my nature," he said. "Got you to remind me of the other options."

We were like old friends, my Frank and I. We'd found the ways to bend and give, just like the oak with its deep roots. I felt blessed to have the time to marvel at the orchids of life, blooming while we climbed out onto strong limbs.

So we had gone to Ohio by way of Pittsburgh, making a little vacation out of it. Frank hadn't wanted me to drive and so we took the train, running again, mostly on schedule. Frank still complained of pain when he got up in the night, and he agreed that after this trip we'd head south to see a specialist in Miami. Tonight we would sleep in Pennsylvania, then board a train in the morning for Ohio.

Pink came to me in the dream.

She wore white gossamer skin. She drifted through the air, her toes a perfect point beneath her, her arms outstretched as she soared over the water of the New River. She was an egret with long eddying plumes. She smiled, her blond hair long again and flowing out behind her even as she dipped into the water and became a fish then, a spinning, fin-driven fish that moved in a dart and swirl up the river, past a lumbering manatee who turned its whiskers to her then moved aside so Pink could see its calf. The fish still had Pink's face and she still smiled, even when she opened up her mouth to take the line drifting in the water, even when the fisherman set the lure, even when she recognized the face of the angler who reeled her up and pulled her out.

I woke up with a start, my heart pounding. My hands felt wet. The pillows had fallen so that I'd been sleeping on my side. Frank stood beside me.

"You were shouting," he said. "About Pink."

"Horrible dream." My hands shook. "Just dreadful. Pink looked so happy and she was a bird, egret-like, and then she was a fish. Oh, so ridiculous. I can't remember it all."

I shook myself, started to cry, and didn't know why.

Frank sat down beside me and slipped his arms around me, his cologne cooling and sharp.

"And then," I said, remembering in a flash, "Pink got caught."

CHAPTER EIGHTEEN

nnie Beck sent the telegram to Pittsburgh though by the next day all the papers carried the news: HURRICANE DESTROYS FT LAUDERDALE. The date was September 18, 1926.

"Does she say how Pink is? DeWitt? Bloxham?" My whole family that I'd gathered there had been caught in the eye.

Frank shook his head. "Just that it happened and to come back."

We couldn't leave Pittsburgh, couldn't get a train ticket, couldn't find out information. It was the worst of feelings to be stranded in the unfamiliar while those you loved struggled far away, grieving, trying to pick up the pieces.

Annie Beck telegraphed again, said that Pink faired fine, a little shaken but they were staying with friends farther inland. Annie was telegraphing for everyone since the phone lines were down. By the third day she sent a wire confirming that all the Cromarties had lived through it.

Over four hundred people hadn't. Bodies were still being discovered as the water receded and volunteers pawed through debris. Thousands arrived in makeshift hospitals in the few buildings left standing. The paper estimated that 50,000 people had lost their homes across the state. "Their homes, Frank! The very stability of their lives."

"Faith, Ivy. That's the stability of a life."

"You're right, of course. But to be so exposed, so unprotected..."

Pictures began appearing in the newspapers before we finally got out of Pittsburgh, and I thought it would prepare us. It had been four days since the storm by the time we arrived. Nothing could have fortified us for what we faced.

The trees said it all. Many still stood, but naked now. Not a single leaf remained on any one of them. Not a palm or pine or oak had leaves, all stripped bare as though a giant had breathed evil onto them, run talons of fingers and twisted every tree, let some stand but exposed, and then had salivated over the devastation leaving dark swirling water in its wake. The famous Sentinel Palm that for years had marked the inlet to the New River had vanished. So had the House of Refuge.

Uprooted telephone poles leaned into lines strung like cobwebs. Tangled masses of lumber lay splintered and tossed from once-sturdy warehouses and fine-painted shops that no longer existed. We climbed over rubble and coconuts and the roots of palm trees and the strands of palmetto when we arrived back at the station. Shredded leaves lay flattened by wind and rain everywhere.

"All this damage. All the people. They've lost so much." I kept saying it over and over, I didn't know why. I gripped Frank's hand.

Our block was a crisscross of bent and toppled trees with coconuts piled so deep near the New River they looked like a pile of rocks meant to reinforce the bank.

"We may not be able to get to the house, Ivy," Frank said. Annie had told us that our home had been seen; it still stood. But there'd been a tidal wave that had rolled up over the beach and come as far as the railroad. The storm destroyed everything from there to the sea. Toward our place, back from the railroad, the area had flooded. How badly, we didn't know.

Debris drifted in the river and in the places where water ran now as though it belonged, over steps and seawalls. Bloated, listless snakes bobbed as they floated by. And when we got to our home, I could see water, a foot and a half deep, maybe more, saturated the main floor. Looking in through the window while Frank scudded the boat close, I spied my small oak footstool with a cross-stitched orchid floating beneath the piano bench. The china cabinet had water almost up to the bottom shelf. Mud spattered against the glass doors. The chocolate set sat serene on the top shelf.

The fish plates still lined the plate wall in the dining room as though no giant wind had roared through. Even most of the windows still held glass.

"We can clean all this up." Frank held me, patting me as I leaned onto his shoulder. "We're alive. We can stay on the second floor while we clean up."

"I know. I know. We're fortunate, we truly are."

"That may be a little too optimistic," he said.

I pulled back from him. He handed me his handkerchief.

"I want to see Pink and DeWitt and the children and Bloxham, make sure they're all out of this. Then I want to go to the camps."

"Next report to the Women's Club and the Red Cross, I'll wager," he said.

"Nothing we can do here until the water goes down."

The beach received the worst of it. Little cottages that had been built with such care near the ocean, with screened-in porches known as Florida rooms and hand-turned railings along the steps, were cut in half, beds and chairs still sitting as though ready for visitors with no reason for walls or doors. For many people, their whole life savings had blown away. Few had insurance. Even fewer would be able to rebuild or keep up the payments on half-destroyed houses. Rebuilding would be difficult as well, with continued supply problems, jobs destroyed, and banks perhaps calling in loans to increase capital.

It took six weeks for us to clean up the street between our home and the river. Frank hired people to roll up our carpets and hang them to dry, to slop up the water off the pine floors. The dark muck around the wallpaper inspired a look at the catalog. We would have to replace it. Frank clenched his teeth as he gave directions to the men and worked himself, shoveling debris.

"I don't think you should be doing that," I said.

"Can't sit around and watch," he said. "Don't you always say it's not the event but how we respond that counts?"

"How we respond, yes. Learning to say, 'Do what must be done and when it's over, what's done is done.' I'll be late this evening," I said then. "I'm helping at the hospital."

"Speaking of hospitals," Frank said, "did I tell you? Tony Tommie's contracted TB. He's in a sanatorium in Oklahoma, where he'd gone to that Indian school. Guess alcohol is still a part of him, too."

"Oh, Frank, that's so sad." I thought of Albert, how he'd died. "Tony was a help in this Dania thing. I'll miss that."

"He might recover," Frank said. "Some people do."

Cleaning up after disaster takes enormous strength, not so much physical, but emotional and spiritual. Beginning again, seeing hope where heaviness lies in waiting, takes courage. Unworthiness joins with futility and swarms like a cloud of hungry insects over leftovers. Yet that was what south Floridians had learned to do since time began here and we would do it all again.

I didn't mind that there were fewer visitors expected for the season. The Red Cross, the Women's Club, the churches, our growing group of Adventists had all we could do to hearten and inspire those I called neighbors, family, and friends.

I dreaded going to the camps, the ones still in the swamps, to see what the storm had done there, but I knew I had to.

I felt a wave of relief when I saw Esther dangling her feet over the walkway. Julia ran back and forth along the raised lumber. Esther and Stretch had stayed behind, had not yet moved to Dania. She waved at me, and I walked past new chickees going up to replace those lost in the storm. "Hide behind hogback, behind rocks," she said, pointing. She took me to where they must have huddled during the storm. The area had potholes to hide in. They'd survived. The tidal wave would not have affected them, only the heavy rains.

"You could have a house at Dania," I encouraged.

"Stretch say good here, good, go when good ready."

Nine miles away, at the reservation, people had fared well.

"Big wind blow barn down," Annie Tommie said as she walked over to where I unloaded crates of foodstuffs from the back of my car.

"Did it? I hadn't noticed when I drove by. Well, certainly now they'll take off the locks and those acres can be available too."

"Want no trouble with white mans," she said.

Squirrels rushed about climbing palmettos and pines that had skimpy leaves left on them. I caught flashes of color, blooms from wild hibiscus and birds with red feathers. The air smelled lush. This was a good place for them, high and dry.

Annie came in to town a few weeks later and told me a new dairy barn had been built.

"For you?" I said, amazed that Spencer had authorized that.

She shook her head.

"They wouldn't!"

"New man there now. Sell us milk, he say. Barn on own land, he tell Jack."

I drove out and saw for myself. He'd chosen a site farther west for the dairy barn. It was possible it was on the private land owned by that Byran. But it would be close. It meant another letter to Spencer.

"You are nothing if not persevering, Mrs. Stranahan," my husband said. "Most would have given up years ago."

"Am I daft, do you think? To do what I do? To believe that it will matter in the end?"

"Not daft. A bit beset. Admirable, really. Don't know if I could do that, abide so long with so little hope of harvest."

"The harvest has been abundant, though, don't you think? They're there now, building; the door to education has at least been peeked into. Even in my own life. Pink's pregnant and healthy at last; and I live in this stimulating place—temporarily without leaves anywhere but on the ground, I would note—but with a man I adore. What more could I wish for?"

"Did you know that the origin of the word *family* is from the Latin word *famulus,* meaning servant?" I asked Frank. We were driving Tillie south to Miami to see the specialist he'd promised he would see, before the storm hit and recovery stole so much of our time.

He shook his head.

"Servant. I find that fascinating, almost spiritual."

"Do you feel you have to wait on me, like a servant?"

I turned to look at him. "Of course not. What a strange thing for you to say, Frank." I turned back to watch the road. "What I do for you, little as it is at times, I do as a joy, not because I feel I must. It's the connection in the words I find so interesting, that *family* and *servant* should have the same root. It implies that they belong together not as a demand of master over servant, not as something of power, but of connection, that to be in a family requires service and a union. I think the image is lovely."

"Might not be so in some families, especially where the need's great," he said. "Expect serving could get old."

We pulled into the parking area, the sun glaring against the white-rock lot. Newly planted lantana flashed shiny green beside the stuccoed building. Yellow blooms teased. I squinted.

"Here we are. Dr. Mortenson. He's supposed to be the best, Frank."

"Getting old," he said. "Not worth a whole lot of extra effort."

"You dear boy, you'll not get away from seeing him by having a pity party, especially not one all by yourself. Come along, let's see what he has to offer us."

Dr. Mortenson stood tall and slender and looked no older than a boy. He had gentle eyes beneath busy blond eyebrows and I was surprised he could have been so skilled in the science of urology, they called it, when he was obviously so young.

The doctor completed a series of tests and I found myself asking questions about their origin and purpose, the sciences of things always forming an interest for me. Then Dr. Mortenson asked if I would mind stepping outside.

"It's not frightening me," I said.

"I'm sure not, Mrs. Stranahan. But I find patients are more relaxed when it's just their doctor and themselves, at times."

Frank didn't protest. It hurt me a bit that he didn't want me there, or at least didn't object to my banishment. Still, I knew he would share with me whatever I needed to know, I felt sure of that.

When we left, Frank told me we needed to fill a prescription at Beck's drugstore, and that the doctor expressed hope that the medication would help his problem.

"Residues from the arsenic damage, in the steel mills," Frank said. "Who would've thought all these years later they'd trace it that far back. Nerves and blood pressure."

"The elimination problems? That's what he thinks is causing it?" Frank opened the door for me and I slipped behind the wheel of Tillie.

"That and my, hmmm, incapacitation." He walked around to the other side of the car and got in.

"Incapacitation?"

"My impotence, Ivy." He slammed the door shut.

"I don't like that word, and you've never chosen to use it until now. It sounds so, powerless, when you've been anything but that all these years. We've had a relationship beyond the physical, one very strong, I'd say, very...what's a good word? Robust. Yes, robust."

"Thank you for that." He stared out the side window and spoke not another word about what the doctor said, despite my persistence and reassurances.

Frank took the medicine and seemed encouraged by it. It bothered me, the use of artificial chemicals, though I knew groups such as the Rosicrucians found merit in alchemy and the study of metals and reactions, chemistry and such. And Alfred's skills were exceptional.

Still, I hoped that Frank could find relief not in the potions Annie Beck's husband was trained to mix but in good foods, sound habits, and faith.

Before November turned into a mild winter season, Frank went back to the bank and sorted out loans and cash flow, listened to people telling of how the storm had affected them, changed their whole lives.

We made a trip south to the doctor almost weekly. Each time Frank and the doctor conferred together while I read older issues of the *Ladies Home Journal* in the waiting area.

"He said I may need a surgical procedure in the future," Frank told me on a return trip in early December.

"To do what?" Rain pelted hard against Tillie's roof, and the windshield wiper labored to keep the small arch free enough of mud and rain for me to keep Tillie on the road. I had trouble hearing over the deluge. The wind whipped against the car, straining my arms to keep it on the slick road.

"Why don't you pull into one of the tourist camps," Frank said, pointing. "We can stay the night and wait out the storm. There's one, with the light by the sign. They have covered areas between the rooms."

It was a relief to stop. Frank stepped over puddles unhurriedly while the wind whipped his cuffed pants around his legs and his tie twisted around toward his shoulder. He stepped into the office and after a brief wait, returned with a key in his hand. He motioned for me to back out and drive to a room at the far end of the string of little houses linked with carports. He shivered beneath the roof while I drove in, turned off the key, and waited for him to open the door where we stepped inside.

The room smelled musty and damp but it was clean and dry. Frank turned on the single lamp and an arc of warm light spilled across a small desk that held a washbowl and pitcher. A patchwork quilt lay on the bed between designs of ironwork at the foot and the head. A single painting of an English cottage engulfed by blooms hung over the bed.

"Good. There's no mirror. I must look a fright."

"Your hat's drenched is all," Frank said and plucked the pin out, putting the palmetto with a saucy bow on the desk.

"Palmetto's getting old," I said, fluffing my hair rolled up at the back. "I need to get a new one."

He sat quiet, not turning my way. "That's what happens to old things, isn't it?"

"Oh, Frank. You're much too morbid. Come here."

I sat on the bed and leaned against the ironwork, fluffing the pillows up to comfort my back. "Put your head on my lap and let's not talk about old things."

"I am old, Ivy." He turned to look at me. I saw the lines leaving his eyes, the dark circles beneath them. "Was when we met. You've kept me young as you could all these years. Those bright eyes, that thick hair that rolls up onto your head, perfect oval, a perfect lift to frame that face." He inhaled. "Warm as a nest of young chicks."

"So poetic you are, sir."

"Old age brings on such things."

"Unless you agree to let me revere you and love you and honor you, I won't let this 'old' subject be dealt with, Frank. You are too young spirited, too vibrant to be wallowing in this place of remorse and regret." I patted the quilt.

He sat on the side of the bed, carefully pulled off his boots, and set them together beneath the cover sham that fluttered against the floor. He leaned back and sighed, let me run my fingers across his forehead and fold back through his hair. I patted the raindrops on his forehead with my fingers. The rain drummed against the tin roof, and an occasional blast of wind puffed the dark green-checkered curtains away from the windowsill.

"Says the surgery would relieve the discomfort," Frank said.

"We should have it done then," I said.

"It will mean a, hmm, tube of some kind, all the time. Very inconvenient...quite, ah, messy."

I could see his fingers tense as he talked, though his hands were folded over his belt buckle. The spots of color on them looked dark in the shad-owed light. His legs were stiff and straight out from him, that high arch covered with dark socks.

"If it would make you more comfortable, Frank, it would be worth it. You deserve that, to be comfortable."

He didn't answer. I thought he might have fallen asleep to the sound of the rain and my fingers caressing his forehead and temples. My mind wan-dered to the Women's Club fund-raiser, a way to bring in northern money to help with the needs without people feeling like charity cases.

But Frank hadn't slept. And when he spoke it had been so long I had to think back to what I had said that he now responded to.

"I deserve so little, Ivy. That kind of surgery, it would make *servant* a much more meaningful word than *family.*"

"I would take care of you, Frank. You know that."

"Want it the other way around, though I don't think you need me," he said. "That's the way it should be."

I didn't know if he meant that I should need him or that he thought it good that I could take care of myself.

Pink and Randall decided that if I was willing, she would stay with Frank and me, just until she passed the fifth month that had always been so trou-bling.

"That sounds just lovely, doesn't it, Frank?"

He nodded once in that way he had and returned to his book, a cup of chamomile tea steaming beside him. The evening felt chilly—light sweater weather.

"Good then, I'll just be bringin' some things by, a little at a time. We'll be right here for Christmas, sister, so you can go ahead and fill my stockin' and hang it by the fireplace."

"Hang it by the fireplace. Just like you were a child."

"I am a ch-*ild*," she said, exaggerating the last word as though it was made of two and she was from the Arkansas south.

"I can't think of anything I'd rather have happen," I said.

Pink stayed in my room upstairs while I shared a room with Frank. Our hands reached across the space between the single beds, and I realized I'd missed that tender touch, one I could gather in the night.

"Even when Pink goes home, I think I'll move back in here. That be all right with you?"

"Suppose so," he said. "Hate to keep waking you when I get up."

"You do that less with the medication. That's a good sign. Everything feels hopeful, Frank."

Pink began having pains so we moved her downstairs, closer to hot tea and activity to distract and where she could be watched more easily all day. The bed fit at an angle in the parlor where she could look out the bay window at the river or let her eyes gaze at the small potted pine tree with a white picket fence around the base that served as our Christmas tree. It stood on the table in the corner.

"We've been here before, Pink," I said patting her hand. "But this time it's earlier. You've taken immediately to bed. We have good medical advice and fine herbs, too. I believe we can get you through it this time."

She smiled. "I am hopin' so myself."

Randall came by every day, took meals with us, and in the evening we played dominoes and sang at the piano before he headed home to feed the hounds they had and two cats. I found I liked the gathering of us under one roof and wondered why it was that families took to separating when they married. Why not stay with compatible people who knew your little quirks and ways and had learned to love you anyway?

Esther and Annie's people were ahead of us, I thought, bringing their husbands into their parents' chickee instead of the young girl and young man being sent out like Hansel and Gretel, forced to follow signs to find their way back to comfort and home.

John Mason knocked on the door about 3:30 P.M. on the afternoon of December 12, 1926. He said he was looking for Randall and had been told he might be here since he wasn't at home. Came from up north he said, a business colleague and old friend.

"He isn't here now," I said, "but you're certainly welcome to wait if you'd like. He usually comes by before long and takes supper with us."

"Fine place to board," he said, his eyes scanning the pine ceilings and paneling of the rooms.

I chuckled. "I guess it is at that. Please. Come in."

"The storm has interrupted a few things for us, and we've had trouble keeping track of land transactions and all. You know how it is with the phone lines down," John Mason said in that familiar way of northerners. "Lovely home you have here, Missus...."

"Stranahan," I said and pushed open the screen door, letting affliction enter my life.

He gave me his hat, and I hung it on the tree and took him around to the dining room through Frank's office so we needn't bother Pink asleep in the parlor. But our movement, our voices, awakened her, and she called out my name.

"Excuse me," I said. "My sister's staying with us." I rose to go into the parlor.

"I'm intruding," he said, standing with me.

"No, please. I'll get us limeade in just a moment. Unless you'd prefer herb tea. Mr. Stranahan and I don't take coffee. The caffeine is so hard on one. Please, stay comfortable."

"No bootleg whiskey, either, I'll venture."

He had a thick, dark mustache that looked like a caterpillar hanging asleep over his lip. He returned to his seat and crossed his legs.

"No bootleg whiskey," I said and left for the parlor.

Pink asked for water which I gave her. She seemed to be running a fever but rejected a cold press of herbs I suggested.

"Just need a distraction or two until Randall gets here. He always lightens my day. Who's your guest?"

It seemed impossible for her not to flutter her eyes at John Mason who had stood again and leaned his broad shoulder against the opening between the living room and parlor. He stared at Pink. He had long eyelashes that rested on his cheekbones for brief moments before opening again to reveal dark eyes.

"This is John Mason. A friend of Randall, he says. From where did you say?"

"Philadelphia."

I wasn't sure why I was uncomfortable. He didn't move closer, had violated no boundaries that I could sense. Pink wore a bed jacket of white lace that covered what the bed linens didn't, right up to her neck. I'd done her hair for her earlier in the day and only a few soft strands fell across her eyes from the side cut. The permanent wave had loosened and looked like spun honey. She was in no way exposed, and yet I felt exposed for her in an odd and presentiment way.

"This is my sister, Pink," I said.

Pink lifted her fingers to him and smiled that face-lighting way she had. He stepped forward to take her hand.

"Randall's wife," I added.

John Mason stopped, his fingers suspended in midair. "Didn't get that, Mrs. Stranahan. Did you say Randall's wife?"

"Randall's wife."

He shook his head, and a small grin eased the caterpillar higher toward his nose.

"Now that sure can't be. Unless you mean a former wife," he said, almost as to himself. "Now that could be."

"Current," I said.

"Well, now, dear lady, that just can't be a fact. Because I know Randall's wife, I surely do. His children play with my children, or did until they got so old they started going to dance parties together. Which is what they do now, his two boys and a girl."

"Randall's children?" Pink said, her voice a faint echo of the words inside my head. "You must be mistaken. Randall and I haven't been able to have children yet. We're confident we will…"

"Got Randall's eyes, his nose, his dimple. All his kids have. His wife is not the looker you are, Miss Pink, but she's sure delivered him children. My Molly and I have been there when they came home from the hospital, babes in arms. Might even have pictures, maybe."

He began patting at his pocket for his wallet and a part of me longed to see the photographs, to prove what he was saying or disprove it, while the rest of me knew without a doubt he had them and could, and it did not matter now.

I watched the color drain from Pink's face. John Mason watched it too.

"I best be going," he said. "I'm staying at the New River Inn. I'll leave my card on the plate. Would you ask Randall to get a hold of me?" He coughed.

By now he had reached the door, lifted his hat, and was backing out through the screen while I stood beside Pink's bed and felt the coolness of her hand.

"I'm sure there's some mistake. As soon as Randall gets here we'll get this all cleared up, I'm sure."

Pink stared after John Mason.

I heard Pink moan. I turned to see her furrowed brows, her small mouth pursed in wonder.

"I did hear that, sister?"

"You did. And while it may well be true, we'll let Randall have a chance to prove it isn't."

"It must be true. It all makes sense, now. The travelin', the times away. How he is with me. Not much interested in havin' babies, sister, not really. I never understood because he loved them so. But I kept insistin' wantin' a family. I never should have pressed him."

"He's a scoundrel, that's what he is. Don't even think that you're at fault in this…this duplicity, this betrayal."

"Oh, but I am, sister. I am. I could neither give him babies nor keep from tryin' and both pushed him from me. I see that now."

The tears made their way from the corners of her eyes, trailing and pooling into her ears as she lay, her face as white as the linen.

"Willin' to risk tryin' but not livin' without them. Now without him."

"You've got to fight this, Pink. Don't let him think this will bother you one bit. Cromarties are stronger than that. We'll show him."

I could feel my teaching voice, my "making things happen" voice rush out of me, trying to cut into the pain her words forced into the air. "You'll have this baby, you'll have what you've always wanted, and you won't need the likes of Randall Moss to raise it either. Your family will do what we need to, Pink, you can count on that."

But she turned her face from me and stared instead out the window at the swirling water of the New River.

Randall did not arrive for dinner.

I suppose John Mason found him, told him what he had revealed and that had made Randall Moss's decision, cowardly as it was, to never see or touch his Florida wife again.

Randall's absence cheated me of my chance to burn my outrage into his skin, to scratch my nails along his face, to give him pain the way I watched it flood across my sister. I'd wait for him in the rocking chair next to her bed, rehearse what I'd say when he arrived then pounce on him like an angry panther.

In the night, Pink's restlessness woke me as I slept in the chair beside her. And when she cried out in pain I could already smell the acrid scent of loss. All the flannel I could gather became a small cotton fluff in an ocean of red.

Blood and a tiny little boy left her body weak and unwilling to go on. I woke Frank, asked him to please call the doctor.

"Maybe you should get Bloxham and Louise, too," he said when he saw the size of the pool I'd soaked up, the sinking image of Pink in the bed. "Frances and DeWitt. Might encourage her."

"In the morning. No sense waking them tonight."

Frank had been appalled when I'd told him of John Mason's visit. He had called around to various places and had not located him nor Randall. I would have feared for Randall's life if Frank had found him; if I had cared. He phoned the doctor and then dressed quietly to saddle the mule and go out into the night, taking the soiled flannel and its contents with him.

The doctor had little to say when he arrived.

"Not much to do. I'll ask Alfred to bring medication by, a prescription for pain. Might help her rest if nothing else." He patted my shoulder. "Annie's on her way."

Annie Beck arrived and I never appreciated her presence more, just a friend who would come at any time of day or night and simply sit, keeping silent, letting sisters sit together as though they sat alone.

When Frank returned, Annie Beck fixed him breakfast so I could stay beside Pink, holding her hands in my prayers.

Bloxham and Louise came, each as stunned as the next over the tragic tale, each trying to remember any little hesitation, any small moment when we might have overlooked the obvious, might have found a way to spare our sister of all this.

DeWitt and Frances brought Dale and Margaret, who played quietly on the porch as dawn came. Frances held her youngest, DeWitt Jr., in her arms.

I searched the past, seeking reason and explanation, moments when I might have made a difference but I hadn't. There were no moments, nothing any of us could put our finger on. Randall had lived a lie for years, and he had lived it well. He had found a way to prevent the venting of our outrage by simply disappearing. He and Will, I thought. He and Will.

"We'll come back later and spell you, Ivy, honey," Louise said. She patted my shoulder and for once I didn't snap at her or resist her offer. "I'll have Daddy bring over his watermelon drink. That'll refresh us all. Maybe send him on up to Okeechobee to let your papa and Gus know. I think'd be all right for them to bring their newest, don't you? So common," she added. "So close together."

"Thank you. And your dad, too. I don't know about a newborn right now. Need to get Pink past this crisis, then we'll see."

"I'd see her," Pink said, overhearing us. "Always liked seein' babies."

The day wore on with Pink breathing as though she had stones on her chest. Traffic moved up and down the river. I could hear the piercing horns of autos on Las Olas. Life and commerce continued.

Pink didn't seem to be sleeping, but she didn't open her eyes when I talked, either. Annie Beck lifted her wrist, gentled it to me so I could feel the weakening pulse. Her heart barely beat.

Alarms pushed against my ears.

"Pink," I said, "I don't want you to go, I don't. More than anything in this world I want you to stay so we can dangle our feet in the river and twirl our parasols at the county fair in Palm Beach and kick our feet in the sand. There are so many things left to do, Pink. The birds to watch. The nieces and nephews to be nurtured. And you can help. I need you to help. At Dania, too, Pink. Please want to stay."

"Never had my showin'," Pink said, "of my paintin'."

"We'll do that. Next spring. Won't we, Annie Beck?"

Annie Beck nodded but she stayed silent.

"Too afraid. Worried how folks would judge. You never worried 'bout that, sister."

"Not wise enough to worry," I said. "Just plunged ahead."

Pink smiled a thin line. She kept her eyes closed as though the effort to keep them open would be too much.

"You were willin' to be exposed," she said, "to be helpin'. Don't be afraid to show your grievin' side, now, sister. There's lessons there for some folks too."

"Pink..."

"You'll do fine without me, sister."

"The doctor says you've got to want to live, Pink. You do, don't you? We all want you to, so much, honest to truth, we do."

"There is a time for everythin'; ain't that Scripture?"

"This doesn't have to be yours. I don't want it to be, Pink." I heard the sob in my voice, tried to keep it from her, but what I wanted made no difference. I couldn't keep her living; I could not make that happen on my own, not with all my will and wish.

"Just let my leavin' go easy on you."

"Oh, Pink. Do you have to?"

She nodded weakly, and I could feel her need and that the way that I could serve her now would be to stay with her for as long as God allowed, then let her go.

"There's a better place, sister, just like Mama said."

She slipped a little more through the night. Frank came to sit beside me for a time.

"You ought to rest," he said.

I shook my head. "You go lie down. If something changes, Annie Beck or I will come get you."

He stayed awhile, watching Pink, remembering, I imagined. Then he nodded, kissed me gently. "Wish I could take this from you, Ive," he said.

"Me too. Honest to truth."

Then while I sat beside her, doves cooing from the porch above, Albert's memory came to me, of how I'd failed to walk beside him when he left us and so had not found a way to say good-bye nor make his last hours full of living.

When Pink woke sometime after the clock had struck two times, I did not try to sweep away what was when she spoke.

"Will you speak the twenty-third psalm with me, sister?"

"I will."

We repeated the words together. Her hand, gentled into mine, squeezed when we came to the part about the valley of the shadow of death.

"There's an Indian version, did you know that? Annie Tommie told me. A part says, 'It may be soon or a long time, He will draw me to a dark valley but I'll not be afraid for it's between those mountains that the Shepherd Chief—that's what Annie said it translated to—will meet me and the hunger that I've had in my heart all through this life will be satisfied. He gives me something to lean on and spreads a table filled with food and puts His hand on my head and all the tired is gone, and later, I'll live with Him forever.' Isn't that lovely?"

"Lovely," Pink said.

"I believe you are in the valley of the shadow of death, Pink." I swallowed, wondering if what I said was what I should.

But she was fully present, her eyes wide open, clear, wet pools of wisdom taking in last moments of life.

"You don't need to be afraid there, because you're not alone," I said. "The Lord is with you, and those of us who love you will be with you for as long as we're allowed. But I won't pretend you're not there, not any longer. Because then I won't be able to say good-bye to you, nor help you say farewell to us."

She took deep breaths and watched me. "It won't be so bad, sister."

"Not for you, I don't think. That's what the Lord promised." My voice choked. The continuous ooze of blood stole her from us.

"You're strong."

"It takes great courage to die well, to let us be with you, to accept our love for you. We want you to stay, but Pink, we can let you go."

She nodded, and a faint smile eased onto her face. After a time she said, "I feel guilty for things I shoulda done and didn't and things I did I best had left alone. I don't like leavin' that behind."

She had trouble breathing, and I wondered if she should talk, if I should tell her to rest and wait. I watched Annie Beck wake up others lying about in the room. What Pink had to say seemed important to be heard. "I was given lots. Didn't give nothin' back."

"I would imagine the most loving, productive, powerful person in the world would feel guilty when it came time to die, Pink." I brushed tendrils of damp hair from her temples. "There's always more to do." I found myself crawling in bed beside her, wanting to hold her, feel her against me as I talked. I stroked her head as though she were an infant. "Maybe regret could be the word, rather than being burdened by guilt."

"Regret's a good word, sister. Thank you. I have regrets. That I didn't pay more attention to people I loved. I never did step out with Will," she said. "And I never did know what happened to him, though I know I set your mind to thinkin' that I did." I squeezed her shoulder. "I'm hopin' the Lord won't mind much, my not doin' all I could've with my life. Do you think He will?"

"He won't," I said. "He knows all about your generous spirit, all you gave to your family and friends. Just who you are. He'll welcome you, Pink, just as we'll grieve your going."

"Will I see Him? When I didn't do enough?"

"We join Him through grace, Pink, through his love. You accepted that, and that's all the invitation needed. None of us can ever do enough. That's the gift. He did it for us."

She smiled then and looked at others stepping close to the bed. She gazed at them then seemed to sleep, her breathing labored but steady.

Just before dawn she awoke again, restless, her hands moving and fluttering, her breathing labored and my thoughts stayed glued like sticky pitch on her, not stuck somewhere past nor running to the future. Just there, with Pink, at her moment of transition.

Annie Beck came in along with Frank, the rest of the family, too, and each talked quietly to Pink of their love and memories. We chanted psalms and sang songs of joy, for she was going to a place warm and wonderful.

"It's almost like a birth, isn't it?" DeWitt said. He stood with his arm around my shoulder while I pressed the tissue to my swollen eyes.

"Is it?"

"The waiting, the expectation, not knowing when or how and yet anticipating, getting through the pain, hoping for something glorious to happen."

"Births have always been so terrifying to me."

"It's another passage, like taking the ferry across the New River."

"Like taking the ferry."

Pink's eyes opened wide suddenly, and she did not seem to have trouble breathing at all but almost held her breath between deep gulps of air that filled her narrow chest. She gazed into the eyes of everyone in the room standing around her bed. It was as though she spoke to us with those eyes, communed in a deep and mystic way, told us not to worry, gave us comfort and a presence to remember. She was comforting us in that moment, gave peace to each of us.

Then she looked upward toward the ceiling and her face became as beautiful as any I had ever seen, a glow almost, a smile and light flooded her face and made her young and beautiful and free of disappointment and betrayal.

"She's seeing something wonderful!" Louise said. Her voice mixed awe with bliss.

"Of heaven," Annie Beck said. "Oh, what a gift to be here, Pink, to be present when you enter into the presence of God. I...I don't know what to say, I feel so privileged." Annie Beck cried quietly, and I wondered why I couldn't now.

And then Pink sank back into the linen, her shoulders narrow against the pillowed bed. I saw a movement, a presence, beginning at her heart and moving up through her body, past the cartilage of clavicle exposed through the opening of her bed jacket; up through each tiny bone of her neck, through her chin, her mouth, past her nose. It moved until it soared out through her eyes and into the dawn light of the room. Pink and her soul had gone. Only the shell of her body remained, sunken in on itself, onto the bed that now held nothing more than the still and once graceful form of my sister.

We buried Pink in the Evergreen Cemetery, in the family plot next to Albert. At the graveside, I looked around at the faces of those who had loved Pink, her friends, the children from the Methodist Sunday school she so faithfully taught. I studied those who had been with her in life and those present when she made her passage from it; and I felt a connection with them, a comforting one, a communion that would bind us together forever.

Papa's shoulders shook in silent sobs as DeWitt helped him back to the car.

My rage toward Randall had not abated, and I looked for him through the crowd of parasols open against the blazing sun as we returned to our autos. He was nowhere about.

I blamed myself for not noticing, for not sensing his treachery, for not protecting my only sister in life; for not preventing her death.

But the courage of Pink's dying said not to waste my time there, that helping her passage meant accepting my own part in it, grieving the loss and letting her go.

I was uncertain about what to do with Pink's things. Their home had been left just as Randall had on the morning John Mason entered our lives. DeWitt agreed to take the hounds; Bloxham and Louise inherited the cats. Eventually, I began packing things, putting her lovely clothes, the waists and tiny shoes and beaded belts, into boxes for the Red Cross. I marked furniture to be given away.

Her paintings, when I found them, brought me to my knees. In addition to the seascapes, she'd painted mere impressions of things, of a blue mule washed beneath a live oak, of a manatee's eyes searching through hyacinth-clustered water; of pale pastels of greens and blues and the light of ocean that looked like dreams almost, color sobbing into color. And at the bottom, in a tissue-wrapped canvas tied with purple string, she'd painted the trading post, porches, windows, seawall, windmill—all as perfectly drawn as though they were a photograph, the promise of the New River ferry moored just out of sight. She painted it the way she thought I'd like to see it, not the way she might have loved to paint it best.

I wept and then brushed off the dust of Pink's life and in the process, began the journey to bury my own despair.

CHAPTER NINETEEN

I had thought we would have had a sad Christmas gathering, but a few of the Osceolas and Tigers had joined us as usual along with old neighbors and friends, and I believed Pink would have found pleasure in it, the spirit of giving and celebrations surrounding the birth of a Baby.

After the service and with Advent completed, Frank drew up inside himself. I knew I had to give to him now, help him get well. I couldn't lose him, too, not while the wounds of Pink's leaving still scratched red and raw.

"Will you have the operation, Frank?"

"Suppose so," he said. "Sometime. Don't worry now, or I won't tell you what the doctor says. You've got things to do, you just do them."

I considered cutting my hair after we buried Pink. Somehow, brushing the lengths hand over hand, as I had all my life, felt too tiring now, too demanding.

"Look just fine as you are," Frank told me.

"Why, thank you," I said and kissed his forehead, "but I think I need a change, something to mark this time as a new beginning."

With a scissors from my sewing basket, I chopped at the lengths, then closer and closer until it settled just over my ears in soft waves. I stood before the mirror, wondering if I ought to begin using some face powder and makeup to cover the lines to my eyes.

"Always did have that natural beauty that didn't need fixing on," Frank said.

"Annie Beck says to wear brighter prints and paisleys and I'll look as though I'm wearing rouge when I'm not."

"Clever, that Annie. She's a good friend to you."

"A good friend, when such are hard to find and keep."

Frank wheezed when I said that and straightened his paper, then buried his face in the text.

⇓

A survey had finally been completed at Dania. The government had paid for it and discovered—to no one's surprise—that the property line of the reservation ran right through the middle of the squatter's new barn.

Once again, Federal marshals were dispatched and this time, Lucien Spencer had requested that the man be allowed to take his barn down, move it still farther west so at last the final vestiges of squatters would be gone.

"I can't believe he's willing to give them another ninety days," I told Frank when I read of it. "This could go on forever."

"That's the way with those who push the law," Frank said. "They wait, figuring the government will tire. They'll have what they want."

"I'll never tire until those men are gone."

"Didn't know they were taking on the 'queen of endurance.' Thought they had a puny adversary, the U.S. of A."

In the spring of 1927, after six years of waiting and urging and praying, the squatters had finally left. A few more families had made their way to the reservation. It pleased me and at the same time saddened me, to think that Pink had not lived to see the houses finished nor the gardens bearing fruit.

"I suppose there'll be all these little things that will just reach up and grab me and make me think of her when I least expect it."

"Suppose so," Frank said.

"I wish I could get Esther's family to consider the move."

"Can't keep pushing things, Ivy."

"I know, I know. But they'd like it once they got there, I'm sure they would."

"Stretch may have his 'source' impaired out there."

"You think he bootlegs?"

"Don't you?"

"But that's terrible. He could be arrested, not to mention the harm he does to his own people."

"Not his."

"His child is."

"Wouldn't worry over arrests much either, history of the squatters any indication. They'd probably want handwritten receipts from those who buy in order to prosecute."

"Oh, Frank, you think?"

"It's the government way."

Then new word came down from Spencer, and I believed I had a way to encourage my friend into a better place.

"If I come to pick you up, in my car, will you come then, just for the day?"

Esther cooked in the cooking chickee, Julia chasing a puppy escaping beneath a platform, its pink tongue all we could see from the shadows there. I handed Esther a heavy spoon when she scanned around for it.

"You wouldn't have to stay. But Annie Tommie and her family have. They're happy there. And you could build a chickee if you wanted. You don't have to live in a house."

"Stretch not go, no goin'."

"He might. You don't know for sure. But you have some say, too, in this. For Julia. There's an agent living there most of the time now. It stays safe for people. Don't you want to be safe?"

"What I know is safe, most safe."

"What you're used to, yes, what's familiar. But just as you made a change that day to come inside my home, to look at yourself in the mirror, to read a book, you'll change if you need to, for your daughter. Those weren't familiar things those years ago, but you did them."

She touched the side of her face.

"Your child won't need to be afraid to learn new things, Esther. She has a mother who modeled courage for her. You didn't have that. Your parents…because of the moonshine. It robbed you, Esther. But it won't rob Julia. You'll do whatever's needed, even though it's frightening, I know you will. You have courage. And what a gift that is, to protect her as you can."

She stirred and stirred with the heavy spoon, looked longingly at Julia and cast a quick glance at Stretch lounging near the gardens, talking and spitting brown juice against the ground.

"You come pick me up, in Tillie, Tillie. I see."

"They want you to come out to Dania," I told Frank that morning in May. Pink's Christmas stocking still hung over the fireplace; I wasn't sure when I'd ever take it down.

I held one of the new insect guns, a green metal tube with a handle and forced a spray along the doorjamb.

"Usually go when you want, no reason for a special invitation."

"They just want to be sure you'll be there."

I set the tube aside, washed my hands, and reached for the thick ironstone bowl for Frank's cereal. I plopped raisins into his dish, and we talked pleasantly about our friends at Dania. Frank said their row of houses reminded him of the tourist camp we'd spent the night in after one of his visits to Miami.

"They are lined up rather stilted," I said. "I hope they'll be able to expand when they start cutting their own timber. We need to pick up Julia and Esther first. Is that all right with you?"

"You're the driver."

Both climbed into the backseat, the scent of buttonwood lingering on their cape dresses. Julia's eyes were wide as I backed us up, then forward, heading out the road. She stuck her head out the window and from the little mirror on the dash I could see the wind blow at her fine, dark hair.

It was an exceptionally beautiful day, the kind of balmy weather with seagulls dipping and calling above us and wild iris in bloom. Red and orange bromiades speared the dark foliage beside the road and we stopped several times for slow-moving turtles.

"Days like these are what bring them all down here," Frank said, a heaviness washing over his words. I could never tell when something would lighten him or wear him down. "Folks from Philadelphia and New York and Minnesota."

"Yes, and the good homes you build is what keeps them here."

I had meant it as a compliment, but Frank had turned his face from me and looked away.

We pulled up through the gate, paused to watch a child lead a bony-shouldered cow across the opening. It was good to see a bovine or two promising milk in a place smoked free of mosquitoes and bugs.

"Here we are. Esther, there are the houses." I pointed and she looked out through the front windshield. Julia opened the door and waddled out. "Not much to speak of, I know, but things could be done with them. And it keeps the rain off."

The little straight row of houses still bothered me, though paths had been lumbered as walkways and the doors were open to the sunlight. I watched Esther watching Julia make her way along the path, so I failed to see the other children until they stood next to the car.

They opened the door and pulled on me, leading me, a few others pushing me like a pup.

"I'm going, I'm coming," I said, flowered dress lifting about my calves in the breeze. I held my hat on with my purse hand. "The next surprise is for Frank. Pull on him. I know what's through there."

They turned to grab at Frank then, and he seemed to like their little fingers tugging against him until we had bent through an overhang of palmetto. Esther had gathered up Julia and followed us.

There stood the building the children were so proud of, the one I had dreamed about for them so long ago. A new building, a rectangle, with windows and one single door stood before us and the sight of it—though I had known it was there—took me back, years and years back, to a place Frank had helped build, to a structure I had once taught in.

"They ran into trouble staffing it so I didn't want to say anything. But they've a teacher now. Imagine that, Frank. They have a teacher and a school. See, Esther? A school."

Esther took the few steps up, Julia in hand. Annie Tommie's large frame filled the door, and the memory of Ada Merritt flashed into my mind. Julia and Esther disappeared through the door followed by a scattering of children deserting Frank and me for the promise of fun inside. Annie waved at us then stepped back inside.

"At least for the first few grades, Frank, these little tykes are going to school."

"And no one's objecting?"

"Not directly." I looked away.

I gathered myself and my feelings, my wish that Pink could be here to share all of this, so pleased that Frank could and would.

"You and Annie Tommie are quite the formidable force, Ivy."

"We just set our sights on a thing, Frank. Had a vision of something. Might take twenty years or more, as this has, but it's worth it, it is."

Could he tell I willed him to want something, to not give up on his health or the changes the hurricane forced or whatever was happening in our finances? Could he feel me infusing him with the promise of the future?

"Never thought it would happen," Frank said. He walked slowly around the building, touching the lumber, picking at the specks of green driven into the walls. "Not the reservation. Certainly not a school." He turned to look at me. "You're a powerful woman, Ivy."

"Not alone, I'm not."

Children sprang back out, got behind Frank and pushed on him.

"Worse than ants," he said, but he let them lead him. He spoke back over his shoulder, then, to me: "Know how to make things happen, long as there's no one to hold you back."

Inside, across the cooler room came the smell of chalk and lumber and the lingering of children and a dozen memories of freckled faces and snakes and little girls with umbrella-dressed dolls. Esther sat at one of the desks, Julia on her lap. This building represented what I thought my teaching career would be, not what it had become.

"Quite a place to go to school." Frank spoke to Esther.

She turned, her large eyes threatening to spill. "For Julia, Julia," she said. "Good school for Julia."

"Suppose you want to teach here, then," Frank said.

I shook my head. "They hope to have an Indian teacher before long, from Oklahoma way. And someday, a Seminole. I'm just sure of that."

"Got cards up there," Frank said, pointing above the blackboard.

"So they do."

Across the top hung the alphabet in huge black letters written in English, both the upper and lower cases.

"They should have been done in color," I said, "The children would pick the words up so much faster."

The Seminole School at Dania officially opened in 1927. A home for the teacher sat painted white just down from the Indian rows of homes. Children clustered in an orderly fashion, without pushing or lining up, to step inside and take their seats. Julia, Esther's girl, was one of them. It was only a primary grade school. Upper grades would still be an issue, but it was a beginning—and an end for me, the realization of a twenty-five-year dream. Fourteen children had come forward to enroll despite the stated tribal prohibition against it.

Afterwards, I still drove out on Sundays and my letter writing told me the Baptists might be interested in establishing a church here in the near future.

"A church," I told Annie Beck. "Imagine that."

The people were receptive, I'd been told. *We are encouraged that some of them even know the Bible stories,* one church planter had written. I didn't bother to explain my lack of surprise. Things just happened in their own time.

Frank's despondency continued through the year. He couldn't seem to be encouraged by the increased construction, that south Floridians were doing what they did best—recovering from the power of storms, neighbors helping neighbors.

"Everything moving too fast for me," Frank said.

There were reports of growing arguments within the city council, about how best to recover, refinance debt, assist with the massive losses some had incurred through mortgage and speculation. I had not given it much concern until Frank mentioned a note he had due. "Need to sell some property," he said. "Trouble is, what we have isn't worth much now."

"It's still land," I said naively.

"I have loans against it, Ivy. Made loans to others with the money and now they can't pay me and I can't pay either."

"Oh. Should I be worried? About our home, I mean?"

He shook his head. "I'll figure out a way." And because he never mentioned it again, I assumed he did.

Even when the state comptroller was indicted in Tallahassee for allowing insolvent banks to remain open, Frank didn't comment. And when people came to see him and talked quietly in the office off the parlor, when he leaned to take papers from the back of the safe set in the stairwell and fingered them with a sad and sullen face, even then I did not worry. I felt hopeful. I was prepared for pain.

I tried to turn the medical trips we made to Miami into adventures, visiting Royal Palm State Park and listening to the soothing sound of birds making a comeback. Frank didn't allow the sights and sounds to soothe him. Instead, he spoke of wishing he weren't such a burden or that the "mess" of caring for him would be too much for me, "such a little slip of a thing you are."

"I've weighed ninety-eight pounds for most of my life and I'm strong as a horse."

"Dark circles under your eyes."

"Has nothing to do with my health. Family trait, that's all that is. I can certainly take care of you, if you let me."

I set about tending to his every need, dusting powder and bluing sheets. Annie convinced me I should change the linens daily. "I do it because we fail to get the evenin' breezes where we live and the house gets so closed up against the bugs. But it is a fine luxury I've found, clean sheets."

"Della might have my hide," I said.

"Land sakes, that woman adores him almost as much as you."

"Frank would rest easier," I decided, "and I'll help her."

I kept my schedule busy and active to show Frank I could care for him and meet my civic obligations. When President Hoover suggested me for the chairman of the Florida Better Homes Committee, I readily agreed to serve. I assisted with the library celebration in early 1928, raising money to expand the collection. A proposal for a children's home for orphans came my way, and I actively worked to see if we could find a building and raise money privately to care for them. Some had lost parents in the storm of '26. I helped start the Campfire Girls, too.

As a diversion, Frank and I drove to the amusement park one afternoon. It had expanded well beyond the roller-skating rink and now included high rides that thrilled children and adults alike.

"We should do that," I told him, my hand shading the sun as I arched my head back to watch people swing in the little iron buckets high in the sky. "Honor your farsightedness in investing in something so wonderfully fine for families."

"You have a pig in your pocket?"

"What?"

"That 'we' part," he said. "We have no interest in going up in that thing, we-e-e surely do not."

"Oh, Frank." I jabbed him lightly with my elbow and beamed inside.

It was the first time in so long that he had teased with me. "The view would be spectacular out over the beach."

He shook his head and smiled and I felt heartened, though I knew if I wanted to see the view I would have to do it with Annie Beck or one of the nephews or nieces.

We drove back through town, and the sounds of hammering and the clop-clop of wagons filled with supplies and the steam from the train arrivals all spoke of progress again, recovery. The government had been bringing people in to shore up the banks of Lake Okeechobee, building levees so if we had another hurricane, the levees would help prevent flooding. These were new ideas and were welcomed as ways of planning ahead, for protection.

Sun glinted off the New River. As a sign of renewed vigor, in November, Frank was once again elected to the city council. He quietly accepted.

On February 16, 1928, the State Bank Frank had been such a part of closed. Two days later it reopened under another name with all the principals originally involved. Except for Frank.

He did not speak to anyone for four days. The hurt in his eyes went beyond description, and though I didn't understand all of it, I knew he'd been devastated both by the bank's need to close and by his exclusion in the reopening.

Some of Frank's friends stopped at the house with worried looks and they spoke with him in hushed voices, strain showing on their faces when they came and still, when they left. He spoke only short sentences for weeks after that.

Then for five long, interminable days in late March, Frank again did not speak. He sat in the chair and stared. I tried everything I could think of: food, music, talk, prayer.

"Let's count the manatees," I said and tugged gently on his cool hand. He didn't budge.

I drove to the reservation and invited one of the Tigertails to come talk with Frank about alligators or hides or simply sit with him on the porch. They did that, rocking in the chair beside Frank and talking to me when I spoke. But Frank didn't. Not to them nor to me. I pointed out a shark tail moving up the New River one day, sure that it would startle Frank into words. It did not.

No one else knew, not Bloxham nor DeWitt. But Annie Beck knew even when I tried to lightly gloss it over.

"You've got to get him to a doctor," she said. "It's his mind, Ivy. He's turned it inside himself."

"But he's done so much! How can he let this bank thing bring him down? He needs to get his back up for excluding him. I certainly intend to have words with Will Kyle. After all these years, how could he do this to Frank! How is it they have money to reinvest while Frank doesn't? What kind of shell game went on there, I'd like to know. He needs to know instead of turning his fury onto himself."

"Not everyone addresses distress as you do, land sakes. Head-on and clear. You know, you always lift your hand before you speak. Like a child in school does."

"Do I? Just a habit, I guess."

"I always know when you need to talk, at the women's club or wherever, by that genteel way you raise your finger." She showed me and I smiled. "They never know what will hit them, of course, once you have the floor."

"I'm not too strident, am I?"

"Not at all."

"Frank's been disappearing for months, hasn't he?"

"You know that."

"No. Yes. I don't understand it."

"Alfred says talk is that Frank made personal guarantees on people's notes, that he'd secure the loans for their homes if the bank would make the loan for them. Word is, it went well until the storm."

"Then they couldn't repay the bank, so they've come to him now. And he hasn't the money either because people can't pay him back. Oh, Annie."

Annie Beck nodded. "That, and that he encouraged people to both take out loans so they could build and others to make deposits. On his word, many did, and then the bank has become, well, almost insolvent. So they closed and reopened. But people have now lost their investments. Their homes."

"Why won't he talk with me about it?"

She shrugged her shoulders. "Embarrassed, I suppose."

"Embarrassed. Yes. He's always been so strong and independent, so able to take care of us and others; and with integrity, that old Alexander complaint not withstanding."

"And with his health…"

"One more thing he can't control, feels he's burdened others. Well, that one I can do something about."

I drove him to Miami and this time insisted I stay while Dr. Mortenson furrowed his brow, pinched his nose over his glasses, and listened to me talk. Frank sat in the car.

The doctor made a phone call or two and gave me directions and Frank was admitted to the sanatorium to help rest his mind.

"I'm confident we can help him, Mrs. Stranahan," an even younger doctor—a psychiatrist—told me. "Just give us some time."

My husband didn't even look distressed when I left him sitting on the side of the bed, his shoulders bent over, his feet precise against tile.

Time. We would take care of this in time.

I actually found the travel back and forth to see Frank restful for me. Alone in the car, I loved seeing the sea grapes and ferns, cranes feeding beside the road, children playing next to schoolhouses; they all gave me confidence. It was prayerful time, too, in my car, considering what God wanted for my life, what new things He had in store for me as He did for each of us up until the moment we die.

Pink came to mind often as I drove. I grieved the empty space her leaving left. I hadn't really sat and cried much with her passing. I wondered about my depth of feeling that I couldn't do that or didn't. But I believed Pink would understand, not want the living to waste much time weeping over the past.

Frank spoke to me on one of the visits.

"You've been away," he said.

"Not me."

"No? Guess it's been me then. Think I'd like to come home."

"I'd like that very much, Frank."

"Got my strength back. Face whatever I need to."

"Good," I said. "We'll do this together, Frank. We will."

Dr. Mortenson had also told us he believed Frank had a kind of cancer. Prostate cancer, he called it, that destroyed slowly, and while a surgery might assist Frank's comfort, it was not essential, he didn't think, right now.

Frank had put on weight eating all that starchy food the sanatorium served, and I was pleased when he asked to take his walk with me in the mornings. I had to slow down for him, but that was fine. His company soothed, and the planning of our day serenaded by curlews and gulls is a memory that nourishes. He'd sit on the sand in the shade of a palm while I had my morning dip in the water. Life was tentative, I thought, as I walked toward him out of the sea. Tentative, but good.

That night I dreamed of a river. It appeared where it wasn't supposed to be. I rode in a car with a stranger, some sort of guide, someone showing me places where new homes could be built. We'd come around a bend and been engulfed by a river, rising up over the fenderless wheels.

"Does the river belong here?"

"No. It's out of its course," he'd said, and we'd continued to drive to a strip of higher land. "We've got to get above it." He motioned me out. We'd begun climbing beneath a waterfall that suddenly turned to mud—black, black muck that cascaded over us. I turned to look out through the ebony veil but the man warned me, "Don't look back."

The wind came up on September 15, 1928. Little blasts at first, not unlike fall weather. Almost two years to the day of the big storm that people said had yielded 130 mile per hour winds. It felt unsettling to have another storm brewing so close to the same date.

Bloxham came by to say ships' captains had received reports of a huge storm, the first of the season. "I'll help you move the chairs off the porch, inside," he said. "Best put the hoes and things into the shed, too. Anything lying about. Got enough food for a few days? Candles?"

Frank nodded, and the two went off to tidy things up. I checked our food stores, put more fruit into the ice chest and pulled candles out of the cupboard. I ran water into the sink and the clawfoot tub upstairs. I hoped the windmill's old arms would hold. In the attic, I closed off the shutters leaving the ones open on the leeward side of the house. The palms were already dipping low, and the phone wires danced like strands of black hair in the air.

Five hours later, the storm hit with a fury, rain drenching as I had never experienced in all my years in the state. Frank and I huddled beside each other in the dark, blankets over our shoulders leaning against the clawfoot tub hoping the size of it would protect us if the wall should give in. And it felt like it might with the blasts and the howl. We could barely speak to each other, the sound of winds roared about our ears. I didn't want to imagine the devastation it would leave when it left.

Even when the quiet of the eye came and we had a moment to light the candle, check windows and doors, I felt glad we couldn't see out toward the river, that it was night.

Then the blowing resumed. We slept fitfully on blankets I'd spread on the pine floor.

No tidal wave rose over us this time, and we thought that we'd been spared when the sun came out. Then we learned the worst. A torrent of rain had filled Lake Okeechobee to overflowing. Angry, greedy wind swept water against dirt levees built for protection. It pushed and clawed and ate away at them in the rain until they broke, sending cascades of black mud like waterfalls gouging out new rivers. The waters surged up over the banks and made rapids of trees and houses and people it deposited all over south Florida.

It was a more devastating hurricane than the one in '26, people said. Ed King, Louise's father, died there on the lake. He'd gone to help repair a boat and with two thousand other souls, mostly black farmworkers who lived close to the lake, Ed King had ended his life in a torrent of water and mud.

My brother and his family and Papa survived the storm. We did too, and the rest of the Cromarties. But it took its toll on south Florida and wore another hole in Frank's fragile spirit.

Cleanup began again. This time, you could feel the futility, the energy drained from the previous storm not yet deposited before facing another demanding withdrawal.

In January of 1929, a County Commissioner, the chairman of the Dania Chamber of Commerce, Mrs. Dickey of the Hollywood Women's Club, and I completed a special investigation of conditions at the reservation at Dania. I sent the report off to the Commissioner of Indian Affairs with recommendations for developing a dairy or at least a cattle industry, suggested a weaving industry, and by providing root stocks for citrus groves, avocados, rough lemons, and guavas, the beginning of new enterprises.

Spencer disagreed with the dairy recommendation when he read his copy of the report. He attached his own comments saying the Indians couldn't be taught to milk twice a day. *I shouldn't think they would be regular enough to serve the cows,* he'd written. We also wanted the school maintained; fourteen children still attended. And we encouraged continued employment off the reserve as well as on, creating dolls and crafts for the tourist industry.

There had been some cases of flu, we'd reported, but the people were generally healthy and sought care from white doctors in the community. We found no disease to speak of there, nor poor sanitary conditions, unlike reports made at other Seminole sites in Florida. There were still problems with liquor. We did note that, too, but that was not unique to the reservation. That was a national problem.

The report was well received though people expressed surprise that adults attended school in the evenings or that the Indians worked for their living outside the reservation or that gardening was a part of every school-child's day. Education, that's what was needed, and by more than just those on the reservation.

After completing the survey, I insisted Frank have his surgery. It took me until February, but I persisted and finally Frank agreed.

He appeared to recover well. It meant he'd need a permanent tube, catheter they called it, but I was prepared to manage that. I wasn't worried about my stamina one bit. I just wanted to get him out of the hospital, and for a time to adjust, I'd decided on an extended trip, up north, to visit his family and friends.

"I don't think that's wise," Dr. Mortenson told me. He looked older, the treating of illnesses perhaps more troubling now that he'd grown older or knew more about the fleetingness and fragility of the human form.

"Why ever not? I love to drive. Frank loves to travel. It'll be a chance to show how well we can do together, that I won't be torn between my service demands and what Frank needs of me."

Dr. Mortenson pinched his nose again in that way he had. "He's been…despondent," he said. "Almost, how should I put this, during the psychiatric sessions. And then, while he was hospitalized he was…self-destructive. He made an attempt."

"Frank? Take his own life?" I felt myself sink into the narrow chair at the doctor's hospital office, slapped like a baby. "Do you think he intended it?"

"I do. He stored up pills. He's quite concerned about you, Mrs. Stranahan, about whether he'll be too much for you."

"But that's exactly why the trip would be so good. He could see that he's the most important value of my life. The reports, the committees, those are nothing, nothing compared to Frank."

"It would be better if you were closer to his psychiatrist here from the sanatorium. In case you needed him."

"I could call. We'll stop in Asheville. They have that fine facility there if we need it. We'd visit family. If he says he wants to, wouldn't that be good? Seems like morose people are made worse by other people making choices for them. I'll just offer it, let him decide."

Dr. Mortenson hesitated but he concurred, and I tried not to sway Frank one way or the other.

Frank chose the trip and he did seem to enjoy the time we spent together. We drove north through Asheville where we'd honeymooned those years before.

"Changed a fair piece," Frank said.

"Haven't we all in twenty-nine years."

We talked of our early years, the way we'd been led to be together, two people with unique "requirements" Frank called it, who had found a deep and abiding, passionate love.

We drove on to Ohio and visited with his aunts and a few cousins and lamented Will's passing, again, whenever it was.

"Just can't explain," Frank said.

"No, you can't," his uncle had agreed. "Got to just accept things as they are. Learned that a long time ago. What's done is done and you just got to move on."

"Least he's missed seeing the devastation," Frank said.

His uncle nodded and the men sat without talking in that quiet way Midwest men can.

The wildflowers had come out in Pennsylvania by April and were a canvas of rolling color. We'd driven on to Niagara Falls and then into Canada. So beautiful, Canada. And through it all Frank and I worked out a routine to care for his needs, washing linens along the way in the little bowls and pitchers provided in the rooms. "Mo-tels" they called them, for the mobile people who stopped for a night or two on their way to somewhere else.

"Feel like a mo-tel myself," Frank said as I dabbed at his body with soft flannel, fluffed powder onto his skin.

"In what way?"

"Just a night or two on this earth," he said. "That's all any of us really has, by comparison to eternity."

I was conscious of raising my finger as if to respond, the way Annie Beck said I did, but I couldn't think of a thing to say.

In late April, we learned of some stock market fluctuations. I was glad we were on the road, away from the looks of Lauderdale folks. Time enough to respond to that challenge.

Then another huge storm hit the coast in May.

We drove into Fort Lauderdale on May 22. Newly set out crotons bloomed profusely and hibiscus stuck their showy blooms out of pots beside store doors. A few northerners were stocking up on shell art, mirrors surrounded with purple fans and the like before heading back to places we'd just left. It would be slow, this recovery, especially with the storm and rumors of stock market skips, but Lauderdale had been spared much of the May storm's wrath. West Palm Beach had taken the hit.

"That's a good sign, Frank. We weren't too hard hit this time."

"All Florida's hit."

I turned off the key and we sat beside our home, our sturdy, Dade pine built home that had harbored us, kept us sheltered. I sensed we were at a place of new beginning, Frank and I, once again.

"I do love this place," I said. "Thank you so much for building it all those years ago." I patted his hand. He sat silent.

"I'll go in and call Bloxy, let him help us unload the car and start freshening up the place. Doesn't home look good, Frank?"

He gazed at it, nodded slightly, then turned to look out across the New River. He saw what I did, I thought: its permanence and promise, the lushness of greenery, the surprise of blossom and bloom. An alligator sunned itself on the seawall then swiggled away toward the lawn and the water, splashing into the late afternoon. The river reflected the beauty of its people who had been drawn here all those years before and the kindness of the Indians who had helped Frank and me survive here. And we'd given back, too, into the cycle of life.

"I'll be right back, Frank. You wait here. Just soak in this sunshine."

"Check on the garden," he said. "I will."

"The garden. Yes. We're a bit behind on all that with our mo-telling around. I'll be back as soon as I call." I leaned and kissed him. I thought he smiled.

Bloxham said he'd be right over, and he could actually see the car he said, from his house across the river, and Frank's walking toward the garden shed.

So I didn't go right back out. I opened a window or two, checked the tabletop with a swipe of finger to see about dust, and began pulling sheets off the furniture.

I heard the splash almost as soon as I heard Bloxham's plaintive cry, his shout and a sob and I thought, how strange. I pushed open the screen to step onto the porch.

"Frank?"

I expected to see him come from around the back, to see what Bloxham shouted about as he ran toward the water and then with a dread, one so deep and so piercing, I knew what my brother's cry meant.

We sought frantically, Bloxy summoning several divers plunging into the New River, coming up with no sign of my husband. After more than an hour, a strong swimmer decided not to go so deep and he found Frank's body caught up at a ledge just below the surface, not even that far downriver. We'd been searching in deeper areas. They pulled my husband's body up, all gruesome and slick, and that young man, an August Burghurd, administered that new technique for drowning victims while Annie Beck gripped my shoulders, a stake beside a shaking plant. But it was too late.

The heavy iron grate Frank had attached to his legs before he plunged in had already sealed his fate.

More than a thousand attended the service we held on the lawn. Frank's lawn of the home he had built and loved in the town he had given his all to.

I sat in a daze beneath the awning, Annie Beck fanning at flies, her free hand holding mine in hers. Bloxham sat on the other side of me, Louise to his left. My family had all come including the youngest, Gus's Alice, age three. She would stay with me after everyone left. "Need someone to share your bed," he said. "Worst thing for a widow, sleeping alone."

"She'll give your mind focus," Annie Beck said. Give it a reason to heal. DeWitt Jr. and his school-age brother and sister sat on chairs behind us and I heard them whisper "Uncle Frank" this and "Uncle Frank" that. Billy, Gus's oldest, leaned his four-year-old head against my brother's chest in the same row I sat in. I looked at his large eyes as they stared. I watched his baby brother, John, just one year old, make his way along knees from his father to his mother while Alice sat straight back on the chair, her feet straight before her. I ached that these children would never know Frank now, not the Frank I loved.

Half the town appeared, along with Frank's former associates. Their presence there on the lawn beneath the flag made no sense without Frank standing there too. I'd been unable to piece it together, this Frank whom I loved, whom I believed together we could weather anything, this Frank was gone. I couldn't understand his leaving as he had, not after we had so enjoyed each others' company. I was sure we had.

"He wouldn't have pretended," Annie Beck assured me. "He didn't have a deceptive bone in his body, Lord knows. Perhaps that's why he did it, because he knew he couldn't deceive you into believing it would be all right. He did mind, I suspect, the idea of your taking care of him, maybe even stopping your work for it."

"My work," I'd said to her as though she had cursed me. "What does 'my work' mean without him?"

"He'd say it means everything. He was so proud of you, Ivy, for your passions, your perseverance. Did I ever tell you how he raved to me about the reservation school one day, about how you'd persisted for twenty-five years, single-handedly, to accomplish a vision? Said he never thought you could bring it about, not the school or the Seminoles' move. You amazed him."

"He called me the 'queen of endurance.'"

"Better than the 'queen of control.'"

"Does Alfred call you that?"

Annie Beck laughed. "Call myself that. I think Frank was proud you gave him the choice of things, this trip and all."

"Suppose I learned something along the way, about not trying to control everything. But I wish I had controlled this, acted so this hadn't happened."

"Regret. That's what you told Pink, don't you know? Not guilt. But regret."

"I'll try to hang on to that."

I hadn't cried. I'd made the arrangements and asked the Methodist choir to sing. Frank had always liked music and their choir, with Lula Marshall in it, was still the loveliest.

They had chosen C. J. Stone's "The Church's One Foundation," and I thought, how fitting. We were of one faith, really: Esther's people and the Methodists and Baptists and Presbyterians who had assisted through the years and of course, my fellowship of Adventists which Frank had accepted for me though had never joined himself: we had a foundation in common.

The fourth stanza truly struck me. I had never really listened to the words before. But there it was, the promise of a time when Frank and I and all the others buttressed by the same foundation would someday meet again.

> Yet she on earth hath union
> With God, the Three in One,
> And mystic sweet communion
> With those whose rest is won;
> O happy ones and holy!
> Lord, give us grace that we,
> Like them, the meek and lowly,
> On high may dwell with Thee.

Pink had won her rest as had Mama and Albert and both of Frank's parents. Perhaps even Will. And the babies: Pink's, Mama's tiny baby that I had failed to save those years before, and all the others she had given life to and lost. Her rest too was won, along with Frank's.

I hoped I could let go, not cling to the outrage over Frank's choice, nor the emptiness of my loss.

Then the Seminoles had come, more than one hundred in full Seminole dress. I'd been dry-eyed until I saw them, the dugouts, swishing along the New River, poled by the men Frank had cared for so much; women draped in beaded necklaces and the swirl of their colorful skirts; children sitting clear-eyed and unsmiling, staring straight ahead, their dogs, with tongues hanging out, perched at the bows.

Their acceptance of us those years before and their presence here now were gifts beyond measure.

While a group of Methodists chanted psalms, I looked at the Seminoles, the men and women who had befriended Frank, helped him those first years, trusted and treated each other with such care despite all of the changes. We'd have been lost without them.

I nodded my head at the Tigertails and Osceolas, the Jumpers and others who'd come to pay their respects to a man who loved them. I know that he loved them, as he had me. Still, he had chosen to leave us just as they had chosen to stay.

Annie Beck squeezed my hand and I watched them, the men in their colorful turbans wrapped around their heads, a plume standing up behind as part of traditional dress. I gazed at their diagonal shirts and skirts as they eased along the New River, now turning to rainbows, filtered through tears.

CHAPTER TWENTY

E veryone departs. Somehow the leaving is emptier, colder, when it follows a funeral. The bereaved are left to mend alone. The days formed a fog for me, worse than with Albert and Mama; worse than when Pink had died. I had lost my husband. Such a strange phrase that was, as though I had been responsible for him and now had misplaced him, like a pair of glasses or favorite sweater.

Gus and Vera's Alice remained with me, a three-year-old with large eyes and a daintiness about her that reminded me of a Spode china teacup even then. I wasn't sure if her staying was the best idea, but the family had insisted it would be good, "just for a time," and I found myself unable to resist.

I felt wrapped in cotton with no sense of ending. I wondered if perhaps the gauze I lived in might kill me too. I almost desired it, shoved deep the guilt of the wish.

As the days wore on, Alice's presence intercepted the pain that threatened to catch me unaware when I'd smell Frank's powder or hear the scrape of a chair and turn to see him, surprised when he wasn't there. I would stand and stare at the table or by his desk, I don't know for how long. Emotions like torrents of rain poured over me: sadness torn open with anger, then outrage followed by guilt would wash into loneliness, separation from myself.

"I would like an orange, Aunt Ivy."

Alice's little voice would lilt like a wind chime cutting into silence and I'd gaze at her, wondering where she'd come from and then I'd remember.

"An orange. And a pineapple, too, I suppose?"

"That would be 'specially nice," she'd say and take the hand I offered. "It prickles my tongue, Auntie."

"Does it? Well, let's see what we can do about that."

"Who painted that picture?" she asked one day. She pointed to the painting with the manatee I had hanging in the hall. I told her of Pink, and promised we'd wait at twilight for the manatees to come in.

I missed Frank most at night, while the mockingbird sang to the moon. We used to discover each other awake for no reason, reach out into the darkness and find the other person's hand there, the touch of our fingers a comforting sigh. I'd wake alone now, Alice asleep in what had been Frank's bed. Tears eased from my eyes, fell into my ears with him not present to dab them away as he would have. I know that he would have. We were so close.

And yet I had missed it, his wishing to die, his choosing to leave me. How had that happened? What hadn't I done?

A letter from Frank's lawyer had invited me in shortly after his death. I sat there, my hands wrapped around the cord of my black purse handle, twisting it while Lon Erickson, Frank's lawyer, told me of my "situation," how Frank had extended loans and mortgaged even our home.

"I knew there was that Biscayne Bay note he had trouble with," I said. "The rest, well, that's a surprise."

"A great many people are struggling, Ivy. You're not alone in this."

"I appreciate that, Lon."

"You have some property you can sell. And the house too. If you sold it right, you could pay off a portion of the old debt."

"I'll not sell my home," I said, firm. "But I will pay off the debts. It may take me years, but I'll find a way. Just give me a little time to take in the figures here, all that you're telling me."

"You've a lot on your mind, Ivy."

"Activity is always a good salve."

"Yes. But it can smother the wound, too. Make sure you give yourself time, get yourself some air. You've had a tremendous shock."

There wasn't much time for myself, as I saw it. I had a pig in my pocket, debts "we-e-e" had made together and thus needed to be paid off. I reviewed the papers and our "situation" and I knew I didn't have much time to gather air. Frank's clock ticked behind me. My eyes ached and I took my glasses off and rubbed at my nose. What's done is done. No sense assigning blame. Do what you can do in the present.

With some effort, I determined which pieces of land, which holdings and the mortgage against them, would permit me the greatest gain if I sold them. Annie and Alfred Beck helped me look things over and served as my check against pretending "all was well."

I worked out agreements with several buyers to deed me back a small portion of each property sold. Just a little section so I could hang on to something while still paying off debt. Each new owner also agreed not to permit the sale of liquor on their property. I thought Frank would have liked that little provision and I stuck with it.

And I dealt with the personal changes, the even more painful ones. "Della, it breaks my heart, honest to truth, to let you go, but I'll be wringing things alone now."

"Miz Ivy, I'd come just for your company."

"I wouldn't feel right about that, my not being able to pay what you're worth."

"Ain't nobody ever got paid what they worth, chile," she'd said and laughed. "Jus' let me give this way, to you and Mr. Frank, too. We like family. You believe in servin' family."

"Service, yes. All right then, if it's for Frank."

Like water flowing under the Everglades, relentless though slow, I paid off on the debt we'd incurred. I hung on to my home.

The wish of it, the hope and prayer of that, to repay the debts and find a way to stay on the New River, kept my focus those years. And I suppose in a way, the activity kept the wound of Frank's leaving at bay, too. I could hardly speak of his death, the way of it. I felt I held a part in it but I didn't know how; I thought his friends had betrayed him and I even chastised Will Kyle with that famous finger of mine and said I'd see him in his grave before I'd forgive him for his part in this, yet didn't know how it all fit.

Lon Erickson, our lawyer, scowled over my main plan to keep the house and had invited me back in for a chat.

"For now, Ivy, I don't think it's wise, really, for you to be renting to northerners, not while you're still staying right there in the house alone."

"Nonsense. I'm not alone. Alice is with me. And every room has an entrance onto the outside porch. It's perfect. There's demand for rental rooms. I keep them scrubbed. The attic is fine for me. Closest room to the bath. I've decided to add a dormer up there, to increase the light."

"And that will be enough to keep you?"

"I have other plans," I said. "To do what I have to."

"Such as?"

"Major and Clifton Breckenridge are interested in having a few little tables in the downstairs. They'd serve Basque dishes, take advantage of the *Saturday Evening Post* series of articles."

"You'd turn your home into a restaurant?"

"If that's what it takes."

And it had, first a Basque restaurant and then later a Swiss chalet, a lease not renewed because I refused to permit the sale of liquor.

Alice stayed a while longer and then returned to her parents, but she was always special to me, visited every summer and always came first to mind when I thought of my living kin. When my eyes went bad, Alice tended me. We'd walk up to Annie Beck's and I'd say, "How're you feeling today, Annie Beck," and Annie Beck'd answer back, "Just fine, Miss Ivy. Today I'm doing just fine." Alice would repeat those phrases in her play. "Just fine, I'm doing just fine." We'd sit on the porch watching the world go by. Annie Beck had an extra long cord put on her phone so she could cook and talk to me for hours when I called, feeling "blue" I called it, feeling lost even though I kept busy, always something to do. Often doing to avoid feeling the sadness Frank's leaving had left.

In later years, when Alice prepared to marry that nice young man, I had a talk with her about taking care of her husband, doing for him in special ways.

"You fix his meals the way he likes. I always did serve meat to Frank though I wish he hadn't eaten it. He could have lived long, like me, if he hadn't."

"Aren't you supposed to be eating an ounce of meat a day now?"

"Who told you?"

"Annie Beck. She's worried about your anemia."

"I cook up what I need for the week on Sunday and keep it in the icebox. Take it like medicine, once a day, because that's what it is."

"I think it's your exercises that help you most."

"That and being an Adventist," I said. "I never would have lived this long if I'd remained a Methodist."

"Oh, Aunt Ivy," she said and bumped her hip to mine the way Pink always did, and laughed. I blinked away tears as she sipped her herbal ice tea.

When the county proposed taxes on homes, I protested. Homes needed some kind of exemption. Without homes, there'd be no permanence, I had argued, no schools or community. I'd had to stand on a chair for them to see my hand raised to speak, but my passion had moved them: they'd passed the exemption.

My life with the Seminoles changed too. I didn't drive out to the reservation as much though I still wrote dozens of letters on their behalf. They'd come to the house when they needed someone to represent them, someone to be their voice in the maze of government ways. New families moved onto the reserve. Betty Mae Tiger, who was about five in years and nearing thirteen in her insights and vision, started school there. I heard at ten years of age, she openly challenged the agent having windows in his house while the Indian people did without.

Trips to Dania continued and I could see that before long, the little lower grade school would be no challenge for the likes of bright girls like Betty Mae. That would be another trial. I could see it coming.

The Indian Reorganization Act went into effect in 1934 and I wrote to get land set aside for cattle for the "new" tribe. Always something to do.

But it was what happened at Dania that brought me such deep and abiding joy I carry it with me still. We began conducting Sunday school and church services in the little Dania school. Sometimes we had a music leader to assist and that brought out the finest ring of voices one could ever want to hear backed up by piano music and the sift-sift sound of the turtle shell rattles. And I, along with those who knew me and what I hoped for, prayed that someday we would have an Indian missionary, someone of their own people, to come to teach and lead them.

One day it happened. A group of Creeks and Seminoles from Oklahoma, remnants of the earliest wars who'd been moved from Florida and taken away, returned. They traveled south. They were Baptists and, much to my great delight, they were received at Dania and encouraged to remain to help build a church and a community of faith.

A small mission grew up on adjacent lands, then, private lands the Southern Baptist Conference bought next to the reservation and several pastors came, all Indian, all Christian. Willie King became one of the first, he and his wife remaining there many years to teach and serve.

There were weddings and baptisms and funerals I attended, each time grateful that all three legs of my little footstool had been completed: education, friendliness toward the government, and introduction to Christ. Many days I spent lifting my little hymnal, raising my voice, so amazed to be there, so joyful that we all knew the church's one foundation.

Over the years, I'd contact senators because of wild ideas the Bureau had to make the Indians pay rent on the houses they'd built themselves or other such nonsense. Spencer had died before he could retire and they'd replaced him with a former pastor named Glenn who worked diligently. Annie Beck said my letters sounded strident.

"The luxury of age allows me to be genteel, I like to think, but formed of steel."

Almost into the forties, my life changed again when the Blackwells took over, lovely people who had the teahouse that Frank and I had eaten at in the twenties. They created the Pioneer House out of my home, signing a twenty-five-year lease for the whole building, minus one room upstairs that I slept in. We enclosed the north porch for use as a sitting room for me, and they lived in the remainder of the upstairs. The light in that porch made it the perfect place to grow begonias and ferns. And I had an entire wall for all the blue ribbons my orchids had won.

Papa came to stay there with me in his later years. He even died there in the closed-in porch. I sat beside him, held his hand, and he promised he'd say hello to Mama for me, and Pink and Albert, and I believe I forgave his wandering, moving ways and the pain I believed he had once caused my mother. No one need judge what happens in another's marriage bed.

In later years, I took my meals downstairs in the Blackwells' restaurant, at my own little table by the window. They always prepared meatless meals for me. In the summers, the Blackwells took me with them to the cool up north, treating me as a member of their family.

The depression astounded us, though we in south Florida had been in it since '26, that's the date I gave its beginning, with the first storm and the land boom built on false hopes.

No more of Tony Tommie's attempts to integrate Fort Lauderdale schools; Tony himself had died in '31 of tuberculosis.

In 1936, the school at Dania, or Hollywood as they now called it, had closed.

We were in the midst of an economic depression and the government had little reserve for anything, let alone a small Seminole school that served only the first few grades anyway. Travel away to the town of Dania or beyond would be necessary.

So I saw what could be done and did it.

I bought clothes for those who wanted to go to the Indian school in Haskell, Kansas, or the Cherokee school in North Carolina. That's where Betty Mae Tiger went, the first of her group to graduate from high school, skipping grades once she got there as though they were stones on a lake. We were all so very proud.

I remember one fall especially at the reservation. I'd come out for church in the building the Baptists had put up. The Seminoles liked the Baptist singing and their gentle way of teaching faith. I suspect they'd have learned of Methodist or Presbyterian or Adventist ways if those denominations had been willing to reach out to them, but it was the Baptists who had and so had won their hearts and souls.

That day, three children approached me and said they wanted to try school in town but they were fearful of the white children and the distance.

"What do you think you can do to solve that problem?"

We were sitting on a log at the reservation eating mangos together.

"You could come to school with us," the tallest boy said. He'd cropped his hair short and straight across his forehead.

"If you'd feel better about it."

"Well, I would," he said. The girls nodded their heads and licked the juice from their fingers.

So the next day I took them with me, him and two little girls, and I sat outside their classroom all day on a little chair the teacher put out for me. I didn't leave once, in case they looked out the door to see if I'd left them, to see if I'd kept my word.

And they did look, once or twice. And there I sat, the netting of my hat over my eyes, my purse perched on my knees, patiently waiting, doing what I had to do, taking some needed time to think.

It wasn't wasted time, no, waiting never is. I spent the day praying for their futures, for their success; and remembering that first year of teaching with the Lauderdale village children and then the Seminoles and their parents and now grandparents, teaching and reaching them as best I could.

The following day, I put the three on the bus and said that I would meet them at school. It was around 1947 or so. I met them and sat outside the door again.

I thought of the patience change took, the trust, love and endurance, the acceptance and faith. How easily Frank and I might have let it all go. Maybe Frank did. Maybe that was what I did not want to forgive him for, even years later: that Frank didn't persevere, didn't trust enough to let God do the work in his life, to let God solve the problems no matter how long it might take.

"I've been angry that he did not keep his promise to never leave me," I told Annie Beck one evening. "Angry and guilty, too, for thinking such things."

"You'll have to forgive yourself, too, Lord knows," Annie Beck said, "for being angry. He was despondent. Something had happened to his thinking. He must have thought he failed you." We sat on the porch facing the New River and shared our day. The crickets blessed the quiet of the night.

"I thought I could protect Frank, fix things."

"'Course you did. You loved him true and true. But you didn't do anything that caused him to choose as he did. If it was you sitting here, that's exactly what you'd tell me."

"Tough things to accept, Annie Beck." A light breeze washed across my face carrying the scent of night-blooming jasmine with it. "I have to trust that God is able to turn every act into a good thing, even if we don't understand it in our time."

"You surely have accomplished what others couldn't have," she said. "Quite a calling you heeded those years ago." She fanned herself with a wide funeral fan stuck on a stick. The moon broke out through a cloud and pierced the river with a shimmering shaft of light then.

Something in the way she said it or the light on the water or the restfulness of exploration that can come beside good friends, tapped deep within me, took me back to another time and place.

"Did I? Accomplish what others couldn't have?"

"Oh, my, yes, how can you even wonder?"

"I had a student once, named Tenley. He died in the Okeechobee flood, but he wrote a poem as a boy, where each line started with a letter from his name."

"How clever."

"The last two lines were 'Every day searching/Yesterday's light.' Those lines always stuck with me for some reason."

"Has a mournful kind of image, doesn't it?"

"His parents had traveled a lot, like mine, I suspect. I always wondered what he searched for in yesterday's light. Something you said just now, about my doing what others hadn't...I think I have just had an epiphany. I may have misunderstood something, a lesson I was to learn. It's true God turned that...tragedy when I was a child into acts of service I might not have performed otherwise, but I don't think that's what He meant at all about my 'doing' things."

"What then?"

"He wanted me to do what 'no one else could do,' only it wasn't to 'do' something at all but to look to yesterday, and accept His forgiveness for what happened, accept it and His love without conditions, let Him be my caretaker, let Him be the one to do what needs to be done. That's what no one else could do. I overcame the fear in most everything but that, in letting Him love me despite my failure."

We sat quietly.

"We all fail, Ivy."

"When I let myself get close to the pain, I just pushed harder, made more things happen." I shook my head. "Wish Pink were here. I'd ask her what she thought about that kind of 'bein' out of control' she said I always needed more of."

"Wouldn't that be just fine to have her sitting here."

"Sometimes, when Frank and I would...just hold each other and be close, my mind would wander, so far away. And he'd say, 'where are you?' and I'd tell him, 'just away' and he'd say 'stay.' And then I'd say the strangest thing. I'd ask him not to leave me! I'd think that other times, too, 'just don't leave me' I'd say, especially when I struggled with something. I thought I was speaking to Frank. But I think now I was talking to myself, telling me not to go away, that I was all right, whether I did something amazing or not. That God loved me just the way I was."

"Maybe that's the light inside your yesterday you've been every day searching," Annie Beck offered.

"Maybe you're right."

On the next day, the third day of school, Billie said it wasn't necessary that I come again to wait outside their door.

"You don't need me?"

"Everyone knows we have a Little White Mother, so no one hurts us. If trouble comes, they know you come back. We take care of things ourselves now."

When I drove home that day in my Oldsmobile, the first with an automatic transmission, I thought of Frank with more fondness than I had in years, without the anger or the guilt and I spoke to him. "So much has changed, you dear boy, since you first came to this river sixty-some years ago. So much."

It had taken only four days this time for the children to see their own strength.

"I need to go through your papers," I said. "And mine, all the 'firsts' books and scrapbooks. Make sure all of them are put in order and given to a historical society, to remember Lauderdale and all that went on here. People should know about this life we made along the river, living side by side with Seminoles, so they can draw their own conclusions about how we did together."

I began that very evening, dragging the books from the attic, paging through newspaper clippings and letters I'd kept while I listened to diners scraping silverware on china in my old dining room below me. I had thought it would be painful, but it wasn't. Instead, it became a celebration of our lives.

How I wished Frank had been there to go through them too. He hadn't seen Billie send me away that day. Billie, all independent and strong now, seeking his education, seeking his future. Me, knowing they didn't need me, knowing that was all right.

But did I still need them? Had we intruded on their lives all these years or been allies? Only time would tell.

A tourist boat chugged along the New River outside my window. I heard its chug-a-chug. "They have the tools, Frank, those Indian children." I spoke into the fading upstairs light. "That's all I ever wanted to give them. And they do just fine now."

Later, I slipped downstairs and waited at the seawall for the manatees. None came that night, but I felt hopeful. Talk was a group to save the manatees had formed, some young people caring for the earth. "A worthy effort," I told Annie Beck, who heartily agreed.

"I don't know anything I'd rather do than listen to the manatees," I told her. "No matter how long I have to wait."

In my dream that night, I walk with a friend, a woman friend, maybe Annie Beck, possibly my sister. We are in a place of gathering with a community of people who work and serve but live separately as though called out by God to be alone and yet in union. A man is showing us the living places, as though we were tourists considering if we wished to spend the season.

We step on freshly lumbered pine boards forming an entry well. Outside this room are relatives of mine, cousins of my mother's people. One, a tall woman named Jeannette, is dressed in red, a color my sister always looked good in though she rarely wore it, believing her color was pink. An aunt I barely remember, seen once near the Peace River when we lived there, talks with her. They have their backs to me but I recognize their voices, the laughter in them and their passion for life as they commune. A part of me is briefly envious, briefly excluded. I do not see faces.

Our guide asks if I will be staying with my friend and he nods to the woman with me, but I tell him no, that my husband will be joining me and it feels correct, precise, an honest to truth. The woman turns to me then and I am surprised to recognize her, to see that it is another side of myself. "Are you prepared to accept?" she asks me and I nod agreement. "To treat your neighbor as yourself?" the guide asks and when I tell him yes, she says she knows I will take care of myself now, having accepted the forgiveness offered in yesterday's light.

The woman walks toward me and in a rush of feeling so powerful and complete, so sweet, she disappears within me and I feel whole. The guide nods in satisfaction as he opens the door at the bottom of the stoop. The wooden door creaks back and I step down inside the room.

It is an old chicken coop, one that has been decorated like a child's playroom, one that resembles a playhouse Papa had made for us, Pink and me, years ago.

Emotion overwhelms me. I am suddenly filled with the memories of my sister, the look and feel of her, the warmth and wit of when we were children. Here we dressed kittens in swatches of clothes made of handkerchiefs and watched them escape across grass. Here we read a single McGuffy Reader together, our towheads touching as her perfect nails moved across the printed page repeating each halting word while I taught. Here we heard Mama call to us to come inside and here we giggled, waited just a moment more before we answered, just enough time to express our power in what we controlled and yet not so much we brought her the pain of worry.

The scent of chicken droppings permeates the room along with lavender, Pink's favorite sachet, and something more, the powder Frank wore to camouflage unwanted scents. The smells lift and settle like ideas onto the muted tones of an old room. Everything is the color of dust over finely etched memory.

The guide quietly closes the door, and I see the wind lift the leaves of the live oak tree outside the single curtained window. I am alone in the room but not lonely for as my eye scans the shelves I see it is full of tiny frames of photographs, ovals and rectangles and squares, as though pressed from a child's workbook of shapes and sizes. Each holds an image of one I loved who has already gone. My mother. Her baby I did not save. Albert. Pink. My father.

Sobs rise from so deep a place they feel heavy and labored. They surface from deep beneath water, deep beneath the throbbing of my heart. I am aware of exposure, of missing them, especially Pink. Oh, how I miss her, the part of me closer to myself than my own mother, though I was of her flesh. Yes, closer than Frank and I. For I was there at her beginning and at her end and her flesh was as mine, her body formed feminine, and I miss her beyond the words of it, beyond the sense of time.

No one outside says for me to hurry as I grieve in this room of my childhood. It is both an invitation and a place to wait and I am aware of healing, of a burden being lifted and drifted away.

Frank's picture isn't among the ones that grace the shelves, but this does not worry me now. He was not a part of my childhood. An opening opposite the outside door promises another room, one I could explore but don't, for I know it is Frank who will be joining me there, when the time is right, when we commune again. Frank will stand with his arms open to me, he will be there along with those who remain in my days; along with the children, all of the children, who move on their own.

The live oak branch scrapes against the outside door now, to bring my eye to it. My friends wait outside. There is no rush. They are willing to let me find nurture here in this place without noise or discord or challenge, this place bathed in acceptance and love. The water of my dream comes from within me, from my tears meant to leave behind. I weep. The tears are real and I know then I am in a dream, in a river of my own making, but I cannot stop the sobbing.

I hear a child's voice. Is it Alice? Julia? Billie? They have need of me? I have need of them.

Without warning, my crying stops. My eyes are not burdened by the rush of tears. I know that there is more to do though the greatest work, of receiving love and healing, has been done. This rest in yesterday's light has been welcome.

I take a deep breath. The door to the outside beckons me. A yellow orchid bursts into bloom as my eyes drift toward the window. People wait like petals of patience. Understanding presses in: no one can prevent change or pain. Human love cannot. It can only prepare, teach, offer service to another with compassion, unhold them from deep within.

Through the glass, the guide notices me stand. I move toward the door and he opens it. The sound of the hinge turns the heads of those waiting. They smile an invitation, young and old alike, and I know that healing lives there, in the warmth of their faces, the tenderness of their eyes. I walk through the door and return to the arms of the living.

AUTHOR'S NOTE

To be faithful to one's beliefs and values and still walk beside others in compassionate and honoring ways is never an easy journey. Frank and Ivy Stranahan very likely would not have used the term "cultural competence," but their sojourn with the Seminole Nation one hundred years ago provides a glimpse into an early understanding of that concept in the blending of beliefs and ideas of two very different peoples.

It has been my privilege to spend time with Ivy and Frank Stranahan, Pink and Mr. Moss, Bloxham and Louise, DeWitt, Gus, Albert, Will, the Kings, the Becks, Tony Tommie, Mary Munroe, Annie Tommie; and more briefly, Betty Mae Tiger, Billie Osceola, Captain Spencer, young Alice Cromartie, and Ivy's first students. All these names represent real people who step out from the past to teach and touch us with their lives.

To the greatest capacity possible, I have remained true to the facts as preserved by the Fort Lauderdale Historical Society, the Stranahan Museum, and family and researcher interviews.

Records support the fact that Augustus Cromartie moved his family often, affecting Ivy's dream for schooling and teaching. She took the teaching test after tutoring by Ada Merritt. Some debate exists about the actual date. Some question also exists over the date of Ivy's mother's death. A page said to be from the family Bible records her death as 1905, well after Ivy married though Ivy's recollection that she had to raise her younger brothers and sister is remembered by most who knew her. Her mother's troubled pregnancies may have been the cause of Ivy's care for her siblings rather than her mother's death. By all reports, Ivy did experience the childhood trauma that so changed her life choices.

Pink's fate and Mr. Moss, Frank's health and financial conditions and circumstances of his death are based on facts. Will did fade from the south Florida scene without fanfare. A small Tote pin believed to be Will's from the secret organization formed to protect the "Red Man," was found in the archeological dig of the trading post compound completed in the late 1970s.

Ivy's role in the plume trade and specific recovery of feathers portrayed, women's suffrage, the planning of Fort Lauderdale, her passion for the land, her attraction to the Seminoles, her views on alcohol and diet, exercise and driving, and especially education and faith and the establishment of permanent homes are all documented. Ivy had a deep and abiding faith that sustained her and guided her passion into service.

The incident with the Seminole woman's death at the post is recorded in an interview in her later years as was her three point plan for providing tools to the Seminole Nation, not to make them like herself, she'd say, but to give the Seminole people all the tools needed to be the best at who they are.

Every effort has been made for accuracy in dating events. The hurricanes and freezes, the swamps and terrain, the landscape changes resulting from the drainage and dredging depicted did affect the settlement of south Florida in unique ways and challenged Ivy's social conscience. It is a region known for sun and restfulness whose development required both hardiness and hope from her persevering pioneers.

Esther, Stretch, and Julia are fictional characters; King Solomon Branham and Mr. Williams, the squatters and their capacity to delay removal from federal land are not. There was a Brother Frost and Holding as well, written of in Ivy's own hand (the letter reproduced almost verbatim in the text). Whether Ivy had a personal confrontation with them is not known; she did leave the Methodist Church around the time of the letter to form the Adventist Church.

Bureau of Indian Affairs Agent Lucien Spencer existed. His role with the Cow Creeks and Seminoles is documented in several places including the Bureau of Indian Affairs archives. At least one of his letters is recorded verbatim in the text.

Ivy did become a spokesperson for the Seminoles as confirmed by letters and documents in her sprawling hand preserved at the National Archives and at the Fort Lauderdale Historical Society. She was once a Methodist, utilized the Presbyterian Sunday school material to interact with Seminole children who did have their term of endearment for her as "little white mother." One of her stated joys was the building of the school and later church at the Hollywood reservation.

Ivy's actions were the catalyst for the Seminole Nation's move as portrayed in this story in 1926. The dates and the events preceding are in some dispute. Documentation by the National Archives correspondence and interviews with Dr. Kersey serve as my inspiration for Tony Tommie's role in the squatter incidents and my use of the 1926 date.

Ivy did later assist with the Seminole cattle industry, she did help start the library, she did serve as chairman of the Federation of Women's Club's Committee on Indian Affairs. She was instrumental in the development of the school at Dania. She was active with the DAR in supporting education for all children but most especially the Seminoles. In later years, she spoke eloquently to pass the Homestead Exemption Act and assisted young Seminole students to attend school including Betty Mae Tiger, the first Seminole to graduate from high school. Dr. Betty Mae Jumper later became the first woman to serve as Tribal Council Chairman of any Indian nation. She is today a distinguished author and respected Tribal Elder.

The Dania Reservation—known as Hollywood—continues to flourish, one of several Florida reservations. The Seminole Nation sets a strong example with its successful orchard and cattle enterprises, its educational programs, and museum.

Ivy did indeed teach formally and informally in Broward County and is remembered fondly as Broward County's first teacher as Frank is remembered as a founding Fort Lauderdale citizen. Ivy's faith and perseverance and her role in the informal teaching of the Seminoles are all substantiated. And she did find a way to keep her home through the devastation of the depression by exercising faith, perseverance, and creativity.

For the contribution she made to the history of Florida and her faithful role with the Seminole people, Ivy Stranahan was inducted into the Florida Women's Hall of Fame posthumously in 1996.

Today the trading post Frank built in 1901 of sturdy Dade pine still stands beside the New River on the original site, not unlike the photo on the cover of this novel. The live oak they planted the first year of their marriage has survived all the storms. The Stranahan home is on the National Historic Register and is maintained as a museum of the 1913 era. It is managed by the Stranahan House Trust. Tours can be arranged by contacting the Stranahan House, PO Box 030164, Fort Lauderdale, FL 33303. It would please Ivy, I believe, to know that school children are valued visitors who tour her home annually.

Ivy died in 1970 at the age of 91 in the room of her home where her tropical plants had flourished. Hundreds grieved her passing, including nieces and nephews, Seminole friends, Garden Club associates, and her friend, Annie Beck. Billie Osceola, the young Seminole boy who sent Ivy home that day long ago, was one of the many who gave eulogies at Ivy's funeral remembering her compassion and commitment to education. He became a Baptist minister and served the Florida Seminoles until his death twenty-five years ago.

I have made every effort to portray Ivy Stranahan, her family, and friends as true to the facts as I know them and with the studied speculations permitted the novelist. It is my hope that through this version of their story, the Stranahan's will continue to inspire the curious student and compassionate teacher in each of us. Thank you for reading it.

Jane Kirkpatrick
www.jkbooks.com